THE LONG GOODBYE

She slipped off of him, pulled on her silk robe and walked to the door. He stared at the wall as the sound of the bolt unlatching crashed to his ears. It was a curious sound, from another world. A male voice. Just a grunt, but male. Then he heard her speak.

"Next time I want more time," she said.

He felt a strong arm grab his wrist. He felt himself being dragged to the bed. A cold collar of steel snapped over his hand, then over the bedpost.

The last thing he heard was her voice in his ear.

Other Avon Books by
Richard Berman

UNJUST DEATH

Avon Books are available at special quantity discounts for bulk purchases for sales promotions, premiums, fund raising or educational use. Special books, or book excerpts, can also be created to fit specific needs.

For details write or telephone the office of the Director of Special Markets, Avon Books, Dept. FP, 1350 Avenue of the Americas, New York, New York 10019, 1-800-238-0658.

HOSTILE WITNESS

RICHARD BERMAN

AVON BOOKS · NEW YORK

> **VISIT OUR WEBSITE AT**
> **http://AvonBooks.com**

HOSTILE WITNESS is an original publication of Avon Books. This work has never before appeared in book form. This work is a novel. Any similarity to actual persons or events is purely coincidental.

AVON BOOKS
A division of
The Hearst Corporation
1350 Avenue of the Americas
New York, New York 10019

Copyright © 1996 by Richard S. Berman
Published by arrangement with the author
Library of Congress Catalog Card Number: 96-96072
ISBN: 0-380-77813-0

All rights reserved, which includes the right to reproduce this book or portions thereof in any form whatsoever except as provided by the U.S. Copyright Law. For information address Gelfman/Schneider Literary Agents, 250 West 57th Street, Suite 1007, New York, New York 10107.

First Avon Books Printing: September 1996

AVON TRADEMARK REG. U.S. PAT. OFF. AND IN OTHER COUNTRIES, MARCA REGISTRADA, HECHO EN U.S.A.

Printed in the U.S.A.

RA 10 9 8 7 6 5 4 3 2 1

> If you purchased this book without a cover, you should be aware that this book is stolen property. It was reported as "unsold and destroyed" to the publisher, and neither the author nor the publisher has received any payment for this "stripped book."

CHAPTER 1

Light ran his hand over the cool surface of the metal cylinder.

"Yep, this here the one. Right here. Saved LeVander's life with this here." He kept running his hands over the pipe, not looking up, just studying the shiny silver. He knew they were looking, could kind of feel their eyes on him, just like he did every day.

"Them Italians had LeVander all pushed up in that alleyway, over by Nostrand and Pacific. They was all set to beat on his ass, then shoot him or cut him up—one." Light banged the pipe on the concrete stoop. He heard the horn honk and he looked up, just like he did every day. Light waved the pipe as LeVander tipped his broad-brimmed hat from the inside of that Mercedes, just like he did every day.

"How come you don't do no work with LeVander and Franklin?"

Light smiled as he watched the Mercedes disappear around the corner. Light didn't have to look to know was one of the new boys had asked that.

"I'll tell you, boy, I never worked a day in my life. Not that there's nothing wrong with work, now. If you want to do it. I just don't." He slipped the pipe behind his back and picked up the brown paper bag with the silver can in it. He pulled the napkin out, leaving the beer in the bag. "Le-

Vander do all right working, and Franklin, he got a history doing things like they was a job anyway, even if they ain't."

Light wrapped the napkin around his untrimmed fingernail and dug into the gully around the edge of the can. "That may be the way it's goin'. Time you grow up, boy, maybe everybody be working." Light worked his way around the can, digging at a resistant speck of dirt. "But not me. I didn't never work, and I ain't gonna start, hear?"

He folded the napkin, stuffed it in the pocket of his nylon shirt, and tapped the top of the can with his fingernail. He could hear the boys shuffling around, getting impatient for the story. He popped the can and ducked down to suck the foam off the top.

"You like a cowboy, Light," the new boy said.

Yeah, Light thought, he liked that, like a cowboy saving this one and that. "Maybe, but that time with LeVander, I wasn't riding no horse. No, they had LeVander pushed way back up in that alley. Wasn't no way I could get to him. They had these two Italians standing at the opening of the alley, you know what I mean?"

Light waited for the murmurs of agreement to die down before continuing. "Them white boys, Italian especially, but all them white boys, they get to lifting weights and working out. Well, these boys was about six-two or six-three, maybe two-eighty, all muscle. But them white boys, no matter how big, they always scared of a black man. That's the truth." Light looked over at the small group of boys, who were twisting away now. "Don't pay no attention to that ruckus down there, just some crazy, doped-up or something. I'm telling you something important here."

The boys were all looking now, ignoring Light. He sighed and picked up his pipe.

He looked over the heads of the boys, over the handrail on the stoop, down to the corner where the white man stood, shaking the white woman. Wasn't white exactly, more like Spanish. Nice though, young with that smooth Spanish skin and that lipstick that was a little too bright and a little too shiny, making her teeth look a little too white.

Not like she was a whore. No, she dressed nice, with that tweed kind of suit they wear downtown. That man had a hold of that suit, by the arms, shaking that woman, making her head snap back and forth, yelling something Light couldn't hear.

The boys were all crowded around the base of the stoop now, leaning forward and looking at the white man and the woman. Light knew his crowd was drifting away.

"Now, boys, you see the difference there between white folks and black folks. You don't never see no black folks doing like that."

"What you talkin' about, you old drunken black fool? It just too early in the day for you to have your ass drunk enough." Evelyn Jefferson looked at her watch. "Be about three in the afternoon 'fore you ready for your fight."

"Oh, Evelyn, don't be givin' me your bullshit this early." Light didn't even want to look at her, standing there with her housedress hanging loose over her bony frame. "Least let me have some peace early in my day. I'm trying to talk to the boys here."

"Talk to the boys? What you gonna tell them, Light, about how you a big man?" Evelyn chortled in that way she had.

Light felt her looking at him, laughing inside at his rising anger. Light slapped the pipe in his hand. Someday he was gonna bury this motherfucker in that sorry bitch's head.

"What you doing now, Light, whippin' you hand with pipe? You one tough motherfucker."

The boys had all drifted away now, down to the corner. Light clutched the pipe with two hands, staring down at the corner, afraid even to look at Evelyn. She had changed over the year since LeVander and Heather moved out and she lost the welfare. She never hesitated to tell anyone who'd listen how she hated that job cleaning city offices, how it cut into her drinking time. And since Light stopped seeing her, she never hesitated to embarrass him in public.

Light followed the boys to the corner, tapping the end of his pipe on the sidewalk like an Englishman with his umbrella. He got a better look at the white man now as he stepped away from the woman. The man looked to be in his mid-sixties or so, his ruddy face with its swelling veins topped by a little shock of white hair, still cut in the same style as when it had been brown.

They were silent, the man glaring at the woman with the kind of hatred Light felt for Evelyn. The woman leaned against the traffic light, her back to him, staring at the curb. Her shoulder-length brown hair hung across her face, its silky strands fanned out like a deck of new cards smoothly spread across a table, looking not disheveled, but as if it had been spread across this beautiful face by a photographer hired to sell conditioner.

She might be a model, Light thought as he studied her, tossing her head to fling hair back, trying to maintain her dignity despite the growing knot of black faces gaping at her.

"Now get in the goddamn car, bitch," the man was saying.

Light felt the bony fingers poking into his kidney. "Now, that the way, huh, Light? That the way a man treat a woman, right?"

Light twisted away, ignoring Evelyn as he watched the white man grab the Spanish woman by the shoulder and yank her roughly to the car. She tried to pull away, but he tightened his grip on her upper arm, jerking her hard. She stumbled, sprawling on the sidewalk, her knee-length skirt flying up, revealing muscular thighs beneath dark hose.

Light leaned forward to get a better look. Yes, sir, she was a fine piece, that one. Might just be a model or an actress. More than likely, though, just another fancy whore getting abused by another john.

She pulled her skirt down with all the dignity she could muster, and curled her legs up under her, staying on the sidewalk. The white man was standing over her now, yelling at her. "Get up!" he roared. "Get up!"

Show over, Light leaned back, only to feel that bony poke at his kidney.

HOSTILE WITNESS

"That's about as close as you gonna get to some fine white pussy. Looking up some lady's dress on the street," she cackled. "Just like them boys. You ain't no different."

Light didn't look around. He stuck his hand on that part of Evelyn where her breasts used to be before the wine and the crack devoured them. Flipping her back like a piece of rice paper in the wind, he turned back to the white man.

The white man had dragged the woman to her feet. She limped, the heel of one of her shoes having broken. As she bent to adjust it, the white man yanked her again. She snapped her arm free and bent to her shoe.

The white man pulled back his right hand and slapped her across the face. Her hair spun like a silky top just yanked free from its string. She fell backward, twisting away from the white man. He held her wrist fast, yanked her again, spinning her hair the other way. She stopped, facing him full on. As her hair settled by her ears, Light glanced back and forth between the welt growing on her cheek and the look of diabolical hatred in her eyes.

"Mmm, that one fine woman, ain't it?" Evelyn cackled. "Yeah, boys, you keep listening to this old drunk and he be telling you that's how you got to be treating a woman. Ain't that right, Light?" Evelyn cackled again, poking him in the back for emphasis.

"You shut your fucking mouth, woman, this minute, or I'll show that white man how it done."

"Now, you listen, boys, he gonna tell how to beat a woman. Go ahead, Light, tell 'em."

"That ain't right, is it Light? To beat a woman?"

Light put his hand lightly on the boy's shoulder. "No, boy, it ain't right. You shouldn't never hit a woman." He turned to look Evelyn in the eye. "No matter how seriously tested you are."

The white man slapped the woman again.

"So what you doing about it, huh, Light? You the big, fucking hero 'round here. Why you ain't show that white man the right thing?"

"Ain't none of my affair."

"You scared, that's what. You didn't do nothing with that pipe for LeVander, no way. I never believed that story." Evelyn stuck her finger deep in his rib now.

Light spun around, slapping her hand away. God, how he wanted to beat the bitch. He spun angrily back to the white man, and pushed his way through the knot of boys toward him. Light could see the Spanish woman's tears now, joined with the matching welts on both cheeks.

Light tapped the end of his pipe on the sidewalk.

The white man spun around, glaring at Light. "What the fuck you want?"

Light stood transfixed. It had never occurred to him that he'd have to say something. He could feel the boys' eyes bearing into him, could almost see Evelyn's mocking him. A siren sounded far in the distance. He took a deep breath. "Ain't right," he said finally, tapping his pipe on the sidewalk.

The man released his grip on the Spanish woman, turning to face Light. "Well, I don't think it's any of your business," he said, looking over Light's shoulder. "So, why don't you and the seven dwarfs over there climb back up your tree or into your cave or wherever you came from." He reached over to the woman, who was huddled by the light post, and roughly shoved her toward the red BMW double-parked near the corner.

Light heard Evelyn sucking breath over her molars. "That's good, Light, that's real good. You doing fine." It sounded as if her voice was fading. Light pushed her voice out of his mind.

The Spanish girl pulled away again, and the white man pulled his hand back. Light snapped the pipe up and drove it end first into the man's stomach.

The white man crumbled to his knees, gagging. Light jumped back as green vomit spewed from the man's mouth. The girl stared at the white man, then at Light, then back to the white man. She hesitated for a second, then knelt by the white man."

"Are you okay?"

The white man groaned, looked up, and shot another wad of green.

The woman deftly dodged the vomit, reached ino his pocket, pulled out keys, and ran to the BMW. She jumped in and roared off. In his confused daze, Light watched the car disappear and vaguely heard Evelyn laughingly shoo the boys home. The white man didn't move.

"All right, freeze."

Light stood staring into the distance into which the BMW had disappeared.

"That's it, just stay there quiet now."

Light shook his head and looked down at the white man gagging at his feet.

"All right, drop that pipe, just let it go. Let it fall right there."

Shit, they talkin' to me, Light realized, spinning around to face the cop.

"Freeze. Don't move a fucking muscle."

"Yes, sir," Light said, letting go of the pipe and raising his hands above his head. The cop stood silently, a slight tremble in his hand. A rookie, thought Light, no more than about twenty-two. First time he had that gun in his hand, from the look of it. That boy be surprised when he find out what happen here. Yes, sir, Light gonna be a hero now, a real hero, so everybody knows about it.

The rookie looked over Light's shoulder as if to another cop. Had to be another. The rookie shoved his gun down into his holster, deliberately snapping the flap closed.

"Good, now I can explain what happened here," Light said, dropping his hands.

"Keep 'em up there. You can tell the judge." The other cop was older, from the sound of him, probably smoked too, from that rattle. Light put his hands on his head.

The rookie pushed him against a parked Chevy, bent him over at the waist, and grabbed his right wrist.

"Now, I can explain this, it ain't what it look like."

The rookie snapped the handcuff shut. "Just shut up."

"Oh, man, you can't just listen?" Light whined as the rookie snapped the other cuff shut. "You can ask any of these people around here."

"Yeah, what people?"

Light looked around. The street was empty: no kids, no Evelyn, no nobody. "Oh, shit, just knock on any door. They tell you. This man was beatin' on some woman. I just trying to help."

The rookie spun Light around to face the white man. The other cop was helping him up.

"Stay right there, sir. The ambulance is on the way."

CHAPTER 2

"What about the brief?"

"I'll do it tonight." David pulled his briefcase from the space between the desk and the wall, opened it, and dropped the legal pad in.

"You can't do him any good, you know."

"He deserves a defense."

Joel dropped his lanky frame into the leather client's chair next to David's desk, hanging a long leg over the arm. "Legal Aid will give him a defense."

"He asked for us," David responded, the irritation creeping into his voice. He stepped over Joel's leg toward the coat rack, shooting Joel a look as he did.

Joel ignored it. "We do private defense. That means retained," Joel said.

David felt the knot in his stomach tighten. "Look, Light did me a favor. I owe him."

"He did a favor for LeVander. You were just LeVander's lawyer."

"And because of LeVander you have that big office with that big chair where your butt should be parked."

"David, I'm trying to look out for you."

David grabbed his coat. He was sorry he had said it, but it had jumped to his mouth. A lot of things had lately. He took a breath and allowed the tension to flow out of him.

"Joel, there are guys I owe, whether they can pay or not. I owe. There aren't many, it doesn't happen much, but once in a while somebody I owe gets in trouble. I'm going to do what I can."

"Okay, okay. What did the crazy drunk do?"

David pulled on his coat. He didn't know why Joel was irritating him so much lately. Joel hadn't changed; he was the same irreverent asshole he had always been. Not even an asshole really, just an irreverent businessman. David dropped the briefcase between his knees and slipped the Daytimer from his jacket pocket.

"Detective says they're holding him on an assault. Slugged some old guy with a pipe."

"Robbery?"

David shook his head. "The detective hadn't gotten the whole story apparently."

"Look, he's not going to get arraigned for two days anyway. You told the cop not to talk to him. That's all you can do: walk across the street, put in a notice, and wait."

David slipped the Daytimer back into his jacket pocket, buttoned his coat, and walked toward the door.

"David, all you're doing is wasting half a day stroking some drunken burglar."

"It's my half day," David said and disappeared.

Bastard wouldn't even talk to him. Like he weren't shit.

"All right, back to the cell, Scott."

Light shook his arm free of the beefy cop's grip and strode back to the cell. That bastard, forgetting what he'd done. Treating him like some old no-account nigger. Light crashed down on the hard wooden bench in the cell, pushed his back up against the cold cinder-block wall, and folded his arms across his chest. Shit, he was the one saved LeVander's ass. Gave that hot-shit, bastard lawyer all that press. People thought that Cohen had saved LeVander's ass. *Shit, no, it was me.*

Light slammed his hand down on the bench. "Fucking

bitch." He clamped his jaw shut and glared out into the squad room.

The beefy cop didn't look up, just stared at paperwork. "Say something, Scott?"

Light said nothing. He hated when cops called him Scott. Ought to be Mr. Scott, but better off the cocksuckers didn't call him nothing.

"Scott, was that a statement?" The older cop got up now, walking over to the cage.

Light turned to face the corner, putting his leg up on the bench. Cocksucker gonna bait him now. Cohen told him don't make no statements. Told the cop too. Light heard it. But this bastard was gonna work Light. Torture him. Light clamped down on his jaw.

"Yeah, that was some story you told, how that man was beating on a woman nobody saw and how there was a whole crowd who saw you save her. That was pretty good. Only trouble was, nobody saw it."

Light pulled his other leg up on the bench, twisting his back as much as possible to the cop.

"That ain't right, putting your feet up on the bench like that, Scott. Ought to have consideration for the next guy, you know?"

The next guy. There shouldn't be no next guy.

"Yeah, Scott, I don't think anybody's gonna buy that story." The cop walked around the cell so he could get as close to Light's back as possible. "But you could help us with a few things. We were trying to figure how come you didn't rob the guy. I mean, you had him down and out. Spittin' up green like that fucking bitch in *The Exorcist*. He wasn't putting up a fight, was he?"

"Fuck you, you cocksucker. You get out there, do your job, talk to them people, you find out what happened." Light reached down and grabbed his knees. He wasn't gonna let no cop fuck with him. The bastard lawyers, always tellin' you don't say nothing, and give me money.

"Whoa, we got a little fury here, Joey. You wanna check Mr. Scott out?"

Light heard the chair squeak clear of the desk and them shiny black shoes clip-clopping on the dirty tile floor. He popped up and walked over to the corner, the real corner where the two cinder-block walls met in the back, away from that beefy detective with the ruddy face.

"What's the matter, Scott, you don't wanna talk to us?"

Light stood in the corner, facing the two walls like he was gonna piss. Yeah, that's what he could do, piss. Serve those bastards right. Make beefy come in here, mop it up. Light reached down in front and took hold of his zipper. He thought better of it. No, they'd probably get some brother, have to come in here and clean the shit up, all the time Tomming to these cocksuckers. No, Light thought as he dropped his hands back to his sides, let those bastards spit their shit. He'd just stand here, ignoring them.

Just like a few minutes ago, before they let Light call the lawyer, when they sat at the two desks, set up facing each other like two faggots who couldn't stand to be apart, even for a minute. Talking loud, to be sure Light heard while they talked about who was gonna call the hospital to check on the white man's condition.

And then when the rookie called and Beefy walked over to the water fountain by the cell so he could yell back to the rookie. All so Light would hear when they said that the white man was getting out of the hospital and coming over to the station to sign a complaint. Spending all this time drinking coffee in the station, yelling across the room just to get him worried or pissed off, all to get him to talk.

They could check out what he said if they'd just go back, walk the streets, and knock on a few doors. But they had their fucking nigger; they didn't need no more. Light hitched up his pants. Yeah, he should piss right here in the cell.

He played with his zipper again, then pushed his hands down into his pockets. No, they'd just charge him with something else, creating a public mess or indecent exposure. Light dropped down on the bench in the corner.

"Complainant will be here in a few minutes, Scott. You want to meet him personally? Maybe if you apologize?"

Apologize to the white bastard that was beating on that woman? Apologize for doing the right thing? Shit, maybe it's better. Light slumped. *I ain't nothing but a drunken nigger. My one heroic moment gone almost a year now.* He looked up at the beefy one. "What I gonna say?"

"Just 'I'm sorry,' Scott. That's all. Bet that old man'll be so overcome, he'll just drop the charges there. He was asking about you on the phone. Right, Joey?"

The rookie looked up from the desk where he was pressing hard to make five carbon copies with a cheap ballpoint. "Yeah, right."

Light looked back to the beefy one. The rookie wasn't even listening.

"Yeah, I think he's just waiting to drop the charges, Scott."

Light looked away. You could never tell from the cop's smirk. Could be just his way. Could be he was getting like cops did when they was scamming. Trying to get him to apologize, 'cause that would be like a confession. Light looked back at the cop. He quick switched from that smirk to that look of concern. Yeah, he was scamming. The cocksucker.

"Seems to me, it's the way to go, Scott. Otherwise, in a big press case like this, you're looking at maxing out on a five to fifteen."

"Fuck you, Beef."

"Suit yourself, Scott. But I think you're missing your chance. You lick this guy's boots a little—this guy, probably a liberal—you'll be out in a heartbeat."

Light spun back to the corner. Definitely a fucking scam. *It was that bitch. Saved her fucking ass, and what happen? She take off with the car, and I wind up in lockup.* If I ever get outta here, I'm going to find that fucking bitch. Kick her little cocksucking ass, till she tell me what's going on and straighten this motherfucker out. Don't matter what them fucking lawyers say. Gonna find that bitch.

* * *

David bent forward as he turned the key, waited the terrible moment while the Toyota decided whether to catch, then sat back as it rumbled roughly to life. Pulling the seatbelt over his shoulder, he wondered for the fifth time this week why he kept the car. Joel's BMW, complete with alarm system, ignition lockout, club, and electronic tracking, sat three cars away, elevated on a web of steel above a 1989 Chevy. It went with the big office.

David pushed the gearshift up into first and inched his way out of the lot. Joel had taken to the success that had come in the wake of the Jefferson case and the publicity it drew: the office overlooking the harbor, the BMW, on TV with somebody every other week. David had resisted the trappings and rarely thought about it.

But he did now, as he swung the Toyota left on Atlantic and headed toward the outback of Brooklyn. He passed the brick and brownstone apartment buildings that stood along Atlantic like four-story cliffs cut Zorro-style, with green and black fire escapes. BMWs didn't seem appropriate somehow. Neither did big offices overlooking the harbor or prancing in front of juries or worrying more about the effect of prancing on other potential clients than on the jury. But since the fame that the Jefferson case had brought, it was Joel who had parlayed the success to BMW level.

David swung the Toyota along Atlantic as it curved next to the elevated LIRR line out toward Nostrand Avenue. David supposed it was good that Joel was worried about BMWs and press. Since the Jefferson case, David had avoided the press. He told himself that staying away from press cases gave him more time to think about the possibilities, the puzzle. It was partly true. That was what he liked about new cases, a new puzzle.

Like Light's puzzle. David was pretty sure there was more to this case than a street robbery. Light had been on the street too long to be reduced to robberies. That, Light would say, was young man's work. And foolish young men at that.

He'd told Light not to say anything, mostly because that

was his job. Never say anything. Look at O.J. But there was another reason, a perverse reason. David spent his time on the way to the station house speculating. It was, in fact, one of his great pleasures in defense, speculation. He always told clients to tell him the truth, always explained the attorney-client privilege, but part of him screamed in protest when a client confessed to him on that first meeting. That part felt cheated of the opportunity to concoct in his mind various and sundry stories about what might have happened.

In some cases the client too was cheated by confessing to the attorney too early. Some of David's best summation red herrings were developed in the ride to the precinct. Light would not be cheated like that. Light had been insistent. The only thing David had let Light say over the phone was that it was bullshit . . . bullshit.

"Mr. Cohen." The words preceded the light slap on the shoulder by a second or two.

David turned. The smiling face was perched atop a thin frame dressed in the formal uniform of a police lieutenant and below straight, salt-and-pepper hair, forced with some sort of Pat Reilly goop diagonally across a balding head.

"Lieutenant," David said, returning the tone of familiarity although he hadn't the foggiest notion of who this lieutenant was or where he had met the man.

"Peterson," the man said, as if David had paused after "Lieutenant," which he hadn't. "You're here to see Mr. Scott?"

David nodded, hiding his surprise. Lieutenants, generally the commanding officers of precincts, usually didn't know every arrest or every lawyer who was popping in to see his client.

"He's indisposed." The lieutenant's hand, still poised on David's shoulder, now guided him gently away from the desk and down a hall. David allowed himself to be led.

"Mr. Scott had had a bit to drink when we picked him up. You understand."

"I've told your men: no statements."

"Of course, we don't even take statements much anymore. The way the courts have interpreted it, seems like the only people you can get an admissible statement from are people without a pending case. In this precinct seems like there aren't many of those." Peterson laughed.

David shifted his shoulders uncomfortably. Peterson wasn't talking like a cop, not even like a lieutenant. And so what if Light was retching his guts out? Some cop was going to be watching him. Usually cops loved to make attorneys see them do dirty work. "I'd like to see my client," David said as sternly as possible.

"In a moment, maybe about ten minutes. You know how it is. This is a delicate case." The hand rested on David's back again, maneuvering him into Interrogation Room 1.

"Delicate?"

"You know, with the congressman involved."

"Congressman." A pale, empty feeling filled David's chest. He allowed himself to be guided into the interrogation room.

The white man stood in the doorway, his ruddy face a little paler than Light remembered it. He glanced around the room uncertainly, the look of a man not used to uncertainty.

Light pushed his back up against the cinder blocks in the corner, enjoying the camouflage of the dark corner. Hardly breathing, he watched the white bastard, the congressman. Nobody to tell him where to go, what to say. No, he just stood there, shaking a little.

The man looked from under his gray hair over to the cell, catching Light's eye as he scanned by. Light glared back, boring in, as if his look could cut the man, slice his brain. The man looked away nervously.

"Congressman Twining, right this way," the rookie said, running up to him, taking the congressman by the hand and leading him to the green metal desk.

Looking nervously over his shoulder at Light, the congressman followed. Light still glared, cutting into the man's eyes. The congressman, no longer able to hold Light's eyes, looked away, back at the desk.

"We have the papers all ready for you. Just sit there and read them over, sign right at the bottom."

"Now's your chance, Scott." The voice shot out in a stage whisper from the side of the cell.

Light jumped a little inside, but not so the beefy one could tell. Clamping down on his jaw, Light turned his glare to the beefy one, standing outside with his hand gripping a bar, watching the rookie and that ruddy white man huddling over the desk.

"If you just call him over, say you're sorry, didn't know who he was. You know what to say. Yep, he'd drop them charges, bet you."

Light looked back to the white man. He was shaking all right, hand with the pen just wouldn't do what he wanted, looked like. Looked a little like Evelyn used to look when she needed that wine, trying to grab his dick and stuff it in her mouth. Light shook his head, thinking about that. How some days she couldn't get it in her mouth, she was shaking so bad. How he'd have to give her some of the wine first, to calm her down so she could get her mouth around it.

That's how that white man looked, with that funny-looking white hair piled on top of his head, like they hadn't given him nothing to drink in the hospital. Musta come straight here.

"Now, what I think is that we shouldn't even prosecute this thing. I don't think you're a bad guy, Scott. Haven't got your sheet, of course, but I'd say your bad crimes are behind you. Know what I mean?"

Beefy was trying to make his voice smooth, but the smoother he made it, the more it irritated Light. Lying to him, lying to that white man.

The white man slammed the pen down on the desk and stared out the window.

"See what I mean, Scott? Just a word from you, he'd drop this whole thing."

"Fuck you, man. You get your ass out there in the street, do your fucking job, you drop this motherfucking thing," Light said, still watching the white man.

"Suit yourself, Scott." Beefy released the bar and turned back to the rookie and the congressman. "I hear Attica's cold this time of year. Better pray for global warming next fifteen years." He started walking over to the desk. "You know, I go fishing up in Canada sometimes. I'll check you out on the way, okay, champ?"

Light scowled at him as he left, but Beefy didn't turn around. Wasn't going to jail behind this shit. No, somebody'd tell the truth. Evelyn, them boys, somebody. Or maybe that Spanish girl, if Jacobs could find her. Or Cohen. Light was a little disappointed that it was Cohen answered the phone. Cohen, okay. Still look good in a suit. Some of the boys still remember when he played point guard at Brooklyn College. But he ain't Jacobs. Ain't the TV star. It's Jacobs people talk to. On TV with that O.J. thing.

Light was a little pissed when Cohen said he'd be over. Hopin' it be Jacobs. He needed Jacobs on this here. And them guys, they owed him. Yeah, thought Light, I need Jacobs on this here. He just shook his head at Beefy. Shook his head and looked down.

Beefy walked back over to the desk, glanced at the rookie, and put his hand lightly on the white man's shoulder, as the rookie spoke in the white man's ear. "Just got to sign right there at the bottom." he said, pointing.

The white man glanced at the rookie then back out the window. The white man was *real* white, not like Beefy or the rookie. They was white but not *white*. The white man had his white hair, that pasty white skin. Whiter now than it was on the corner. Like there something wrong with him. The white man started to say something, whispered almost, still looking out the window.

Light got up and went to the front of the cell, closer to the white man and the rookie. He wanted to be close so he could hear.

The rookie pushed the paper a little closer. "Press hard," he said, "you're making five copies."

The white man sighed a little and picked up the pen. The rookie sat back. The white man stopped. "Can't we just forget about this?"

Beefy dropped a chair between the white man and the rookie. "Not a good idea, here, Congressman. See, this is a bad guy, this Scott."

The white man turned to Beefy, then looked over Beefy's shoulder to the cell.

"See, we been after this guy for years. A slick one." Beefy spun around, his holster cracking across the wooden rungs on the back of the chair.

Light tried to look peaceful despite his growing anger.

"He doesn't look it, but he's a bad one."

"Well, I just don't need the attention," the white man said, turning back to the paper.

"A public servant like yourself, Congressman, I'm sure you'd want what's best for the community, not just yourself."

The white man didn't answer but picked up the paper, reading it again.

"The community would thank you for getting this guy off the streets," Beefy said, putting his hand on the white man's back. "I think you'd get a few votes out of this, I really do."

"I don't really need the publicity."

"Can't help you there, Congressman," Beefy said, squeezing the congressman's shoulder and standing. "The unusual is already out. Can't stop these things, you know."

The white man looked up, shock spreading over his face. Light could tell Beefy was trying to look sympathetic, just as he did with Light. It was that fake sympathy, that expression that says on the front, "Too bad," but in back there's a smirk just waiting to burst through.

Beefy walked over to his desk, opened the bottom drawer, and pulled out a leather-covered flask. "You been through a lot, Congressman. Have a shot. May calm you down. Help you think.''

The white man hesitated a second before taking the flask. For the first time since he was hitting that Spanish woman on the corner, he seemed to know what to do. As he screwed the top back on, the color come back to his face—not all over, but in little rivers and creeks, mostly on his nose. The white man grabbed the papers.

"Push hard now, you don't want the judge to have to strain," the rookie said, smiling. Beefy was smiling. Light plopped down on the bench, folded his arms, and stared at his shoes. He didn't feel like smiling.

"Look, I need to see my client now," David said, slapping his open hand on the Formica-topped table. The third request needed the slap for emphasis. The first two had succeeded only in getting Peterson to drone on about how well loved Harrison Twining was and how Light had made a very bad choice in assaulting this particular congressman.

David had a right to see Light, of course, and see him immediately. But enforcing that right required a writ of habeas corpus, a process involving preparing papers and getting a judge's attention. As a practical matter, there was nothing David could do, nothing but wait . . . wait until Peterson and the detectives were finished with whatever they were doing. It was certainly not anything like beating. Except in Suffolk County, cops had stopped doing that years ago. No percentage. David would wait and have his conversation with Light when Peterson was ready to give it to him.

David paid no attention to the soft tap on the door until Peterson slapped his knees and stood. "Let's see if Mr. Scott is ready for you, shall we?"

David rose to follow. *Shall we?* No cop talked like that except under extreme pressure. A congressman complainant, could that be enough pressure? Of course, it could. There'd be press in this case for the cops too. Just paranoia, David thought, as he followed Peterson up the stairs to the PIU. Time to forget paranoia and put on the client face.

"Mr. Scott, how you doing?" David asked, faking his best cheerful mood.

Light scowled back. It was the same scowl Light had shot David when he walked over to the two cops, introduced himself, and told them again not to talk to Light. Light didn't move from the bench at the far side of the cell.

David shuffled his feet. "Listen, don't talk to them. Don't say anything at all. Except your name and that stuff, okay?"

Light folded his arms and glared silently at David, who pushed his irritation down. That wouldn't do anybody any good now. The question was, would he be able to get any more of the story out of Light today? Doubtful, but David decided to make one try.

David pulled out his Daytimer as if checking the appointments he had for the rest of the day, looked up hurriedly, and said, "Okay, and this is important, don't even talk to me, right?"

Light's eyes darted left and right as if confused. His mouth opened and closed but no words came out.

"Good. I'll see you in court then." David spun to the door.

"When?" Light said the word without moving a muscle.

Perfect timing. "Not today." David said. "Maybe tomorrow. Arraignments are backed up."

Light sat, silent and motionless.

He was a sad-looking figure, his basketball belly poking out through the blue nylon shirt, straining the two bottom buttons. The rest of his body sat in angry repose, like a three-year-old on a five-minute hunger strike. The electric blue of the shirt clashed with the dull tans and grays of the cell. David wondered why clients always clashed with the surroundings. Bright colors in dank surroundings. The light that dappled through the dust-encrusted casement windows didn't penetrate to the cell, tucked as it was in the corner, but Light's blue shirt still flashed, even without sunlight to reflect. Maybe that was it: trying to carry his own light, sparkle up the drabness of life with himself. But the drabness of the cell had soaked up Light's sparkle. Soaked it dry.

David stood up straight and slapped the bars of Light's cell. "Anything else?" David asked.

Light met David's eye for a second, then looked down, his face softening slightly. "When we can talk?"

David pretended to ignore the crack in Light's voice. The angry demeanor was broken now. It was what David was hoping for, the crack that would let David through, would allow him to represent Light effectively. David had done his job, but he felt some sadness, watching Light staring at the blank walls, his spirit, now nicely broken, seeming to match the gray concrete.

"Won't be really safe until after arraignments," David said slowly and quietly.

"Can't pay," Light said without moving his eyes from the concrete.

"We'll talk about that later, after the arraignment." David hesitated for a second before tapping the bars. He motioned to the detectives that he needed privacy, and they walked to the other side of the room. David turned back to Light, gesturing that he should join him at the bars.

Light reluctantly pushed himself up from the bench and came toward David with a half-hearted angry strut that looked out of place on his fifty-two-year-old body. Making the journey without eye contact, he leaned against the bars and looked over David's shoulder to the room beyond.

He told the story to the empty room in hushed tones. The answers to David's questions came without acknowledgment of David's presence, as if the room beyond David's shoulder needed the information.

"You know about attorney-client privilege, right? Anything you say to me in confidence, I can't tell anyone else."

"Mr. Cohen, I know it hard to believe, but this the truth. This the one right thing I done in my life. This and that thing with LeVander." Light's face crinkled as if he were trying to hold back tears.

Pulling out his Daytimer, David flipped a page, just to have something to do, just to cut the tension.

"Can you describe the woman?" he asked.

Light shrugged. "Spanish-looking, young, pretty. Kind of silky brown hair. Short, like shoulder's, you know?"

"Could you identify her?"

Light shrugged, still staring over David's shoulder. Then, face hardening, he said, "Yeah, I know her. You bring that bitch here, I identify her."

David snapped his notebook closed, told Light he'd see him in arraignments, and headed down the stairs. One thing he was sure of: if he found a woman, Light would identify her. But he had better find the right woman.

Vance tapped the toes of his loafers on the wooden saddle. He loved this time and the brief respite it gave him. The heavy door groaned before opening to his push. The bad part of this time of day: the door reminding him the vigorous days of his youth had passed.

Pulling off his tweed sport coat, he realized that the mood the walk by the reflecting pool had so methodically built was already undermined. It was time for a vacation, he thought as he plopped down on the well-worn chair next to the fire Mabel had so thoughtfully started. *MAHbel*, he said to himself, the proper Spanish pronunciation. He had, in a moment of exasperation, almost spat out in raised volume the English pronunciation. He had caught himself, both in the exasperation and the pronunciation. That wouldn't have done, to mispronounce the housekeeper's name. A person's name was hers and not subject to the linguistic rigidity that age and American English chauvinism set upon it. The housekeeper deserved the same consideration on this score as did his clients. Vance picked up the newspaper and snapped it open to the front page. Perhaps more. At least the housekeepers of this world tried to do their jobs honestly, which was more than he could say about some of his clients.

He briefly read the congressional news and scanned the world news before punching his answering machine. The machine crackled, beeped, and was silent before a resigned voice spoke. The voice shook slightly as it introduced itself, as if Vance would not have recognized it as Twining's in its occasional sobriety. Perhaps Twining was trying to collect his thoughts. That would be a nice change, Vance thought as he flipped open his black, leather-bound notepad and pulled the ballpoint pen fashioned in the shape of a quill from a blond wood desk set.

"Sorry to bother you," the voice said. "But since you're not there, I guess I'm not bothering you, am I?" The voice hesitated.

Vance let the pen hang over the pad. Twining, he realized, was turning into one of those drunks who make more sense drunk than sober. It might be hard to talk around that to the voters, even in Brooklyn, where having homosexual affairs with congressional pages was not considered a bar to reelection.

The voice continued. Vance jotted the salient points in the black notebook. He waited until the beep sounded and the tape began to rewind. He was hoping for more, like a phone number, a precinct, some way of getting in touch. Twining had managed to ruin a perfectly good morning without giving Vance the slightest opportunity to do him any good.

Slipping the artificial quill back in the wooden holder, Vance snapped the leather notepad closed. Twining would do the wrong thing; of that, Vance was certain. Twining always seemed to do the wrong thing. Exasperation rising, Vance picked up the phone. Exasperation and guilt. Twining was an idiot, and Vance had helped elect him.

CHAPTER 3

David pulled to the curb and stood for a second, scanning the neighborhood. It was that section of Brooklyn, stretched like runny chocolate icing over the top of a marble cake, that white cops referred to as "black." Its residents might think of themselves as living in Brownsville, East New York, or Flatbush, might think of themselves as Americans, Africans, Haitians, Trinidadians, Bahamians, but the white cops knew, they knew as they rode back to their suburban homes on Long Island and in Rockland County.

David tossed his briefcase in the trunk, locked it, dropped the keys in his pocket, and walked over toward the knot of blackness, tying and untying itself in front of the corner bodega. He hated the approach, even when he had done it with cops, cops who had made the approach for years. Each had his own method: the boisterous, covering their insecurity with volume; the shy, alternating their gaze between the notepad clutched in front and their shoes, projecting the image of a damn fool, just trying to do his job; or that of the kindly father, really here to help all these people.

David shook himself to try to make this his own approach. The knot was already beginning to twist slowly as it became aware of him. Its individual fibers, each clutching a brown paper–bagged beer, turned, trying desperately to face another fiber without facing the oncoming suited white man, trying not to be the first to whom he spoke.

David stopped a few feet from the knot, confronted with a solid wall of backs. The faces behind the wall shifted uncomfortably, avoiding eye contact. All but one: a short man, glaring out between two shoulders, a man who looked as if he could have been a fighter once, a flyweight, but who had ballooned over the years so now he could qualify only for light heavy.

His eyes locked onto David's. The eyes looked as though they had anger trapped in them, anger from long ago.

The shoulders closed as the backs began to move, the spell broken.

David shifted his weight and cleared his throat. "Any of you know Light?"

The knot held for a second, silently suspended in space. The backs shifted slowly, gaps opening in the wall, until those eyes again glared through, softening slightly, confusion still dominating but another emotion, curiosity, peering through. David locked onto the eyes and said, loudly enough so that his voice could defuse through the group, "I'm his lawyer."

David kept his eyes on the short man and let the other eyes play over him, evaluating. David had long since lost control of his approach, as any of the many cops he'd accompanied would have gladly pointed out. For the cops, the knot had won at this point and the case would remain a Puerto Rican mystery, precinct shorthand for a crime with a hundred eyewitnesses who had seen nothing.

David broke eye contact and reached in his pocket. "Well, if any of you know anything about what happened with that congressman, you can call me." David held up his card as the backs closed to him. He shrugged, stuffed the card back in his pocket, and walked toward the bodega.

So much for friendship, he thought. Two days before, Light would have been there, rolling with that knot, sucking down a few and then a few more, until the conversation deteriorated to ghetto bottom: one word repeated with various inflections, interrupted by crackling laughter erupting from the back of mouths and punctuated with bursts of anger and bouts of pouting.

David pulled an Amstel from the upright refrigerator and slapped it and two dollars on the counter. The middle-aged Spanish man with the salt-and-pepper beard smiled a wordless hello and pulled a bottle-sized brown paper bag from a small pile on the counter. Opening the bag with a practiced flip of the wrist, he slipped the bottle silently inside.

As the man lifted the two dollars from the counter, David asked him if he'd been working when Light was arrested.

He grunted in the affirmative and dropped two quarters on the glass counter. "Was watching from right here, out that window. Couldn't see much, nothing but that congressman on the ground, Light with that pipe, waving it around, yelling at that man to get up. Like he wanted to hit that man some more." The Spanish man put both his arms on the counter and leaned forward, bringing his face to within a foot of David's.

David stepped back a pace and twisted the top off his bottle. "Funny, he didn't just take him off then."

"No, not Light. He don't care about money. That man been kind a crazy since that thing with LeVander. Remember that?"

David leaned back against the refrigerator. "Yeah, that thing where the lawyer got shot downtown?"

"Yeah, that's the one."

"So, Light just bopped that guy, huh? Just bopped him?"

"Yeah, I guess. And it was weird, kind of, with that girl takin' off in that BMW."

David took a long pull on his beer, trying to appear as calm as possible. He stopped the beer with his tongue as he thought. Someone who saw the girl. Someone else saw the woman. A confirmation that his crazy client was telling the truth. "Know her?" David asked.

The man behind the counter shook his head. "Some whore, I guess. But sure took that car like she thought it was hers." He paused for a minute. "She wasn't like a street girl. Clean, good skin. But I couldn't see much from here."

"Anybody around who could see better?"

The man shrugged. "I was in here. I could only see the corner, just that patch of corner over there, see? Anybody around could have seen better, but I don't know who was around."

"Anybody in the store?"

"People, I guess, but I don't know who." The man pulled a rag from under the counter and started rubbing the glass covering the front pages of the week's tabloids. "You a cop?"

"Lawyer," David said. "Light's lawyer."

The man nodded to the glass countertop. "You could ask around, but just don't say I said nothing. People don't like to get involved, unless it's on television. You know what I mean?"

"Yeah, sure. Light ever come in here?"

"Yeah, Light come in here all the time. He bought his Old English here. Every day."

David thanked the man and walked outside. Good enough to sell his Old English, but not to help out in time of trouble. Life in the big city.

As David walked over to the 1979 Chevy and half leaned, half sat on the hood, few heads turned in his direction. The knot got quiet. David watched as the pack tried to decide whether to move or accept its unwelcome visitor. Finally they decided to ignore him and went back to their conversation.

David ignored them, sucked on his beer, and enjoyed the feeling of mild inebriation coming over him. He didn't notice the light heavy until he was standing apart from the knot, glaring straight at David. The knot nervously swelled and twisted, its conversation reduced to grunts, as the man and David eyed each other.

Anger was in the eyes, but it was diffused, not directed at David.

David took another swig of his beer and looked away. He wasn't nervous, just uncomfortable. He wished the man would say something or go back to the knot.

David looked up the street. Two blocks up was another knot in front of another bodega. David decided he'd check with them next, to cover his bases, though they were probably too far away to have seen anything. And knots usually stuck to their own bodegas, so it was unlikely any of the members of that knot had been down here when Light was arrested.

Light had said there were kids around. They must have seen something. Then there was Evelyn Jefferson. But Light said not to talk to her. She didn't want to help. Light had been adamant, but David would talk to her too, maybe after he found some of the kids.

David took another hit from his beer. The man hadn't moved; he was still standing motionless on the sidewalk in front of David, still silent. Finally the man jerked his head in the direction of the opposite corner. There wasn't anger in it, more like an invitation. David allowed his eyes to follow the man's head.

The building was old: an abandoned storefront on the ground floor, red brick shrouding green casement windows on the second. A wooden sign hanging vertically near the corner window proclaimed in green lettering, "Billiards." David shrugged, drained the beer, dropped the empty in a wire trash can, and walked toward the pool hall. The man might look like a boxer, but that was a lot of years ago.

The door, painted the same shade of green as the upstairs windows, resisted the first push. The man pushed David aside and put his shoulder to the door. It groaned but gave way. David followed the man up the rickety stairs and into a carpeted room scented with blue chalk and the must of uncleaned corners.

Standing next to David, the boxer maintained his silence. David nodded to the two older men holding cues at a table near the window. They nodded back, then turned to the window, leaving the balls laying undisturbed in the rack. David took a step to the desk and the fat black man who sat behind it.

The fat man pushed back his baseball cap and gestured

to the twelve tables running in two rows from the desk to the windows. "Table, sir?" Except for the two men at the table in the front, the place was empty.

"Table," David mumbled, failing to make eye contact.

The fat man pushed himself off his stool and bent slowly for a plastic brace of balls. "Yo, Squeaky," he said, just before his head disappeared behind the counter.

A voice responded from the doorway behind David. "This here white man is gonna be paying for a table for him and me." Squeaky was named against type.

The fat man looked at David and David nodded. "Don't care who pays, just pay before you leave, gentlemen," he said, dropping the balls on the counter. "Table ten."

"Don't mind that 'Squeaky,'" Squeaky said, putting his hand on David's shoulder and guiding him to table ten. "See, they just call me that. Street name."

"How come?"

"'Cause I talks too much. Talking all the time, that's me. Can't hardly shut me up." Squeaky grabbed the square rack, dumped the balls on the table, put the chalk on the rail, and pointed to the triangular rack below the table. "You rack, seein' as how I'm going to break."

"Eight ball?"

Squeaky nodded. "Eight ball, five dollars a game. Got your money?"

David nodded and racked. As he pulled the black plastic away from the balls, the cue ball came crashing into the pack.

"George don't get many white men down here playing." Squeaky watched as the three ball dropped in the corner. "Ever since he heard about this thing with pool becoming upscale, George been waiting to be discovered. He like some young actress with stars in his eyes." Squeaky laughed. "Four ball." A second later the four ball dropped in the corner pocket.

"Can't hurt to have dreams," David said.

"See, that's the problem with these here niggers." Squeaky hesitated for a moment, as if trying to decide if he'd insulted David or his people with the term. Apparently deciding it didn't matter, he continued. "They got a dream, but it all depend on the white man. The devil, I say."

"White man the devil?"

"That's Muslim shit. That just the same shit. See, that way the white man define. It ain't us. We just get to react to the white man, same as before. Just we invent some god to be on our side. Then look at the white man Bible, and try to prove Jesus be black. Don't matter." Squeaky paused and looked at the table. "One ball."

David watched quietly as Squeaky walked to the side of the table and sighted the one ball. David dabbed some chalk on his cue. He looked up as Squeaky stroked.

"We got to make it our own selves. Why you want to Tom up to the devil?" The one ball dropped softly in the side pocket.

"Why are you talking to me?"

Squeaky straightened up and looked at David for the first time. "See, them boys down there don't understand it. They just don't talk to the white man if they can help it. Only white men we get down here regular is cops and landlords, or storeowners, one. They down here takin', orderin', bossin'." Squeaky paused to chalk his cue. He walked to the other side of the table and bent for a better look.

David scanned the table. Squeaky hadn't left himself a good position and was staring at a three-ball combination.

"But you may be different. See, you come for what you want, but all you want is information. Some a your shit come down here and fuck up. You trying to help a brother. Most a them don't see it that way. Seven ball." Squeaky bent low, sighted down the cue, moved slightly to the right, and smoothly stroked the ball. There was a series of clicks, like a rear-end collision on a Los Angeles freeway, and the seven ball rolled to the lip of the corner pocket, teetered there for a second, and fell in.

"And five dollars a game?"

"You willing to help us, but it don't come free."

David nodded, then waited while Squeaky lined up the

six ball. "So you saw that incident with Light?"

Squeaky looked up. "This here game ain't over. I figure I'll remember after about ten games." Bending low, he studied the path the six would have to traverse, squeezing between two high balls and into the corner.

David chalked his cue. Fifty dollars. The man wanted fifty dollars for information David didn't even know he had. "If I'm going to lose fifty dollars, then I should know what I'm going to get." He said the "fifty dollars" a little loudly, loudly enough so the two old men poking balls by the front window could hear. The men looked over.

Squeaky raised his voice, taking the challenge. "You getting like all them other white men, looking for something for nothing. Maybe I was wrong 'bout you. Six ball."

David watched as the six ball squeezed through the two highs and dropped in the middle of the pocket.

"Just another white man come down here when he need something. When he need something from us. Needs votes, needs us buying more a his bullshit." Squeaky walked over to the three balls frozen together. "Now see here, no white man would shoot this here shit. You know why? Because it ain't sure shit. Just like you, want sure shit. White man talk about taking risk, but he don't take no risk, not really. He want everything lined up perfect so it just drop in place for him. But watch, see I'm gonna hit that five ball, that two ball gonna come off the end, kiss the nine and drop right in that pocket. No white man try that shot." Squeaky walked back, sighted down the cue stick, and rolled the cue toward the pack. The two kissed the nine, rolled toward the pocket, hit the jaw and rimmed out, setting up in front of the pocket. "See, I got that shit blocked for you. That's what people miss, not takin' risks. Even when you don't get what you trying for, you get some shit."

The two old men came over from their game, drawn by Squeaky's commotion.

The only ball David could see was the ten, sitting next to the twelve and parallel to the cue ball, which was an inch from the first dot near the side pocket.

HOSTILE WITNESS   33

One of the old men looked at the shot and shook his head. "Like to see you win, mister. Like to see anybody shut Squeaky up."

"Better make the most of it, Mr. Lawyer. That the best shot you gonna see today." Squeaky laughed, a high-pitched squeal that sounded like a subway hitting a corner too fast.

"Ten, kissing the twelve, in the corner." David bent over the cue, sighting the shot, then looked up at Squeaky. He locked onto Squeaky's eyes and stroked the shot.

A second later the ten was in the corner. Thirty seconds later David was shooting the eight with a one-foot, forty-five-degree shot. The two old men had forgotten the window.

David walked over to Squeaky, stood next to him, looking at the table, and whispered, "Looks like you got your choice, Squeaky. I drop this ball and the cue in the corner, you get five dollars and tell me what you know. Or we play ten games, you owe me fifty dollars, and you tell me what you know." David looked around the room. He stopped, staring at fat George sitting behind the desk. "Now, I'm not coming back, so I don't care. But you wouldn't want to have a white man beat you ten times in a row, right here, when he could choke, just like white men always do. See, it's this risk thing. We don't have the nerves." David paused. "Up to you."

Squeaky was quiet for a long moment. The old men stood over by the window, silhouetted by the sun peaking through the dusty glass. "How you gonna be sure you scratch?" he asked finally.

"What choice you got?"

Squeaky took a deep breath. "Okay, but then we play another and you lose."

"Okay, one more, but sink some balls, will you? I got work to do."

Five minutes later Squeaky led David out the door, along the side street, down another, and around a corner, all the time assaulting David's ears with his constant babble. David tuned it out as he walked alongside, surprised by Squeaky's pace. He didn't slow until they reached a quiet block lined with abandoned buildings on both sides. Smiling crookedly at David, Squeaky gestured with his head.

David looked into the buildings as he passed, noticing the eyes of the junkies peering out at him from slits in the basement walls. Shivering, David continued. Maybe he should have lost the fifty dollars. At least Squeaky wouldn't have revenge as a motive.

"Come on, Mr. Lawyer. I thought you was a risk taker." Squeaky turned back to the front and laughed. "See, the white man, he always back off. You just got to take him far enough. This ain't like no pool table, right Mr. Lawyer? Can't be predictin' here."

David didn't answer, but possibilities ran through his mind. He didn't even know where this man was leading him. Maybe to some evidence, a witness, maybe the woman. Or maybe an alley, there to be jumped by a gang of some kind, beaten, maybe killed, robbed of the money he had in his pockets, and left. Left to be stripped, like urban carrion. Stripped by the scavengers. First the jewelry, then the clothes, finally the gold in his teeth, ripped from his mouth and sold for a vial of crack.

David shook his head. He was a better judge of character than that. This man was too old, too talkative. Too many people had seen them. Besides, David wasn't going in any alleys. He followed Squeaky into the middle of the street. The streetlights cut the gloom a little more here, he thought as he looked back to shadows near those slits. Even Squeaky wasn't comfortable here, in this deserted street.

Squeaky continued across the street, right over to a line of parked cars. Suddenly he stopped, pointing proudly to a red BMW. "This it. That motherfucker peel out right after Light hit that man. Just peel motherfuckin' out."

David felt a little foolish. Squeaky was crossing the street to get to the other side, the other side where the BMW was. The great and brave lawyer wiped the nervous sweat from his forehead and walked to the front of the car. The plates

HOSTILE WITNESS 35

were on it. The doors were unlocked but the stripping of the car had not yet begun.

"This is the car the woman drove away in?"

"Squealing off that curb."

David pulled open the passenger door. The alarm sounded, but David ignored it. So would everyone else in the area. Except the junkies and the crack heads, David imagined, ready now to pounce on the car as soon as David left.

He flipped open the glove compartment. Pushed among the usual assortment of maps was a plastic envelope with the registration and owner's manual. He stuffed the plastic in his pocket and flipped through the maps.

He closed the glove compartment and went through the seat pockets, which were empty. In the compartment between the seats he found a business card. He pocketed it and got out. He checked the license plate against the registration. It matched.

He looked across to Squeaky, who was standing by the car, smiling. "Where is there a pay phone close by?"

Squeaky gestured with his head and David followed.

"You follow the car afterward?"

"Nope. Walk down this street on the way home from George's. Recognized it. Actually took down the plate." Squeaky fumbled through his pockets, finally pulling out a scrap of paper. "See here," he said, shoving the paper toward David.

The plate number was roughly scrawled on the back of a grocery receipt. David handed the receipt back to Squeaky. They walked to the corner in silence. Thanking Squeaky, David ducked into a phone booth.

CHAPTER 4

David dropped the phone back in the cradle. Satisfaction began to cover the anger. Light had been telling the truth, at least in part. The part about the woman, about the BMW. That had been true, and the cops' story about no evidence was bullshit. Jenson's voice had fluttered just a little when David told him about the red BMW and a little more when he told him the owner was Congressman Twining.

David spun the registration in his hand. He hadn't told Jenson about that though. Instead he'd told him he'd checked through Motor Vehicles. He had, of course. It had taken only five minutes with the computer, but that was just to cover his tracks. Dropping the registration into a small manila envelope, he pulled out the business card. Maybe he should have called Jenson first. After all, the junkies might be on the car by now. He shrugged as he flipped the business card between his fingers.

The card was a woman's, Coyce Loyn. Interesting name. It identified its owner as a provider of business services, with no indication of what kind. There was a phone number, no address. David punched in the number.

"Business Services," a soft female voice answered seductively.

David paused for a moment before answering. He tried

to make his voice as businesslike as possible. "Coyce Loyn, please."

There was a pause on the other end of the line, then a click as David felt himself put on hold. Whoever had answered the phone was definitely not a front-office type. David flipped the card over with his fingers. There was nothing on the back, only what he saw. He supposed "business services" could refer to servicing out of town businessmen. It fit the name.

The phone clicked again and David was rescued from hold.

"Hi," the voice said, "this is Coyce. I'm busy right now, but if you leave your number, I'll call you back in no more than twenty minutes."

David gave his number.

"If that is your home number, press one. If it is an office number, press two."

David wondered how an automated answering machine could be so sexy.

"If discretion is required on the call back, press one. If no discretion is required, press two."

David pressed one. He thought of disillusioning Lois, the new receptionist. What the hell? She was eighteen, old enough to be disillusioned about men. But he didn't. The romantic Victorian in him won out.

The machine continued. "If emergency service is required, press one. If this call is to schedule routine maintenance, press two."

David realized how much of an emergency it was as he remembered how long it had been since he'd had routine maintenance. Janie had been in Florida for the past year and seemed intent on remaining. David pressed one.

The voice of the machine did not respond at once. It just breathed, slowly, rhythmically. David could feel the breath, first on one erogenous zone, then another. Just as he was about boiling, the voice spoke.

"Stay by the phone, I'll call right back."

David was silent as the breathing resumed, first on the

inside of his thighs, then on his scrotum. "When?" his loins screamed, but the machine clicked off.

David resoulutely placed his hands on top of his desk and slowed his breathing. He was a professional, he reminded himself. A professional working on a case. It took a few minutes, but eventually his blood flow returned to normal. Then the phone rang.

He grabbed it before Lois could. The breathing was back. He assumed it was live, although he didn't know why. The fidelity of the recording had been astoundingly good.

The voice breathed through her introductions. It was Coyce. She spoke a few more words.

David felt his loins scream, "When?" He believed it was in response to a question.

"Seven?" Coyce asked between erectile breaths.

"Where?" His loins again.

Coyce gave him the address, which he scribbled down. David sat quietly for a moment as he collected his thoughts. Coyce didn't sound Spanish, but she was close enough to the congressman that he carried her card with him. David didn't know what that meant, except that he'd meet her at seven and see how erectile breathing sounded live.

David took a deep breath before walking through the black iron gates into the Criminal Court Building. Somehow that last gulp of what passed for fresh air in Brooklyn made the atmosphere of the courthouse a little easier to take. Slipping past the line and through the side door, he flashed his yellow pass and walked into the main foyer, straight back, past the reporters milling in front of the arraignment part, through the clerk's office, and into the rear entrance to the courtroom.

He nodded a greeting to a court officer as he entered the courtroom. The benches were about a quarter full. The occupants sat in the half stupor David had gotten used to over the years. He slapped the court officer's desk quietly.

Looking up from his dog-eared copy of the *Daily News*,

the unshaven officer raised one eyebrow but otherwise maintained civil-service detachment.

"Leroy Scott?"

"Downstairs." The officer showed little animation. "Judge said to pull him up soon as you got here."

"Wants to get rid of me, huh?"

The officer pushed himself away from the desk. "Not you. The press."

David nodded and watched as the court officer lumbered over to the pen door and disappeared behind it. Squeezing behind a fat lawyer arguing bail for his client, David found a seat in the first row of the gallery. A cop shifted slightly, making room. The lawyers' row had been taken over by the press, leaping aboard like scavengers on carrion.

David looked around. Congressman Carrion wasn't there. Not a surprise. Other than the pencils and pads in the hands of the small knot of overweight, overage men, it was a typical arraignment day.

The judge avoided eye contact, assuring David he was aware of David's presence. His Honor nervously fiddled with some notes as he discussed a plea with the attorneys. Snapping open his briefcase, David pulled out his file. It was going to be another one of those: the judge trying to get off the stage as quickly as possible without anyone remembering his name, trying to be the perfect third man in the ring. Not that it mattered. No judge would give Light bail that he could make, which was none. Besides, despite finding the BMW, David wasn't sure Light hadn't tried to rob the congressman.

The door to the pens opened with the court officer behind it, beckoning.

Slipping behind the court officers and the defendant, David followed the officer into the tiny pen behind the judge's bench. The heavy steel door slammed shut as the officer pushed his way through the crowd of ten prisoners jammed into the six-foot-square room. He quickly unlocked a wire mesh gate, slipped through it to a makeshift office, and sat behind an aging wooden desk.

David remained in the cubicle. The two interview carrels on the right and left were occupied. He stood, breathing through his mouth, a defense against the atmosphere of the room where prisoners had been trapped in the system for two to three days, without showers or changes of clothes, most of them afraid even to shit.

Light stood against the wire mesh, arms folded, scowling. David weaved his way over to him.

"Soon as one of these cubicles opens up, we'll talk."

Light grunted, sullenly staring straight ahead into the back of another prisoner.

David put his back against the wire and stared straight ahead with him. "Don't say anything now," he said, folding his arms.

They stood together, silently waiting for several minutes, until one of the doors to the left crack opened. A Legal Aid lawyer, short, chubby, balding, and bored, threw his rumpled corduroy jacket over his shoulder and ducked out of the room. David grabbed the door just ahead of another Legal Aid attorney, and he motioned Light to the other door.

They closed the doors, David sitting on one side of a chest-high counter, Light on the other. Light leaned back against the partition, as far from David as he could get. Taking a deep breath, David prepared for the struggle.

"All right, listen up, Mr. Scott," David hoped the "Mr. Scott" might help, but he doubted it. "I want you to know what's happened and what's going to happen out there today."

Light glared silently.

David breathed a little easier. At least Light was glaring at him now, not over his shoulder. "I don't think you're going to get out today."

"Why the fuck not? Everybody see what happened."

"Well, maybe. But everybody's not talking to me. In fact, nobody is."

"Why the fuck they don't talk to you?"

"How should I know? You want to talk about what we do have?"

"What we got? We got a congressman saying I rob his ass, and we got you sitting on your fucking white ass while my black ass locked up, that's what we got."

David hesitated for a moment, letting himself cool down. He took a deep breath and continued. "What we do have is, we found the BMW."

Light was silent for a moment. "What you mean, 'We found the BMW'?"

"The one the woman drove off in, we found it."

"Where you find it?"

"About ten blocks away."

"How you find it? I thought nobody wouldn't talk to you."

"They wouldn't. Somebody finally did."

"Squeaky."

David nodded.

"Yeah, Squeaky can't stop talking."

"Squeaky and I played some pool."

"How much it cost you?" Light grunted.

"Ten."

"You lucky," Light said as he walked around the tiny cubicle like a dazed zoo leopard just regaining his senses. It was a minute or two before he was aware of the silence and looked up.

"The BMW was registered to Twining," David continued. "It'll give him some questions to answer."

Light nodded. "So how come I ain't gettin out today?"

David shrugged. "It'll turn out to be an embarrassment to Twining, but it doesn't affect the facts in the case. Besides, there's a load of reporters prancing around out there. Judge won't risk cutting you loose in this case. Probably keep you in on bail for at least five days to see if the DA wants to indict."

"Indict? I didn't do nothing," Light said, storming around the cubicle, grabbing at air, as if he were looking for something to throw. "I was doing the right fucking thing. I done shit in my life. You can believe that. Everybody know that. But this time I do right." The anger seemed to drain from Light as he turned to David. "I really done right."

David tapped Light's hand, smiled tightly, and slipped his papers back into his briefcase. He hoped this case didn't go to trial. Preparing Light would be torture. *Now, Light, stay calm, no matter what they ask on cross.* Yeah, right.

"We'll be called in a few minutes. Try to calm down by then." David opened the door and pushed his way through the crowd and into the courtroom.

"Scott, Leroy!"

David caught the bridgeman's eye. The bridgeman shrugged as if to say it was the judge's idea. David walked around the rail, dropped his briefcase between his knees, and pulled out Light's file.

The door popped back open and two NYPD officers pushed Light into the courtroom.

Light stumbled in, stopped, and spun on the officers. "I can walk," he snapped.

The skinny blue shirt, about thirty with black hair slicked straight back, grabbed Light by the arm, shook him, and said something David could not hear. His more phlegmatic partner grasped Light's handcuff and gave it a quick twist.

Light bent over double and screamed something ill formed but meant to be obscene. By the time the judge looked up from his paperwork, the officer had snorted, run his hand up to above Light's elbow, and was inquiring solicitously about "Mr. Scott's" welfare.

"Your Honor, do we have to put up with this kind of torture in the courtroom?" David was sorry he had said it before the words left his mouth.

Light shook free of the officers and walked to the defendant's spot. "Just leave my ass alone," he said, "I know the routine. You don't have to be torturing me." Light spun—first toward the officers, who tried to look like innocent children, falsely accused, then toward the judge.

The judge took the offer, running his gaze first over the officers, then over Light, finally allowing it to rest for an uncomfortable minute on David, as if to say he expected this kind of behavior from the younger siblings, the cops and criminals, but not from David.

David held the judge's eye for just a second too long before glancing at the bridgeman.

As if thusly cued, the bridgeman started to read: "Scott, Leroy, 120.05, 110/160.05 . . ."

Assault and attempted robbery; David tuned out the rest. It was what he had expected. David looked up when the bridgeman stopped and said, "So waived." The bridgeman droned on.

"Waved? They fucking torturing my ass, and you waving at the fucking judge?" Light muttered.

David started to explain, but thought better of it.

"I want Jacobs. He don't wave at no fucking judges."

The bridgeman had stopped droning, and the assistant district attorney had taken over. "Your Honor, this man was arrested brandishing a four-foot length of steel pipe, this steel pipe," the ADA said, brandishing a four-foot length of steel pipe, "over the crumpled body of Congressman Harrison Twining."

"Your Honor, in the interest of maintaining some level of veracity before this court, I must point out that Congressman Twining is alive and well and, as far as I know, in excellent health," David broke in.

"Thanks only to the bravery of Officer Seaford and Detective Jenson, who rescued him from this . . . this monster." The ADA gestured at Light.

"Ain't you going to say nothing?" Light asked, spinning around to face David.

The cop grabbed Light and roughly spun him back toward the judge. "Face the judge."

"Face the motherfucking judge," Light muttered.

The cop fingered the handcuffs, beginning to twist gently. Light turned front and said nothing.

"We are asking for $100,000 bail," the ADA concluded.

David looked at him as he finished, hesitating. He was young, twenty-six maybe. Never been in front of the press before. *Any minute now, he'll look up, notice.* David waited.

The ADA looked up. David caught his eye. *Now he'll hesitate, get self-conscious, start looking around.* David loved this part. It was like that lifetime in an instant some athletes talked about. The ADA started to shake.

"What?" he asked.

David turned calmly to the judge. "Assistant district attorneys are immune from prosecution for perjury in this state, Your Honor, and I suppose that's just as well. After all, we don't know if this man is a fully involved coconspirator or merely a dupe, sent, like the Six Hundred, to do and die. Because in our system, we don't punish people for ignorance..." David paused to glare softly at the ADA. "... or eccentricity or merely doing the bidding of others. No, we punish people for their crimes. The ones they commit, not the ones it's convenient for someone in power to accuse them of."

The judge glared down at David impatiently. "Mr. Cohen, are you saying there was no crime committed here?"

David hesitated a moment. He felt the reporters in the gallery inching closer, heard their pencils scribbling ferociously.

"Oh, there was a crime committed here. And there was a hero. It's just that, for reasons best known to those in the district attorney's office and those in Congressman Twining's office, roles are being switched. You see, Your Honor, I presented evidence to the New York City Police Department and the district attorney's office, just yesterday, confirming what the defendant has said all along." David paused for effect. "That there was an assault, but that Congressman Twining was not the victim of that assault. No, he was the *perpetrator* of that assault."

The ADA jumped toward the bench. "Your Honor, is counsel going to use the cloak of his immunity to libel the congressman?"

"Your Honor, it is my intention to libel the district attorney's office, not the congressman. After all, it is the district attorney who has chosen not to come clean with the court and disclose all the evidence in this matter." David paused as he strained to hear the scribbling behind him.

Judge Williams looked at David, as if to make sure he was finished, but really, David believed, to try to compose a dignified response which would seem judicial and not burn any political bridges. Judge Williams was a large man, a presence in the courtroom, with his dark black skin glistening with sweat despite the air conditioning. He undid the blue-backed papers with his large hands, flipping the pages of the file deliberately. He wasn't reading. There was nothing in the papers to read, each page bearing a coded symbol that obviated the need to read.

He stopped at the computer printout of Light's record. David had stopped counting after page five; so did the judge. After this point the length of the record actually worked to the defendant's advantage. If his crimes had been serious, he would have done more time. And besides, he had a track record of returning to court. Judge Williams dropped the papers to the desk and looked over to the ADA.

"Mr. District Attorney?"

"Your Honor, I don't know what Mr. Cohen is talking about."

David, expecting a longer defense, had turned to the audience, now separated, like cheap ice cream, suits near the rail, jeans and sweats in the back, seated, waiting quietly for the show to be over and the real action to begin.

David spun back to the judge. "Well, in that case, I suggest the DA talk to his superiors."

"Well, Counselor, I can't direct the man to do that. And if you don't have more, then I'll have to rule on what I have here."

"Your Honor, I don't think it's in my client's best interest to prejudice the police investigation by giving out the information at this time."

Light spun around. "Getting my black ass out of this jail is in my fucking interest, and that's all," he whispered.

The skinny cop grabbed him and spun him back to the front.

Judge Williams waited for another second, looking back

and forth between David and the DA. Hearing nothing, he began to write on the papers.

"In view of the seriousness of the offense and the record of the defendant, I'm going to set bail in the amount of $500,000." The judge smiled and tossed the papers across his desk to the clerk waiting with his stamps.

David silently pushed his way past the newspapermen in the courtroom and hallway, muttering, "No comment" to the midwestern teeth hovering around their news vans outside the courthouse. He glanced at the calendar on his watch: Monday, June 10. He'd give them until Wednesday. He turned sideways to slink through the normal crowds of society's parasites and their parasites in law enforcement.

He was half a block away when he turned back to the press crush, hovering around the entrance to the courthouse, waiting to attack an interview, any interview. Yeah, the Wednesday morning papers would have her name, probably her address too.

"Just meet this guy, David." Joel sprawled in his oversized chair, his six-six frame spread against the glass wall behind his desk.

David looked over Joel's shoulder to the skyline of downtown Manhattan and the Statue of Liberty beyond.

Swinging his leg off the arm of the chair and slapping it down on the plastic carpet guard, Joel continued, "You're good at this stuff."

David silently stared at the sun gleaming off the Manhattan skyline.

"It does us good. Names in the paper, business through the door."

"Everything isn't about new business, Joel," David said quietly.

"No," Joel said, standing and folding his arms. "Some of it's about representing clients, getting them off."

"Exactly. And what does my meeting this guy do for Light?"

"I'll tell you what it does, it gets the press started on Twining. They make it hot for Twining, he cools off on prosecution."

A pale, empty feeling filled David's chest. "The press is going to pursue this thing anyway. What good does it do us or Light to talk to them?"

"What harm does it do? I'm not asking you to have a goddamn press conference, just meet with this guy. Have a goddamn conversation."

David turned back to the river. He hadn't always had this aversion to the press. Just since Jefferson. Just since Janie left. "I still don't see what difference it makes if I talk to them or not," David said more calmly.

Joel took a deep breath and spun around to watch the river with David. "We don't know which way they'll take this story. Could go two ways. How dangerous the streets are. How even a congressman can get mugged. Or how a guy is getting railroaded by sloppy police work. TV goes with the pictures, print goes with the quotes. We don't give 'em quotes, they'll only have quotes from the other side."

David silently turned to the door. Joel was right. David didn't like it, but Joel was right.

David stood, bumping his head on the low-hanging plant. The man who was approaching had no concern about bumping his head. He wasn't short, or at least he wouldn't have been had he been standing at his full height. But stooped forward enough to make his thin, gray hair fall forward over his forehead, he was short. The body faced David straight on, but the face, dropped and twisted, faced him only three quarters. The part of the face David could see was smiling a thin smile through the gray pallor of his skin.

"Crawford Walsh," the man said, taking David's hand and clasping it briefly, without pressure.

"David Cohen," David said, gesturing to the empty chair across the table. Awkwardly, David adjusted his own chair as Walsh heavily dropped his case to the floor next to his.

Walsh bent into the chair, his twisted spine looking more

natural in the sitting position than it had standing. Reaching into his vest pocket, he withdrew a spiral pad, which he carefully opened. He pushed the used leaves up, meticulously working them over the bent spiral until they lay flat on the back of the pad. He then laid the pad on the table next to the unused place setting, reached into his shirt pocket, and withdrew a Mont Blanc pen, which he uncapped and brought down next to the pad. Finished, he looked up expectantly.

David wondered what he was expected to say. Walsh waited, his expression unchanged, the smile frozen, the dull eyes carrying sadness with them. Perhaps it was the head, tilted just slightly so that Walsh's gray hair hung toward his aquiline nose, that made Walsh look inquisitive. Perhaps too many years as a reporter, a sitting reporter.

Walsh's expression finally changed. The smile remained, but his mouth, which had been slightly open, now closed, his lips pursed. With that slight change the face became a demand, a harsh demand.

"Sorry, my mind wandered," David said.

"Your partner said you have some news on Twining." What had seemed an affectation when Walsh had introduced himself became an English public school accent when heard in full sentence.

David hid his surprise. "I don't know how much news, but we have a client in jail who's accused of assaulting Twining." David explained the facts briefly.

"Who was the woman?"

David shrugged. "Nobody saw her but Light."

Walsh's smile disappeared as he scratched a few notes with his Mont Blanc. The waitress appeared and Walsh waved her off. "I won't be staying," he said.

"No news?" David asked, hearing the relief in his own voice.

"No woman," Walsh answered. The smile gone, he took on the appearance of a man in a hurry. He pushed the cap back on the pen and stuck it into his pocket. "You see, we're a weekly."

"Tabloid?"

Walsh looked hurt at the appellation but nodded his assent. "But the point is weekly. Without a woman, this story will last a day, possibly two. If we spend our time on this, we get nothing. We like the kind of stories we can work over week after week. You know, a new revelation every week."

"Like the two-headed Martian boy?"

Walsh flipped the pad closed. "Don't laugh. We've as many repeat customers curious about the fate of the two-headed Martian boy as the *Times* has crossword lovers." He slipped the pad into his vest pocket, straightened his jacket, and stood. "However, I was referring to those non-fabricated stories over which we have control."

"Sex."

"Quite. More particularly, the sexual peccadilloes of those in high places. The 'legitimate press,' as they call themselves, the *New York Times*, and so on, stay away from breaking these stories."

"But pick up your leads."

"Precisely. Without a woman this is just a street mugging. A two-day story, tops." A smile twisted across Walsh's thin lips. "With a woman we could run Twining for a year."

David forced a smile as he shook Walsh's hand. He didn't like the man. Just being in Walsh's presence made David feel as if the life were being sucked from him. But there was the client's interest to think of.

"In any event, many lawyers look forward to working with us," Walsh continued, releasing David's hand too quickly. "Not only do they get their names in the paper once, but every week for a whole series. If we can find the woman, we may be able to provide the same service for you and your firm."

David dropped the smile as Walsh turned to the door. If they could find the woman. David's ardor for the search dropped.

* * *

David straightened his tie while looking at his reflection in the glass of the lobby. "Loyn," he said.

The doorman smiled and picked up the phone.

David tried to remember he wasn't nervous. After all, it wasn't as if he'd never had a first date before. A prostitute was just like another woman underneath it all.

"4B."

A few minutes later the door to 4B opened. Coyce brushed her reddish blond hair out of her eyes, stepped aside, and gestured David in.

He walked through, carefully avoiding the filmy robe that hid little and the soft skin of her thigh, extended as if to trip him. He turned and stood nervously as she closed the door. She turned, careless to her exposure of pubic hair—or maybe carefully careless. She smiled.

David noticed his hands were clasped in front of him, protecting that part of him that ostensibly needed attention. He quickly re-clasped them behind.

"I'm sorry I wasn't available earlier."

"Oh, don't worry." David tried his ingratiating smile but felt like a schoolboy.

"How did you get my name?" Coyce asked, sitting on the bed that dominated the left side of the room. Her robe parted as she sat, spreading in a circle on the bed, obscuring the floral pattern of the bedspread, and revealing a large section of inner thigh.

David didn't answer but followed uncertainly. Why he was uncertain was beyond that part of him that judged his behavior. He was paying $250 to touch her, and that would be difficult from across the room.

She patted the bed in encouragement.

He hadn't noticed before, but her thighs were slightly plump, as were her breasts. That was good; he was calming down enough to notice details. His lawyer's mind was coming back.

She patted the bed again, and he obediently walked over and sat. She began with the tie, loosening it in a most sensual way. "How did you come to call, then?"

"A friend." David pulled his tie off and started on his shirt himself. "Referral, I guess you'd say."

A moment later they were both naked and the flowered bedspread was at their ankles.

"I wonder who?" Coyce paused just long enough to catch her breath and allow David to fall from the brink of inevitability, before dropping her head back in his lap.

"Mmmm," David said.

"Who referred you?" Coyce started up his midsection, dragging her tongue along his navel and up to his nipples.

"Twining."

There was only a second's hesitation, then she was on his mouth, then his dick. But she was noticeably tenser. "That's surprising," Coyce gasped. Her work increased in tempo, as if she wanted him to come and be gone.

He did not cooperate. Instead he gently guided her face up to his.

"No funny business," she said.

David shook his head.

She guided her hips over his and took him inside her. He wanted to ask what kind of funny business she was talking about, but speech was difficult at the moment. He was glad she hadn't asked a question.

"Why would he recommend me?"

David groaned louder. There it was, the question. Well, he couldn't be expected to answer while he was coming.

David finished before he spoke. "I can see why he'd recommend you." He bent to kiss her.

She turned her cheek.

"What kind of funny business?" David asked as he pulled on his underwear.

She lay naked on the bed, her right leg hanging off the edge, her left knee raised like a mountain peak. She didn't speak.

David wanted to ask if another ride would cost another $250, but he didn't. He pulled on his pants.

She slipped her hand down the front of his pants before he was able to snap them closed. "You'll be able to come again, won't you?" she asked, massaging him back to life.

David thought it curious that she would be working him again, when she'd already earned her money. He pulled her close and whispered in her ear. "What happened with Twining?"

He felt his earlobe being sucked into her mouth and gently beaten by her tongue. "We can't talk about that," she said, "but I don't see him anymore."

David felt his pants falling around his knees. He wasn't thinking about another two fifty.

A half hour later David was on his feet and in her well-stocked bathroom. Pulling off a length of flavored dental floss, he started with the molars. He'd already selected a new toothbrush, in the container, and a hotel-size bottle of mouthwash. He turned on the water in the sink.

Twining had something more to be embarrassed about than a simple case of wandering lust. For someone named Coyce Loyn to be so upset by his attentions that she had cut him off. David couldn't imagine what it was, but it wouldn't play well in the papers.

"We can't just drop the thing."

Twining was into his bellowing stage, Vance thought as he watched the man stomp across the Persian carpet spread in front of Vance's desk.

"We can, and I think we shall." Satisfied that his voice had remained low and steady, Vance leaned back in his leather chair, folding his hands behind his head.

"Jesus Christ, Edwin, what'll the press do with that?"

"The press will do what it wishes. You've seen to that with your philandering. The more pertinent question is, what will that lawyer do to you if you pursue it?"

"That's relevant?"

"I suspect so, if the man who beat you raises defense of another, as I'm sure he will."

"Anacleta will never testify," Twining said more quietly.

"She won't have to. He'll simply raise the defense, find a couple of others who saw the incident, and get himself an acquittal. And you a nice scandal just in time for re-election."

Twining slumped into the chair across from Vance. "It isn't philandering, not really."

"So you want to marry the girl, do you? Well, the voters will see it as philandering... or something worse. She's twenty-two and you're near sixty. Get a grip, man."

Twining pulled the tumbler toward him. "Maybe I should just quit, retire." Twining looked up as if inspired by the idea.

Vance shook his head. "I'm afraid that's out too." Vance pulled the manila envelope from his top desk drawer, opened the flap and fished out the photos. A nice likeness of Twining and Anacleta, leaving a restaurant, clearly lovers. Vance pushed them across to Twining.

Twining picked them up, a resigned look on his face. He flipped through them slowly. "Anacleta was very friendly that night," he said, the spirit gone from his voice.

"There was a note with those," Vance continued, ignoring Twining's comment. "Shall I read it?"

Twining shook his head.

Vance slid the note over, watching as Twining slipped the note, unread, and the photos into his vest pocket. Vance felt for Twining as he drained his glass, reached across the desk, and shook Vance's hand. Vance felt a twinge of remorse as Twining trudged toward the door. Flashes of the campaigns in which Vance had helped elect and reelect this man popped into his head, but Vance pushed them away. After all, Twining was an adult. He had made his own decisions. They all had.

David tossed some change across the counter of the kiosk and picked up the three dailies. The *Times* had a dignified article in the "Metro" section, but the *Post* and the *News* were playing the sex and violence angles. And most important, as Joel would say, they all got the name right. "Leroy Scott's attorney, David Cohen, refused all comment, saying he would rather wait for the system, with all its weaknesses, to do its work." They even had cleaned up the quote for him. Maybe he wouldn't have to deal with the press on this; maybe they could handle it by themselves.

David folded the papers and stuffed them under his arm. Yes, the papers were getting the story right without him. But more important, the papers were right on schedule. The city editors would be working on their reporters to take this story to the next level. To do that, they needed the name of the woman.

"Walsh called," Joel said before the door had closed. He stuffed the note in David's pocket. "Wants you to call back."

David thought of making a comment, even resisting, but he knew he had to make the call.

Grabbing the slip, David strolled into his office and punched out the number. A moment later he was on hold, listening to a particularly obnoxious brand of Muzak, which cut of with a click.

"Walsh." The voice seemed to crackle through a thin veneer of mucus.

David identified himself and went through the fake pleasantries.

"Have to talk to you," Walsh's voice cracked through the line. Had tension been in his voice at the restaurant, or was it just today? David didn't know; he remembered only that face. He didn't remember tension. "About Twining."

David grunted.

"We have to meet."

"Why?"

"I've some competition. *Times, Post.* The big boys. We can't compete."

"I thought they wouldn't go with the sex for sex's sake."

"They are on this one."

"Why?"

"Don't know. But I have to talk to you."

"Crawford, this isn't life and death here. It's just a story."

"You're joking. The editor said to me, 'You've an inside on this, right?' So I said, 'Yes.' I saw the papers this morning. Now the question occurs. Do I?"

"Well, I'm talking to you." David wished the damn Englishman would get to the point.

"What I propose is that we collaborate."

"I'm a lawyer, not a reporter."

"Right. I wouldn't suggest anything that violated your ethics. Not at all. But I suspect this prosecution will be abated. Don't you agree?"

"They may dismiss at some point." David did agree.

"Right. Well, then. You supply me with what stories you can, consistant with ethical considerations, of course, and I give you any news items I come up with before they go out."

"And what are you likely to get me for risking the wrath of the discipinary committee?"

"You need pictures?"

"Of what?"

"The girls in Twining's life. Just like in *Playboy.*"

David sat up. "Girls, plural?"

"The girls. Twining has had a series of mistresses." Walsh was trying to sound grandfatherly now, as if he were both offended by it and reconciled to the fact that these things go on. But more than that, it was his subtle trust voice, the one that said you have to be able to trust someone who spent this much time on an accent. That it was okay. David didn't feel it was okay. He felt he was about to tread on very thin ice. If he wasn't careful, both he and Joel could end up owing this man.

"I don't know how, but these guys always seem to end up with young mistresses. Aphrodisiac of power, I guess," Walsh continued, ignoring David's silence.

"I suppose the pictures could help." David kept his voice satisfactorily even.

"Good, I thought they might. I need a favor from you too."

Here it comes, the touch. "Emm." Don't use words, they come out sounding like something they're not. Just sounds. A cop had told David that once.

"Nothing immediate. But you see, all the reporters have the photos, all the photos. However, after you show them to your client, then I'll be the first who knows the identity of the lucky winner."

"If I tell you."

"But in return for the photos . . ."

"Which I could get from any reporter. They all have them, didn't you say?"

The voice didn't answer right away. David could almost hear, in the raspy breath, Walsh composing his answer. "That's true. But who else is going to guarantee you big play in the story?"

David had never thought Walsh would give him the press out of friendship, but his editor thought he had an inside. Walsh's own self-interest and ego would push him to play David big.

"All right," David said, "send them over."

David hung up, leaned back in his chair, propped his feet up on the desk, and looked out the window over downtown Brooklyn. Just wait here for the crazy bicycle messenger to ride up with the pictures and then he'd drop over to see Light.

Twining stared at the glass in front of him, three quarters filled with clear liquid. Water. It had been years since Twining started the day with water. Maybe law school. Maybe then. He remembered law school, the idealistic days. His fingers slipped down the condensation on the outside of the glass. He remembered some professor, couldn't remember the name or see the face, but he remembered him talking about slippery slopes.

Slippery slopes. Twining laughed as he pulled from the glass. He hadn't understood what they were. Now he did. It was like Gutenberg. In grade school he thought Gutenberg had invented a printing press on wheels, a moveable type printing press. Thought that for years. Knew the words, knew the definition, always passed the test, but never understood.

He pushed himself out of his chair and walked to the window. It was a nice apartment, overlooking the East River. He'd come far. How had it started, the slippery slope? Maybe with that first term? No, before that. That first campaign, maybe the first time he decided to run. No, the first campaign.

That woman. She and her group had wanted some street repaired in their neighborhood. Hadn't been able to get it done. Would he help? she'd asked. They had many voters, would vote for him, pass out literature, all that. Sure, he said without looking at the project. He did look at the project later. Not a bad project, not the best use of the money, but not bad. He had pushed it, and he'd been elected.

The first step on the slippery slope. No one would have called that blackmail, corruption, bribery. No one. It was good politics. No one but his professor, sitting in the Ivory Tower. The Ivory Tower with sheer walls, no slippery slopes.

Twining took another swallow. It tasted bitter. How could water taste bitter? Everything tasted bitter today. It hadn't always. Not during that first term, when everyone had wanted to talk to him. The lobbyists crowding around. The junket weekends, the promises of campaign contributions. Just need a vote on this legislation. What's a vote between friends? That's what this is, isn't it, friendship?

Yes, he'd said. After all, everyone else was doing it. He was no different. The contributions came, junkets, favors, the re-elections. That's when it started. Water had tasted good up until that first term; then it changed. It wasn't the taste, not really. It was the thoughts, that voice in his head, that idealistic voice. Is this what you wanted to do? Is this what you ran for? The voice wouldn't stop, not as long as he drank water.

But vodka, that magic elixir. Made the voices funny. No longer condemning, threatening. How could he be afraid of voices slurring words? He laughed at them. Then came more votes, more junkets, more contributions.

He drained the water, went back to the refrigerator, and poured another glass. He stared at the water for another second. He would have continued, just continued . . . until the call. He gulped the water. Maybe the note. Just said they found those pictures. Thought it might be better if he had them. It might not be good for him if they were out and about in Washington. Just doing him a favor. That's all, they'd said, just doing him a favor.

Twining had seen the bottom, seen others there, but never himself. Never thought he would be at the bottom. He was a congressman. A very important man. Then this call. Just a brief call, a minute or so. It didn't say anything, not really. But he was at the bottom now. Three minutes after the call came the messenger. A sealed envelope. That much respect at least. He'd cut it open. At first it was just joy, pure relief. The negatives. Neglected to send them the first time, the note said.

The second call came three minutes later. Just helping out their friend, the voice had said. It was dangerous to be out like that, when there was so much press. Fortunately the real press wasn't there, but sometimes we become overconfident. Yes, yes, Twining had said. Yes, he understood. He must be more careful, at least until this blows over.

The voice said he had been happy to help. And about that vote, the one Twining had said he didn't think he could make, against the best interests, etc. The voice thought he should reconsider. Hated to bring up the subject at a time like this. No connection, of course, but while he was on the phone . . . It was important. He was the ranking Democrat and had great power. The second-ranking democrat was in favor, as was the chairman. They both thought it was in the country's best interest. The voice sounded reasonable. Maybe Twining should be also. He could reconsider. If not this term, then next, after the election.

Twining sat for an hour after he hung up the phone. Blackmail, it was direct blackmail. Then Twining had started drinking water. The last step on the slippery slope. He gulped down the water and reached for the vodka. Was it any more blackmail than that road repair so many years ago? What was quid pro quo other than blackmail? Where was the line in that slippery slope that divided politics from bribery, from blackmail, from corruption?

He poured three fingers. He didn't know. Not unless it was the first step, that decision to run. After that it was all the same, different forms, but the content was the same.

He looked at the vodka. Well, he had had enough. He needed this, at least for a few more days, he needed this. He gulped it down and reached for the phone.

CHAPTER 5

The heavy iron door clanged shut behind David. That sound still unnerved him. One is never sure for whom the door clangs. David shook the thought off.

He pulled out the wooden chair, dropped into it, and snapped open the briefcase. Twining had taste, he thought, as he pulled out the photos. Three women, each more beautiful than the last. But it was the last one, the one who looked Hispanic: full face, smooth olive skin, and those eyes. They seemed to cut through him, promising she could take him to heights he'd never experienced . . . but wouldn't.

No, she wouldn't. Not now. Even if she had been a co-worker of Coyce Loyn's, she had moved out of that class. She didn't have the look of a Coyce Loyn now. None of that cheap slut look that a misspelled body part indicated. Instead there was a look of haughty confidence. No . . . arrogance.

But she wasn't the child of South American aristocracy. The look acknowledged her roots, but acknowledged the fantasies of her lovers too. They wanted haughty; she'd give them haughty. Give the customer the fantasy he wants, even if the service is identical to the freebie down the hall.

Maybe we do have something in common, David thought, as he slapped the pictures together and slipped them into his jacket pocket. A heavy iron key rattled in the door at the opposite end of the conference room. Through the one small window, David could see Light's face, bobbing, first with a surly glare, then a blank expression.

The door swung open and Light bounced in, followed by his jailer. The stride communicated a lifetime to David, a lifetime of powerlessness all balled up in a show of arrogant superiority . . . superiority Light didn't feel. If he could convince David he actually did feel superior, and the price was a lifetime in jail, Light might call it an even bargain.

David decided not to fight over old battles again. "We've got work to do."

"We got work to do, shit," Light said, flopping down in the seat opposite David, avoiding eye contact. He sat sideways in the chair, looking back at the iron door, through the small window. Then, as if realizing that was not where he wanted to go either, he spun completely around and stared out the window behind him.

David waited. He knew he wasn't going to get overt cooperation, but if he waited, he might get something. Light reminded David a little of his cat. Left alone for a weekend, the cat would ignore David when he returned. Act as if he were doing David a big favor by eating the food he put out. David had found that ignoring the cat usually brought it around quickly. The same strategy sometimes worked with clients.

Light kept his body facing out the window but allowed his head to turn so that David could see three quarters of his ear. David waited for a full ear. Light uncrossed his legs, bringing the top one down with a bang on the floor, before allowing the other to swing on top. He turned just a little more, facing the iron door again.

"So what kind of work we gotta do?"

David pulled out the top picture, slapped it on the table face up, and slid it across at Light. "Ever see her before?"

Light turned his head quickly and glanced at the picture. "Yeah, that her," he said.

David pulled back the picture. "Are you sure?" he asked,

slipping the second picture in its place and sliding it across.

Light glanced at it for a second longer before nodding.

David pulled the picture back. "Who was it?"

"That girl. That one with that white man."

"That Spanish-looking one?"

Light nodded.

"With the dark hair, right?"

"Yeah, right."

David slammed the first picture down. "Light, that picture, that one. Look at it." David waited while he did. "That woman has blond hair. Blond hair." David glared at him now. "You didn't even look at it."

"What you expect?" Light snapped back. "I sitting in here for doing the right thing. That bastard out after beating on that woman." Light turned back to the window.

"Okay. Tell you what I'll do then." David snapped back to the three-quarter ear. "I'll just go out there and tell everybody that this is the woman you saw, 'cause that's what you told me. Then we find out that this woman was with her husband in Seattle or some fucking place and everybody says, 'Yeah, I knew from jump that nigger lying.' How's that?" David waited a second for an answer before continuing. "I tell you how that is. You go in for beating on this cocksucker. With your record you get maybe five years. For something you didn't do. And you know why? Because you wanted to make your lawyer pay."

Light kept staring out the window for a minute before looking back to David. His mouth was curled in a tight pout, his eyebrows tense. "How about you, you asshole? Coming in here, got two pictures . . . lying on me. Making it like it was only one."

"Light, I'm trying to help you. Trying to get you out of this. I've got to be sure you're telling the truth."

"You coulda started by telling me the truth."

David was silent for a minute, before pulling the three photos out of his pocket. "Okay," he said, sliding the three photos at Light. "I'll start here. These are three women Twining has been seen with."

Light glared again at David and then down at the pictures. Moving the three pictures alongside each other in a row, he fingered each one, finally flipping the one on the right back to David. It was the blond. He picked up the one on the left, tossing it like a Frisbee at David. "This one," Light said, holding the third card in his hand. "This the one."

David slipped the first two into his pocket, taking the third from Light. It was the Spanish girl with the olive skin.

David pushed his way through the revolving doors into the Supreme Court Building. The elevators in the lobby were packed. Nine thirty on a weekday. Sardine time at the courthouse.

David squeezed past the litigants and the lawyers standing around the information desk and joined the mob pushing for the down elevators, just to be inside when they returned from the basement. He felt a hand on his arm.

"Counselor."

David turned. It had to be a cop or a court officer; other people used names.

The hand tightened and pulled David toward him. A pocked face atop a burly chest and an over-ample stomach pushing out a blue suit stood stern-faced in front of him.

"You made a mistake, counselor," the man said.

"You're referring to my arriving here the same time you did, officer?"

"You know what I'm referring to."

David searched his memory. "Jenson. You're Detective Jenson."

Jenson grimaced. "You embarrassed me, and the department."

"Well, consider that you might have embarrassed yourself, detective. Should have done some investigation."

"You didn't have to do it that way." The grip tightened.

"What way?"

"In court. In front of the press like that."

David twisted his arm free. "Everything that day was in front of the press. I got a client to represent." David hesitated. "You got the wrong man because you didn't ask any questions."

"That woman told us. Told us what your skell did."

"Look, officer, you could have knocked on a few doors, found out who else saw what else. But you didn't."

Jenson pushed up closer in the crowd and spoke more quietly. "We can't do a door to door on every case."

"Where you've got a congressman, you're going to have press. You've been around long enough to know that."

An elevator opened and a small herd of people pushed in.

"Counselor, this is what I know. Your guy beat up that congressman, and it wasn't because he was protecting some bim. There's something more going on." Another elevator popped opened. "I'm going to find out what, and then your guy is going down." He disappeared into the elevator.

David stared as the door bounced shut.

CHAPTER 6

Light stamped his feet once or twice, getting the shirt to hang straight. He opened his trousers, slipped the shirt in, and folded part over against each hip. Make it look like a military fold. Like he was in the army. Judge'd like that. Light wouldn't say so, didn't want to lie to a judge, not over something like that, something they could check up on. But most of the time the judge would see that fold and assume. If he was a military man, he'd assume.

Light looked around the cage. Shit, who was he kidding? The judge'd never look at him. Just look at the lawyers, talk to them. Light'd never get to say a word. He wasn't really there, never was. Just like a letter in the sorting room of some post office. Them lawyers and the judge just deciding what zip code he belong in, upstate, Rikers, probation, or home. It didn't make a fuckin' bit of difference how he tuck his fuckin' shirt.

The court officer bent over his black leather belt with the tools of his trade attached and pushed the skeleton key in the iron gate. Light didn't move until the lock snapped open. Bastard could be fooling with him again. But the door opened and the officer waved Light out into the hall. Light waited calmly with his hands behind his back as the officer snapped the cuffs on and gently pushed Light toward the brown door at the end of the hall. Light waited once more as the officer reached around and pulled open the door, paid no attention when the officer inside the courtroom yelled something that included "Leroy Scott." Instead, Light squinted into the brighter light of the courtroom. Cohen.

And that white-haired bastard. That white-haired bastard was standing up there, next to the prosecutor. That woman beater, standing there, standing there nervous, balancing on one leg then the other, looking around. Yeah, the bastard should be nervous.

Light walked over next to Cohen and looked straight forward, not looking at Cohen. Not going to neither, not until Cohen said why Jacobs wasn't there.

Cohen held Light's arm. "Something's happening," he said.

Of course something happening. I'm fucking here, Light thought. But he said nothing, just kept staring straight ahead, looking up at the judge. The judge was looking back, smiling at him. "Good morning, Mr. Scott," the judge said.

"Good morning, Mr. Scott?" What the fuck was this?

"Something big," Cohen said. "Twining, the congressman, is here. He shouldn't be here. Not for this."

Light still stared straight ahead. The bastard wasn't saying nothing about where Jacobs at. Well, Light was going to stare straight ahead until he did. Light shifted his weight, first on one leg then the other. Trouble was, Cohen didn't seem to be noticing Light's ignoring him. Light turned his back to Cohen, looking over to the wall.

"Your Honor, I have been informed by the complainant that he wishes to drop the charges," the DA said.

Light spun around. "What he say?"

"They're dropping the charges."

"What about the last three days?"

"What do you mean?"

"Case dismissed," the judge said.

"What about the last three days?" Light asked, louder now.

The judge looked down at him as the court officer pulled him toward the door in the back.

"You'll be released from the back," the judge continued, smiling beatifically down at Light.

"What about the three days I spend in there?"

"You're getting out, Light," Cohen said in his ear.

Light spun around to Cohen. "I don't care about that. What about the three days I spend inside 'cause a that man's lies?" Light shouted. He could hear the commotion behind him, the people getting up and crowding toward the rail.

"Mr. Scott," the judge said, more sternly now. "This is a criminal case. That case is over. If you have complaints about the prosecution or Congressman Twining, you have civil remedies. Your lawyer will tell you about them. But this case is over."

"What he talking about, 'civil remedies'? That white bastard admit he lying or what?"

Cohen put a hand on Light's back and gently started to rub it up and down. "Light, we can talk about that later."

"We can talk about it now," Light screamed, pulling away from Cohen. "We can talk about it now. That white bastard say he lying about that woman or what?"

"He didn't admit anything."

"Then this whole thing just over? He the good guy 'cause he ain't prosecuting me? 'Cause he stop lying?"

The court officer pulled Light's arm, dragging him toward the door and back to the pens. "This way, Scott. You'll be released from the pens."

"I don't want to be released from no pens. I want that bastard admittin' he lied." Light spun around and was staring into the gallery crowded with reporters and artists, struggling to get the image of Light being dragged from the courtroom down on paper.

"That bastard lie. Motherfucker lie. Ruin my motherfuckin' reputation," Light screamed as the door slammed behind him.

CHAPTER 7

Santeria nodded to Julio. The man moved, burly chest first, as if pulled by some guiding light. Santeria thought about how much he liked this man, as Julio pushed the videocassette into the machine without a word. That's what Santeria liked about this man: not a word. Never a word. The TV flashed to life. A man who just did his job.

Unlike the man whose face appeared on the TV. Julio was trim, barrel-chested, but trim. Always in shape. He was younger than the man on the TV, of course, but that wasn't it. Santeria moved his glass, allowing the ice to clink against the sides, chilling the Perrier still more. The man did not complain about bringing Santeria his Perrier; even with all his training he did not complain.

The VCR played on. It showed Twining moving, talking, explaining. Twining was relaxed, more confident than Santeria had seen him in years. That should have given him his clue, but it did not. In fact, Santeria had not even turned on the camera. It had been Julio. Julio, who usually tuned out English, had listened this time... listened and flipped the switch. He had understood, had seen it right away. Perhaps I am slipping, Santeria thought. Perhaps it was the lack of understanding that gave Julio better understanding.

Santeria signaled to Julio, who turned down the volume. The man understood immediately, without words. Twining went on with words... many, many words. Confidently. Santeria was uncomfortable with Twining's confidence, but Julio was confident. Santeria liked that. The difference must be the training. Yes, the training. Twining wasn't trained; he had just floundered into the job and floundered through it. Training had taught Julio how to handle orders. Not to give them, but taught many ways to carry them out.

Perhaps it was like the Eastern cultures. People knew and were satisfied with their roles. A man could make a career out of serving tea. A lifetime learning to get it just right, perfectly carrying out the ritual. That's what Julio had, that's what our culture has, Santeria thought. That is what these *norteamericanos* have lost. A country of leaders. The fatal flaw of democracy.

On the screen Twining sat back and gestured with his arm. Perhaps Twining was the fatal flaw of democracy, Twining and all like him. People who had no idea what they were doing but believed they should... trying desperately to keep their ignorance hidden. How this country had become the world leader with leadership like this was beyond Santeria. A man who is intended to lead should be trained for leadership. Training from the beginning. Trained like Julio was. Trained in the arts he was expected to use. In Twining's case the arts of leadership. Not the arts of corruption. It was too easy to corrupt these people.

The screen flickered and Twining stretched his arm again. chThere, there... Santeria could see it there. Just a flash, a flash of black wire under the sleeve of his jacket. It was Julio who had noticed it first. Noticed it just before he flipped on the camera. That was the thing, Santeria thought. Julio hadn't made a fuss, hadn't run in to tell Santeria. He had just flipped a switch. Then he could show Santeria the film and let Santeria make the decisions. It was these decisions for which Santeria had been prepared. It was interacting with dead people for which Julio had been prepared

And he had learned. He had, Santeria supposed, learned to recognize dead people.

CHAPTER 8

"You should call her," Joel said, leaning forward, over his beer.

David silently scanned the bar: the usual group of after-work lawyers, judges, and court workers jammed around the bar or huddled over small tables covered with maroon-and-white checked tablecloths.

"How long has it been?"

"A year," David said, without making eye contact. He didn't particularly want to have this conversation, but Joel probably wouldn't be deterred.

"A year. That's a long time."

"You think the statute of frauds applies to agreements to make a clean break?" David smiled with a mirth he didn't feel.

"Maybe it should. Isn't a year enough time for her to recover?"

David hunched over his beer, pulling it close and staring at the middle of the table. Joel was right, of course. He missed Janie. He wanted to call, but he hadn't—and wouldn't.

"I saw this chit today," Joel said, pulling a slip from his pocket. "Investigative services to Coyce Loyn? We'd have a better chance if you said it was dinner and you misspelled."

"Wasn't that choice, actually."

"Arnie will think it was." Joel leaned back. "I can see him now. 'Coyce Loyn, Investigator. Whatta ya kidding me wit dis shit here? Waddam I gonna tell de IRS wit dis shit, hanh?' "

David laughed at the picture of the accountant, crouched over the books, his mouth working an unlit cigar, popping up and stamping into David's office. David would jump up, then trundle the chubby little man with the slicked-back black hair and the pencil mustache back to the library with an admonition that would be heeded only until the next item caught the attention of his internal IRS man.

"What are we going to tell the IRS?"

"The truth: it was an investigative expense. She was Twining's whore."

" 'Oh Christ, now I gotta figure da mileage, personal use, what? Ten percent? The bastards'll never buy that shit.' I don't want to be there, David," Joel said, dropping the Arnie act.

"I'll pay it," David said.

"No, that's not the point," Joel said. "We'll slip it in. It was an expense. The point is you jumping this Coyce Loyn's bones. I mean if it were me, there'd be no question. But you were always one of those . . ." Joel put his fingers together, cocked his head to the right, and continued in a falsetto, "who wanted to be in love."

David gave an embarrassed chuckle as he looked around the bar. The drunks were attending to their own business.

"Call her, David."

"I can't."

"Why not?"

David hesitated a second, then turned to Joel full on. "I just spent $250 of the firm's money on a prostitute because I thought she could throw some light on a case with a client who can't pay us and doesn't even like me because he thought he got a raw deal."

"Yeah, so he did."

"Right, but he's gotten great deals from the system all

his life. If this were Iran, he'd have no hands, no feet, and no life.''

"David, that's what we do. We get people breaks. That's the system. That's a lawyer's job."

"With me it's a passion." David said softly. "I get a case and I can't let go." He pulled the beer toward him and studied its fallen head for a second before taking a hit. "Last time I didn't let go, she got hurt." David drained the beer, dropped a five on the maroon-and-white tablecloth, and left.

Light pulled the maroon jacket forward, adjusting the collar so it lay flat. After ten years it still fit. Fit just right. If, that is, you didn't count the belly sticking out between the folds in the front. Light didn't count that. Smoothing the tie down and shrugging the shoulders into place, he checked once more to see that the pocket was laying flat. It was.

People didn't understand that good B&E—*good* B&E, not like that show-off kinda shit Franklin did, but the good stuff—it wasn't done with fancy tools or like that. It was done with props, like this jacket. Light had spent an hour getting ready, picking his hair out real neat, shaving, doing his nails. He wanted to look like an actor or a singer right out of some little town in the Midwest, looking for his break.

He'd seen enough of them, coming to New York, thinking they was going be the black somebody and winding up just another black nobody. But he'd seen them . . . seen them and noticed. And copied. He copied them back when he was Lightfoot. He loved the way he told them people to turn around while he moved somewhere, making them think he couldn't be heard. Shit, that was the show. The real thing, that was like this here.

Light walked behind a group of white people going to a party or something. They were laughing like they hadn't been drunk in six months. Light scrunched his face, mocking the amateurishness, then remembered his role. Time for games later.

He followed the people past the storefront office with the

sign painted on the window. "Congressman Harrison Twining" in gold letters curved in a semicircle across the top of the window. Below, painted in a straight line, "Brooklyn Office." The shades were pulled and a metal-mesh gate was pulled down over the window. It was dark inside.

Light continued a few paces behind the white amateurs until they reached the corner. They went straight; Light turned. The side street was darker, with four-story brownstones fronted by tall, old oaks crowding the street on one side. Twining's office was cut into the corner of a seven-story apartment building, balanced by the drugstore on the other side of the main entrance. Light continued down the side street until he came to the back of the building. As he figured, there was a small space cut behind the building.

Quickly looking around and seeing no one, Light slipped into the space. It was a garbage alley, but it wasn't as dirty as the alleys on Nostrand. The garbage cans were lined up neatly along the back of the building. Above the cans, dark windows were cut into the wall. The glass was covered with dust, stuck to the windows with grease. The combination looked to have been there for years. Light walked down the other side, coming to another cut in the building, a short entry leading to a large green door with a brass handle. It was propped open.

Light peered in. A fat man in a dark-green uniform with a white, oval name patch over the pocket sat in a chair propped against the wall, feet on the ground, front two legs floating in midair. He was fast asleep.

Light crept back down the alley. Reaching into one of the cans, he tore open a garbage bag and pulled out a dirty paper towel. He crumpled it, spit on one side, rubbed it against itself to spread the saliva, then pushed it against the window. The greasy dirt slowly moved away, revealing a swirly picture of the area within.

A white Sheetrock wall faced Light from about ten feet away. It went all the way across the room, with desks pushed up against it, corkboards hung from it, and various scraps of paper stuck to the cork. The window had a standard brass lock, activated simply by thumb pressure.

Pulling a small butter knife from his pocket, Light slipped it between the top frame of the window and the bottom. *Turn that sucker just so.* Light felt his mouth and tongue twist as he tried to get the knife to hook the window latch.

There, hooked.

Light gently pulled the bottom of the knife toward him, so that the top pushed the latch out.

Not moving, push a little harder.

The knife raced toward his face. He stepped back, almost kicking the garbage can. Catching himself, he stepped back and looked at the latch. Still closed. The butter knife bent.

Light slipped the knife back into his pocket and extracted a glass cutter. After checking up and down the alley, Light cut a small semicircle in the pane above the lock. He dropped the cutter in his pocket, picked up a piece of brick, and rapped the glass. The glass broke away, falling to the floor with a deafening crash. At least it seemed deafening to Light. No one else seemed to notice.

Light waited a moment while the noise died and his emotions quieted. *Yeah, this was going to be easy.* He didn't know what he was going to look for once he got in there, but getting in was the hard part. He'd find something, something that would show that Twining had been with that woman and maybe that Twining was beating her. Prove it, that's what. That'd show them boys.

Light reached his hand through the broken glass. The semicircular cut hadn't done much good; shards of the shattered pane hung like stalactites above the lock. Light's hand shook as he reached for the lock. For a moment he wished he'd had a beer before coming here, but then thought better. He wanted to be alert for this caper.

Reaching through the hole, he twisted his hand onto the latch and pushed with his thumb. The lock gave with a sudden snap, releasing a shard on his hand. The glass knifed away a section of his finger. Light pulled back his hand, sticking his finger in his mouth and sucking the blood away. He grabbed the greasy paper towel and jammed it on the finger. Swearing softly, he looked up and down the alley and pressed the paper towel tighter.

What the hell. He pulled up the window and silently crawled in.

As Twining rubbed his cheek against the portion of her breasts that her low-cut dress revealed, she thought about the office where she had spent so many evenings. Sometimes they went there because he was busy, had only a few hours to himself. Sometimes because it was more thrilling. Twining knew what it would mean if he was caught, how his career could come tumbling down. Now he knew the risk was even greater. He'd started to hate her when he found out, started the violence. But the risk seemed to energize him, to increase his passion. Still, most of the time they did it at her apartment. It was safer there, he'd said. A big building. No one knew where he was going.

But today, today with the press probably hanging around her apartment, today they had to come here. Like most men, Twining liked the risk, as long as it wasn't a real risk.

Twining also liked her breasts. He had turned his face to them, kissing them wetly. She tingled while her eyes were closed, but as she opened them, the tingle changed. She stroked his gray hair, and the tingle mixed with a sense of revulsion. The slight gagging she felt prevented her from speaking. Despite that, she felt she was making the right decisions, doing what had to be done. But the revulsion was there, the gagging and that feeling in the pit of her stomach, as if his fluids burned like raw sewage. She shook off the feeling and gently guided Twining's head off her chest.

They had stopped in front of the office. The driver sat silently, the tinted divider still up between him and the passenger compartment behind. Twining blinked and looked around, groggily getting his bearings.

He grunted once, then, in more understandable English, told the driver to meet him here at eight tomorrow with a change of clothes. Taking Anacleta's hand, he led her onto the sidewalk, where they stood for a moment as the limo disappeared around a corner. Anacleta stared after it, saying nothing, showing nothing. They would make love, he would call a car service, and she would disappear, arriving home at two or three in the morning. That's the way he did it, saying he didn't want the publicity. She felt the muscles of her lower jaw tense. She shook it off. Later, there'd be time to gag later. Shit, there'd be time to vomit later, she thought as she followed him into the office.

Light pushed the window down, squeezing it shut and reactivating the lock. There was only a little blood on the sill. No one would notice. He looked around the room. It was a long, narrow tube with papers piled and stuck everywhere. About six or seven people could sit and work, manning phones. The whole place looked like a battle room for a re-election campaign, a permanent re-election campaign.

A lightly stained wooden door in the middle of the room dominated the opposite wall. Light crept toward it, spun the knob, and pushed. He stared at a short hall with office doors on both sides and a large room facing the front windows at the end. He slipped into the hallway.

He didn't know why he was being so quiet. The maintenance man couldn't hear anything and wouldn't think anything of it if he did. Just some of the people working late. Light moved quietly just the same. Habit, or maybe he was thinking of his reputation and what Evelyn would say if she found out a maintenance guy heard him through two walls and thirty feet.

So Light crouched low as he reached for the knob on the office door to his left. The brass knob turned easily in his hand. A metallic crack split the silence. Light froze. His eyes shot to the front door. The metallic crack sounded again, slightly deeper this time, more like a thud. The front door started to move.

Light pushed the office door open and slid in, pushing the door closed behind him. Collapsing near the door, he cringed as the spring bolt clicked into place. This wasn't what he had in mind. *Fucked up this one good.* He listened as a pair of heavy feet entered the room, then another, lighter, quieter. Two people. Yellow light glimmered through the space under the door. Voices. One man, one woman. Then the sounds of kissing, sloppy kissing.

The voices started again. Light couldn't make out the words, but the woman, the woman sounded vaguely Spanish.

Twining let her go then pulled her back again, kissing her wildly, driving his tongue into her mouth. She gently pushed him away, whispering she had to get ready. Dropping her purse and coat on the sofa in the waiting room, she looked back toward Twining, kissed the air in front of her, kicked off her heels, and walked seductively toward the door.

She opened the door and slipped in. The convertible by the back wall sat folded, bed inside made, ready to be opened, used, and pushed back when they had finished. She wondered what the workers thought when they came in in the morning, smelling her smells mixed with the smells of passion. The small window opened only on an air shaft and could not clear the room. She shrugged. It wasn't her problem.

It wasn't her problem. She repeated it as a mantra over the next few minutes. Repeated it as she opened the door to allow Twining in, repeated it as he kissed her. She was even able to act happy, to giggle.

Anacleta giggled as she wiped saliva off the edge of her mouth. She dropped her head again, this time kissing his neck. He shivered as she lightly ran her tongue along the top of his shoulder. She rhythmically rolled her hips over his thigh, rubbing her genitals lightly up and down. It was less disgusting if she didn't have to look at him.

She reached down and touched his member, stroking it softly. It was almost over, she thought as she moved down, kissing his nipples, his navel, and pubic hairs on the way. She looked up at him, holding his penis in front of her face. She knew she had that glazed look in her eyes, those puffy lips, that blush that always drove him crazy. She wrapped her swollen lips around his penis and closed her eyes. If she closed her eyes, she couldn't tell whose it was and it didn't seem so bad.

The door across the hall clicked shut. He had to get out of there, with or without evidence. He knew that was what he was supposed to think, supposed to do. It was the smart thing. He knew now, knew for sure, but no one would believe him any more now than they had before.

He turned the knob gently. The spring bolt snapped back. Light froze. The sounds from across the hall continued.

They was into it, those two.

He pulled the door open and slipped out. Stopping for a moment in the hall as he pulled the door behind him, he left it slightly ajar. He didn't want that snap again.

He listened to the breathing in the other room. It sounded early, the breath. Not panting yet. He still had time. Only the streetlight dappling through the mesh gate in the front cut the darkness. It wasn't much.

Light picked his way to the front of the large room, avoiding the large pieces of furniture on the way. Where could he find evidence, evidence that she had been here? He looked at the reception desk. It was clear except for a large appointment calendar in the center.

Light slid the receptionist's chair away from the desk. It squeaked. Light froze. The breathing in the room seemed to stop for a second. Light waited, glanced under the desk . . . there was room. He heard a grunt from the room, then another. They were back to it.

Light flipped open the calendar. The page was filled with entries. Names of people, but no Lucas. Shit, this wouldn't prove nothing. He looked around the room. It was clean, only two coats and the purse tossed carelessly on the sofa. The purse. Light crept over to the sofa. He ran his hand through the pockets of the coats quickly. Nothing. Then he picked up the purse. The breathing in the room intensified. They panted breathlessly. Wouldn't be much longer.

Snapping open the purse, he stuck his hand inside and pushed aside the cosmetics, keys, and tissues. Had to be something. There, at the bottom. Light grabbed the book, listened for a moment more, then turned back to the book. Red and thin, it was small enough to fit in the palm of his hand. He opened it. A calendar of some kind. Flipped a few pages. An appointment book. He snapped it back to the front page. Anacleta Lucas. Stuffing it in his pocket, he crept back past the offices to the door in the back. He turned the knob. The spring bolt clicked. The breathing in the other room stopped. Light froze.

The door clicked open and the woman walked out. Crouching behind a chair, he peered into the room. The woman was naked, the dim light from the room gleamed off the sweat covering her smooth, tan skin. Light licked his lips involuntarily. She walked across the hallway and disappeared behind a partition.

The bathroom, she was going to the bathroom. She might look in her purse, for makeup. Women he knew sometimes put on fresh makeup in the middle of fucking, but he'd never been with a woman like this one. He wanted to be out of there with the evidence. He wanted to be back in the neighborhood, showing it to Evelyn, making her admit she was wrong.

He crept back to the window, put his hand on the sill, and pushed up on the sash. It made a crack through the quiet night. Nobody responded but he couldn't open the window the rest of the way and expect nobody to hear.

He slipped back against the wall between the offices and the back room. He'd wait. Wait until they left or started fucking and hope they didn't need something in the back.

Light waited for what seemed like hours but was probably only a few minutes. He heard the congressman call from the bedroom for her to come back. She made some sound but didn't return right away. He called again, starting to sound impatient now. Light popped up on his toes, wanting to be ready when she came back and they started fucking again. Nobody would check a window in the middle of fucking.

He heard her walk across the rug and back into the room, heard the door click shut. The room darkened, illuminated only by the light leaking through the dirty glass. He waited. He heard a smack, maybe like he was hitting her. Light smiled to himself. Not this time. He wouldn't make that mistake again. He'd just wait.

In a minute he heard the springs squeak as someone landed on the bed. Then the springs squeaked again and the breathing started. Light grabbed the lower window and waited. The breathing from the other room became heavier. He shoved the window open. The window squeaked, but the breathing continued. Hopping up on the sill, he squeezed through the window and looked both ways. No one. He jumped down between garbage cans and stayed low where he landed, hiding between the cans.

Light scanned in front of him. The street at the end of the alley was deserted. He swung slowly around behind him to where the green door still stood, propped open, a large, dark shadow standing at the door, looking toward the back of the alley. Then the shadow swung around and looked to the front. Light glanced up at the window. It was still open. He looked back to the man. The man was on the same plane as the window, couldn't see it.

The squeaks still came from the bed. Shit, that old man could really pump. Light looked back to the shadow. The shadow heard the squeaks too. The shadow stepped down the stairs to where there was enough light for Light to see the green uniform and the oval white name patch over his pocket. He took a step toward Light. Now the shadow could see, could see the window wide open. Light sucked in his breath. *Shit, that bastard coming back just to close the window.* Light spun around. Nowhere to hide. He slid his foot carefully between the garbage cans, allowing his body to follow only after it had found free area. It wasn't enough. The man would see.

The man looked straight at the window and stopped. The squeaks from inside continued. Light couldn't hold his breath much longer, but if he let it out now the man would surely hear. Light clamped down on his teeth and pursed his lips. Hold just another second.

The man listened to the squeak for a minute, cocked his head as if to hear better, . . . then smiled. Shit, he was going to walk back. He thought they had opened the window to get some air. The man just stood there, smiling. *Shit,* Light thought, holding his mouth clamped shut, *this cocksucker is a fucking auditory voyeur.* But the man turned around and walked back to the door. He climbed the three steps to the door level and stood looking out over the night sky.

Light couldn't hold his breath any longer. He opened the side of his mouth and let the air out in a slow, steady stream. The man looked over but saw nothing except cans and looked back to the sky. Light exhaled it all, but his lungs begged for more air. The man stood impassively at the door. Light opened his mouth, forming a small "O" with his lips, allowing the air to come in slowly, silently. He could wait now. Could wait the man out as long as he could breathe. Yeah, except for his knees stiffening up, he was just fine.

A flurry of squeaks burst from the room, followed by a slow rhythmic winding down. The man looked back and smiled again. *Like a fucking old woman, this cocksucker.* A desperate thought hit Light. They'd be up soon and would notice the window opened. He couldn't move with the man standing there.

The bastard, first he sleeping on the job and now just standing there.

Light heard the door inside click and saw soft light break from the open window. The shadow looked over, took a deep breath, and turned back to the hallway. Now was his chance, Light thought. Light pushed hard on his knees and they creaked up straight. He took a step to the back and stumbled, pitching forward toward the entrance to the alley. His weight went forward, his legs trying to catch up but unable to. He stumbled again, falling into the street. Crawling to his knees, he swung his head back toward the door. The man was peering down the alley at Light.

He was on the sidewalk now, clearly outside the man's

jurisdiction. *Could be just a drunk.* Pushing himself to his feet unsteadily, he stumbled, emphasizing the unsteadiness. He looked back to the man, stumbling again. *Important not to overdo it now.* He tried to remember he was supposed to look like a drunk trying to look sober, not like the sober drunk he was, trying to look drunk. His mind gave up on trying to figure out that puzzle, and he stumbled down the sidewalk.

CHAPTER 9

Light popped out of the subway, bounced up the steps, and headed straight for Evelyn Jefferson's house. Bitch'd be in her apartment on the third floor now. Probably all piped up, but maybe not. Light glanced at the clock hanging off the bank. 10:45. She'd only be back about a hour from work. Maybe she didn't have no bottles.

He danced up the stairs to the third floor, clutching the book in his left hand. Yeah, she'd be impressed. Have to believe him now. Have to tell everybody too. Light wanted to show it to the boys, but he didn't know what it said. Not really. He could recognize names, read a little, if it was printed. But reading a woman's handwriting. Above his education. But Evelyn could tell him. Besides, the boys wasn't on the street.

Light rapped on the door. He heard a commotion inside and Evelyn's voice saying she was coming, to wait. She sounded excited, like she was expecting somebody, not Light. Light rapped again. Make her nervous.

The door snapped open. Evelyn stood, her housedress pressed, her bony face softened by the application of makeup. Even her teeth looked better. Somehow the brown spots and the eaten-away parts looked smaller.

Light snapped back to himself. It wouldn't be no good to let her see him like this. Looking like he was impressed. He pushed his forearm into her side and shoved past her. "You see what I got here?" he asked.

"I see you ain't coming into my house uninvited," she said, recovering her balance.

"Look at what I got here."

"It better be you got some money there, 'cause a man coming over here to give me some money."

"This better than money. It prove what I been saying about that congressman and that woman." Light stopped for a second. "And it prove you nothing but a liar."

"Let me see that," she said, grabbing the book from his hand. She snapped it open. "Anacleta Lucas." She flipped pages. "So this her address book."

"Yeah, and look . . . that congressman's name."

She looked at him suspiciously, then back to the book. "Yeah, his name here, so what?"

"That prove it. That prove she know him."

Evelyn didn't answer, but kept flipping through the book, stopping at a page here and there and reading a section.

Light stood nervously. He wanted to know what she was reading, but knew that asking would give her the advantage. "Give me that book back," he said finally.

She snapped the book away from him, turning her shoulder to him almost playfully, like a little girl flirting. "I think I keep this," she said lightly.

Light grabbed her shoulder, ripped her toward him, and grabbed the book. She held it, but he grabbed her wrist and twisted. She gave a wince of pain as she released the book.

"Now you know you lying," he said, backing out the door. "And tomorrow everybody know."

He skipped down the stairs, nodding to the heavy man who passed him on the way up.

Evelyn watched as Light crossed the street, walked up the block, and disappeared into his building. She glanced at her watch. It'd take him a couple of minutes to go up, drop the book off, and come back down. Then he'd be across the street to the bodega, buy him his Old English, and be back on the stoop in less than ten. Not enough time. Nope, she'd have to wait.

She heard the big man pulling off his shoes in the bedroom. She wasn't as interested as she had been a few minutes ago. The big man's twenty dollars, two caps, didn't seem as important. She hesitated by the table in the living room and picked up the *Daily News*. The story about the congressman was front page. Not the main story, the one with the picture. That was about two little girls roasted alive in a fire in the Bronx. But it was there, a little note up in the top, with a picture of the congressman and a caption: "Congressman Twining dismisses charges."

She didn't know about the press, not really. But she knew the story wouldn't be hot forever. She kicked off her shoes and padded barefoot toward the bedroom. Twenty dollars was twenty dollars, she thought as she pulled open the door and put on a big smile.

"So now you're defending a case for nothing."

"Not the first time."

"First time we've defended a murder for nothing." Joel folded his huge arms across his chest.

"We can't just cut him loose because he's accused of murder." David picked up his briefcase. "Besides, he didn't do it."

"Oh, now you know he didn't do it."

"This is Light. Only thing he ever damaged was a keyhole."

"Well, we're in serious danger of his hurting our bank account."

"Is this the same guy who insisted I talk to some anemic Englishman for the publicity?" David asked, slipping a file into his briefcase.

"Right, and you're the guy who puts in chits for two fifty for investigative services on Coyce Loyn."

Scowling, David folded his arms and waited for Joel's point.

"You go down there, we're taking on a murder case," Joel said.

"We don't even know if it is murder. Squeaky said he thinks it's murder. The only thing we know for sure is that Jenson came down and picked up Light."

"And that Twining is dead."

"And that Twining is dead," David repeated more softly.

"And that Jenson thinks Light's involved in something with Twining more than just beating up some woman." Joel sat across from David and leaned forward. "I never believed that story anyway."

"What, that Twining was beating up a woman? We have witnesses."

"The store clerk saw the woman. Squeaky saw her take off. Nobody saw Twining throw a blow. At least nobody who's talked to you."

David sat back. He felt Joel crowding him, but Joel was right. The only thing David had to prove Twining had been beating the woman was Light's word. The real witnesses, fifteen or twenty, from what Light said, hadn't come forward.

"I know you believe Light, but remember, Light has made his living on scams."

"He's a fence."

"What do you think that is? He's a salesman. The stuff that's hot he gets more for by convincing people it's not, and the stuff that's not he gets more for by convincing them it is. And if he can get a top lawyer by convincing him he's innocent, you think he's not going to?"

"He's telling the truth on this. I feel it," David lied. He didn't. He didn't feel it, and he hadn't convinced Joel he felt it.

Joel took a deep breath and blew it out. "David, be sure on this. Because we're not court appointed. We can't make a motion for experts' fees. We either have to pay ourselves or go without. We may not be doing Light a favor by taking this case."

David looked over Joel's shoulder to the certificates on

the wall. Admitted to the bar, to the Southern District, to the Eastern District, to the Second Circuit. The awards he got from various organizations after the Jefferson case. What did it mean? He couldn't do a better job than some first-year legal aid or some court-appointed lawyer doing his first criminal trial because he wouldn't have access to the experts, not unless he and Joel paid for them themselves. David picked up his bag. "Maybe we'll make a pro bono application."

Joel nodded, grabbed David's shoulder and spun him around. "Check this out, David, before we submit a notice."

David felt drained when he arrived at the precinct. He wanted to be mad at Joel, with Joel's interfering with his crusading, but Joel was right. It wasn't only his crusade. Light had the right to the best defense he could get, whether he was telling the truth or not. And the best defense might be legal aid, not Cohen and Jacobs.

Pushing open the door, David walked past the sergeant and up the stairs to the PIU. He peered through the tiny window in the center of the swinging door. Jenson stood in the room, arms folded across his chest like a conquering hero, pocked face staring at the far desk where another detective was telling a joke. David straightened his tie and pulled himself to his full height. Time to make an entrance.

"Detective Jenson," David said, as he pushed open the door and strode across the room, hand extended.

Jenson took it without relish. "Counselor, I assume you don't want me to talk to your client."

"Correct."

"Didn't even try in this case. Don't need to," Jenson said, leading David to one of the pair of steel desks in the corner. "We got everything we need at the murder scene." Jenson picked up a manila folder from the desk and handed it derisively to David.

Feeling strangely unsettled by Jenson's confidence, David took the folder. Jenson called it the "murder scene." That answered one question. They had reason to believe it was a murder.

The folder contained a single white, 8½-by-11 form. Printed from top to bottom, the sheet had two blank lines. In one was written "No statements"; the other, "No property recovered."

David handed the folder back. "That all you found at the murder scene?"

"Nope," Jenson said proudly. "Your client left a big fat print, in blood. We didn't even have to dust. Just take a photo." Jenson pulled a slide from a manila envelope marked "Evidence" and handed it to David.

"Where'd he get the blood?" David asked, taking the photo.

"His own."

Holding the slide up to the fluorescent light, David muttered, "Uh huh." The slide clearly showed a print on a broken window. "Matched?"

"Came back positive this morning."

"And you picked him up this afternoon after you checked the body for Light's blood."

Jenson looked as if he were about to bust.

David didn't look up immediately. Letting Jenson stew for a second, he flipped the slide over in his hand.

"Did the forensic guy explain to you the difference between presence and participation?"

Jenson reddened.

"So you don't have blood on the body. You have any transfer evidence? You know, fibers, anything like that? Anything that proves Light touched Twining?"

Jenson ripped open a desk drawer and dropped the evidence envelope in. "You want to see your client?" he asked, slamming the drawer.

"Sure," David answered and followed Jenson toward the pens. "No transfer evidence, huh? Well, doesn't matter that much. Not like you have to touch somebody to kill them these days? What was the cause of death, anyway?"

"Heart failure." Jenson disappeared through the double swinging doors and right down the hall.

David stopped in his tracks, confusion gripping him. What the hell was Jenson doing? Could he be this stupid? Not likely, David thought, scurrying to catch up. Something more here.

"So, ah, heart attack, huh? And no transfer evidence. You figure Light scared him to death, that it?"

Jenson spun around to David, pinning him against the wall. "Look, I'm trying to do a job here. You embarrassed me once with that crap in court, now you're doing it here. I don't like it."

Turning his head to escape Jenson's cop breath, David slid to the side. "Look, Detective, I'm sorry if I've offended you, but it is a little unusual, don't you think?"

"We both know this shit about your client saving some woman from being smacked around by the congressman is a crock."

"I don't know that." David maneuvered another foot between himself and Jenson.

Jenson gave him the room. "Well, I know that. There's something else here. It stinks. Like how does he afford a hot shot like you?"

"Wish I knew," David muttered. "But look, you've got to have more. What does the autopsy say? It's got to be more than a heart attack."

"Heart failure, and I ain't giving you nothing more, wise-ass."

"As soon as you have an indictment, I get it anyway. Why not give it to me now?"

"Because you pissed me off." Jenson stopped in front of an open door cut into the tile wall. "Down the end, last cell. Show the officer your pass."

"That's it, Detective? You're gonna charge this guy with a homicide on this shit?"

"The DA'll be here in a couple of hours. Just let me know if your scumbag wants to confess now or later." Jenson turned the corner, disappearing through the double doors and back into the PIU.

David stood for a second as the false bravado faded and his consoling personality took over. Jenson wanted Light, that was clear. But whether he had the horses in this case, that was another question. David flashed his pass to the uniformed officer sitting behind the card table next to the cells.

The officer pushed himself up, pulled a ring of keys from his belt, and led David down a narrow hall with four holding cells on the right and a plain white wall on the left. Prisoners were crowded along benches in each of the four cells and shifted as David passed, settling back into their boredom as the next cell began to shuffle.

The officer stopped at the last cell, made quick eye contact with Light, and bent to the work of pushing the giant steel key into the giant lock.

Light stood, shoulders hunched as if awaiting another blow, and worked his way toward the door. David made eye contact, but Light looked down as though he didn't want to talk, not yet. David maintained his silence and followed Light and the officer to the interview room around the corner. Light and David sat but remained silent until the officer pushed the steel door closed and turned the key.

Slumped over the table, Light began picking at a callus at the base of his ring finger. The subdued man who sat before him seemed a stranger to David. Certainly it wasn't the Light he had known for the past year.

"I guess you know I need some answers," David began quietly.

Light nodded, then looked up, his face looking as if it were trying to maintain the hard facade, but the resolve was crumbling behind. Independent twitches arrhythmically fluttered each of his eyes and the left corner of his mouth. Tiny muscles, firing and reloading, acting independently of Light's will.

Not even noticeable, unless you were watching, David thought. "Twining's dead. I guess you know that," David said, bending over, snapping open his briefcase, and pulling out a yellow legal pad. "Detective Jenson thinks you had something to do with it."

"What the fuck that asshole want from me?"

"A confession, he says."

"Confession, shit." Light leaned back, the spirit apparently drained from him. "I didn't do nothing. Don't know nothing a what they talking about."

"Ever been to Congressman Twining's Brooklyn office?"

"Yeah, right. I go up there regular to check what he doing with the street people pac money." Light folded his arms, turned toward the single window just below the ten-foot ceiling, and peered out.

At least Light was showing some life. "You left something there."

Light shifted but said nothing.

"A fingerprint." David wondered if he could really see the color drain from a black man's face, as he could from a white man's. That's what it looked like, although it could be that the muscles of Light's face just gave up.

"You gotta check that shit out. Could be like that guy making photocopies of prints then saying he found 'em at the scene. Could be like that."

David shook his head. "I saw a photo of the print. You left it in blood."

Light curled his head down, studying the calluses on his thumb. "On the window."

"On the window."

"So what I gonna get on a burglary?"

"Murder."

Light spun around. "I didn't do no murder. I broke in, but I didn't do no murder."

"What happened?"

Light looked back to the window and took a deep breath. David pulled out a pen. It looked like it was going to be a long story.

* * *

David turned the key and fluttered the accelerator as the Toyota rumbled to life. He had that same sort of unsettled feeling in his stomach. Light's story was plausible, but what were the odds? Same day he's there, somebody wastes Twining. Swinging left onto Atlantic, David pulled his beeper from his pocket. Light just didn't figure to be a killer, but he'd need more than that to convince a jury.

Between glancing at traffic, David ran through the messages. Nothing urgent. Nothing more urgent than finding out how you cause heart failure.

CHAPTER 10

The door had barely closed before she reached up and kissed his cheek. He endured it, even smiled, before walking to the white sofa near the window and sitting. It would be a moment before the woman would ask him if he wanted tea, a few minutes more before the games began.

"You want tea, honey?"

Julio grunted. He mostly grunted with this woman. His English wasn't the best, but with this woman he felt illiterate. Other gringos he could make understand, those better trained.

"I can never remember, honey, you take sugar?"

Julio wanted to grunt again, but realized that might result in sugar in his tea, which he didn't want. "No sugar."

"I love it when you speak Spanish to me, love."

Julio said nothing. He was angry at himself. He had been in this country for over a year and still had an accent. Santeria had told him not to worry, it would fade as he spent more time with these people, but it hadn't. He hadn't spent much time with these people either. Only what was necessary. That was his fault too. He needed to learn the ways of the *norteamericanos*. He needed to take the time.

Santeria said so too. Julio thought perhaps Santeria could give him more time, but quickly pushed the thought down. After all, he could make the time. Santeria had said the work must be done and the time must be made. Julio could make the time.

The woman came with the tea, appearing from behind the wall that separated the kitchen from the rest of the apartment. He didn't like the way she flounced. Was that the English word? He didn't know. It made her skirt bounce and made Julio think she would fall off her heels. She didn't, even managing, with a sudden movement of her hips, to place the tray on the coffee table in front of him.

"You know, I think I'm beginning to pick up some Spanish," the woman said as she nestled in next to him, slipping her shoes from her feet and tucking them up under her ass.

He slipped his arm around her, brushing the dry, blond hair from her shoulder. He did not like the hair, dry and tangled as it was. He liked hair like Anacleta's, dark and straight, each strand hanging independently.

"That word for sugar, I understood that. Even though I knew what you said 'cause you was answerin' my question. I knew. What's that Spanish word, lover, the one for sugar?"

"The word I used was sugar," Julio said slowly in his best English. "The English word. In Spanish, the word is *azúcar*."

"I could have understood that, if you'd said it in Spanish." She wiggled closer, pushing her head against Julio's chest. "Talk to me in Spanish," she said, "so I can practice hearing it."

Julio thought of telling her in Spanish that she was stupid, one of the stupidest women he had ever met. That would have been pointless, however, so he said nothing. Besides, she might have understood. He needed this woman, at least for now, and insulting her would serve no purpose.

She nuzzled his chest, apparently disappointed that Julio would not speak Spanish to her. Or maybe that he would not speak at all. She let her hand slip carelessly down his stomach, then to his lap, finally allowing it to fondle him casually.

This, the woman knew something about, thought Julio.

Not that she had training, but experience. That, this woman did have. Julio slipped his arm around her waist and gently guided her up.

"You're gonna get me in the mood first, aren't you? You know how I like it when you get me in the mood."

Julio bent to kiss her lips gently. Yes, he would get her in the mood. Getting her in the mood would get him in the mood, and he needed to be in the mood. In fact, this was all pointless if he wasn't in the mood.

CHAPTER 11

Evans Steinberg opened the door to his tiny fourth-floor apartment, kicked the pizza box into the corner, and waved David in. Following Evan gingerly through the empty Kentucky Fried Chicken boxes, Burger King bags, and other assorted fast-food leavings, David tried to speak but was drowned out by Campos.

Evans dropped his three hundred–pound carcass into a worn recliner, punched a button on a receiver buried beneath a pile of books, and gestured toward a stained, red leather chair.

"Just knock those boxes on the floor; kick them over toward the door. I'll pick them up as soon as I get to it," Evans said.

David did as ordered and sat on the edge of the chair.

"So, what brings you to see me?"

David hesitated a moment, taking in the ambience and trying to soften his entry. Evans was like no other Haitian he knew. The man had lost his accent completely, although he spoke French and Creole as well as Spanish fluently. His sweaty black torso extended from under his shirt, gleaming in the distorting light of the single lamp near the cluttered desk. David listened to the raspy breathing for a moment before he picked up a small hardcover volume on the arm of his chair.

"*Shamanistic Plants of the Amazon?*" he asked.

Evans laughed that sort of loud, embarrassed laugh in which obese people specialize. "A new interest. Can't spend all my time studying zombies, you know." Evans picked up a cup from the arm of his recliner, pushed the chair back with a squeak, and looked out of the bottom of his eyes at David. "Are you interested in zombies or shamanistic plants of the Amazon? Huh? Or something else?"

"Something else." David leaned back. "What do you know about heart attacks?"

"Other than that my doctor tells me to lose weight or I'll be having one, nothing."

"I guess I should be more specific. Causes of heart attacks."

"Oh, well that's far different. They're caused by the heart stopping. How's that?"

"Not exactly what I had in mind." David leaned forward. "If you wanted to give someone a heart attack, how would you go about it?"

"Ah, now I understand. It's a woman. You've either been too successful with her and now she wants to monopolize you, or you haven't been successful enough and you want to punish her. Which is it?"

"Neither. It's about a case. A possible murder."

"Murder by heart attack. Very unusual. I hope you're defending."

"Why?"

"Because it is very difficult to prove that a heart attack was caused by a foreign agent. You see, the heart stops for one of two reasons. First, there is an occlusion or blockage of the arteries leading to the heart. This literally starves the heart of the oxygen or fuel it needs. Second, there could be an interference with the electrical impulses that tell the heart when and how fast to beat. Which way do you want to kill?"

"I don't know." David looked up from the book in his hands at Evans. "No, I mean, I don't want to kill anybody. I don't know how it was done."

"What was done?"

"This killing. See, they say my client was a witness to a murder, but it apparently was a heart attack. But they suspect murder."

"Got the autopsy?"

David shook his head. "Not yet."

Evans pushed his great bulk against the recliner, the chair complaining then slamming back down to the floor. He silently walked over to the desk, pushed aside one of the dusty piles, and pulled a less dusty file from the bottom of another pile. "Had this case a few years ago," he said, turning back to David. "Somebody should have caught hell for this, would have if it had happened in the U.S."

"What happened?"

"Electrolyte death."

"Come on, some runner ate too many bananas?" David laughed.

"Close. Doctor wanted to put a guy on a respirator. In order to do that, you have to prevent the muscles from fighting the machine. If you notice when you breathe, it's mostly relaxing, not contracting. Well, if you try to make a machine do it, the patient relaxes when he should contract and contracts when he should relax."

Evans walked over to the bookcase against the wall and pulled down an oversized book with color anatomical drawings and plastic overleaves which added additional systems to the pictures. He flipped it to a page and dropped it on David's lap.

"These muscles, the skeletal muscles, have to relax, so the patient is paralyzed. Then the lung machine is hooked up and the patient lives. Except if the patient gets too much potassium."

"Electrolytes?"

"Electrolytes."

Evans walked back to his chair, pulling two sheets out of the middle of the file and tossing them to David. "Just look at them here, and never admit you got them from me."

David caught the papers and read the top. "Autopsy report of Franciso Vega." *Loreto, Peru.* David scanned the page for the date. Almost four years ago.

"You doing malpractice cases in Peru?" David asked.

Evans shook his head. "They found him in the jungle. Not within fifty miles of a hospital." Evans pulled two Dr Peppers from a half-height refrigerator next to his desk. "A cop of some kind found him. The hospital was offering a bounty for cadavers, for the medical school. The cop decided to make a few dollars."

Evans tossed one of the Dr Peppers to David. "The body was pretty mealy by this time, but they did an autopsy, mostly just a teaching exercise, and they foud the heart stopped. No reason that they could establish. Couldn't figure it."

"And you could?"

Evans shrugged. "The doctor had read my book about the voodoo herbs of Haiti. Thought I might know something and called."

"What did you find?"

"Found nothing. Came to the same conclusion he did. Electrolyte death. Had all the earmarks."

"You could kill somebody by giving him enough potassium?"

"Yep. But they probably paralyzed him first."

"But he was in the middle of the jungle, not near a hospital."

Evans reached up to the wall over his desk and pulled down a large map of South America. "See here?"

"Yeah, looks like the Amazon."

"Right. Biggest hospital dispensary in the world. More different species of plant life there than anywhere else, by far. Ninety percent of it not even cataloged by Western science. And ninety percent of that ninety percent not even investigated by the local shamans."

"So a plant could yield some paralytic?"

"Or anything else. See, the plants and the insect predators are in a war down there, always. The insects threaten to eat a plant species into extinction. The plant responds with a chemical that makes the plant taste bad to the insect. The plant is saved for a while, until the insect changes its taste buds to like the bad-tasting plant. The plant ups the ante, makes itself poisonous. The insect mutates to be immune to the poison . . . the plant makes a more potent poison."

"All this mutating must take millions of years."

Evanss shrugged. "Time the jungle has."

"These things are poisonous to people?"

"Sometimes. Take curare for instance. Insects and humans use the same neurotransmitters to move muscles. Curare blocks those transmitters. Works on humans same as insects."

"So you think somebody used curare?"

"Possible. Or something else. Never be able to trace it if you didn't know what it was."

"So this was murder?"

"We'll never know."

David opened his mouth as if to ask another question, then closed it. He had no more questions.

Evans smiled. "Look, David, what I'm telling you is that if somebody knows what they're doing and wants to kill somebody by stopping their heart, they could do it in a thousand ways, and we'd never be able to trace it. Unless the autopsy is done quickly, . . . forget it. Even if it is . . ." Evans shrugged.

"So what we know is, Light has a plausible story," Joel said, folding his arms and leaning back.

"Right."

"The prosecution is going to rely on some kind of medical evidence of induced heart attack."

"They could never prove that Light could even begin to understand."

"But they could prove that Light could stick the congressman with a needle tipped with curare or something like it."

"Come on."

"I mean it, David. The sticker's end of this is very simple. This would mean Light wasn't the main guy, but he could be the dupe. Just the sticker."

"Which means they're going to want to turn him."

"Which means they're going to push it."

David absently pulled the pen from his pocket. "Which means an indictment..."

"A doctor to testify..."

"And that we have to hire an expert."

"At five thousand a day."

David's eyes drifted away from Joel, who was framed by the setting sun behind him. He realized how much he liked Joel's office: the bookshelves recessed into the blond wood paneling, the plants, the view of Manhattan behind Joel, where the entire wall had been replaced by one of glass. Why was it that every time he came in here, he wound up feeling bad?

"We can't afford it." It was not an order or a decision, as Joel spoke the words, more a statement of fact. And it was true.

"Light didn't do it."

Joel nodded.

"Legal aid or worse, some 18B hound won't do much."

"Might not even make the motion for a court-appointed expert."

"So we've got to keep it."

"You want to spend $2,500 of your own money on this case?" Joel tapped the glass behind him. "And $2,500 of mine. Two months rent."

"Look, Joel, there's no way Light could have done this on his own. In fact, we both agree there's no way he could have done it at all, right?"

"Right."

"But either way, there's somebody behind this. Somebody who could have put something together."

"Who?"

"That's what we have to find out. Before the DA."

"How do we do that?"

"We can start with the woman." David slapped the arm of the chair and got up.

"Is this going to cost another two fifty?"

"Maybe more. I might have to pay for dinner," David called over his shoulder as he left Joel's office. A moment later he was rummaging through his file cabinet, searching for Light's evidence file. Finding it, he tossed it on the desk and flipped it open to the manila envelope Acco-clipped to the top of the file. Opening the envelope, he pulled out the photo of the Spanish woman and flipped it over. Anacleta Lucas.

David checked the Manhattan address on the back. Walsh had been kind enough to include the phone number. David realized the excitement he felt creeping through him was silly. After all, here was a woman used to being beaten up by congressmen. Surely she wouldn't be interested in dating a back-street criminal lawyer from Brooklyn, a lawyer who'd never even hit a woman, except his sister, and she didn't count; he'd only been ten. But David's logical mind had never had good control of his fantasy life, not enough to control the tingles as he picked up the phone.

The phone clicked up after the second ring. There was silence for a second before the voice on the other end said, "Hello." The voice indeed had a Spanish accent, just a hint, and a tentative quality, as if the speaker were eight years old, cast adrift in an adult world. But the voice was adult, full of that mature flowing music that makes a woman's voice a delight to male ears.

David shook himself loose from the trap of her voice and shot his own hello back. "Is this Anacleta Lucas?"

The voice hesitated, as if it had to check with some internal censor before answering. "Yes . . ." came the tentative answer at last.

"I heard about your loss. I'm sorry."

"Thank you. Who is this?"

David introduced himself, then waited a second while she said nothing. "I am a defense attorney—"

"The man with the pipe," she broke in.

"Right. I wonder if I could meet you to discuss—"

"That will be impossible." An adult voice this time.

"It's important. It's very important to a man, to a man's life."

"That will be impossible," the voice said firmly. But her voice was less sure now, wavering.

"It will only take a few minutes. We could meet in your neighborhood."

"That will be impossible." Even more unsteady this time.

"I won't use your name. It will be just you and me," David lied, trying hard to hold his voice steady.

"That will be impossible."

David sighed. "I guess I'll just have to send the press then. I tried to save you that."

There was silence. Only her breathing crackled through the line. It was different, rapid, uneven. David could almost hear the circuits opening and closing in her brain.

Finally the breathing became even again. "You must do what you must." The voice spoke evenly just before the phone clicked off.

"You shouldn't have done that," said Walsh, who, having nothing to write, tapped the top of his Mont Blanc against the cloth napkin. "I told you I would arrange things."

David didn't like the tone of the man's voice, a haughty gruffness. The man was a reporter, David reminded himself. Not even really a reporter, more like a weasel transformed into a man for one lifetime in order to feed upon the carrion of the famous. A karmic devil, here today to visit upon Twining. But David said nothing. He stared into his beer and said nothing.

"You made it tougher," Walsh said, flipping a page of his spiral notebook back and smoothing the page over the metal spiral. "I had to threaten."

"Threaten what?"

Walsh shrugged. The shrug left his smile undisturbed but

flipped his gray hair down from his forehead until the leading edge curled around the high ridge of his nose. "You shouldn't have said anything about the press. That made it harder."

"Come on."

Walsh drained his martini and signaled to the waitress. "You mention the press and people think of the *New York Times*. Nobody's really afraid of the *Times*. You have to be more specific and reveal it slowly."

"So you're a master of the threat?" The idea of this skinny, hunchbacked Englishman being a master of threat was laughable. Still, there was something mildly disturbing about the man's focus. David looked over Walsh's shoulder to the bar, where the waitress called in an order, jabbed a duplicate on the spike, and swung her tray away toward another table. At their first meeting Walsh had been interested in David's reaction. He'd been trying to charm a potential source. David felt his status in Walsh's mind had shifted. David was now an instrument to be used for Walsh's purpose.

"One must deliver a threat as if it is not a threat," Walsh continued. "As if you are caught, as helpless as the threatened. The threatened must believe that only she has the power to save you from the threat."

"And you had a threat?"

Walsh leaned back as the waitress deposited the new martini in front of him. "I had to go higher on the threat ladder than I wished," Walsh answered when the waitress had disappeared.

David sipped at his own beer. He'd nursed this one since he arrived a half hour ago. He didn't like people who were late, but it was hard to hold it against someone he had never met. Besides, he didn't know if Walsh had told her to arrive later so they could have this conversation or if she was on South American time. And David still didn't know what this conversation was about.

"I don't understand what you need me for," David said.

"Someone has to talk to the woman."

"You speak well enough."

"Even with the accent, huh?" Walsh laughed. Not a real laugh. It stopped abruptly, Walsh's face coming back to its fixed smile. "Some people find me upsetting. I called her in your name."

"You didn't give your name?"

Walsh shook his head. "I will not be meeting her. You'll be on your own," Walsh said, pushing his chair out, "but I expect a full report."

David watched as Walsh disappeared through the double cut-glass doors and into the street. Picking up his glass, David walked to an empty table near the window, pushing ferns out of the way as he went. Walsh jaywalked across Second Avenue and disappeared behind a green subway railing.

David turned his thoughts to Anacleta. As repellent as meeting Walsh had been, meeting Anacleta was exciting. All David knew about her was that she was beautiful. No, that wasn't true. He knew she had those eyes, looking slightly dead in the photo, dead but alive. As if they looked through the camera and out the other side to her own thoughts. Piercing the thoughts and concerns of this world, of those trapped in the world where photographs were important. An interesting woman, David was sure.

He saw her first on the corner, waiting for the traffic light. She was wearing one of those grayish white dresses that hung loosely, clinging occasionally to a hip or a breast, with the skirt swinging in rhythmic counterbalance to the rest of her body. As the light changed and she started to cross, David felt only slightly guilty hiding in the ferns like a licentious ferret, watching her approach.

Her body moved with freedom and rhythm, bouncing slightly at each step, head held high, face encased by shoulder-length auburn hair which swung in perfect harmony with her skirt. That carriage and that body should be capped by a radiantly smiling face, begging to meet the day's challenges.

It wasn't. Her face was pure light tan, unblemished, unlined. And blank, almost unearthly in its passivity. The face was not angry, not annoyed, not mildly irritated. Not even interested. Just passive.

David watched her walk to the door, the fabric of her dress clinging statically to her hip for a second before slipping off. The perfect curve of her hip standing in sharp relief for a second, before the image slipped, transferred as if by magic to the other hip.

David shook himself free from the image. He had to introduce himself. He got up and started toward the door just as she opened it.

She looked around the bar quickly, spotted him, and without a word, without a smile, slipped between the tables. Settling into the chair across from him, she ordered white wine.

David felt the words again, ready to ramble out, but he held himself back. He had the power here, he reminded himself. He choked the words back and sat silently, staring at the woman. She sat . . . motionless, her hands folded in front of her, gazing at a fern, as if the leaves held some insight.

David waited, watching the waitress approach, slip a glass under Anacleta's gaze, and slide away with a glance at David. David nodded, as if he were in control of this situation and the waitress didn't have to worry. The woman delicately moved the glass to her lips and sipped.

She replaced it carefully before speaking. "Congressman Twining and I had been together for about a year," she said as if reading a prepared statement. "It has been difficult." With this last she glanced up and caught David's eyes. The hint of a smile, just the minimal curling of the corners of the mouth, a playful sparkle in her eye, then as quickly, she looked back to the fern.

"Difficult in what way?" he asked.

"He was under so much pressure, you know?" She flicked a white spot off the dark red of her nails.

"So he beat you?"

She smiled, not the real one of a moment ago, but a

pasted-on one, meant to be false and to be read as false. "I deserved it," she said.

"Deserved to be hit?"

She nodded. "I wanted to leave, just walk away," she continued. "You can't do that."

David wanted to ask why not, but he didn't, afraid it would lead the conversation into a discussion of cultures which he wouldn't have won or even understood. Instead he asked, "What hold did he have over you?"

"None," she said. "Other than he had been my man." She put down her drink, leaving her hand on the table.

"You know that man, the one who hit the congressman, he's in jail," David said, allowing his hand to rest on the table near hers.

Again that hint of a smile, that playful smile.

David touched her hand, just his forefinger on her palm. He could have claimed it was an accident, if he had to, but they both would have known it wasn't.

"We need to get him out," he said.

"We," she said, turning her hand suddenly, trapping his forefinger under hers. "We used to play a game when I was young. When the girl caught the boy with her finger, like this, he was hers."

"For how long?"

She shrugged, releasing his finger. "As long as the game lasted." The playfulness left her eyes. "That depended on him, I suppose." She pulled her hand back in her lap. "I cannot help," she said.

"Yes, you can," David said, the words starting to tumble again. He clamped his mouth shut and started over. "Yes, you can."

"How?"

"Tell me about Twining. Who were his enemies?"

She finished the wine and pulled her purse on her lap.

"That man, the man with the pipe, they may charge him with murder."

The surprised look again swept over Anacleta's face. A second later it was blank. "I cannot help."

"I'll have to tell the press," David said quietly. "I don't want to."

She rose and started toward the door.

"I won't have any choice," David said, following her. "I have to protect my client."

She stopped at the corner, took his hand and smiled. It was a smile that could melt men, that David felt in the middle of his chest, disrupting natural rhythms, moving outward in concentric circles until his hands shook in little tremors under hers, until his knees started to buckle.

David broke his eyes away. Look over at the green awning across the street, the dirty one with the stains, that's it. He grabbed his body back, tensing the muscles, locking his legs in place. But he still felt her hands.

"If you did, David, it would hurt me deeply," she said, then turned and walked away, disappearing into the crowds across the street.

David didn't like the feelings that ran through him as he watched the crowds swallow Anacleta. In the year since Janie moved, he hadn't had those feelings. Not once. Maybe a couple of times, talking to a woman, he'd felt the emptiness. But when he'd turned away, the feeling had gone. This time it didn't. Anacleta had been gone for ten minutes, yet David stood rooted to the spot.

It wasn't her, he told himself. It was just that he couldn't turn away. He was trapped this time. She was a witness. Witnesses had to be talked to, no matter what feelings the lawyer had.

David thought of the other things he had to do before he'd have to see Anacleta again, like get the autopsy report and find out if they were really going to indict Light for murder. It felt a little better, planning his attack, but the empty feeling remained.

It was still there twenty minutes later when David walked into his office, picked up the phone, and punched in the medical examiner's number. A female voice came on the line.

"I need a copy of an autopsy report."

"Just one moment." The voice had the shrillness of experienced officiousness. David imagined its owner had been shuffling calls for close to fifty years.

A new voice crackled through the line. "May I help you?"

"Yes, I need a copy of an autopsy report."

"And to whom am I speaking?"

"David Cohen. I'm a lawyer."

"Yes, Counselor. Now, what is the name of the case?"

A new voice, but shrill just the same. "Harrison Twining."

David heard a keyboard working in the background. "That's the defendant?"

"No, the decedant."

"Oh." The voice paused, the pitch lower and dropping fast. "I'm afraid we can't help you."

"Why not?"

"Well, there hasn't been an arrest. What I mean is, who are you?"

"I told you, David Cohen. A lawyer."

"Yes, well that doesn't do much for you, does it? Being a lawyer. I mean you're nothing until you get a client, right?"

"I beg your pardon."

"What I mean is, I was a secretary for years and I couldn't just send out autopsy reports, not until I got this job, don't you see?"

David said he didn't and the voice clicked off, assuring David there would be another voice along presently.

"Yes, sir, can I help you?" The voice was male this time. Some sexist part of David felt reassured.

"Yes, I need a copy of the autopsy report of Harrison Twining."

"And you're a lawyer for . . ."

"A witness." David thought it prudent to change his story.

"A witness? A witness to what?"

"To the murder."

"Well, we don't have this as a murder. Heart failure, that's what we have."

"Okay, he's a witness to the heart attack."

"Don't know that you can witness heart failure, not really. More like a witness to someone gasping for breath. Doesn't help us much, having a witness to a heart failure."

"Look, can you just send me a copy of the autopsy report?"

"Not to a witness. No. Can you imagine what would happen if every witness wanted a copy of the autopsy report of every heart failure they saw? Bedlam, I can tell you. People's hearts fail every day. On the street, in cars."

"But this wasn't in a car. It was in an office, and there's a murder investigation."

"No, we have this as a heart attack. Natural. There's no investigation."

"I can tell you there is."

"You can't tell me, not if we don't have it in the records. It wouldn't matter anyway. We can't give a report to witnesses. No, no witnesses." The voice paused. "Have your client go out and kill someone if he really wants an autopsy report."

The phone clicked dead. David felt the boil. He'd need a subpoena, which meant starting a case, which meant paying a filing fee. All for a client who wasn't a client and had no money to boot. How was he going to explain this to Joel and Arnie the accountant? God, David hated bureaucracy.

CHAPTER 12

She pulled him close, kissing his cheek, then his ear, then whispering, "Get me in the mood first, honey, won't you?"

Julio moved to her neck, softly kissing his way down to her breasts. He hated the way this woman used *eufemismo*—what was it in English? Euphemism. *Get me in the mood.* What did that mean when she was shivering with expectation already?

He moved down her abdomen, kissing her lightly until he reached her genitals. There he paused while she shifted her weight and spread her legs expectantly. He didn't mind getting this one in the mood. The only thing he worried about was getting her past the mood. Running his tongue along her labia, he felt her arousal. This is the important part, he thought, feeling her arousal, her emotion, feeling it as if it were mine. He paused as her arousal moved toward the peak, allowing her to back off before brushing her thigh with his cheek. Her arousal washed through him. She was ready.

He gently guided her left hip up as he relocated his body.

"Oh, honey, step over like you did last time."

He glared back at her.

She moved her straggly, dry, blond hair out of her face and pinned it behind her head. "So I can have your balls in my face when you do it. Just for that, honey. You know how I love it like that."

Julio reached down next to the bed for the leather case.

"Last time you said it was better for you too, honey. You remember, don't you?"

Julio remembered. He remembered how she talked him into doing it differently. He remembered how the emotion ran through him, her emotion, his. He couldn't even tell. He remembered how every time he touched her, his body exploded. How he couldn't hold his hand still. It was no good like that.

Julio ran his hand over her breasts, palming the nipples lightly and moving them in little circles. Watching her smile, he remembered how much he enjoyed it. Her mouth was parted just slightly, just enough to show the hint of her pink tongue between her even teeth. It was discipline, he thought, as he pulled the leather case closer and stepped over her face.

"Slide back just an inch, can you, honey?" she said. "And hunker down a little lower, so I don't have to reach when the time comes, okay?"

Julio moved the case a little closer, slid his hips back a bit, and moved down until he could feel her warm breath on his scrotum. He bent an inch more until he felt her lips and nose, waited until she sighed and moved back.

"Right there, honey, that's just perfect," she said, moving her left leg over her right.

Julio ran his hand over the smooth skin of the outside of her thigh, up over her hip, over the bumps, allowing his hand to fall lightly with the curve of her body as it fell to her waist. He liked it when women laid on their sides, the way their hips rose. It made them more beautiful. That's what Julio thought.

It is more difficult this way, he thought, as he reached for the box. But this one is cooperative. It may not be so bad. He pressed the button on the brass latch. He smiled at the sound of the latch flying open. Such a small metal piece giving such a deep, resonant sound. He considered closing the latch and opening it again, just to hear that sound, but he did not.

Resting his hand on her hip, he lifted the maroon leather top of the box. The top opened easily on the hinges. German, he thought. German machines were so well made. Things as small as German hinges or latches, machined precisely so they would move easily. Julio liked that the box was made carefully. A man is as good as his tools, they had said. Julio felt his tools should be the best. There were few tools he needed. His mind, his hands . . .

He slid the box near her hip. He ran his fingers over the bumps again, more carefully this time, more slowly. The main line ran diagonally from back to front, about forty-five degrees down. It had been treated three times.

His fingers ran along the surface of the open box. They stopped. He liked selecting the knives by feel. Like a divining rod, his fingers knew the right weapon. He smiled at his mistake, as he pulled a scalpel from the case. Tool. The word was tool, not weapon, he reminded himself.

The tool fell into his hand easily. Held like a pen, it oriented itself to the diagonal scar and sliced easily along its surface. Julio smiled as the thin line of blood oozed. It was a second before she felt the pain and a millisecond after that that Julio did. He hunkered down that extra inch. Not until he felt her lips on his scrotum, her tongue flitting across the surface, did he pull the skin apart. Her sudden intake of breath rushing across his damp testicles chilled him momentarily. Then her emotions came: the pain, then fear, then arousal.

"You'll love me more after you're finished, right?" she asked just before he felt the damp presence again.

"Of course," he said, "but I need to concentrate just now."

Julio felt the warm, damp massage begin again, then bent to blot the blood. Mustn't let it heal too quickly, he thought, looking at the design. There was a spot of fresh skin. The tool almost leaped upon it and began cutting. She made a sound, a sound of pain. That's better, he thought, as he pulled the wound apart with his thumb and forefinger.

She whimpered.

A brave woman to only whimper, he thought.

"Tell me again why you like women with scars?" she asked.

He cleaned the scalpel in alcohol. It was the only bad part. Talking to this *gringa* about love.

CHAPTER 13

Light curled into the tan blocks where they joined to form the corner. The benches didn't quite meet, causing Light to shift around for a comfortable perch. It was at least a little better now, at least they had him moving. Now down to the courthouse. Didn't know why they was moving him. Didn't know why he was here, but he was. Never seemed to make much difference if he knew why or not, things just happened.

"Leroy Scott." The officer shouted the name without looking up from the paper in his hand.

Light pushed himself up and walked slowly over to the bars. Didn't want to walk too fast here. Just make 'em think you was anxious. That'd give 'em the power.

"Peter Simpson," the officer called out.

Another man stood and walked over next to where Light stood. The officer called three more names. Five men stood near the bars. The officer opened the cell and escorted the men to the end of the hall and into another holding cell with cubicles on one side. Light peered into all of them. No Cohen.

"Leroy Scott," the officer called again. A minute later Light was in a courtroom. Mr. Cohen was speaking to the judge and ignoring Light. Light said nothing, but stared up over the judge's shoulder to the wall behind. Nothing there, but that made it as good a place to stare as any.

"Your Honor, they've held him now for over twenty-four hours without a charge and without even telling me what charges they intend to bring."

Judge Williams looked relaxed this morning, looking out over his courtroom and realizing the press had not noticed the habeas corpus motion. David had been surprised too. The prosecution had not seen fit to notify the press, which could mean several things, most of which were beneficial to Light. It also meant that the worst thing for Light, that he was about to be charged with murder, was not going to happen. No district attorney would avoid milking that for all the press he could.

Judge Williams turned to the DA and raised his dark eyebrows above his dark-rimmed glasses. "Mr. DA."

"Your Honor, we actually didn't know anything about this arrest or detention until we got the papers last night."

"And you've talked to the officer?"

"Detective Jenson, yes, sir. We have. He's right here in fact. He tells me there's now a charge of burglary."

"Burglary? Mr. Cohen, I thought you said this was a homicide investigation."

"Still investigating that, Your Honor," Jenson said from behind the DA.

"May I ask then, Your Honor, what proof the detective has that there was a burglary," David said, recovering from his surprise.

Judge Williams turned to the prosecution side and opened his mouth, only to be cut off by Jenson, now pushing his way in front of the DA.

"A big, fat, bloody fingerprint," Jenson said.

"If I may, Your Honor, the fingerprint was found on the window of the premises. Even if it were the defendant's fingerprint, that would only establish his presence, at some time, at the window, not necessarily at the place of death nor at the time of death. But even conceding that, it only

HOSTILE WITNESS   117

proves one half of a charge of burglary. What was the crime counsel alleges the defendant was planning to commit inside?"

The young assistant district attorney turned to Jenson who promptly looked at the thick wire mesh covering the floor-to-ceiling windows of the Brooklyn House of Detention across the street.

The ADA turned back to Judge Williams. "I think it's premature to ask that question, Your Honor."

Judge Williams hesitated, then folded his large hands before him, looked down at the DA, and spoke slowly in a deep Southern drawl. "Well, this whole thing has me a little suspicious. Your office didn't know about this. High-profile case like this and the detective didn't see fit to tell you. Then telling Mr. Cohen that it was a murder investigation and showing up here talking like it was a burglary all the time. Nothing about what was stolen, if anything. This entire matter has me deeply suspicious."

He pulled a rubber band off a set of blue papers, unfolding them before continuing. "Now I have been provided by Mr. Cohen with court papers concerning Mr. Scott's arrest for assault and later dismissal. Looking at Mr. Scott's record, I see that he has lived at the same address for the past fifteen years, except for short periods during which he was a guest of the city," the judge said, peering over his glasses at David. "I see no evidence that there would be any difficulty at all in locating Mr. Scott, if and when you have a case against him, and arresting him at that time, gentlemen." This time the judge paused to glare at Jenson. "Therefore I am going to order the release of Mr. Scott, subject, of course, to rearrest if and when the police have a case they are prepared to go forward with."

David turned and faced Light for the first time.

"What that mean?"

"You're going home," David said.

Light nodded, turned, and followed the court officer back to the cell.

*   *   *

Santeria carefully folded the *New York Times*, placed it on the corner of his desk, and nodded to Julio. Anacleta tried to remain calm. That was her job, she reminded herself, to stay calm. But Santeria always unnerved her, ever since the first time she met him, six years ago. She'd only been sixteen, she reminded herself. Only sixteen and he older than her father, she guessed.

"This is a problem," Santeria said.

He spoke in that voice she had first heard when she was sixteen. It wasn't his only voice, just the only one he used when speaking to her. She wondered if he were trained. She tried to imagine *Señor* Santeria as a young man, a teenager, walking with a master, practicing with this voice and that until he got it right and the master hugged him. No, the master wouldn't hug, not like *una doña*. There would be a slap on the back, a trip to a brothel maybe if the student needed a hug. But no hug from the master.

Anacleta felt herself smiling at the thought, then looked up into the disapproving eyes of *el señor*. The smile was replaced by a chill, a chill that had not changed since she was sixteen. *El señor* could still deliver a chill.

"This is not amusing, *señorita*."

Anacleta folded her hands in her lap and stared at them. She wasn't exactly clear why it was so upsetting to him. Lifting her head, she looked over *Señor* Santeria's shoulder, through the window behind his desk to where Julio sat impassively. She wondered who had decided that Julio should sit outside. Did Julio know what they were discussing? Did Julio even read the paper?

"Tell me again what you remember."

"It was two days after Harrison died," she began, turning her attention back to *Señor* Santeria. "It was not until then that I needed to look at my appointments."

"And it was gone?"

Anacleta nodded. He was acting as if her appointment book were a great loss. She was a lover of powerful men. That was her life. Anyone who cared could have known that just by following her. The diary would tell them only when she and Twining had made love. All the page said was that she was to meet Twining at ten.

"Why this page?" Santeria asked.

Anacleta said nothing. She could not have known the answer, so he must not be asking her. That's what she thought until she felt his eyes boring into her. Then she shrugged.

Santeria flipped open the *Times* again. "A day ten days before Twining's death." He looked up at her. "A nothing day. Why would the *Times* pick that day?"

"I don't even remember the day," she answered.

"It's not news." Frustration was apparent in Santeria's voice now.

"There's that old drunk."

"The one who saved you from the white-haired monster?"

Anacleta looked back to her hands. She didn't like it when Santeria was sarcastic like that. The man meant well. He was probably the only man who'd ever tried to help her without wanting something in return. That deserved more than mockery, but she said nothing. It wasn't her place. She looked again at Julio. He smiled. She wondered if he'd help her without wanting anything.

"They mention him in the article."

"Holding him for the murder," Anacleta said.

"Released him this morning." Santeria ran his long, thin fingers over the text, as if they could pull more meaning from it than his eyes. "The paper is being fed." Santeria spoke with conviction.

"Fed?"

"If they had had the whole book, they wouldn't have printed this page. It is a nothing."

"Who?"

"Cohen. The lawyer."

Anacleta said nothing. Santeria was smart. He understood these things far better than she. That is what *la doña* said. "Anacleta," she said, "you will be trained to read the emotions of life. But remember, others are better trained to read the ambitions of life. Stick to your expertise." Anacleta's expertise said that Santeria was angry . . . and a little afraid.

"You must see the lawyer again," Santeria said as if it were final.

Anacleta felt a wave of pleasure run through her body. Cohen was a young man. A new experience, she thought, but she pushed the pleasure away. This was business, she reminded herself. Business.

Light looked back at the courthouse once, then snapped his collar up, pulled his jacket around him, and started down Atlantic Avenue. *Don't want to see that courthouse no more*, he thought as he walked. *Stayed out that place for ten years doing crime, been in and out that place three times since I decided to do a good deed.*

That reporter, the skinny one with the gray hair, come up asking him if he saw the *Times*. How he gonna see the *Times* in jail? On the way out he saw the *Times* just like he saw it every day, laying there on the newsstand, too many words and not enough pictures, that's what. Did he see the *Times*?

But that reporter, he walk along right beside, talking about this or that, opening the *Times* to some page in the middle, scannin' the page, then rippin' to another page, like he was in a hurry to find some shit. Light kept walking, making that old man skip along to keep up. Light felt bad about that, that old man skippin', but the old man could've just let him go. Light didn't want to talk to no old man about nothing, not even if he was a reporter. No, just want to forget about it, Light thought. *Just forget this whole thing happen, just forget about how I wanted to be a good guy. Showin' off for them boys. That's what. Ain't never gonna do that no more.*

Light turned the corner, heading up Atlantic and back toward home. Didn't want to get on no bus, not yet. That reporter just get on beside him, sit down there, rippin' through his *Times* till he find some article say what a scumbag this Leroy Scott is. How dangerous the world is. Then this reporter gonna ask for comment. *And what comment I gonna give? Gonna say yes, I'm a scumbag. Been a scumbag all my life. Shoulda never tried to convince nobody I wasn't. Shoulda just took what Evelyn dish out on me. That's what I should tell him. Then a hour later Cohen on the phone saying what I say that shit for. Saying how it look bad, how they gonna read that shit to the jury. So I gotta ride on a bus all the way home, ignoring that reporter with the gray skin, while he insult me more and more just to get me to say something. No, I just walk.*

Light listened to the reporter's heavy breathing as he walked by a church. He quickened his pace. The reporter grabbed his arm.

"Here it is."

Light stopped and looked at the page the reporter stuffed under his nose.

"Ever see that before?"

A box dominated the upper-left corner of the page. Inside was what looked like a page from that diary, the one he took from that woman's purse. But that couldn't be. That book was still home in his dresser. Still safe right there. That was the proof, the proof he had that that congressman had been with that woman. The proof was going to prove him innocent. Of course, it was a little different now that he was accused of murder. That diary was going to prove that he was there the night Twining died. That wasn't so good. But it didn't look like that diary was in his dresser now. Somebody from the *Times* had it.

"Any comment?" the reporter asked.

Ain't gonna make no comment now, Light thought as he started home. *Not gonna take no bus.* Light left that reporter standing, taking notes in front of that church.

Light's legs were tired by the time he turned right from under the elevated train and up Nostrand Avenue, but his mind was clear. *Had to be Evelyn took that diary. Hadn't told nobody else he had it. Had to be. She hear about that and she figure she gonna take that shit and sell it to some reporter. Go right to the top, right to the* Times. *Evelyn don't have no shame, she go right to the top. She get her some money for that shit, money should by rights be mine.*

Trouble is, if I go straight at her, she just lie. Contrariest bitch I ever knew. Got to trick her, just like some lawyer cross-examining. I'll figure it out.

Light went to his apartment and checked the dresser. Sure enough, it was gone. He changed his shirt, tucked his copy of the *Times* under his arm, went over to Evelyn's apartment, and knocked on the door.

Light waited as the door clicked and opened a crack. An eye peered through. Light jammed his arm through the crack toward the eye and pushed.

"Out a jail no more than about a hour and you beatin' on more women," Evelyn said, stumbling backward.

"I don't never beat on women," Light said as he stepped into the apartment, ignoring Evelyn's futile attempts to regain her balance. The woman looked a wreck. Hair hadn't had no order for a week, looked like. Big sore on her cheek, dress still hanging on her bones like the devil dress up death.

She slumped against the wall, steadied herself, then pushed herself slowly up to a standing position. "I forgot. You beat on old men."

"Don't beat no old men. Don't steal nothing from nobody on the block neither."

"What somebody steal something from you," Evelyn cackled.

Cackled, that what she done, thought Light. *Noise just leaking out her mouth like there weren't no right hole for it to come out.* He turned away from Evelyn and walked to the living room near the front of the building.

"What you doin'? I distinctly don't remember invitin' you in this house," Evelyn said, clambering after Light.

"I don't remember invitin' you to mine, neither," Light said, looking around the room. A table to the right was covered with all manner of flotsam but not books. A sofa and a TV were to the left; nothing there either.

"You think I the one steal from you?" Evelyn cackled

again, moving up close behind Light, pushing that cackle in his ear. "What you got I could want?"

Light spun around, his nose in Evelyn's face. "You see the *Times*?"

"See the *Times*?" Evelyn asked, stepping back.

Light followed her, keeping close. He could hear the crack in her voice, the weakness. "The *Times*," he repeated.

"What you think? I some fancy downtown whore, entertaining gentlemen . . ." she said, stepping away from Light and extending her hand, waving it in the air like a fancy whore.

Light grabbed her by the neck, pushed her against the wall, and held her tight against it. Her eyes showed fear. *Felt good, making that woman fear,* Light thought. *Could bust her skinny-ass, cracked-up neck with just a twist. Just a little twist,* Light thought as he twisted. Her eyes were bulging now, wide and bright. First time since the crack Light saw them bright like that. He gave her neck a little more twist until he heard the crack. Just a little crack, like a background crack. Light released her. *Should be enough to scare her,* he thought. *Enough to scare me.*

Evelyn stepped back and wiggled her neck from side to side. The look of fear left her and the defiant look returned as she stepped back, keeping her distance. "Want to kill me?" she asked in a voice still weak, as if testing her throat.

"More than you know."

"Want to kill me?" she repeated, voice stronger this time.

"Not like you don't deserve it, stealing from me like that."

"Stealing what?"

Light threw the *Times* at her. "Page thirty-five."

Sneering, she bent down, picked it up, and dropped on the sofa as if settling in for an evening of reading. Light's hand started to twitch, he wanted to kill her so badly. Just get that neck back in his hand like it was. *One little twist, get the big crack this time, not no little snap.*

Evelyn dropped the paper. "So, they printing some diary."

"That diary I show you, before I got arrested."

"Same diary?" Evelyn asked with a rise in her voice, like it was a curiosity.

"That same diary you stole from me." Light felt the anger growing. Couldn't really kill her. Not here, anyway. But he could make her think so. He took a step toward her.

She cringed back on the sofa. "Didn't steal no diary from you."

The sound of the crack hit Light before the awareness of the blow. He stepped back, watching Evelyn tumble across the sofa, ending up sprawled, head hanging over the edge, legs straddling the sofa's back, blood trickling from her cheek. Light shook his right hand. It stung.

Evelyn gathered herself in a ball in the corner of the couch. "Every time a man come to me, it appears he want to beat on me."

Light heard the tear in her voice and, for a second, felt for her. He shook off the feeling. This was the woman who stole his diary. Stole his proof. The anger came back. "Why you sell that shit to the *Times?*"

"Just so I could have another man to beat on me, I guess."

Light remembered this one, all the way from the time he pulled his hand back to when it hit her cheek, same place as the last. He even felt when the blood squished under his hand. It was better when he remembered.

Evelyn's squeal escaped from her mouth, as if she were trying to hold it in, not give Light the pleasure. But it leaped out before she had a chance to clamp down on it.

"Why you sell that shit to the *Times?*"

"Why you think?"

Light raised his hand again.

"Money," she yelled. "I sold it for money, what you think?"

Light hesitated. He surely did want to hit the bitch again. But it wouldn't be right if she were telling the truth. "You had it."

Evelyn nodded. "I had it. Took right out the dresser."

She smiled and shook her head. "Light don't never hide nothing in the dresser. That's were everybody hide shit."

"Don't worry about where everybody hide shit, just tell me. You still got that book?"

Evelyn shook her head.

"Who?"

"Some man."

Light raised his hand again. "Some man. Who?"

"Don't know who. Some white man."

"Describe him."

Evelyn shook her head. "He was covered, had a hat, sunglasses, long coat. Couldn't see nothing."

Light felt the frustration. He wasn't going after no white man. Not when admitting he had the diary would mean that he'd been there the night Twining died. No, this was the end, Light thought as he picked up the paper.

Evelyn moved to the edge of the couch and draped herself over the redwood end table. Caressed it like it the only thing she could get comfort from.

At least that something, Light thought. *Some punishment, the bitch not havin' nobody to hug.*

CHAPTER 14

Jenson liked the way her cheekbones popped up high when she smiled like she did in the picture. Liked it and didn't like it at the same time, he thought, dropping the three-by-five to the desk. Forty-two and he had just made detective. That wasn't right. He should've made it before. Should've made it in his thirties.

Jenson leaned back in his chair, watching Seaford over at his desk, squaring the corners, putting the papers into those hanging files, like a grandmother. Like a ninny grandmother. Jenson couldn't figure how the army was making faggots. It wasn't that Clinton had let them in; it was that the service was making 'em. It had started when he was in, after Nam. It got important to get the papers right. Supposed to be about killing people, or being ready to at least. Instead it got to be about remembering where you left stuff. Same here on this job.

Seaford probably had been good in the service. Navy. Had to be the navy. That man could store more papers neater in less space than anybody Jenson had ever seen. Spent hours doing it too. But he had the right idea. Go in the service, do your time, then come right out and be a cop.

Not like I did, thought Jenson. Spending six years, too much. Then taking three for college and dropping out. Then wasting ten more in uniform. By the time he'd decided it was time to move to detective, they all told him, take your twenty and retire. Fuck it. Don't get as much overtime with a gold shield. Worse pension.

But Jenson did it anyway. Then his first case, first fucking case, this Cohen makes a fool of him. How was he supposed to know? Every little fucking collar, do a house to house. So the fuck what if it was a congressman. All the more reason. Congressman ain't gonna be doing nobody right in the street. Senator maybe, they got six-year terms, got some time to let the population forget. But congressmen, they run every fucking minute.

"Christ, I got a partner in a trance," Seaford said, looking up from his file drawer.

Jenson looked away. Trance, yeah, that was it, a trance. "So tell me, Seaford, how is it we get the only fucking congressman in the fucking country stupid enough to do his dirt on Main-fucking-Street?"

"This is Brooklyn." Seaford laughed. "Nobody here can read no names. They read 'dem' and pull the lever."

"Yeah, what about Giuliani?"

Seaford leaned across the desk and lowered his voice. "They can read 'nig' better even than 'dem.' "

And "pol" better then either, Jenson thought as he watched Seaford head downstairs. Being a pol is worse than either, that's where Jenson had made his mistake. The people loved to hammer their leaders, and the reporters knew it. The reporters and the lawyers. Yeah, Cohen knew and Jenson hadn't. Jenson had figured it was another nigger beating on white man case. But it wasn't.

Now the congressman is dead, maybe because of this, and Jenson's next step is through this woman. This beautiful fucking woman. Jenson pushed his copy of the *Daily News* to the side, so he could see the picture better. He'd been trying to ignore the story on the front page about that cop in the Seven Five making eight large a week selling the coke he shook down from the dealers. The paper had started to run pictures of the women he'd run with. This fuckup, twenty-eight, been fucking the finest of the fine, while Jenson's celebrating with his wife, his overweight wife, with the bad teeth and the pussy that seems to sprout yeast like a fucking bakery. Celebrating his worthless, pension-sucking gold shield.

Jenson looked again at the Spanish one, Anacleta Lucas. So his first case is with a dead congressman, a wiseass lawyer, and this fucking women. This gorgeous fucking woman.

David tossed the autopsy report across the cluttered desk. Evans drained his Dr Pepper before picking it up.

"Where'd you get it?"

"A reporter." David felt the irritation as he said it. How could Walsh just walk in and do what David couldn't, get information that David couldn't? He'd told Walsh about the interaction with the ME's office, and Walsh had said, "Oh, I have it. Want a copy?" Casually, like it was nothing.

"Anything?" Evans asked.

"Not so far as I could tell." David said. "No reason to think it was murder by that report."

Evans pushed the photo under the lamp hanging over his desk and bent low. "Pricks," he said.

"Yeah, I was thinking the same thing. And why? That's what I can't figure."

"Pinpricks."

"Pinpricks?"

"Or needle pricks." Evans flipped to a color copy of the photo, stapled to the back of the report. "Could be needles."

"What?" David grabbed the photo and studied the body. Hard to identify anything from the photo.

"Have to get the substance somehow."

"The substance. But how do you know there was a substance?"

"I don't," Evans said, reaching over his shoulder, popping open the refrigerator, and pulling out two Dr Peppers. "Neither does the medical examiner, but he does have pinpricks."

"Every time there's pinpricks, the ME starts an investigation?"

"No, but this is a politician. First, not likely to be a drug abuser, so the pricks are not likely to be self-inflicted, especially in the neck." Evans slid a Dr Pepper over to David. "Second, there's always the possibility of an assassination."

David absently rubbed the top of the can with the bottom of his tie. "So, they have no evidence it's an assassination."

"The pricks. But as I said, there are any number of ways to induce a heart attack without being traced. But it's clear they need more evidence."

"Clear." David felt his grasp of the case floating away.

Evans pulled a pair of scissors from the top drawer of his desk. "Why else show their hand on Light? They could have just held him on the burglary. Could have indicted him on the burglary and not given Judge Williams a chance to cut him loose, right?"

David nodded. Strange that David hadn't thought of it before. He could hear O'Neil standing in his office in Homicide and bellowing even now. "Unless the defendant's going to run, don't make that arrest until you have the evidence to indict." No reason to spook a suspect if you'd just have to cut him loose five days later. Yet that's just what they did in this case.

"So they let him out, keep an eye on him, see what he leads them to." Evans turned the plastic six-pack holder toward him, cutting the loops clockwise around the outside. When he finished, he tossed it on the floor, flipped the autopsy report closed, and handed it to David. "They'll be keeping their eye on Light, I suspect. And talking to anyone else around."

"Any way to tell what the drug was?"

"As I said, can't even tell if, but the actual test results would help. The only way to tell for sure, though, is for Twining to come back to life to tell us his symptoms."

David drained his Dr Pepper. So maybe Jenson *was* using Light. Maybe he had nothing. No, that wasn't right. He had the burglary. If he hadn't played with the homicide and forced David to bring that habeas, Light would still be safely in jail.

David leaned on the mahogany rail, blinking the sleep from his eyes. He hadn't held much hope for this motion even before he'd stayed up half the night trying to find law to support him. There wasn't much. He wished again he had one of those computer-research services; then he might have some support. Joel had been quick to point out that they could probably afford the service if David would quit staying up half the night working on cases for clients who couldn't pay.

The court officer slapped the front of the bench and rolled into his "hear ye's." "Hear ye" was never intended for a Bensonhurst accent, David thought as he strode before the bench. "People versus Scott."

"Counselor, I thought we went through this yesterday," Judge Williams began without waiting for David's introduction.

"Your Honor, I believe that the police or prosecution in this case are engaged in an investigation of an alleged homicide with my client as a target. It is prejudicial to the defense of that case that we be denied access to the test results and other data collected at the autopsy."

"Mr. DA?"

"We are unaware of any investigation of Mr. Cohen's client for anything but a burglary."

"Your Honor, I have had discussions with Detective Jenson in this regard..."

"Your Honor, I have talked to the detective and he tells me that when the arrest was first made, there was some suspicion, but the medical examiner did not produce any evidence of murder in this matter."

"Which doesn't mean that they aren't investigating."

"Counsel, slow down," Judge Williams said slowly. "It seems to me that if they say there is no evidence of murder, then the issue is dead."

"I would agree, if that's what they said. But it isn't. The

ADA said that the medical examiner had produced no evidence of murder. But they do have a dead body. That's all the medical examiner has to produce. If the police find other evidence that indicates murder, all the medical examiner has to say is there is indeed a dead body."

"Mr. DA, to your knowledge, is any of the evidence that Mr. Cohen has requested perishable?"

"No, Your Honor. It is all preserved."

"The evidence may not be perishable, but time is. Witnesses disappear, memories fade . . ."

"Then we won't have a case."

"Or maybe they will and Mr. Scott won't have a defense."

The judge bent to scribble a note on the papers before him, tossed them over to the court officer next to his desk, and looked up. "I'm sorry, Counselor, I have no basis in a burglary to give you access to the test results."

David nodded to the judge, tossed his papers in his briefcase, and turned for the door. Another night wasted for five minutes of discussion and ruling and maybe the five minutes it had taken the judge to breeze through the papers. All David could think about was a nap.

"Counselor."

The voice tried to sound energetic but failed. David turned and looked into a gray face.

"Bad luck that," Walsh said, shaking his head.

David turned away. "Expected it."

"Yes, I suppose. But it would be nice to have access to those results, wouldn't it?"

"That's what the motion was for."

Walsh slapped him on the back. "Good, then meet me out front at eleven tonight. And bring your expert."

David turned back to the gray face, but it had disappeared into the crowd.

Jenson pulled out a fresh legal pad and began copying. He wasn't going to allow a secretary at these notes, he thought, as he started jotting on the fresh pad. AB negative, he wrote on top of the pad. Rare. Not rare enough to determine identity, but rare enough to raise a suspicion. He held the pen motionless above the next line. It wasn't that he wouldn't have had the scraping done if he were only going to have a blood type done. No, he wouldn't have done the scraping if he hadn't known what Anacleta looked like. He laughed inside to cover the embarrassment from the more rational parts of himself. Ridiculous. The thought of getting a charge from touching the spent, drying or dried gitz of a beautiful woman. He was one small step from Marla Maples's shoes.

Jenson pushed his feet into the rug and bent over the desk. Anacleta was present the night Twining died, he wrote. It was clear, he thought, but he had no proof. The only way to get proof was to get a mucus sample from Miss Lucas and compare the DNA to the dried gitz found on Twining.

No judge would give an order with the evidence Jenson could present. Where is the proof that it was a murder? Even if it had been Anacleta, what proof is there of murder?

No, he would not be able to get an order to investigate this death. Jenson was a minor official in the prosecution team. No power. He thought about that scandal in the Seventy-fifth Precinct. That cop making eight thousand a week shaking down drug dealers, reselling the drugs. There was a time when Jenson would have been outraged at a law-enforcement officer doing that. He would have been holier than thou, that's the way his wife described it, holier than thou.

Jenson pushed the fresh pad aside. The notes didn't matter. He wasn't going to the DA with any requests. Jenson thought of his life, his house in the suburbs, the commute every day. His wife. He didn't even have a picture of his wife in the office anymore. He rarely thought of her, except when her presence demanded it. She hadn't been beautiful when he married her, and time hadn't been kind to her. Not kind at all. He hardly ever thought about fucking her anymore . . . and he doubted she thought about it either. The desire hadn't passed him by—just the desire for her. He looked again at the picture of Anacleta Lucas. Forty-two and he'd never had a beautiful woman. Never in his life.

He wondered how many women that drug dealing cop had. More than he could handle, from what the *News* said. He thought of the director, J. Edgar. Probably had young boys parading in and out of his office bending over for him and Clyde. Thought about Kennedy, about both Kennedys. The rest of those politicians. Even Twining, for Christ sake. And himself . . . getting nothing . . . nothing, and he had to catch this case. With this woman.

Jenson picked up the phone and punched in the number. Just had to keep on keeping on.

CHAPTER 15

David leaned back against the black paint covering the iron bars that extended from the top of the concrete alcove to the bottom. The iron rings which hung like giant door knockers against the painted iron plate made the evening scene look like the set of a fifties horror movie. David had never seen the gate he leaned on open, or the one to his right closed.

The pedestrian traffic to the left, mothers and girlfriends walking in to see their sons and lovers, had ebbed and flowed during his ten-minute wait. A couple huddled in the corner, sharing a cigarette, or was it a joint? Either way, David wished Evans would get here, or Walsh. Standing alone in front of Criminal Court at 10:30 at night wasn't what David had figured his future as a lawyer to be.

Stepping away from the iron bars, glancing up Schermerhorn toward the clock, David wondered what his expectations had been. To practice in the country with his grandfather, that expectation he remembered. And to go dashing after the absolute, unvarnished truth, as his grandfather had. "If you don't know the entire unvarnished truth," his grandfather had told him, "you're just a clerk. Not a lawyer, just a clerk."

So David had gone chasing the unvarnished truth. And lost Janie in the process. The wash of loneliness swept over him again. It was worse at night, he thought, as he looked up at the clock tower. 10:30. Just the time he and Janie would sit down, dinner done, whatever work they'd brought home done or put away for the night. Still a half hour before they'd think about bed.

It was this half hour he missed most. Sitting on the couch, sometimes reading, sometimes talking about nothing, just to hear each other's voices. Eleven would come all too soon. David would follow her to bed reluctantly. Bed meant sleep—or lovemaking then sleep. And sleep meant loss of consciousness. She'd be right there next to him, of course, but he wouldn't know it. He wondered if he thought that way when she was there, or only now that she was gone. Either way, she was gone.

He felt the soft thump in his back before he stumbled forward.

"That clock have your attention, does it?"

David turned and shook Evans's hand. On those rare occasions when he saw the Haitian outside, he was surprised by the man's stature. He was, of course, obese, but outside his squalid apartment he appeared taller. That height combined with his girth hanging over his belt gave the man a presence . . . a presence that now dominated the two-story arch. Even the couple with the joint seemed to huddle a little more closely.

"You're early," Evans said, stuffing his hand into the oversized pockets of his oversized topcoat. "Trolling for clients?"

David ignored the question, peering instead down Schermerhorn Street toward the clock. He didn't know if it was Walsh's habit to be early or late. At 10:58 he was not yet either.

"So, am I being retained as an expert or taken advantage of as a friend?" Evans pulled out a plastic six-pack with three Dr Peppers still attached to it.

"Only pay you'll get is free press, I'm afraid."

"I'm not even sure I want that on this caper. Sounds a little underhanded." Evans pulled one of the sodas off and offered the remainder to David, who shook his head. Evans shrugged and dropped the free cans in his coat pocket. "Walsh told you nothing but meet him here?"

"That's all," David said, looking down the broad expanse of Schermerhorn Street once more.

Evans thrust the pudgy index and middle fingers of both hands through the plastic rings and, with a grunt, yanked. The plastic stretched then snapped, sending the cans still bound in the plastic flying. The plastic six-pack swung around Evans's pinky, doing a 360 before Evans brought it under control and stuffed it in his coat pocket. "You trust this guy?"

David shrugged. "His information has been good. He's a little odd."

"Odd. White hair, kind of pasty complexion?"

"Right."

"Drives a green Jag?" Evans asked, opening a car door.

David looked down. Indeed it was Walsh in a new, deep-green Jaguar. Climbing in, David made introductions and immediately turned to the window. He wished he hadn't thought about Janie. Keeping memories of her at bay had been difficult for the first several months but had gotten easier since. Now suddenly they were back, back with a vengeance.

The Brooklyn scenery rushed by, scenery David had stopped seeing over the years. Avoiding the small talk tossed back and forth between Evans and Walsh, he found the scenery to be an outlet ... an escape. First the antique shops, then the schlock, the movie theater converted into an evangelical church, the abandoned bathhouse with "Men" and "Women" carved in opposite doors. Men and women. No escape. The world kept pushing it back at him.

David turned to the two men in the car, the lull in their conversation drawing their eyes to him. David pushed his shoulder against the passenger seat. He didn't even feel competent to guide this conversation at the moment.

"Where?" he asked. That much he felt competent to do.

"The morgue," Walsh said cheerfully.

"Do you know the etymology of the word?" Evans asked, adding his own Haitian brand of cheer to the subject.

David turned back to the window. A choice between listening to two giddy necrophiliacs and thinking about his own fractured love life. A blue van rushed by David's window. "Flowers for all occasions." David watched the van disappearing ahead as Walsh turned left into the parking lot at the back of King's County Hospital. It was refreshingly dark as they climbed out of the car.

"The gentlemen is a friend," Walsh said over his shoulder. "Or should we say a business acquaintance?" Laughing, Walsh led them into a room.

The room had the smell one imagined Dr. Frankenstein's laboratory to have but none of the sights. In fact, the white-on-white room was spotless . . . and empty. The tables were clear, the metal storage facilities closed and wiped clean . . . and a short, fat man wearing a white uniform with his name, Mario, sewn in red over the breast pocket crouched in the corner, gloved hand in a bucket. He flashed Walsh a quick smile, pulled a sponge out, squeezed it dry, and attacked the corner.

"Just this last part here, Crawford," Mario said, "then I'll be with you."

David had never considered Walsh a "Crawford." In fact, he found it difficult to believe anyone would call Walsh by any first name.

Mario dropped the sponge in the bucket, pulled off the glove, and waddled toward the trio. He was about five-six but carried his three-hundred-plus pounds with surprising grace. The grease on his hair seemed natural, as did the oil on his palm. David cut the handshake as short as possible consistent with good manners.

The man didn't seem to notice. He greeted Evans, then Walsh, like a lost friend and led them into a small room in the back. Perching himself on a stool behind a blond wood bench, he gestured to other stools for Walsh, David, and Evans.

"You're the expert, then," Mario said to Evans.

When Evans nodded, Mario pushed a pile of papers across the bench.

"It'll take some time," Evans said, flipping through the pages.

The man nodded and led David and Walsh out to the main room, then led Walsh to a corner away from David. Turning his broad back to David and pinning Walsh in the corner, the man spoke softly. Walsh smiled, extending his curled hand palm up. The man shook it, turned to David, nodded, and disappeared down the hall.

"Like a pro," David said after the man had disappeared.

Walsh held his finger to his lips. "The walls," he said.

David nodded, watching Walsh walk toward him. The reporter fit here. Comfortable in these surroundings, his walk took on a swagger. David wondered if he had delivered it all. Even more, he wondered why Walsh took the risk.

"What's your interest in this?"

"A story," Walsh said.

"You make deliveries like that for every story?"

A smile curled Walsh's thin, gray lips. "Saw that, did you?"

David nodded.

Leaning on the table next to David, Walsh stared straight ahead as he spoke. "The paper pays."

"Does the paper supply the product?"

Walsh shrugged. "I save the paper money where I can."

"You make a habit of taking that kind of risk?"

Folding his arms across his chest, Walsh spoke slowly. "You're asking if this story is special, then?" Walsh waited until he sensed David's nod, then continued. "It is. I've been on it for a long time."

"On Twining?"

"On the story."

"What story?"

Walsh pursed his lips in a tight smile and said nothing.

"What have I walked into here?"

"The case of a lifetime perhaps."

David stepped in front of Walsh. "What is the case of a lifetime about?"

"Not now," Walsh said, shifting uncomfortably.

David grabbed his jacket. "Why not now?"

Walsh gently touched David's hand, pushing his thumb into the meat between David's thumb and forefinger and lifted.

David gave a yelp and released Walsh's jacket.

"When you've worked for years on a story, a story that can bring you the prize, you don't want it out too soon," Walsh said, releasing David's hand. "It must play like a symphony."

Stepping back from Walsh, David realized he was not going to get the unvarnished truth, not from Walsh. He rubbed his hand. And he wasn't going to beat it out of Walsh either. So Walsh was guiding him to "the story." Not so bad. Not so bad as long as he got the whole story by the time Light needed it.

Not so bad, but the gnawing at David's gut continued. He didn't like being led, especially by Walsh. He liked being in charge of the investigation. Nothing was coming from Walsh, but there were other sources. Light. Light knew more than he told David. He was there the night of the murder, there for some reason. If David couldn't get anything from Walsh, he could get something from Light.

The door to the small room popped open and Evans strode out. Silently, he walked through the large room and, with a gesture to David, into the hall. David and Walsh followed. A moment later they were in the car, heading back downtown.

Walsh opened his mouth to speak, but Evans cut him off.

"I'll have to think about it," Evans said with a tone of finality.

Stone-faced, Walsh turned back to the road.

It was an uncomfortable ride back. Feeling unsettled, David stared out the window through the tense silence. In less than a half hour Walsh dropped them in front of the Criminal Court. Evans and David stood in silence as the green Jaguar disappeared.

"Murder?" David asked.

"Yes," Evans replied. "But I don't know how." They walked toward Court Street. "Very sophisticated."

"How?"

"There was heart failure, but no bruises, no sign of motion. Like his heart just stopped."

Like his heart just stopped. The phrase had troubled David all night, interrupting his sleep. It bothered him still, as he pulled the blue paper coffee cup across the glass desk cover. How could the man have had an attack and not known it? Not that people couldn't have heart attacks and not know it, that was common, Evans had said. But they move, struggle when the oxygen fades. Not Twining. Twining hadn't moved.

The speaker phone crackled. David punched a button.

"Detective Jenson on the line."

"What does he want?"

The other end clicked off wordlessly. Lois would extract the information without giving a hint of David's whereabouts, allowing him the privilege of being in court without leaving the comfort of his swivel chair. The intercom snapped back.

"Leroy Scott."

David picked up the phone. "Detective," he said, "what can I do for you?"

"It's about your client, Mr. Scott."

"Yeah, what?"

"He's down here at King's County Hospital."

"KCH? Gunshot?"

"No. Damnedest thing. You better get down here."

"Critical?"

"No, nothing like that. He'll be fine. But I'd rather have the doctors explain it."

A half hour later David slammed the door of the Toyota in the parking lot of the main building of King's County

Hospital. In the daylight it gave a different impression than the morgue a few feet away had last night.

The main building rose like the medieval castle of some Eastern European vampire, the gray stone walls seemingly alive with the stench of blood. Around the main building stood others, erected at various times in various styles, with bricks seemingly mortared in place with the blood of Brooklyn's poor and ignorant.

The inside gave a different impression. The employees seemed like escapees from some United Nations training course, the nurses and clerical workers slumping the halls in their hard Caribbean obesity, their English struggling for supremacy with the lilts of various creoles, and the doctors, more exotic to be sure, struggling harder with English, knowing the words but ignoring the accent that makes a language intelligible.

David walked to the desk, asked about Light, and was directed to the surgical recovery room. Microsurgery, she said. He walked toward the hall where she directed him. A blue uniform leaned against the wall in a hallway to the left.

"Detective Jenson?" David asked.

The officer jerked his head backward. "Room twelve," he said.

Jenson sat on a small plastic chair, trying to look over his magazine and up the dress of a young Hispanic nurse. She spun artfully away and, with a smile and a wink, left the room.

David caught Jenson's eye, but Jenson just pointed with his chin to a white-suited, emaciated Chinese man who poked his head frenetically inside the room, allowing his eyes to dart from patient to patient like a giant sparrow.

David rose as the doctor's chiseled features turned to him, puzzled, as if unable to categorize the man with the curly, black hair. Introducing himself, complete with his relationship to Light, David waited for a response.

The doctor hesitated, then the words came out, tumbling over themselves.

David blinked, said, "Excuse me," and bent lower.

The doctor gulped and apologized. "It is this language. I think if I speak it faster, you will understand." He turned and moved away, angular, jerky steps carrying him out into the hallway.

David followed.

"It is better not to talk in front of the patient, don't you agree?"

David nodded, never having considered what to say in front of or behind a patient and wondering how this doctor could think that Light would understand one word of any speech he made.

"I was very impressed. A very straight cut. Very straight." The doctor examined his hands, held out in front with fingers spread. "I don't know if I could do it. No, hands not so good as hands of the man. Very straight."

The doctor continued down the hallway, with David struggling to keep up.

"Not a woman, not like he say. No, not a woman."

David dodged a gurney carrying a comatose body on its way to a surgical theater and struggled up next to the doctor again. "Doctor, ah . . . I didn't get your name."

The doctor nodded to a colleague as they passed. "Chin," he said, turning quickly to shake David's hand.

"I don't really know what happened," David said as he accepted the doctor's hand.

"Not so unusual, the injury. Not so unusual as people think. I have five . . . maybe six cases a year. But not straight like this. Not so straight." Chin stopped and looked at David. "And depth. The depth, just right whole time." Chin turned into a room and disappeared.

David hesitated for a second at the door, not sure whether to follow. Chin was several steps inside the room before he glanced back, a glance David took for an invitation and followed.

Chin picked up the chart from the base of the bed, examined a few pages, and scribbled a note before resuming. "If you find this man, I want to meet him. Must be doctor. Not just doctor, surgeon." Chin repeated the procedure at the beds of the other three patients in the room in silence. Finally he replaced the chart on the last bed and walked back into the hallway.

"Very easy to cut through, all the way through. When we do surgery like this, we make two cuts, first the skin, then the tissues below. But this, one cut."

"One cut?"

"Yes, definitely one cut. Only one cut."

"What exactly did he cut?"

Chin looked up, surprised. "Urethra, of course."

David took a step back. Light's dick. Somebody sliced his dick.

Chin grabbed David's hand and shook it, bowing ever so slightly. "One cut. One very straight cut." Chin turned and walked away.

David stood for a second, staring after the disappearing figure of the doctor. The image of the blood seeping out of Light's dick faded, but the questions remained. *Who? Why?*

David felt even pressure on his upper arm. Turning, he saw Jenson, unsmiling, standing behind him.

"Come on," Jenson said, "let's take a walk. This place is too real."

David followed as Jenson led him quickly out the front door, into the parking lot, and toward some bushes hugging the wall of the castle. Reaching them, he turned abruptly to David.

"The thing is, your guy won't talk. Says nothing."

"Nothing?"

"Nothing. Well, almost nothing. He makes up some bullshit about his girlfriend was pissed at him or something."

"Possible, isn't it?"

Jenson shook his head. "Girlfriends sometimes get pissed and do some damage. Shit, I've had 'em dump boiling oil on the scumbag's scumbag, if you know what I mean." Jenson pulled out a cigarette and lit it. "You ever seen all the skin burned off the bat and balls. It's something. Like a visible V-8."

"So," David said, moving slightly out of the windblown column of smoke, "it could have been, right?"

"No, every time a woman does it, it's passion. You know how they are. A guy can beat them for years, rape 'em, whatever. As long as he comes back, they don't care. Then he goes and beats up some other bim, and they go nuts." Jenson took a drag and shook his head. "No, this was too precise. A bitch would have sliced it off. Like that woman down south, remember?"

David nodded.

"Or maybe she would have killed him." Jenson stared off across the parking lot. "But this. You heard what Chin said. It was too straight. Like a surgeon's scalpel. Sliced right along the urethra. The doctor said that it had to be done slowly to be that accurate. The guy would be in pain, wiggling. . . . Sadistic." Jenson stared off across the parking lot to the emergency room entrance.

David looked away, following Jenson's eyes. Jenson was moved by this case; you could see that in his eyes. After Jenson's many years on the force, after the way he had acted in the precinct, it actually got to him.

"Talk to the neighbors?" David asked finally.

Jenson shrugged. "Puerto Rican mystery. Nobody saw nothing. One guy said he saw two guys knocking at the door but couldn't ID them."

"What do you want from me?"

"Look, I won't make a secret of it, you embarrassed me and I didn't like it. Still don't. I think you were wrong. What I told you at the time, I still believe. But there's something more here. It's connected to that Twining thing. I don't know how, but it is. Your guy doesn't trust me. I can't blame him, but he needs to."

"After you set him up?"

Jenson looked surprised, then turned his head, avoiding David's eyes.

"That's why the murder arrest, then the release, am I right?"

Jenson fidgeted with his radio. "What am I supposed to

do?" he asked. "A congressman dead on my watch. I had to do something."

"So you make a big show of arresting Light for murder, drop that charge, and see where he goes."

"Something like that."

"But where were you?"

"So we missed it. That's history. Your guy's in trouble now. Needs this as much as we do." Jenson paused. "Talk to your guy. See what this is about."

David broke eye contact and stared off to the apartment buildings in the distance. Light was going to be suspicious. After all, this was the cop who pushed the Twining thing. Hell, David himself was suspicious. Jenson wasn't one to build confidence, but Light was going to have to trust somebody. And David had the advantage of being a lawyer. There was still attorney-client privilege.

David nodded to Jenson, turned his back, and walked back into the castle.

He hated hospitals. The antiseptic smell reminded him of death . . . death and a dentist's office. A nurse hustled by, leading a gurney with a white sheet, a man with a twisted grimace on his face, and another man pushing the gurney. If not death, misery, David thought, as he squeezed by and walked to room fifteen.

Light was reclining, back propped up in a reading position but with no book in sight. Instead Light glared around the room, eyes prowling, like a mad predator searching for a new victim. David hesitated for a second outside the door, peering in, taking a breath, preparing himself for the approach. Light was not inclined to talk about the incident—if he were, he would have already.

The curtain around Light was half pulled, allowing him to see the entire four-patient room except the patient across from him, an old man who appeared to be breathing his labored last. It was unclear whether the curtain was pulled to protect Light from watching death or to protect the old man from entering the next world with his last memory of this one being a sliced penis.

Light's gaze drifted over to the window opposite the door. David blew out his breath and walked straight to Light's bedside, grabbed the curtain, and said a loud "good morning." Before Light could relax, David snapped the curtain around the aluminum runner, pulling it closed.

Light looked for a moment as if he were about to complain, but as the curtain closed, he glanced to the chair. "Don't like that cop," he said quietly. "Can't trust him."

David sat silently, hoping Light would continue.

"Tried to railroad me on that shit with the congressman. Now he talking like he my buddy on this here." Light snorted and looked away.

"What did happen?"

Light snorted again, looked at David, then turned away again. "Like I said, girlfriend."

"Who?" David tried to sound as if he needed the information to protect Light, not accusatory, even though he knew Light was lying.

Light rolled to his side, peering out the window as if something of great interest were happening in the parking lot. "I'll take care of it," Light said.

"You get in trouble that way."

"I won't hurt her," Light said, still staring out the window. "I won't hurt her," he repeated, "just take care of it."

David sat by the bed for a second, waiting for Light to turn back to him. Light did not. David got up, mumbled something, and snapped the curtain back.

Light spun around quickly. "Be careful," he said, his eyes locking David's. It was the first eye contact he had made. Light, whose eyes usually bored into David with that seething rage of old drunks, this time had a look that might have been genuine concern. "Be careful," he repeated.

"Of what?" David asked.

Light turned back to the window. "Just be careful. You know. Just be careful."

David waited a second, but there was nothing more. He turned and left the room. Like Jenson had said, something was going on here, something more than a pissed-off girlfriend. David took a deep breath and blew it out.

David's eyes had not yet adjusted to the bright sunlight before he felt Jenson's presence next to him.

"I was right."

David grunted.

"There's something, right?"

An interesting gambit, David thought. *Any answer gives Jenson some information.* So David said nothing but started walking slowly toward the Toyota. He didn't want to give Jenson the impression that he didn't want to listen, just that he didn't want to talk.

"See, I figure your guy either stumbled into something and is blackmailing somebody, or he just stumbled into something and he don't know what to do."

David looked straight ahead but felt Jenson flicking a glance up in David's face every second or two, just to gauge reaction. David kept his face even.

"But see, I don't see your guy as real bad in this. I mean, we can all agree he was pounding on the congressman, and that wasn't because of no bim."

David stopped at the gate, turned, and faced Jenson, who was still speaking.

"No, see, how I see it is like this. Your guy comes across something that that congressman's got to hide. You know those guys are always hiding something. Right?" He waited for David to make a noncommittal eyebrow gesture before continuing. "Right. So your guy figures he should be getting something, either from the congressman himself or from the government, you know?" This time Jenson didn't wait for an answer. "So I figure your guy's interest and my interest are the same. We both want to get the guy who killed the congressman."

"Which is who exactly?"

Jenson stepped back. "Well, I don't know that exactly. That's what I figure your guy can help me with."

"If Light knows who did this guy, then he must be involved, no?"

"No, not necessarily. Listen up. Your guy knows who sliced him. You gotta figure, right? I mean he's got to have some idea. Well then, who's that gonna be? They gotta be the killers, right?"

David stood silently, which Jenson apparently took for disagreement.

"Okay, look here, counselor. They come in and slice up the man's dick. Now, I don't know too much about these things, but I know when the loan sharks get out there, they don't start up with no kneecapping. You know what I mean? They start out with smacking the guy around, then they build up. You know why that is?

"I'll tell you," Jenson said without waiting for an answer. "This guy, some punk, you know? He tells me it ain't about so the guy can still work. He says it's a question of how you go up. I mean you smack a guy around, you could go up. You could break a bone next time. Where do you go from slicing a guy's penis? I mean the next stop is the throat, right?"

"So?"

"So, how does somebody get so upset about this thing so fast? It's got to be murder, right? I mean, these guys, they gonna go to slicing a dick to cover like bribes or some shit? For taking bribes, these guys, they do eight months in some place in North Carolina where they get to write a book between sets of tennis."

"So you think whoever killed the congressman sliced Light's dick?"

"Right."

"And you want me to help you."

"Right. It'll help your guy too. I mean, he's in some trouble with these guys. Am I right?"

"Apparently so. But I have one question. How do you know it was murder? The forensic evidence is equivocal."

Jenson took David's arm and guided him onto the sidewalk. "Walk with me, Counselor. Don't know who has ears here." Jenson turned right, walking past the parking lot before stopping near the corner. "Look, there was something else here. When the congressman died, there was this thing going down."

"What thing?"

"See, Twining talked to me after that thing where he dismissed the charges. A couple of days later, he talked to me. Called me up out of the blue. I don't know why he picked me. Maybe just 'cause he knew me."

"Picked you for what?"

"He said he couldn't trust nobody else. Not the FBI or nobody, it was so big. Well, I been hearing this shit all my life. Like everybody. If you vote for me, I'm gonna do this big thing or whatever. So I figure it's just how these guys talk, you know? Anyway, we set up a meet, and he tells me about how he's being blackmailed. Telling him how to vote. He says that he don't want to be in Congress no more. He just wants out, but they won't let him. They got something on him or something. He wouldn't exactly say. So we set him up with a wire, and we get some stuff."

"On who?"

"This guy."

"What guy?"

"Well, see, that's the thing, we don't know exactly who it is. See, this congressman, he's not really a truster, so he don't want no backup."

"So you got tapes, but . . ."

"We don't know who the guy is. But the tapes, see, they weren't that clear. Twining's done a great job incriminating himself. But the guy was smart, he don't say nothing clear, you know?"

"Then?"

"Next day, Twining's found dead."

"How does that bring Light into it?"

"That's what I was hoping you could help us with."

David was silent for a moment. It made some sense. If Twining was killed because he was blowing the whistle on blackmail of some kind, then the killers might be sophisticated. Might even be sophisticated enough to make it look like a heart attack, but with enough questions that the people who were supposed to be scared by it would be.

Now Jenson wanted to work with David as a partner. David couldn't do it, of course. His first duty was to his client.

"So, what you got for me?"

David looked up, startled. "Oh, Light told me to be careful."

"That's it?"

"That's it. Except that it was his girlfriend who did him."

David crossed the street to his car, leaving Jenson looking disappointed and more than a little pissed.

CHAPTER 16

Julio twisted the dial as far to the right as possible and watched the flame leap skyward. He liked the way the flame on this burner jumped, as if it were a genie too long trapped in a bottle. Julio felt that way sometimes, he thought as he pulled open the cabinet and selected a frying pan. A small one, cast iron, black, well seasoned. He always used the same one, purchased back home many years ago. It was the only piece of cookware with which he traveled.

In airports the customs people were surprised sometimes. A man carrying a frying pan. "You do not look like a chef," they said to him. He forced a smile and mumbled something like "sentimental." Some customs people would look confused, some would smile, most would look slightly angry that they couldn't keep the "contraband" out of their country, but all would wave him through.

As the pan heated, he turned on the hot water in the sink. He put his hand under the stream of water, testing its heat. It was hot, but he would wait, wait until the water was at its hottest before he slipped the metal bowl under the stream, squirted the soap into the bowl, and began.

"*Meticuloso.*" That's how Santeria had described Julio. "And that's what I need," Santeria had said, "*meticulosidad.*"

Julio had been proud when Santeria had said that. He was

proud still as he heard the words in his ears. Pushing the bowl under the stream of water, he squeezed the soap into the bowl and waited while the bowl filled. It would not take long, but it was important. That's what the trainers had said. And you can not improve your technique unless you practice. Julio enjoyed the practice. He always had.

He bent over the pan, running his hand close to the surface. It was hot, not yet glowing red, but hot. He would wait until it smoked. A few minutes, he thought, as he pulled up the leather box, snapped it open, and placed it on the counter. He pulled the scalpel from the plastic bag.

He had wiped it, of course, but that would not eliminate the evidence. For that he needed the soap. Dipping the scalpel into the water, Julio began to scrub. *Meticuloso,* Julio thought as the water burned his hands. A minute later Julio placed the scalpel, clean and gleaming, back into the maroon leather case and snapped it closed.

No one would be able to trace the thin black man's penis to this leather case. Julio was happy with that. This case of tools had been the best he had had. He would, of course, have to leave them at some time, but he was happy that that time had not yet come. He would get to use them again. Maybe on the thin black man again. Maybe on the lawyer. Maybe on someone else.

There were many opportunities for his expertise in this situation, he thought, pushing the leather case back into the drawer and closing it securely. Many, many. Julio slipped his left hand into the oven mitt and took hold of the handle of the pan. He felt the heat through the mitt. The pan glowed red in the middle, and smoke began to rise from it.

Julio pulled the bottle of olive oil toward him with his right hand and unscrewed the cap with index and thumb, placing the cap on the counter next to the bottle. Checking to see if it was in the right position, he adjusted. *Meticuloso,* he thought, as he pushed the fingertips of his right hand onto the glowing portion of the frying pan. The pain rippled up through his arm and shoulder. It felt good to feel the pain.

His trainers had always said it was a sick man, a corrupt man, who could dispense pain but not receive it. Julio was not such a man. He remembered the thin black man's pain. Julio had felt the man's pain as he squatted over him, the man's pain rushing from his chest, where Julio's haunches had lightly brushed against it. The thin black man's pain had coursed up through Julio's body.

Julio pulled his fingers from the pan. He had not felt the black man's pain as if it were his own. No, this pain today was infinitely greater. But he had not squealed, not cried out, he thought as he poured the olive oil into the pan, the pain rushing through his burnt fingers again. Not like the thin black man, whom they eventually had to gag because of the commotion he made.

It is good to have both sides of pain, Julio thought, as he turned on the cold water. It would be a few seconds before the water got really cold, a few seconds before he could plunge his hand under the water and the pain would stop. Julio smiled. Even *meticuloso* in the abatement of pain.

David closed the door to his office. He had felt a little unsteady since leaving Light, but it was Jenson's suspicions that really set him off. If Twining was killed, and the killer was out there doing things like slicing penises...

Not that it couldn't have been a woman, as Light said. It happened every day in Brooklyn. He remembered that day he was in arraignments, his first year in the district attorney's office, maybe his first month. As the ADA, he used to stand there, pick up files, read the hundred-word blurb, and make the request of the judge that was listed in the file. A good risk-free way to get over one's nerves. No risk; just follow the bouncing ball.

It was about ten P.M. Arraignments was an eighteen-hour operation in Brooklyn. David was the only ADA working. The bridgeman called out a case; David picked up the file and flipped it open. The blurb was written in red, in giant block letters. HIGH BAIL. $500,000.00 MIN. He looked down the page. A sixteen-year-old had shot and killed his father.

David shrugged. Even after only a month this wasn't an unusual case. He thought of some of the fights he'd had with his father when he was sixteen. He might have. One never knows.

David didn't look up during the argument. He was a little tired. In fact, he barely made eye contact with the judge. He finished making his pitch, heinous crime, etc. Then the defense attorney began. "Extenuating circumstances," he said. Extenuating circumstances for patricide. David almost laughed. He looked up at the judge, who was looking down from the bench with compassion in his eyes.

David, acting the tough guy, looked over. A face stared back at him from next to the legal aid. No, not a face, a pair of eyes. A pair of eyes that looked as if they had been created by Spielberg. The neck was black, the hands, even parts of the forehead, but the face was that mottled mixture of black and white left when lye drips away.

Those eyes opened wide, asking how the DA, the ally of the good, could be asking half a million bail on this, the victim. How could eyes have expression, have feeling, when their encasement had melted away? David snapped back, the blood draining from his head. How could one imagine this? An innocent victim of his father's anger. The lye, convenient at the moment, thrown in his son's face.

David took a deep breath. It was possible. Yes, a crazed girlfriend, high on crack or drink, could have taken a blade to what was perceived at the moment to be her oppressor. Yeah, it could have happened that way.

But then there was what the doctor said. A woman did that in passion. A drunk did that in passion. This was a straight cut. And then what Light said. *Be careful.* Be careful of what? Light didn't think David had a girlfriend with a knife and a predilection for slicing penises. No, there was something more. And Light was lying. Light was definitely lying.

Then there was this phone call. Walsh. Wanted to do some more investigation, talk to some more witnesses.

* * *

"Sorry about the stain there, ma'am." Jenson pulled the pile of books across the bench seat in the Ford Fairlane. "Hop in."

Anacleta placed one heeled shoe on the burgundy carpet and twisted her hips onto the seat. Jenson wanted to make some tasteless comment about her ass, anything to cover the tightening in his groin. He sure as hell didn't want to show that. But he kept silent, allowing her to snap her seat belt as he turned into traffic.

"Ms. Lucas, I wanted to talk to you about the death of your, ah . . . friend, Congressman Twining." Jenson glanced at Anacleta as he spoke, then turned back to the traffic pulling to a stop at the light. She didn't react, just sat there, like she was the cat and he the mouse. Jenson wiggled uncomfortably. He hated it when women gave him the silent treatment, especially in a situation like this. He didn't really want to come right out and tell her . . . threaten her, but her silence was leaving him little choice.

"Ms. Lucas, the thing is, we found Mr. Twining in . . . ah, what I mean is . . ."

"You believe the congressman had recently made love." Anacleta finished his sentence without moving her eyes from the road ahead. "The light has turned green," she said, her voice playful.

Jenson turned back to the roadway. He thought she smiled, as if it didn't really matter to her, as if it was just something that happened. The car jerked forward. *Shit, automatics aren't supposed to jerk.* He gripped the wheel. The interview was getting away fast.

"Did you know it was me, or did you just guess?"

Jenson gulped. "Well, the papers, you know. I just kind of figured."

"What is it you would like to know?" Anacleta had pushed her knees in his direction, her right leg crossed tightly over her left.

David dropped the black leather briefcase between his legs, and kicked it back against the wooden bench. 6:20 A.M.

Too early. Too early for anything, but especially too early to be waiting for a train. He pushed his thumb and index finger into his shirt pocket, pulled out the note, and twisted it open as he would fan a bridge hand. *Meet me,* it said, *front of Union Station, D.C., 10:30 A.M. Important.* 10:30. That gave him twenty-eight minutes for Metroliner delays.

David sighed and stuck the note back in his pocket. In a few more minutes he'd be on the train and back asleep. Two hours and forty minutes later, give or take, he'd be in D.C. A few minutes after that he'd know what was so damn important.

What was so damn important? What was so important that David even gave a shit? After all, as Joel vociferously pointed out last night, not only didn't they have a paying client, they didn't even have a cooperative client. They had David's curiosity and some vague promise of favorable publicity from Walsh. Favorable publicity that would probably not turn into a single client. The demographics, as Joel had pointed out, were wrong. People who liked to read about violent crimes were usually disinclined to commit them.

A voice crackled over the speaker, too lively for the early morning, annoucing that the Metroliner was boarding. Joining a gaggle of other passengers, David walked toward the platform. He wondered, as he swung the briefcase from right to left hands, why he had brought it. Part of the uniform, he supposed. He couldn't imagine taking this trip without wearing a suit, even though it might be totally inappropriate to the task he would be called upon to perform. Would a lawyer be as intimidating, or as hated, without a briefcase?

It was a question without an answer, he thought, as he skipped down the steps, onto the platform, and onto the train. He found a window seat, dropped the case between his legs, put his head back against the rest, and closed his eyes. Hopefully he wouldn't wake up until Baltimore.

It had been easier than Jenson had thought. By the time she had invited him to see her apartment, he was sure it was her idea. All that about how she liked older men, it wasn't that Twining had been a congressman or the power or any of that. Jenson knew he was sucking up a load of shit, but he kept sucking. He couldn't help himself. He'd never taken anything, in all the years on this job. Never. He chuckled to himself. Not until now. But who was going to know? And he could justify it. After all, this was investigation.

He sat nervously on the edge of the bed. He hated the frilly things that hung over it. Never knew what to do with them or what they were for. Just to look good, his wife said. A lot of work to look good, and to look good for who? Who ever saw it? Just the two of them. It wasn't like they invited people to their bedroom.

He reached under the cover with the frilly edges. Felt like silk under there. Maybe some nylon shit. That at least was functional. They could feel that. His wife had bought one set about four years ago. She'd read some book about reviving their sex life, how they should do it differently, with silk sheets, the author had said. The author had never said she should lose fifty pounds and get her teeth fixed. That would have done more for fixing their sex life. But she got the silk sheets.

Jenson figured Anacleta had ten sets of silk sheets. Probably slept on them every night. How else would she have known to put them on today? She hadn't known what he was going to look like, about that crew cut or the gray around the temples that always drove her crazy. Or about that black mole on his neck that reminded her of a Spanish movie star she remembered from when she was a kid. She couldn't have known about that.

Jenson pulled at the elastic of his white cotton Jockey shorts. He wished she'd hurry. He pulled the elastic out again. He'd been terrified at first. He'd never expected that it would be this easy . . . that he'd be in so easy. But it had been all right. He let it snap back. Maybe the noise would bring her out. He wondered what she was doing that took so long.

He threw his legs over the side of the bed, pulled them up, and laid his head on the pillows. The bathroom door opened, and she slipped through the doorway. The first thing he wondered was how silk sounded rubbing against silk. The silk nightie barely covered her genitals. In fact, some of the auburn hair peeked out as the silk slid from side to side as she walked. Not much, just enough to start making him crazy.

It was a long walk to the bed from the door, at least for a New York apartment. He didn't take his eyes off her as she walked. He thought he could smell her—not the perfume, even though she applied it judiciously; he could smell that. No, he felt he could smell her essence. As she got closer, he thought he could taste her. He felt the back of his Jockey shorts, just inside the elastic. It was there. Pretty soon.

She placed her knee on the bottom of the bed and slipped up to him. He never had been able to understand how women, so inferior athletically to men, could move in bed so much better. Like cats. She moved the mole . . . gently kissed it. Jenson thought he felt it get hard. He definitely knew other things were getting hard. She moved to his lips and slipped her tongue from between pastel lips into his mouth. The shiver went from his tongue to the tips of his toes and back. He almost lost himself. Not yet. He wanted to taste it first.

He slipped her onto her back. He tried to be gentle, to act experienced, like she wasn't the first stunningly beautiful woman he had ever slept with . . . like he did it all the time. He kissed her neck . . . down that soft, smooth, unconscionably smooth skin, down to the top of her breasts. He fumbled for just a second before she delicately pulled the black silk strings that tied the front together. He returned to her breasts, pulling the strings down the sides, one by one, until she lay bared. He softly caressed and kissed her breasts as his other hand reached down to caress her genitals. He didn't want to get there too soon. Her breathing got heavier, more rhythmic.

He kissed down her midline, sliding his hips down before his head. Kissing the top of her pubic hair, he reached behind him, slipped his hand in his shorts, and pulled. She moaned softly. He glanced up. Her eyes were closed, her mouth open. He pulled again. The damn thing was stuck. With his free hand he parted the lips of her vagina. He couldn't stay down here forever. It was getting more difficult to concentrate; his arousal was overcoming him. He allowed his thoughts to stray to his wife's genitals. *There, that's better.*

He ran his tongue along the top of the labia. Better than his wife's. He hoped she wouldn't notice his hand behind his back. He dug his fingernail under the tape, working it. It started to pop free. He pushed his tongue along her softness as the tape pulled free. Holding the plastic between his thumb and forefinger, he pulled it toward his mouth.

He rubbed his cheek against her genitals. She continued to moan. Putting the plastic in his mouth, he pulled off the top, then kissed her clitoris. She shivered. No more of that; he didn't want her cooked in the middle. He moved the vial into the bottom of her vagina and slipped his thumb into the soft space, pushing the clear, viscous liquid into the vial. She wiggled slightly. Hell, to be caught at this. He kissed her clitoris again. She shivered again, more vehemently this time. Slipping the top on the bottle, he reattached it to the tape.

He pulled off his Jockeys and threw them with the rest of his clothes before kissing his way up to her breasts. He touched himself. Yes, it was his wife. Not middle age, his wife. Anacleta grabbed him and plunged her tongue in his mouth, at the same time touching him. Just like that, it was on. It was too bad. He would have taken the risk with this woman. It was probably his last chance with a really beautiful woman. He felt his penis slip into her . . . or barely felt it. She wrapped her legs around him. At least she hadn't asked him to use a dental dam.

CHAPTER 17

The flame shot from his shoulder blade to his head. David blinked, then moved his neck again, more slowly this time. He'd forgotten how uncomfortable sleeping in a train can be, especially when your head flops. Pressing his neck toward his right shoulder, he decided it was okay if he moved slowly. Not great, but okay. He rolled his neck clockwise. It was loosening.

The conductor walked by, saying something about Union Station. Picking his case up, David wished he'd woken earlier. He didn't want to meet Walsh angry. And he would be angry if his muscles didn't loosen. Maybe that's why old people are so irritable, stiff muscles.

The train lurched to a stop, the doors opened, and the crowds poured out onto the platform. David allowed himself to be swept along. There were good reasons to be irritated, in addition to his stiff neck. He still didn't know why he was here. He didn't know why Walsh didn't meet the train. *Meet me out front.* Vague directions. David wasn't even sure what was the front of Union Station.

He followed the crowd out a large entryway into the main station. No time to notice the fast-food restuarants encased in mahogany. A moment later he was walking out the door.

Wondering why he had trusted Walsh, David scanned the street out front. A line of taxis stretched to the right; a few cars idled on the left. Jaw clenched, David walked toward the line of private cars to the left. It was the Jaguar, that deep green that looked almost blue on a cloudy day. David bent and peered through the partially open passenger window. Walsh smiled back. The door clicked and slowly floated open.

"Important?" David asked, slamming the door.

"And a good morning to you too, Counselor. Have a good trip?"

David spun to glare at Walsh, but he was already pulling into traffic, head craned behind, looking for an opening. The old man wouldn't even let him glare, David scowled. An old lady holding a leash to a Pekingese piddling on a *Washington Post* vending machine glared back. Probably ruined her day, David thought.

"What's important?"

"An interview. Part of your continuing investigation of the Twining matter."

"What investigation? They've got no case."

"Callous, Counselor, callous. You've a man's reputation at stake here."

"This is what's so important? What stopped you from telling me on the phone?"

Walsh swung left, pulled to the light, and stopped. "You did, Counselor."

"Me?"

"Would you have come if I told you?" Walsh pulled away from the corner and switched to the middle lane before continuing. "Of course you wouldn't."

"So you lied."

"No, I misjudged. It might not be as important as I thought. At least not to you. To me it's very important."

David glared at the road ahead. He hadn't thought his mood could have gotten worse than it had been when he got off the train, but it had. In fact, he had expected to act angry for a minute or two, do whatever had to be done, then leave, happy with the diversion. Now he actually was angry.

"Who?"

"Edwin Vance. Political consultant to the stars."

"To Twining."

"Right."

"You'll be there?"

"No, sorry to say, I can't make it. I will be nearby, however."

David felt his curiosity overcoming his anger. "What am I supposed to ask this guy?"

"Get 'round to the women in Twining's life." Walsh swung right, pulled to a light. "I shouldn't start there, though. Shouldn't want to make him think it's a setup."

"Why shouldn't he think it's a setup? What else would Light's lawyer want to ask him about?"

Walsh pulled up to the curb near the reflecting pool. "Well, you're not to be Light's lawyer, you see."

The anger came bubbling back. "Who am I to be?" David asked slowly, heaping self-control on every syllable.

"A reporter would be the easiest, I suppose. A concerned citizen. Or maybe just a friend."

The boil was rolling now. "The interview's not set up."

"Not precisely set up, no. But Mr. Vance is very approachable." Walsh pointed across the pool. "There he is now."

White-knuckled, David gripped the door handle. "Walsh, you just wasted my day."

"I hope not, old chap. Here, take this. For good luck."

He slipped a silver disk into David's shirt pocket.

"A good-luck piece?"

Walsh nodded.

David stepped out of the car. "I'll be sure to give it back before I beat the shit out of you." David slammed the door. "Back in Brooklyn, where I know the cops."

Jenson pulled his toothbrush from the dopp kit he had slipped into the glove compartment. He didn't want to brush his teeth, not really. He wanted them to smell it. For the first time in a long while, his breath smelled like good poon.

Not like that diseased pus his wife pushed out. No, he wanted them to know.

But he grabbed the toothbrush, smeared a little Crest on it, and stuck it in his mouth. He worked his molars as he pulled into traffic. After all, they might ask who. And who could he say? A suspect in the congressman's murder? No. He had to keep this one to himself. All to himself.

He was working on the back of his front lowers as he swung onto the Brooklyn Bridge. He finished, stuck the soggy brush back in the dopp kit, and slammed the glove compartment door. He rolled down the window and hesitated. Traffic slowed near some construction, and he leaned out and spit. Anacleta had even said something about meeting again. Maybe it was that he was a great lover, just buried in his wife's limited resources, like a primitive artist undiscovered in the same rural pit.

He swung onto the BQE. One more stop to make this morning, he thought as he patted the plastic vial in his shirt pocket and the two-gram packet underneath. Some statement about anonymity and he was done. He'd have to rinse his mouth first. That wouldn't do, telling the punk about how some good Samaritan had given him the gitz while talking with a mouth still full of Crest foam. A few minutes later he pulled up in front of a deli and jumped out. He grabbed a bottle of Evian, dropped a buck ten by the register, and went back toward the car. He took a big swallow and spit it down a sewer.

A homeless man grabbed his arm and made some unintelligible sound with his hand out. Jenson handed him the bottle of water and slammed the car door.

The clear morning in New York had given way to a damp, overcast Washington. Vance walked quickly, his gray tweed sport jacket hanging open, flipping against his thin body with every step. David moved next to him.

"Good morning, young man," Vance said, maintaining his brisk pace. "Although not as good as some."

"No," David said, then fumbled with the next word.

"Well, young man, what is it, a job or a story?"

"Beg your pardon?"

"Has to be one. No young man in a suit approaches a man in his fifties in Washington without wanting one or the other."

David laughed. This might be easier than he expected. Even a little of the anger at Walsh started to dissipate. "Story actually, about one of your charges."

"What paper?"

"Paper, sir?"

"TV then. No, TV does it more formally. Freelance."

David nodded. Freelance, that'd work.

"Have a contract?"

"No, sir, actually I thought I'd just try to put together a story, a little story and try to sell it."

"Careful with that, young man. They can like the story, then give it to one of their own boys to write up. Leave you out when it was your idea. Have to protect yourself."

"Yes," David said, struggling now to keep up, "I'll remember that." Going well, he thought, going well. "The story I had in mind, it's, well, a little embarrassing, but it's about sex in Washington."

"Good, good, we have that here. Good story too. It always sells. Stories about the peccadilloes of those in power. I'll bet there were stories about Henry the Eighth. Little booklets, I'll bet. Henry couldn't read, so he probably didn't care or even know."

"Yes, well, that's why I thought you could help me. I was thinking of this angle of putting what comes out now about political figures in line with what we now know historically. I mean, everyone talks about how all our best presidents were screwing someone that they shouldn't have been, and it seems that it was true in other periods. So I was thinking that no one has put together a real story about it."

"Good idea, good idea."

"Yes, well, what brought me to you, Mr. Vance, is that one of your clients . . ." David reached into his pocket and fumbled with a notebook. Important not to overplay the idiot, he thought. "Where is it?"

"Twining, Harrison Twining."

"Yes, that's the one. Well, there has been something in the news, and I thought perhaps you could tell me . . ."

"Certainly. What do you need to know, young man?"

"Well, I guess first, is it true?"

"Of course not." Vance stopped walking and gestured to a concrete bench along the path. "Shall we sit?"

David nodded and joined Vance on the bench. Making a show of flipping his notebook open, adjusting it on his lap, then placing pen near paper, he looked up.

"But what is important is that no one in Washington, no one political, that is, will admit that anyone for whom they are responsible is having an affair. They all are, of course, and if you ask someone with something against them, they'll tell you who, when, and what are the man's favorite perversions."

"Who would I ask about Twining?" David smiled. He tried to make it the smile of an innocent, but he didn't know if he was successful.

Vance returned the smile. "Harrison was a special case. He hadn't many enemies."

"No enemies?"

"Harrison was the consummate politician. Took very few positions. Just did his job, stroked the voters, and was reelected every year. I doubt you'll find anyone in Washington who was that angry with him." Vance smiled again. "Not that there's anything they could tell you anyway."

"It's been reported that he was connected with a woman, a . . . Anacleta Lucas, I believe her name was. Do you know Miss Lucas?"

Vance was silent. David could feel the tension in the man even as he bent over, nose in his notebook.

"Is that a no?"

Vance bent forward, whispering near David's ear. "Look," he said, "Harrison was separated. Had been for over ten years. He was allowed." Vance folded his hands in his lap. "Besides, the poor man is dead."

"I guess that's why I came to you. He's gone now. You know. I thought it would be easier to get the story."

Vance smiled and patted David's shoulder. "We have to consider the next client, young man. As soon as this client leaves, whether it be by death or otherwise, we have to find a new one. And our reputation goes with us. Even if Harrison had done anything, I wouldn't tell you. And, of course, he didn't."

"So you don't know anything about Coyce Loyn?"

Vance sat back, his body tense. "Coyce is a two-bit whore."

"Was she Harrison Twining's two-bit whore?"

Vance's face was hard, eyes boring in. David felt his own face harden as well. The fumbling-new-reporter act had gone, disappeared, replaced by the cross-examining attorney.

"Off the record?"

David nodded. Vance still believed the reporter act—probably not the fumbling novice, but reporter.

"Harrison has had some problems with women. Haven't we all?"

"Did he ever beat a lover?"

Vance stood, fire emanating from his eyes now. "I'll not stand by and let a man's good acts be tarnished by this sort of publicity, young man."

David stood and extended his hand. "Nor shall I, Mr. Vance."

Vance hesitated a moment, confused, then shook David's hand, turned on his heel, and strode off.

David watched until Vance disappeared. He hadn't realized it until this conversation, but he did care what they thought of Light. He did care that a poor man's reputation and perhaps his life were being sacrificed for the reputation of a powerful one. In the grand scheme of things, it didn't mean much, but in his personal scheme it did.

He turned to where Walsh had parked. The green Jaguar

was gone. Scanning up and down the street revealed nothing. David shrugged. The anger of this morning had vanished completely. Perhaps Walsh was right. He'd manipulated David, no question. But now David had a crusade. He liked having a crusade, especially when the next step in the crusade involved setting up another lunch with Anacleta Lucas.

David walked into his office and closed the door. Closing the door was something he rarely did, but he wanted no company for the next few minutes. He told himself it was because he needed information to help Light, but another part of him knew it was his curiosity. He punched out the number and waited. Probably get an answering machine, he thought, but the phone clicked up on the second ring.

"Anacleta," David said, his voice rising high in his throat, out of his control.

"Yes," she said, her deep voice demonstrating the self-confidence he was so obviously lacking.

He cleared his throat. "I wanted to talk to you." He hesitated. "To tell you again how sorry I am about your loss." Shit, he thought, makes me sound like an apartment hunter checking the obits. "I didn't really get a chance to convey that before. It was awkward." Not half as awkward as now, he thought.

She didn't answer immediately, breathing softly into the phone instead. Each breath sent a tingle down his spine, so intense that he clamped down on his chest, cutting the feeling. He'd never get through this. He moved the phone away from his mouth so she couldn't hear his nervous gasps.

"Thank you," she finally said. "I feel terribly alone."

His heart jumped, despite his muscular clamps. "You shouldn't be," he said. "I mean, at a time like this."

She said nothing, just breathed.

He felt the pressure grow. He had to say it, say it now or he couldn't live with himself. "Maybe we could get together, have dinner or something, take your mind off it." *Right*, he thought, *maybe since your ex-lover is dead now, has been over an hour, you'd like to get right back in the market. She'll see right through that.*

She didn't say anything for a second, only making a slightly wet sound with her lips, as if she were licking them close to the phone. David instinctively reached down and touched himself. It was getting there.

"Would today be all right?" she asked. "I really don't want to be alone."

Would today be all right? Right now would be all right. I could come in about five seconds, but it would probably be better if I waited until I got there. But he just said, "Sure."

David dropped the phone in the cradle, making a mental note not to have professional relationships with any more South Americans or Caribbeans. He glanced at his watch. 7:30. Only a half hour to get to Anacleta's. Not that she'd be ready on the dot of eight, David thought as he pulled on a sweater; she was a South American too.

Grabbing the keys off the bureau and dashing out the door, he remembered Miss Garcia, his ninth-grade Spanish teacher. She shouldn't have been a miss, he'd thought then, not the way she wore those dresses that were too short and too tight and pranced around as she spoke Spanish. Miss Garcia must have been pushing fifty, David thought, but she still looked good to him. She didn't want to be miss, David had been sure of that, but she did like the way the boys tried to look up her dress. David had especially liked the glaze she got in her eyes when she talked about *tiempo norteamericano,* or *tiempo alemán.*

"It is just our way," she said. "We will be late." She had talked about how some blamed it on the climate, but she didn't think so. She thought it was the South American belief that life was too short to fill with work.

David wasn't sure of the reason, but he was sure that the southern cultures didn't have the same sense of time. Evans had proven that, David thought as he feathered the accelerator. Timing, however, was another thing. If Evans had no sense of time, he had a disastrous sense of timing. A half hour before David was to meet Anacleta, Evans had to call.

At first David hadn't wanted to answer. The answering machine sat ready to allow him an evening relatively free from worry, but something had taken hold of his hand and directed it to the receiver. Force of habit perhaps, some force that would not permit him a strictly pleasurable evening of open-ended interrogation and seduction. No, this call had to come at just the right time to put an edge on.

The Toyota rumbled to an even roar before David dropped it into gear. One of the dubious advantages of an old car, David thought, was that one could open the hood and understand what went on. The other side was that it needed periodic tune-ups. David had resisted replacing the Toyota; it was a connection to that part of him that wanted to understand things, that sense of mastery that came from being able to understand, even if you could not control. The Toyota could conk out any time, leaving David stranded, but he could pop open the hood, see the problem, and understand his dilemma. Not so with the computerized modern cars. Computers should be left out of some things.

Evans shouldn't have a computer. It just wasn't right. Haitians shouldn't have computers. Sure, Evans might have gotten the information without a computer, but not tonight. Not just now. David pulled out of the parking lot and headed toward the bridge. If Evans hadn't had a computer, David wouldn't have known.

Damn Internet. The whole fucking world, right at your keyboard. David pulled the Toyota to a stop at the rear of a three-lane backup. The big orange "Road Work" sign was there, the same one that had been there last night when he ignored it. David slammed his hand into the steering wheel. Last thing he wanted was to be late.

Second to last thing. The last thing was to be questioning Anacleta about two murders. One, that would have been okay. It could happen; she just had been with a guy whose time was up. But two, that wouldn't work. David popped the car into gear and followed the traffic moving slowly toward the bridge. Now he'd not only have to question her, not only question her so she didn't suspect he was questioning her, but he'd have to wait for the privilege. Wait and worry.

CHAPTER 18

Anacleta folded the *New York Times* so it covered the corner of the coffee table, front page outward. The story wasn't on the front page, of course. In fact it was buried on page forty-three, but just the paper's being there would allow the conversation to drift to it. An attractor, Santeria called it. Something from some book on physics he was reading. Anacleta had picked it up while Santeria had gone in the other room to discuss business.

She did not see anything about attractors, but something about the weather and a man in New York and how he had stumbled by accident on some theory. It just seemed like an interesting story, not something Santeria should have been so mad she had read. But he was mad. He said it was important that he read such things so he would know how to work better. But, he said, it was important that others not read such books. Anacleta, he said, should concentrate on her work and leave the books to him.

She had said nothing, of course. She would never disagree with Santeria. But the book had seemed harmless. Maybe if she had gotten to the part about the attractors, it would have been dangerous for her. Maybe then she would have understood why it was dangerous, but then, perhaps it would have been too late.

So she didn't understand why the newspaper had to be

an attractor now. Why couldn't it be a conversation piece, like they always said before? Anyway, she knew what she had to do. She had to help the attractor to attract the conversation. And find out what David knew about the diary. The rest, Santeria said, was up to her. How to do it, what to do with the man was her affair. No one would question her.

She had looked back and forth between Julio and Santeria as the older man spoke. Santeria had the look of a father, giving his child her wings. Julio had another look. It was a look she had seen many times, that look the blond-haired boy with the small nose and the straight, white teeth had had when she was six. That same look that many men had when she saw them. That look that said that possessing her would change their lives, would make them whole. More than lust, more like salvation.

She had been surprised to see Julio with that look. Julio was not a six-year-old, not a politician who could not see other people. No, he had been trained. But the look had been there just the same.

Anacleta did not turned to Julio after she saw that look. Concentrating on Santeria and his words, she waited until she heard her instructions. They were not difficult. To find out what the lawyer knows about the diary and to make him love her. Neither would be a difficult task.

She listened carefully for another reason as well, but Santeria did not mentioned the cop once. At first she thought he would know. He surely would know. Santeria always seemed to know, as had *la doña* before him. Anacleta had always assumed they would know. But today he had given no indictation that he knew, except the statement about her having the choice, about having her freedom. Santeria had never said that before.

Perhaps he was telling her that he knew and approved, saying that he trusted her judgment to take actions for the group. Perhaps it was like a promotion. She had felt a hand clutch at her guts. Perhaps it had been a warning. Perhaps Santeria had been giving her a chance to tell him, then and there, about the cop. Perhaps by not telling she proved herself unworthy.

No, she thought, as she checked the fresh silk sheets again. No, Santeria had never been one to be subtle. Had it been a threat, he would have told her. He had always told the girls before.

It was the way the light reflected off her auburn hair that struck David first. The fact that her robe had a fur collar was second.

"Am I early?" David asked hesitantly.

Anacleta smiled and silently moved aside, allowing him to pass.

He ran his finger across the white fur as he did. "There are groups who'd have at you for this."

"The dinosaurs don't have a group yet." She smiled. "I thought we should order in," she said, following him to the couch.

Better than I could have hoped, he thought, glancing at the *Times*. And worse.

"One of the reasons," she said, following his eyes.

David nodded. He hadn't read it, despite the fact that Joel had tossed it conspicuously on his desk. It had been his second foray into the David-and-Anacleta debate. "What if she asks you about this," Joel had asked, pointing to the paper. It was now apparent she would.

She sat next to David, slipping her shoulder under his arm and draping it across the soft fur of her neck piece. She hesitated for a moment, then, as if discomfort had overcome her, turned and pushed one arm behind his back and the other around his stomach.

This is a woman who can make a congressman love her, Joel had said. *What do you have for her?* David shifted uncomfortably. It wasn't Anacleta who made him uncomfortable; it was Joel in his head. And the fact that Joel in his head was right. Joel had kidded about a woman who'd been beaten by a congressman being interested in being beaten by David, but it was true. Who did David think he was, a savior?

"I don't like to go out anymore," she said.

"The press?"

She shook her head, still buried in his chest, every movement giving David a comfort he hadn't felt since Janie left. "No," she said, "not yet. But I suspect."

What if you fall for her? Joel asked. David insisted he wouldn't. *What if there's a conflict?* Joel stressed the conflict until it represented duty and loyalty and ethics. *I've faced that dilemma before,* David said angrily. *I came through.*

Anacleta squeezed him gently, running her hand across his lap. David wanted to push her away but didn't. That combination of comfort and thrill held him there.

"It's that diary," she said. "Every time I think it's over, another page appears."

What if she asks you about the diary, David? Joel almost threw the newspaper at him. *Why would she?* David wanted to know. *Because it disappeared and Light was there the night Twining died. It doesn't take a genius.* David grabbed his jacket and stormed out of the office.

Not a genius, David thought now, but a man with his eyes open, willing to see. He should get up, walk out of the apartment right now, but instead he squeezed Anacleta tighter.

You're in control, Joel called after him, *you've been pining over Janie for a year and won't even call her.* David slammed the door and left, but Joel's voice did not. He hadn't called Janie because she said not to. *It wouldn't work,* she'd said, *better to make a clean break.*

He should have dated others though. Maybe if he had, he wouldn't have this feeling that all was right with the world just because a woman was listening to his heartbeat, brushing her thigh against his, and allowing her warm breath to ripple the fabric of his shirt.

They remained nearly motionless for ten minutes, until Anacleta stirred. "I'm so happy," she said, breaking away from David's chest. "I'd be perfectly happy, if I had that diary back." She kissed David lightly on the lips and stood. "Chinese?" she asked.

Look at this gringo, she thought as she watched David scrape the last morsels from the container. *He is* un puerco, *digging for that last bit as if there will not be another bite of food. It is not him who suffered with hunger, but I, and Julio and the others, while these* norteamericanos *lived like kings.*

She took the paper container from his hands. "You will eat the paper next," she said with a smile, taking it toward the kitchen. *Why is it then that this gringo is interesting to me? Why this gringo and not the others?* There were the obvious reasons: he was young and good-looking as opposed to the rest of the gringos she had dated. But it was more than that. He cared about her. She could feel it as she listened to his heart. She could tell the heart of a caring man, the heart of a self-absorbed man, the heart of a heartless man. Some of the girls had trouble with the hearts, but she had learned it right away. She could usually tell a man's heart without listening.

She remembered the day *la doña* had listened to her heart. She had stood with many other young girls. She was six and one of the youngest. *La doña* had stopped in front of each little girl and bent low, pressing her ear to the girl's heart. She had listened for a moment, made a note on a paper, and told the girl where to wait. When she got to Analceta and bent low to press her ear to Anacleta's chest, Anacleta could hear her own heart beating. *La doña* had not seemed to notice, but straightened up and gazed into Anacleta's eyes.

"You have a good heart," *la doña,* had begun, "but you need training. You can be very good with training."

Anacleta remembered her excitement as she had told *la doña* how hard she would work. *La doña* had smiled a tight little smile, her thin lips moving straight across her face.

"You will begin today," she had said. "You will begin today at a very special school."

Anacleta smiled as she remembered her first days at that school, and the times important men had asked her about the hearts of this man or that. They had listened as she spoke, nervously at first, then with more confidence. No one had asked her about David Cohen's heart, not yet. But she would say that he had a good heart, a strong heart, but more good than strong.

She poured hot water into the teapot, put it on the tray with the cups, and backed out the kitchen door. This man with his heart, more good than strong, would drink tea with her, would talk with her, and would sleep with her. His good heart would love her very soon. Then his good heart would get her the diary.

He kissed her lightly on the part of her forehead that sloped toward her temples. This was the part he hated, he thought, as he inhaled her scents. He stood and touched his penis, still erect, still filling the blue condom with tiny bubbles near the glans.

"Don't go."

"Just the bathroom," he replied, "I'll be right back."

He wondered if he looked as guilty as he felt. The only thing driving him through it was Joel's voice ringing in his ear. *What about when she asks you about the diary? When you have to decide between your dick and your client? What about then?* Well, he was answering that question, wasn't he? Or was he?

He picked up his blue jeans, tossed them over his shoulder, and left the room, wondering if he'd made that look natural, wondering if she'd ask him what he needed his jeans for when all he was going to do was toss a fucking scumbag. But she didn't say anything, and David safely closed the bathroom door behind him, lowered the lid, and dropped down on it.

It had been wonderful, David thought as he dug his fingers under the open end of the condom, taking care to touch only the top band. He had never paid attention to how he took off a rubber before, and it was a more tedious process than he thought. A moment later, however, the rubber was tied in the middle and dropped in a Ziploc bag.

He pulled a toothbrush from his jeans, squeezed a little paste from her tube, and stepped to the mirror. A moment later, jeans draped over his shoulder, he was back in Anacleta's bedroom.

"Always bring your toothbrush?" she asked.

Tossing his jeans on the floor, next to his other clothes, David crawled over the bed and kissed her. Maybe the guilt would fade for the second time, he thought as she reached up and lightly stroked his butt.

Light moved his butt over into the wheelchair, not knowing why he had to be rolled out. He had spent the last two days with that muscle-bound bitch, telling him he didn't know how to walk no more just cause his dick was sliced. Didn't make no difference how he walked with that bitch. It didn't sound right coming out that bitch how he was walking good. Mostly he wanted to punch her in the mouth just for having bigger shoulders than he did.

He settled in the chair and the white-uniformed boy started pushing. Talking about how it was a nice day, about how Light could walk real good, that's what it said in the records, but they had to push him out anyway, cause a the rules. Light didn't care nothing about no rules, he was thinking about what he was goin' do when he caught the one that done this. How he was goin' beat that boy's ass.

They slid past the hallway doors and into the lobby. The boy worked him through the lobby. Light said, "That's enough," but the boy put his hand on Light's shoulder and held him there.

"Got to stay put till we get to the front. That's rules."

Fuckin' rules. Wasn't no rules when that guy cut up his penis . . . now he got to be following rules. Light sat back for the rest of the ride, not enjoying it. He was tense, felt the back of his neck. Felt those two balls of muscle on his shoulders, right next to his neck. Just holding, like they was waiting for him to hit bottom and didn't want no whiplash. Light moved his feet back on the footrests while the boy slammed through the swinging front doors and out into the sunlight. The boy stopped just at the edge of the driveway.

Light looked back. "Now?"

The boy nodded.

Light thanked him, stood up, and walked down the driveway toward the sidewalk. Didn't even know where he was exactly. Shoulda asked that boy about where the subway was or where the buses stopped, one. Light looked up and down the street. Looked busier to the right. He thought about asking the man in the car across the street. Caught his eye for a second, but then he didn't ask. The man didn't look that friendly, like he was waiting on someone he didn't like that much.

Light shrugged and turned right, toward the busier street. His dick didn't hurt that much when he walked. The doctors had it all strapped up, gauze and tape, then strapped to his right leg. His pants were a little tight. Light laughed, Maybe he'd strut around the neighborhood a little, let all them women see him like that, couldn't use it now, but later. The publicity'd be good.

Light turned around, glanced over his shoulder. Car with the man'd pulled out. Nothing else going on. Light spun back to the busy street. Doctors said that the wound, that's what they called it, the wound, like they didn't want to talk about a man's dick. Anyway, they said the wound would heal, but it would take a while. Start to hurt worse 'fore it got better.

Light didn't notice. He felt a little doped up, with that shit they been giving him for the pain, and that shit they give him so he wouldn't get a hard-on. He was next to a parking lot now, a big parking lot in front of the hospital. Across the street was another one. Light glanced over, noticed that car with the man cruising along next to him, matching his stride. Light snapped his head back front. Man didn't say nothing, just staring at him like he a freak. That man some kind a faggot or what?

Light felt those muscles in his neck tighten up again. Like that fall coming. He didn't want to turn, see the guy again. Just ignore him, that's all.

The car pulled up past him. The window rolled down, and the man stuck his head out.

Light kept walking. Don't look. Just like a little kid, don't never take no rides with strangers. Light came up next to the back of the car.

"Hey, buddy." The voice was a little high, Spanish like.

Light ignored it, walked past. He was next to the car now, right next to the man.

"Hey, Scott." The man paused.

Just trying to see if I react, him knowing my name. Just walk. Ain't ready to take on that motherfucker again. Not ready for any motherfucker, not now.

The car moved slowly along with him. The man popped a beer. "Scott, want to make some money?"

Money, shit. Would like a beer, but the edge off now after three days sober. Light almost chuckled. Could go to a meeting now, tell 'em he got three days. But the joke fell flat, even inside.

The car pulled up in front, stopped, and the man got out. Light ignored him. The man stood in front of Light, pushed a beer in his hand. Light glanced down. It was an Old English, top been cleaned. The man did his homework.

"We just want to talk, Scott."

Light took a swig of the beer. He allowed the cool bubbles to tickle his mouth before they ran down his throat. It was good. He looked at the man. White, but with that Mexican look, about six feet. Light thought about how he could tell the boys he coulda taken him, but he knew he couldn't. The man worked out. Looked like he didn't like working out, but liked hurting people. Had that look. Same look as the other night. Light took another swig.

"About what?"

The man smiled. Like he wasn't really happy, but this

was what was supposed to happen so he should act happy. "The man inside," the white man said, pointing his head over toward the car, "he wants to talk."

Light turned to look to the backseat of the car. The man's hand shot out and grabbed his chin, snapped Light's face back front. "The man doesn't want to be seen, just heard." The Spanish sound was more pronounced now, like the man had worked hard not to have it no more, but when he talk fast, it come back.

Light worked his memory. Could be the guy. Had been hard to see 'cause of the dark, but by the sound, could be.

"Smoked glass back there, anyway. All I saw," Light finally said, gulping down some more beer. He wasn't sure he wanted to get in the car with this man, not the way the man didn't want to be seen. Light unconsciously touched his groin. He didn't want to risk no more with no strangers.

He looked down at the beer, drained it, and handed the empty to the man. "Don't feel so much like talking now," he said, moving to the man's right and sliding by.

The man's arm grabbed Light by the upper arm. Light felt himself being lifted almost off the ground. "It is not polite to leave on a free one," the man said. "The man wants to talk to you."

Light looked around, but the area was deserted except for an overweight lady who stood across the street, staring. She had a kind of smile on her face. The kind that white people get when they see a nigger gettin' beat up. Like he gettin' what he deserve. Pretty hopeless. Light shrugged and moved toward the car.

He carefully kept his eyes forward as he got in the car, but he could see the divider between front and back, like the kind they have in cabs, except this one was smoked. The man waited until Light was in, slammed the door behind him, and walked around to the driver's side.

"Mr. Scott." The voice came from behind him, sounded older but authoritative, like the man was used to being obeyed. "We have discussed with you the whereabouts of a certain diary."

"Yeah, that was me," Light answered, "but if that what you call a discussion, I don't think I want to talk no more." Light reached for the door. It was locked.

"This will be a much more decorous discussion, Mr. Scott. That was just to let you know how important that diary is to us."

Light said nothing as the car moved slowly away from the curb. "Drive toward Mr. Scott's home."

The man swung the car to the right and continued slowly toward Flatbush Avenue.

"You had three discussions with your attorney, Mr. Cohen, while you were in the hospital. Is that right?"

Light nodded, then realizing that the man couldn't see his motions, said "Yes."

"You discussed the whereabouts of this diary?"

"No, I didn't say nothing about that."

"He does have it?"

Light looked out the side window. He was thinking about how he wished he never had that diary, never heard of it, but he didn't say that; he didn't say nothing.

"I don't hear, Mr. Scott."

"I didn't say nothing." Light hesitated for another second. The man driving looked over. He had a smile on his face, a different smile, like a real one this time, like he was really happy. "I think he have it."

"You think?" the voice in the back said.

The driver's hand reached over and gave Light's knee a squeeze.

"See, I had it. I did." Light was blurting now. He knew it, but he couldn't stop. "But somebody took it from me. He the only one knew I had it." Light looked down. "'Cept Evelyn," He continued, almost under his breath.

"You didn't discuss it with Mr. Cohen?"

"No, I didn't tell him nothing about nothing. Told him my girlfriend cut me. He don't know nothing about this."

"You led me to believe that you gave it to Mr. Cohen."

"No, I didn't led you to believe nothing. I just said that's who I thought had it."

The voice was silent for a long time. Light stared straight ahead, trying hard to ignore the man driving the car, the man looking eagerly over at Light, like Light was a pegged lobster, helplessly banging his claws against the glass of a death-row aquarium. Light didn't know why he had gotten in this car. Don't never get in no place you don't know how to get out of, that's what he tell the boys. Always better they do you outside, if they do you. Might get caught that way, might somebody see. They know that so they ain't going to do you so quick. He always tell the boys that.

Maybe it was that beer. Maybe that dope the doctor give him for his dick. But something going on and he ain't thinking so well, not today anyway. The car swung out to the left, going 'round one a them Flatbush dollar vans. That voice still not saying nothing.

The man pulled to a stop at a light. He turned full on Light now, that smile, genuine, from deep down. Just for Light now.

The voice come from the back again. "It isn't right to mislead my people, Mr. Scott."

Light felt his mouth go dry. This going to be it, right here. He looked around. Too much traffic. They wasn't going to do nothing here.

The light changed. The man turned back to the front and spun the wheel to the left.

"Where you going?"

The driver didn't answer. The voice was silent. They drove through a couple of run-down blocks and turned right onto a totally deserted one. There were buildings on both sides, the windows gaps with black charred scars along their edges. The man pulled between an abandoned truck and a charred green dumpster, now a playground for rats. The man turned to Light, displaying his teeth, perfectly straight, white porcelain appliances.

Light spun back toward the smoked backseat. The driver's hand shot out, grabbing Light hard by the chin, pulling his head back to face the driver's smiling teeth.

Light's heart pounded now, his mouth dry. The man held

him helpless with his one hand. No, he couldn't even lie about this one to Charlie or the boys. But then he probably didn't have to worry about no more lying.

"You will never again mislead my people, Mr. Scott," the voice said. There were two taps on the smoked-glass divider.

Light heard a click behind him. The man released his grip on Light's chin. There was a terrible moment of silence, then the man reached his powerful hand across and rested it on Light's neck. He reached his other hand across and pulled the door handle. The door swung open.

Light stuck a leg out of the car, gulped some returning saliva down, and pushed his ass after his leg.

"Mr. Scott." The voice in the back was firmer now. "You will not tell Mr. Cohen any of this."

Light nodded. Out of the car now, he bent down so the driver could see his face, as if the driver was the voice's face, as if the voice could see through the driver's eyes.

"And you will not mislead us again."

Light nodded as the door pulled closed and the man pulled out around the abandoned truck.

Julio pulled the limo to the corner and stopped. He saw the skinny man with the bulbous stomach and the cut penis stumble toward the wall, then lean against it. Julio waited. He wanted the man to know he was watching. That is what Santeria wanted, so Julio wanted it too. It is what the training did, he thought, made him want what Santeria wanted, what the organization wanted. The training had been good that way, efficient.

The man touched his penis, looked back at the car, and stumbled away. He looked as if he wanted to make a gesture, but he didn't. That was good. That is what Santeria wanted to see, if the man would make a gesture. The gesture wouldn't make Santeria mad. At least that's what Santeria had said in the past. But it would make him realize that the man was not fully cowed. It was a word Julio had heard only Santeria use. He supposed it meant to act like a cow, but he wasn't sure.

The man with the cut penis walked down the block, away from the car. Julio waited for the tap on the smoked-glass divider, then turned to the right. It would be a few minutes until they were back on Flatbush, another half hour or so until they were on the Manhattan Bridge. Santeria would flip on the light in the back, even though it was a bright day. The smoked glass cut the light from outside, and this light inside replaced it. Very inefficient.

Much about the North American way of life seemed inefficient to Julio, yet they ruled the world. So far. Julio wondered if he would see the inefficiencies and the waste of North American life had he not had the training. It was one of the things the trainers repeated over and over. Waste and inefficiency, and how we had to be better. Julio glanced in the rearview mirror, through the smoked-glass divider, at the shadow of Santeria. Julio didn't know. He thought perhaps *el señor* had forgotten some of his training.

Julio did not even know if *el señor* had had training. The man was old, perhaps there since the beginning. Perhaps those so high up didn't need training. Maybe that is why *el señor* wasted light like a *norteamericano*. It was not for him to think such things, Julio thought as he swung the car onto Flatbush.

No, Julio had his specialty, and to that he should stick. He weaved the car through the double-parked traffic on Flatbush Avenue, past the delivery trucks, between cars entering and escaping from parking places. Julio would have liked to take another street, but *el señor* liked Flatbush. He said he liked it because it showed the teeming streets of North America, showed that with all its riches, it was no different. Reminded him, he said, of the streets of his youth.

Julio stopped behind two cars, each halfway across the center line, each attempting to pass a truck double-parked for a delivery. Julio didn't view the scene with the same nostalgia, but then he had not grown up in the teeming streets of Bogotá, but in the countryside teeming with insects, snakes, life of all descriptions. Julio did not understand nostalgia. He felt himself well rid of the teeming life, with its disease and poverty.

The drivers ahead had stopped yelling, and one of them had backed up a little. The other, the driver ahead of Julio, inched forward. Julio stayed close to his rear bumper. When the car in front of Julio popped free, he eased the limo into the vacated spot. He heard the screaming of the driver who had backed up, but he said nothing. It reminded him of the story one of the trainers had told, the story of Atlas and Hercules. Don't be fooled by honest words, the trainer had said, don't be like Atlas.

Julio had liked that part of the training, even though it had had nothing to do with the skill for which he was being trained. But that trainer did instill in him the need to be constantly reading, to be always upgrading his skills, to be learning from the others. Julio pushed the limo forward. He wanted to be back at the office. He had reminded himself of the research he was doing.

He had read almost as much as he could. He needed practical experience now. He had had some with the penis, but *el señor* had said to stop after one cut. Still, Julio was proud of that one cut. Straight as an arrow, just the right depth. Although Julio had been sitting on the man's chest and had tied him spread-eagle to the bed, still he could tell the man had pain. Julio had been careful to stuff his mouth with cotton before taping it around the head. Pulling the tape off caused a little more pain, but by that time the man was in full agony from the cut.

Julio had found, both from his own experience and from his research, that there was a limit to pain. One could feel only so much. He had taped the penis to the man's body, being careful to hold it straight, covering just enough of the glans to hold it steady. He had wanted to be able to make a small incision there if *el señor* wanted him to. *El señor* had not.

The books he had read had talked about how to experience a man's pain through all the senses. Julio could certainly hear it. But hearing was not a good barometer, the ancients said, since a man can yell from fear as well as pain. Julio had sat lightly on the man's chest, putting most of his weight on his feet, allowing his buttocks to touch the man's chest only lightly. He had worn thin cotton pants. The vibrations of pain had come through to him as he sliced. It was most satisfying.

The traffic cleared as they reached Prospect Park. It would be only a moment before they were on the bridge and a moment more until they were in the office. A moment after that Julio would be back to the Chinese texts. It was the ancient Chinese who had written the most about the science of torture. Julio would read once more about cutting for maximum pain. He had felt the pain wash through the man, felt the vibrations through his own body. He had stopped, waited. Waited for the shivers to cease, for the man to think it was over. Only when the man was convinced he was saved did Julio continue, a millimeter more, a centimeter at most, until the shivers of pain again traveled from the man's chest up through Julio's buttocks, ripping through his body.

Julio pulled the limo onto the bridge, onto the upper level. He liked to see the tops of the buildings shine in the light on a bright, clear day like this one. There was a glory in God's light glimmering off man's works. There was a special glory in the combination of God's works and man's.

Yes, Julio wanted to read over the ancient texts. He wanted to see if he had gotten the most pain out of the man, or if he could get even more.

He remembered back to his training, to the rats, especially the white ones. How they had pinned the rats down. How the students had held their fingers on the rat's neck, feeling first the rat's fear, then, after the cutting began, the pain. How they had learned with their fingers to tell how much fear, how much pain. They had spent weeks on rats before working with people.

Julio smiled as he watched the sunlight shine off the Chrysler Building. It had been pain that the black man had felt. Julio had done his job well.

CHAPTER 19

David dropped off the plastic bag with Evans and headed out to see Light. Eight o'clock. He'd catch Light before his morning round of beer and conversation and, with luck, after Anacleta's glow had dissipated.

Her questions about the diary had burned at him through the night and morning. Joel was right; the diary was important to someone—whoever had cut Light, Anacleta's handlers. But why? From the two items in the paper, there appeared to be nothing important in it, just a series of appointments, with Twining, hairdressers, and one with Vance. It might have embarrassment value, but not to a dead congressman. It made no sense, but Light was cut up and Anacleta had made a point that the diary's being in the paper bothered her.

Other than what she said, it hadn't seemed to bother her that much. And why should it? Certainly she couldn't be embarrassed about being a congressman's young lover. She'd had that role for a while. No, something was going on here, and it had to do with the diary. David pulled in front of Light's house.

A moment later David knocked on Light's door. No answer. He tried the knob, which turned in his hand. Stepping into the dark apartment, he peered through the cone of light streaking in from the hall, looking for a switch. He found it and flipped it on before letting the door swing shut.

A door opened across the hall and a groggy sound emanated from deep in a mucusy throat before Light's head appeared in the doorway.

"Good morning, Mr. Scott," David said pushing the bedroom door open. "Slept well?"

Light groaned and fell back into bed, squinting against the light.

"I want to talk about a diary."

"Oh, shit, my dick, he needs a rest."

"I don't want to talk to your dick, Mr. Scott."

"What this Mr. Scott shit?"

"You've been lying to me, so I figure that requires more formality."

Light pulled himself up, threw his legs over the side of the bed, and sat up. "Too early to be talking about lying and what's formal."

"How about this, Mr. Scott? You went to Twining's office, found that diary, and stole it. After you killed Twining."

"Fucking bullshit. Whose side you on?"

"Then you figured you could make some money, so you sold it to the papers, to the *Times*."

"I didn't sell nothing."

"But unfortunately, someone else wants that diary, and they picked you up and tried to get the information out of you."

Light got up unsteadily and stumbled toward the door. "I had it," he said.

"Who has it now?"

"Evelyn, I think."

"Who?"

"Evelyn Jefferson. I told her 'bout it, right after I stole it. Then it disappear next day."

"You told those guys this Evelyn had it?"

Light shook his head. "I told 'em you had it."

David felt the energy and anger wash out of him. They

thought he had it. Anacleta thought he had it. That explained why she wanted to talk about it, why she said it bothered her. They wanted it back. She wanted it back. But why?

"Where's Evelyn?"

Light shrugged. "She disappear a couple a days ago. Nobody seen her."

David dropped into the leather chair, his body strangely angled, twisted as if it didn't want to support him, not for this.

Ignoring David, Walsh looked over his shoulder. "Never can get the waitress when you're thirsty." He spun back with a smile, revealing perfect white porcelains, in stark contrast to the gray pallor of his face. But the face was unlined, as if the smile was genuine. Not confused, not conflicted. "What's this about, lad?"

"I need that diary."

"Yeah, so I hear." Walsh stuck his bony hand in the air as the waitress looked over. "So I hear."

David was silent as Walsh ordered. The waitress smiled, but David waved her off.

"They got your client locked up again?"

David shook his head.

"Sliced him up good, so I hear."

"We need the diary."

The waitress dropped a martini in front of Walsh, smiled at David again, and walked away. David pulled his legs under him and pushed his back up straight. It was the first time in a while he hadn't thought of Anacleta.

"Funny how that slut's diary is making somebody so angry."

David's chest leaped forward before the rest of his body held him back. Couldn't get out of control here.

"Who, though? That's the question. I mean, from what I've read, there's nothing that outrageous in the thing. Nobody is really mentioned."

"Look, Crawford, I'd like to honor your professional curiosity, but we need it back. Light needs to get it back to those people."

"Oh, Light will be all right. They know he doesn't have it."

"I don't know what he told them, other than that his girlfriend cut him," David lied.

"David, trust me, there's nothing in that diary. Nothing."

"You've read it?"

Walsh nodded with that infuriating smile.

"But it was in the *Times*."

"And the *Times* got it from me."

"You? Why?"

"We're a weekly, as I've told you. We can't pursue this story day to day."

"So you sold the diary to the *Times*?"

"A page here and there."

"Saving the best for yourself."

"Saving the story for myself. When the story breaks, we'll come out with it. As long as I control the story, I control when it comes out."

Walsh was orchestrating this whole story, selling a page at a time, letting the story build. When it had, he would bring the entire matter out. A reporter with foresight, David thought, but a reporter with different goals than David or his client. David felt the anger growing in his belly, but he forced it down. He had to play this right.

"So, you've read the whole diary?" David asked, keeping his voice as calm as possible.

Walsh maneuvered the martini to his lips and sucked off the top quarter inch. "Not all, but enough," he said after he'd replaced the glass.

"So make a photocopy and give it to me."

"I'm sorry, I cannot."

"Why not?"

"I don't have it, my boy."

"Don't have it?"

"Don't have it." Walsh shook his head. "Nope. I get it page by page from a lady."

"Evelyn Jefferson."

Walsh silently sipped his martini.

"Where is she?"

"Can't tell you that, my boy."

David felt the anger bubbling up from the pit of his being. "Why?" David managed to croak out.

"Privilege."

"There's no privilege."

"I suppose you're right, but we must protect our sources."

The bastard, sitting there talking about some privilege, freedom of the press, First Amendment bullshit, when Light had his dick sliced nearly through and Anacleta was trembling. David's hand reached across the table. It wasn't him, just his hand, operating independently. David watched as it grabbed Walsh's shirt, gathered the cotton, and twisted. David's hand enjoyed Walsh's wince as the chest hairs were twisted out.

"You're going to get me that woman's address," David heard his mouth say, "and any other fucking thing you know about this."

"David, understand," Walsh's voice croaked. His tie dipped in the martini. "I can't. If I did, then I'd never have another source."

David looked around. Faces stared from around the bar. Faces peered between the ferns like so many jungle eyes, staring disapprovingly. David's hand, once more under his control, released Walsh. "Light's facing something with this."

"I know. I'm sorry about that." Walsh's voice choked slightly. He squeezed the liquid out of the red silk and back into his glass. He sounded sorry, but maybe it was only his tie. "I can't. I can't."

David sat back. He had to get that diary, first for Light, but also for Anacleta. And he wasn't going to let some cynical pig with a two-tone silk tie stop him.

"How do you get it?"

"A page at a time."

"How much?"

"Five hundred a page."

"How do you pay?"

"Cash."

No surprise. No records. "How are the pages delivered?"

"Express Mail."

"From where?"

"Brooklyn. 11217."

David paused a second. "Address." He said it slowly, forcefully.

Walsh looked down at his martini, fibers of silk floating in it. He pulled it to his mouth. "I can't," he said.

The crack of the glass against his teeth seemed to startle him more than the splash of the liquid across the rest of his tie. David held the base of the glass in his hand, its open mouth perched by Walsh's lips. David ignored the bouncer dodging between tables. "Address," he demanded.

Walsh glanced at the bouncer as if it were okay. He brushed David's hand away.

David allowed it. He knew he wouldn't have carried the threat through. Allowing the fire to remain in his eyes a moment longer, he returned the broken glass to the table.

The bouncer eased back but kept a wary eye on the table.

Walsh leaned forward. "Let's reason together, shall we?"

David ignored the satiric lilt and nodded.

"Let's say you get the diary and give it back to them, whoever them is." Walsh waited while David nodded. "*They* get it back. Then *they* wonder who you are and how much you've read."

"Same is true of Light."

"Not exactly. Let's say Light read it, gave it back, and decided to talk to someone about what was in it. The evidence is supported only by his word. The word of a career petty burglar against presumably well-respected men."

"He could have made a copy."

"And admit how he got it?"

"And you believe that he broke into the office and stole it?"

"How else?"

David was beginning to see Walsh's point.

"You, however," Walsh continued, "would have nothing to fear by revealing either a copy or your memory of the contents. No crime in your background. You don't even have to say where you got it. Attorney-client privilege. You can't even identify the client."

"So they wait until they get the diary and kill me."

"There is that possibility."

"You've seen it and you say there's nothing."

"I haven't read it all, but there's nothing in what I've seen. Just a diary, appointments, travel plans." Walsh paused and looked David up and down as if taking stock of him again, as if the question of whether to take David into his confidence once again had been raised. "I think it's a time bomb."

"A time bomb?"

"Meaning there's something there, but it has to be connected. Something in the diary that, if printed, someone, somewhere would connect with another bit of information that would lead somewhere. A bit in a puzzle."

"So they want it back before it's printed?"

"Yes. And you don't want to produce it. You don't want them to know you ever had it."

"Why?"

"Because you might stumble across that bit of information."

"And Light probably wouldn't?"

"Not likely." Walsh paused, picking a shard of glass from his tie. "Despite appearances, these people don't like to kill. Messy. Leaves clues."

"You know them?"

Silently, Walsh spun the glass stem between his thumb and forefinger, a crooked smile stretching across his lips. "I have followed their careers."

"Who are they?"

"Not yet. The story has never really come out, at least not fully. That is why I'm here, you see. If I get this story

... well, my career will be something. My life actually..."
Walsh paused, staring toward the window as if the fern hanging between tables had suddenly captured his interest. "We all need some meaning in our lives, don't we?"

David paused to allow the philosophical meandering to fade. It had been spoken like a grandfather, pondering his life and regrets. David had never been good with reflections. Perhaps he was too young. David raised his mug to his lips. What was Walsh suggesting, other than that he not deliver the diary? That he and Walsh find it and keep it? That didn't seem so safe either.

"What do we do?" David asked.

"Right. I've an idea. If we can get the diary, we may be able to find the time bomb and work from the bomb backward."

"But if you can get the diary, why haven't you?"

"I can't, but you may be able to. You do have some contacts with Miss Jefferson."

"Me?"

Walsh rose regally, as if making an exit from an English theater. "LeVander Jefferson, your former client. Evelyn is his mother," Walsh said, smiling. He nodded and turned toward the door.

How did the man know that Evelyn Jefferson's son was his client? How was it reporters could get information that lawyers struggled for? And how was it that everything took his mind back to Janie? Took his mind back to that choice he'd made more than a year ago to keep his first big press case as a defense attorney, to allow it to build the firm's practice, allow it to endanger Janie, all for the pursuit of fame and fortune. And this odd Englishman had brought his mind back to that.

Focus on the man, David told himself as he picked up the bill. Focus on anything to get your mind off Janie. Focus on that odd man.

David allowed his feelings about Walsh to run through him as he thought about who Walsh was. David wasn't sure if it was just the way Walsh looked, the grayness of his skin, or if it was more. A man didn't control the way he looked, or did he? Perhaps his manner was the key to the man's soul. David pulled a bill from his wallet and handed it to the waitress walking by. He had represented odd-looking people, junkies, crackheads, drunks beyond count. None gave him the feeling in the stomach this man did. Even before the man reminded him of Janie, David had felt a foreboding around the man. Of course, David had been able to walk away from the junkies, crackheads, and the others. None of them followed him home.

Walsh crossed the street on legs that seemed too thin and weak to carry his weight. But they did, and did so admirably. But it gave his movements a ghostly look. David remembered Evans once, humoring the voodoo part of his Haitian background, talking about how a man's character seeped to the surface, revealing his intentions to those who cared. Not, he had said, in a way that could be explained with words, but in the gut.

David took his change and stood. It didn't matter. What Walsh had said was true. David had little choice. If he delivered the diary, he might be a marked man. But if they could get the diary and find the *time bomb,* at least they'd have a chance to control how the story came out. A chance. A chance that both he and Light could be safe.

A screech came from outside the restaurant. David looked up. A cab had stopped inches from a stroller pushed into the street by a young mother. The cab driver popped his head out and began screaming Semitic insults. The woman responded in Spanish. The only word David picked up was *culo.*

David moved toward the door. Well, maybe not safe exactly.

David skipped up the steps toward the mahogany-stained door, beckoning Light to follow.

Light did, a little reluctantly it seemed to David as he pressed the buzzer and turned to see Light only halfway up the steps. The sound of footsteps echoed from the back of the house.

"Don't want to see that woman."

"She won't be here," David said, a little impatiently.

The door opened and LeVander stood there, a little taller than last year but still a shortish teen, slightly stooped as if he didn't want to cut too big a swath and be noticed by those with larger stature. He stepped aside and gestured them in.

Light mumbled something unintelligible to LeVander, who responded in kind. They followed LeVander to the living room, where Light and David sat together on the white sofa and LeVander took Franklin's chair.

Clearing his throat, David began. "It's about your mother," he said, going through the story of the diary and how they knew she had it. When he got to the part about Light, Light leaned forward.

"Them bastards, four of 'em, they grab my ass, held me down, cut on me. Just to get that damn thing back." Light hung his head. "Couldn't fight 'em all off. Couldn't."

"Now they think I have it," David continued.

"And you want me tell you where my mother is at?" LeVander asked.

David nodded.

"If I do, what stop them from getting one a you, cuttin' on you again, and then you tellin' them where she at?"

David looked away. He'd thought of that question and knew he had no answer. After all, it was true, if somebody was about to take a knife to his dick, he'd give him the keys to a nuclear silo if he had them.

"Look, I been cut 'cause a that woman. Know what it's like to piss out a trough, walk around with a fucking bag hanging out you side." Light was up now, gesturing wildly. "'Cause of that bitch you call a mother."

Light shook a little, as if he were sorry he'd said it. After all, despite her problems, Evelyn was LeVander's mother.

LeVander didn't react angrily. "Can't do it" was all he said, standing up.

"You know where she is?"

LeVander shook his head.

"You could find out," David continued. "You could find out and get the diary from her. We don't care about her. Neither do those guys, they just want the diary." David knew he was sounding desperate.

"Ain't gonna expose my mother."

Light grabbed him. "Ain't gonna expose your mother? What about what we done for you last year? What about with them Italians?"

LeVander looked back and forth between them. "Wasn't my mother. She didn't have nothing to do with that shit."

"Neither did Light," David broke in. "Neither did Franklin, for that matter, but they came through for you."

"Risked our fuckin' necks for your worthless black ass." Light scowled and stormed out the door.

David stayed behind. "These guys mean business. How do you think I know your mother has the diary?" When LeVander didn't answer, David continued. "Well, the same way I found out, they can. And when they do, they'll find your mother, and they'll be cutting off body parts like there's no tomorrow."

LeVander's face remained blank, but there was a slight twitch near the mouth, as if part of him wanted to say something but the larger part resisted.

David turned to the door. "In fact, the only way she'll be safe is if she gives up the diary."

LeVander's mouth opened this time, but still he said nothing.

David handed LeVander a card and said, "Call me." He slipped out the door.

The door closed quietly behind them.

Jenson slipped the NYPD card in the front windshield as he eased the car into the no-parking zone. He slammed the door and took a deep breath. This was going to be a much more difficult meeting than he had thought. He had considered this meeting and how he would handle it for some time, but never from precisely this angle. He stepped listlessly toward the door, realized he had an impression to make, and adopted a more resolute posture. It was a posture that did not reflect his feelings.

Mario opened the door with a barely closed terry bathrobe covering his corpulence. Jenson wasn't impressed with people who weren't dressed by ten A.M., wasn't impressed with people who were obese, and found the two frequently went together. He pushed past Mario, glanced around the room he found around him, grunted a sound that might have passed as a greeting, and sat on the edge of a fold-out bed.

Mario fell into the only chair in the room, a green easy chair with a large tear across the back and the cotton innards leaking out. He had an irritating smirk on his face between the times he rubbed the bridge of his nose, which was about every two seconds. It was that smirk that said he had the power here. It pissed Jenson off, thinking this little junkie had the power and knew it, made Jenson almost want to clock the fucker. But he couldn't, not until this thing was taken care of.

"Well, it's about this thing. This test."

Mario twitched a little, rubbed his nose, and nodded.

Jenson relaxed a little. The little bastard needs some go. That kind of evened up this power thing. But Jenson hadn't liked the way his voice had sounded, like this thing was important. Like he was worried. It wasn't like he visited Mario on a regular basis. Guy would've figured it was important anyway. But that crack. Jenson shook it off. Too late now.

"I brought this to you, outside channels, for a little privacy. It's a delicate thing." *A delicate thing. That's good.*

Mario cracked a quick smile. "A delicate thing, right. I was going to ask you how you got cunt juice. Didn't know the courts gave those kind of orders."

Jenson looked down. He didn't like this guy. Pompous, that's what he was . . . pompous. "Yeah," Jenson continued, "I've had judges order dick scrapings in the right case, herpes or some such. And they'd do it in the right case. But that was the point here." There, it was going much better now. Much better.

Mario shifted in his seat. "What was the point here?"

"Well, you see, this was the vaginal mucus of his girlfriend, it had a right to be there, if you see what I mean. Had a right."

"Had a right?"

"Yes, well sort of. I mean for the purpose of a criminal investigation, if it was someone else's mucus, another woman's, then we could use the DNA to find something out about her, about this woman, and maybe find her. Have a witness to the death, see if it was suspicious. You see what I mean?" Jenson sat back when he had finished. This was going very well. He almost believed it himself.

Mario pushed his chair back. "So now you think it wasn't suspicious?"

"Not now. No, with the woman who was with him his girlfriend, and a girlfriend of some time at that, no, I think it wasn't suspicious."

"What about the pinprick on his neck?"

"Oh, that could have happened anytime. The M.E. was right to ignore it the first time. Just that it came out so late. Looked suspicious, just like all that stuff that came out about Kennedy, just like all that stuff." Jenson felt his voice trailing off. "The thing is, you see, we need to close up this investigation. Close it up. Haven't got anything. So I want to thank you for all your help."

"And you want me to forget what I did. Forget it ever happened."

"Yes, well right. You see, considering the nature of the case, it seemed the best way to go, the delicate nature of the investigation and all that. It seemed the best way to go. And now . . ."

Mario stood and took a couple of nervous steps before turning back. "If it came out, it would be embarrassing for whoever collected the sample, embarrassing for the NYPD to have collected samples in this way."

"Yes, but I want you to understand it was an informant,

not us, an informant who collected it, but still, with the papers the way they are, you understand."

Mario nodded. "You may be interested in this. I found something on Twining's neck. Just a trace." He handed a sheet of paper to Jenson.

There was an indecipherable word written across the bottom of a computer-generated chart. Jenson looked up.

"A chemical analysis of a scraping taken from the deceased's neck. Most of the stuff found there was to be expected, but that chemical was not. It's an alkaloid, plant origin, one I've never seen before. It shouldn't be there."

Jenson handed the paper back. "Well, if you've never heard of it before, then it's unlikely that an assassin has. Besides, who knows what could have gotten on him during the autopsy."

Mario shrugged.

Jenson got up to leave. "The investigation is closed," he said firmly.

Mario stood up and took Jenson's outstretched hand. He withdrew it and looked in his hand. One small packet. Confusion and anger mixed on his face. "You owe me the other half."

"The investigation's over. I couldn't . . ."

"I did the work, man. I did it. Just 'cause you don't want it . . ."

Jenson shrugged. "Nothing I can do." Trying to suppress the smile that wanted to erupt from his face, he turned to the door. It felt good to shut that little bastard up. It felt good.

CHAPTER 20

LeVander shook his head. "I tried, but she don't want to come out. Said those pages was all she got."

David sat across the fake oak table in the conference room overlooking downtown Brooklyn. Walsh crouched at one end, his forehead nearly touching the lamp that hung over the center of the table. Walsh's eerie presence continued to unnerve David. LeVander seemed to take no notice, and Light sprawled over the far end of the table, snoring, wholly unconcerned with Walsh's gray pallor, curved spine, and pointed nose.

No diary, no Evelyn Jefferson. David couldn't blame her. After all, the word was around, and no matter what she thought of Light's dick these days, it was enough to keep you in hiding.

"So we have nothing," Walsh said. "Nothing at all."

LeVander pushed a bundle of papers fastened with a rubber band across the table toward Walsh. "She want me to deliver these to somebody name Walsh. Said to get her some money for 'em."

Walsh ruffled through the papers and slid them across to David.

David pulled the rubber band off and pulled down the covering sheet. Copies of the diary, it looked like. The whole diary. David looked up at LeVander. "She's still got the original."

LeVander nodded. "Had me go make the copies."

David took the bundle and left the room. A moment later he reappeared with three stacks. He slid one to Walsh, one to LeVander, and kept one himself. It was an hour before David looked up. Walsh and LeVander were staring at him.

"Nothing so far as I can see," Walsh said, ruffling the pages as if the noise would somehow bring the puzzle together.

A travel log of appointments and trips, but no names. Other than Vance and Twining, no names at all. Why was this diary so important to someone, anyone? Something embarrassing politically? But what could be more embarrassing to a politician than fucking a twenty-two-year-old when you're sixty-some and looking for older women's votes?

"David, do you remember the Profumo affair?" Walsh asked.

David shook his head.

"That English defense-department guy in the sixties?" LeVander asked.

Surprised, David shot a look at LeVander.

LeVander couldn't hold David's eyes. He looked to Walsh then down, embarrassed. "I started college," he said, hanging his head. "Contemporary history."

Walsh shook his head. "One isn't sure how one feels about having lived through history, contemporary or otherwise." Walsh's smile turned his pallor into a mottle of pink and gray. "In any event, this Profumo was keeping company with a call girl . . . I don't remember her name. A real beauty. The tabloids had a field day and she helped them along, posing for all the photos they needed." Walsh paused. "Actually that was the first story that got me interested in the field." Walsh's mottled cheeks showed a modicum of embarrassment in glowing patches of red.

David waited until Walsh's face returned to a uniform gray before speaking. "So?"

"Yes, well apparently it wasn't the fact that Profumo was

sleeping with a lady of the evening that upset the populace. There is a long and proud upper-class history of that in England. The problem, you see, was another of her clients.''

"Who?"

"A Soviet diplomat."

"So," David finished, "the question was what secrets passed over the pillow from Profumo to the girl . . ."

"And from the girl to the Soviet."

"And if Anacleta was sleeping with someone else, it might be that someone didn't want that known."

"Ain't no sane man gonna beat up no whore 'cause she fucking somebody else." Light was up now, seemingly enlivened by the subject matter. "That's what they supposed to do."

David felt the color coming to his cheeks again. "Well, I don't think she's a whore," he said.

"But she wouldn't be completely loyal to Twining either. After all, she did have her own agenda." Walsh smiled patronizingly at David.

David turned away from the smile and looked out the window. Maybe she was a whore. How would he know? The woman had slept with him quickly enough, and quickly enough after her previous lover had died. And that previous lover had been an old man who beat her. David pushed the thought away. "Who was in the diary? Nobody."

Walsh nodded.

"But maybe," LeVander spoke, "whoever doing the hurtin' don't know that."

"Correct," Walsh said. "No one has read the diary, except Anacleta and now us. The slicing gentleman may not have known the contents."

David didn't like the drift of the conversation, first that Anacleta was a whore, then that she was sleeping with killers. David could take the first easier than the second. "Who killed Twining then?"

Walsh was silent.

"Nobody would kill Twining to take him out, if they could do a Profumo," David said.

"Unless they couldn't do no Profumo without bringing it all down on themselves," LeVander said slowly.

David stared out the window at the green church steeple dominating the view across Atlantic Avenue. So Twining had been into something with somebody who could have killed him. But what? He did nothing, was nothing, a zero. And who would make a green church steeple? David stood and walked to the window while the conversation went on behind him. Maybe the view of Brooklyn was better. That green steeple set the view, the flat tops of the brownstones stretching as far as the eye could see. It was beautiful in its own way. The hill leading up to Prospect Park in the background, Brooklyn seeming to rush up to meet the sky, a clear blue today, dotted with puffy cumulus clouds.

"So, you can do that, Mr. Cohen?" LeVander's voice was raised above the din that the conversation behind him had become.

Maybe the steeple was copper and tarnished green.

"Wednesday, could you do it Wednesday?" LeVander's voice came again.

They had to have known that would happen. Copper had always tarnished, back to the Greeks and Romans.

"Yeah, I gonna show this boy how do some work. None a that fancy show-off shit, the real work."

David spun around to see LeVander giving Light a "you're embarassing me" look.

"So, you can take her out on Wednesday? Keep her out for a while?"

"Anacleta? Sure. Sure. Why?"

"I may not like my mother, but I gotta protect her." LeVander slid his chair out and got up, beckoning Light to follow. "I think maybe it should only be two people on this here, Light. Just Walsh and me," LeVander said as the door closed behind them.

David watched until the door closed completely. *Accessory to Burg One, David. You're moving up in the world.*

* * *

Light watched LeVander pedal away. This gonna be good. Finally get a chance to show LeVander what real burglary about. Not that show-off kind a shit that Franklin do. Light snorted as he turned toward the bodega. *College robber. Ain't right. Got to get you burglary chops on the street, not from some dean.* Light laughed. *Always thought Franklin got that scholarship from bending over for that dean.* Light opened the glass case and pulled out a forty of Old English, dropped two dollars on the counter, and walked out into the spring sunshine, strolling over to his stoop.

Yeah, that's what, bent over for some dean. Now the real burg is like the one he done on that Twining office. That's the real burg. Don't need no preparation or nothing. Just your wits about you, that's all. Light pulled a napkin out and slowly wiped the sides of the bottle. LeVander going over to look the place over. You didn't need none a that. Just keep your wits about you.

Light took a deep pull on the forty and looked around the neighborhood. The boys not coming over to him no more, not since that thing with the congressman. Well, he get LeVander back after this here, then those boys come back. Yeah, he'd explain it all to LeVander, all about how you do burgs.

LeVander slowly pedaled up Eighty-sixth Street. He hadn't used the bicycle-messenger outfit since that thing with the Palintinos. It felt funny, the canvas bag with the Velcro fasteners hanging from his shoulder. The doormen still stood by the doorway, the same ones as a half hour before. Pushing himself up in the saddle, he started pedaling toward the park.

He saw Light's face as it had looked when LeVander left him standing on Nostrand and Pacific. He didn't want to listen to Light talking about no real burglaries. Told Light had to do some prep. Told him three, four times, but Light don't listen. LeVander tried suggestin', orderin', nothing worked. Light just keep on talkin' about real burglaries. How he was gonna show LeVander.

LeVander swung the bike right up Madison. He didn't want Light along; that was the truth. Certainly not for the setup. Maybe later. Maybe later he could give Light something make him feel like he somebody. LeVander owed Light something. Light had introduced him to Franklin, taught him at first. Then Franklin taught him. Taught him all the important stuff about alarms, locks, security. All the important stuff. Then after, Franklin started that business, installing alarms. Took LeVander on as a partner. Franklin taught him a lot too.

Don't let emotion control, that's what Franklin say. It's a business, not no friends thing. Yeah, LeVander didn't want Light along. LeVander glanced at his watch. 3:30. Probably change at four. That what Franklin say. Eight to four and four to twelve. That's what them doormen work.

The bastard. That's what, a bastard. Mario wiped down the table, hard. Had been all day, wiping down the table hard. Wasn't right, that's what Mario thought, wasn't right when a man does the work he says he's gonna do for another man to just say "fuck you." Wasn't right. Wasn't, that's all, just wasn't.

"Night, Mario."

Dr. Mansfield. Always the last to go. Mario grunted at him. Didn't really answer, just a grunt. All he'd done today, just grunted at this one and that. They ignored him. Just Mario, they'd think, in another of his funks. Just that asshole Mario, wiping down after our work. Wiping down the last of all that dead shit that floats out of bodies. Just Mario. *Shit, just Mario,* Mario thought with his finger astride his nose.

And that bastard cop, Jenson. Thinking just 'cause Mario likes a little toot, he some kind of less than life. Wasn't like Mario was doing crack. Just a little toot when the opportunity arose. Besides, he just did it 'cause when he had it he had some women. That was the reason. Wasn't so much that he wanted the toot or the high. No, it was different. He was a fat, fucking Italian, he knew that. But when he had a couple of grams, then the women were all over him. He wondered when the last time that bastard Jenson had women all over him. Maybe that's why he fucked with Mario. Just so he could show off his power.

Mario listened while the door closed behind Dr. Mansfield. Well, Mario didn't care about power over a cop. That was shit. What he cared about was the women. That's what, and it wasn't like that bastard cop could stop him from getting that kind of power. Let Jenson have his little power. Mario'd have his. That's what.

Pulling off his gloves, Mario walked into the office and

picked up the phone. If that bastard cop wouldn't, then Mario'd just go elsewhere. He'd call Walsh, that's what he'd do. Another bastard, most likely. But that gray-skinned bastard was different. He knew how to get what he wanted from people with coke. Known that shit for years, that gray. The phone was picked up.

"Walsh," Mario said, "we gotta talk."

CHAPTER 21

"Quit playing with that thing, Turt," Light said, pulling his cup over to him. "Don't never stop with that thing. Always got to be pushin' or pullin' on somethin'."

LeVander flipped the white plastic box closed and glanced out the window of the coffee shop. Nobody much called him Turt no more. Just Light and sometimes his mother. It had changed since that thing last year and the job. Didn't feel like he needed no street name no more. He felt like a regular member of society now. A nine to five. That is, up till today.

LeVander wondered what they looked like here. Out of place for sure. Most of the people in the coffee shop looked like regulars, bored with the view of Anacleta's building. It'd take about five seconds for anybody to get bored with it, but LeVander kept on looking. It helped him ignore Light's lectures coming one after another, first about one topic then another, with a connection that seemed logical only to Light's mind. Maybe they seem like a father and son.

LeVander let his mind wander as Light rambled on about what LeVander needed to know about this and that. Always using some kind a euphemism for saying stealin'. LeVander didn't respond when he talked about Franklin showing off. He felt a little irritation but he pushed it down. It wouldn't do no good to take on Light. Nobody paid Light no mind anyway.

LeVander glanced at his watch. No cops, no private guards. They had stopped after the first night. He pulled out the white box again.

"You listening to me?" Light glared at the box. "You boys don't do nothing but play with them little gadget boxes. Don't do nothing for your mind."

LeVander ignored him. He liked the way Franklin had taught him to put the remote activator in a Game Boy box. Nobody think nothing of a young nigger playing with a Game Boy, 'cept maybe what Light say, wasting you mind. LeVander had played with that Game Boy for the last three days, since he put that short in the alarm. He press the button, the alarm go through to the cops and the private guards. The police stopped after the third call, just like Franklin say. No privates came. That meant they wasn't on no private company service. That was lucky. LeVander didn't have a plan to take care of private company having their people there all night.

Second day the alarm company come out, but they couldn't find nothing wrong. Not the way LeVander laid it in, they wouldn't. They'd have to go over the whole installation. So they'd hit tonight, about eleven. Come in on one shift, out on another.

LeVander glanced at his watch. David should be picking her up right now. Two hours. LeVander turned back to Light. Two hours more of Light's drone.

David gulped as the elevator groaned to a stop at the twenty-seventh floor. He'd been fairly relaxed until LeVander had started with the questions. Did the apartment have an alarm? David had no idea. The only thing he remembered was seeing Anacleta go into a closet, hearing a few beeps like a phone pad. LeVander had scowled, looked down, and started to repack his black bag. In a moment David would know about the alarm.

Reaching into his pocket, David flipped the switch.

LeVander had made him feel very uneasy. Just taking Anacleta out to dinner, there was maximum plausible deniability, as Nixon had said. But now... David slipped his hand out of his pocket. Concrete evidence.

It was a moment before Anacleta answered his ring. The door swung open and she gave him a quick kiss, pulling him inside with her right hand.

"I'll just be a moment," she said, leading him to the living room.

David again fought the nervousness, guilt, and anxiety. A moment was too long. He just wanted to get out. He fingered the switch in his pocket. Just drop it somewhere, leave it on the floor or behind the couch, and get out.

"You've never met my brother, Julio, have you, David?"

David stopped short. A man was rising from the couch. Stocky, with that brownish tan color of the South American mix of Spanish and Indian. The big smile, the hand coming at him. Act cool. David took the hand and returned the smile as best he could.

"Live here?" David blurted out.

"No," he said with a Spanish accent. "Just arrive. Only staying with Anacleta a few weeks. See *cuidad grande.*"

David loosened his grip. What now? He had to plant the device, but... LeVander didn't know anyone was here. The man sat and gestured David to the couch next to him.

"I'll be right back." Anacleta disappeared into the bedroom.

The bathroom. "May I?" David gestured.

The man spread his hands expansively, but stopped short of *mi casa es tu casa.*

David nodded and disappeared behind the closed door. Spotless. The fucking bathroom was spotless. He'd have no problem hiding the box in his bathroom. Stick it under three dirty towels and nobody'd find it for a week. Looked like Anacleta didn't have dirty towels.

David slid open the medicine cabinet. Metal, of course. Metal trash can with not a speck of trash in it. Toilet. Porcelain. What the fuck was porcelain? Well, whatever it was, it wasn't metal. He pulled open the cover of the tank. Water to within an inch of the top. He dropped the cover.

Leave it in the corner? Brother Julio would definitely see it. David looked around desperately. Nothing. He looked at the corner, behind the toilet. Julio had just arrived. That might mean he doesn't know what she has where. David pulled the box out of his pocket. Just a black box. Could be anything. No reason to be suspicious.

David pulled back the shower curtain. A hanging plastic shelf next to the soap. Have to hope Brother Julio wouldn't take a shower in the next two hours. Shit, that was the least of the problems. LeVander was going to be walking into an occupied apartment. David slid the box onto the shelf next to the soap, pulled the shower curtain closed, and turned to leave. Have to do.

A moment later they were out the door. A last-minute offer for Julio to join them accepted, David followed Anacleta and Julio to the elevator. *It'll have to do. Just have to do.* A feeling of dread mixed with the guilt and anxiety.

LeVander pushed the Game Boy back in his pocket, picked up his bag, and walked to the entrance, Light chasing after him.

"Now, listen here, we got to be careful here walking in. Can't just walk in a place like this."

LeVander ignored Light's protestations. He didn't even turn to look back at him but crossed Second Avenue and slipped into the bushes on Eighty-seventh Street, just behind Anacleta's building. Light crept up beside him.

"How we gonna get through that door? Lock and all. We got to go up front, fake in. That's the way."

LeVander shushed him with a hand motion and reached into his bag. He pulled out a small cylindrical, metal object and held it against the door. He put an earphone in his ear.

"What the fuck you doin' now? More a that asshole Franklin show-off shit."

LeVander waved for quiet more forcefully.

"Don't do nothing but make sure you get convicted when

you get caught, that shit,'' Light mumbled, looking over to the street. "Think you a fucking doctor with his stethoscope or some shit."

LeVander scowled at Light and turned back to the laser microphone. No sounds came from the earpiece. No one in the basement, at least close to the door. LeVander pulled the earphone out, rolled the cord around the mike, and stuffed it back in the bag.

"You gonna listen now? What that shit about?"

"Laser mike, can hear inside with that. Nobody home," LeVander mumbled as he reached into his pocket.

"Fine, ain't nobody inside, but how we gonna get through that door? Big, green, steel monster with a big Segal lock. Ain't never gonna get through that." Light scowled and turned away.

Ignoring him, LeVander pulled a ring of keys out of his pocket, selected one, and slipped it in the lock. He wiggled it for a second until the lock flipped.

Light followed him inside. "Where you get a key? If I knowed you had a key, then this here woulda been different. Would a done it same way. Where you get it?"

"Made it," LeVander mumbled. He didn't have the time or the inclination to explain the electronic pick he had used the other day or the system by which, once the pick opened the door, it recorded the pattern of the lock and had allowed him to make a key to fit. Nor how he had made a dozen or so identical keys so that in case an anomaly of one made it unusable, some other might work.

LeVander checked the alarm-system board next to the door. It flashed, activating an alarm to the police and the service. It would be ignored. He said nothing about it to Light.

Carefully closing the door behind Light, LeVander hurried down the hall, waving Light to follow. The green work uniforms should keep them above suspicion as they walked the halls, which should be a short time anyway. They found the service elevator, jumped in, and pressed twenty-seven. This was the easy part. Getting in the apartment and finding whatever it was they were looking for would be harder.

LeVander was a little confused about what they wanted. More diaries, Mr. Cohen had said. Something that would help him make sense of this diary. The diary itself hadn't been of much use. A list of times of meetings, some names, but not much. Something else, anything else, that's what Mr. Cohen had said. The last minute before they left, Walsh had been clear. He pulled LeVander aside and whispered. Videotapes, he said. Unmarked videos. Walsh acted as if he were sure.

The door opened on the twenty-seventh floor, and LeVander stepped out. Light followed, crouching and looking very much the burglar, not a green-clad workman. LeVander motioned for him to stand up. Light obeyed, but reluctantly. LeVander turned to look for apartment 27F.

Around the corner, past the elevators, he found it, next to the laundry room, just as David had said. Perfect. Glancing in the laundry room and seeing no one, he slipped in, with Light following.

"What you doing now? Gonna fix some washing machines?"

LeVander waved him to silence and zipped open the bag. He ignored the sound as Light collapsed in a heap next to him. LeVander pulled out a small box and pushed it against the wall. Placing the earphone in his ear, he flipped the switch.

Light let his head hang and spoke in a defeated voice. "Another mike?"

LeVander shook his head. "Remote switch. Mr. Cohen supposed to leave a tape." A noise crackled through the earphone. Conversation, Cohen, a woman's voice. LeVander stopped. Another man's. That meant there had been someone else in the apartment; someone may still be there. He bent to listen further. A few more minutes of conversation and then silence. The door opening, a few words, several beeps. Then silence.

The apartment was empty, burglar alarm set. It sounded like an Ademco. Could slip the door, then have thirty seconds to disarm it. Flipping the switch to rewind, LeVander found the part with the beeps, hooked the earphone to the descrambler, and flipped the switch. Four numbers popped up on the screen: 7-6-3-5. LeVander flipped the switch off, repacked the machines, and stuffed them in his bag.

He gestured for Light to follow as he left the laundry room and walked to 27F. Light started to speak, but LeVander gestured him to silence. LeVander slipped the picks from his shirt pocket; a moment later they were in.

Light closed the door. "There's an alarm. What you do now?"

LeVander said nothing but pulled on a pair of tight gloves, gesturing Light to do the same, walked to the pad, and punched in 7-6-3-5. Nothing. The red light remained on and the machine seemed to pulse as if ready to blow. LeVander punched the numbers again. Again nothing. He glanced at his watch. Twenty seconds. He pulled out the descrambler, checked the numbers again. 7-6-3-5. Set for Ademco. He check the brand. No, it was Napco. Frantically, Levander flipped the switch to the new alarm maker and punched the convert button. 8-7-4-6 popped up. He punched those numbers. The light switched to green.

Light shook his head. "Too much fancy-ass shit."

LeVander waved him to silence. "Check out anything looks like a diary," he whispered. "Put it all back just like it was. Don't want nobody to know we was here."

Light nodded and walked toward the bedroom. LeVander flipped the remote switch and followed the beep to the bathroom. There, on the shelf. Grabbing the box, he put it on top of his bag in the living room. He glanced at his watch. 11:30. They had a half hour at least, maybe more. Should be enough.

David glanced at his watch. Eleven. The service had been fast for a fancy restaurant, and they had dallied as much as could be expected. If it were just him and Anacleta, they could walk in the moonlight. He could try to get her to his place, maybe succeed. But what could he do with Julio? If Julio left now, he'd catch LeVander.

David dropped his American Express card on the table. He'd have to think of something else, but what? If he was too obvious, they'd suspect him when they discovered the burglary.

They were on the street, walking toward the park. Julio was shaking David's hand, thanking him. David watched helplessly as Julio disappeared into a cab. Anacleta snuggled close.

"You live in Brooklyn, right?" she whispered in his ear, as if it were an invitation to the experience of a lifetime.

David guided her toward a cab. It might be, he thought, as he slipped his arm around her trim waist. He wondered if sex or worry was the stronger drive in Jewish men.

Wasn't nothing here. No diary, no notes, no nothing. Not that he'd know. He wasn't too good at reading printed stuff, he wasn't shit at reading handwriting. Light poked through another drawer of papers. Wasn't gonna tell LeVander. Told one, be all over neighborhood by night. He wasn't gonna tell nobody. Didn't matter. There wasn't nothing here no way.

Light shoved the door closed and moved over toward the TV. Moved past the bed, that big kind with the brass around the top and the pillars. Over to the TV. Nice TV, one a those big ones, twenty-seven inch. All fit in its own cabinet, set right into the wall. All that fake wood, shiny and nice. Light ran his gloved fingers over the red wooden case, over the doors underneath, with the brass fixtures. That's what he need, a TV. Big fucker. Like this. Whole neighborhood come over, watch the Knicks. Yeah, that'd show 'em.

Have to get this sucker out the cabinet though. Couldn't get it out a here with this cabinet, no way. Light ran his fingers along the edges of the TV, between the TV and the cabinet. Not much room. Tight fit. Built right in. Tight motherfuckin' fit. Just that wood right up against that TV. Nothing along the edge but that little bit of brass with the writin' on. Light ran his fingers over it. It give a little, like a button. He pushed. Just a little, but it make a motor whir, make the door panel under the TV slide open. Inside was tapes, just like in the video store, row after row. But they was in blank boxes. Just plain, some . . . company name on others. JVC, Maxell.

Light pulled one out. LeVander be there for hours, poking through this and that. Franklin got him being a fucking accountant, cataloguing all that shit. Light slipped it in the VCR. Franklin doing all that fancy-ass college shit. Shouldn't be no burglar going to college. Have LeVander going to college now. If I'd known then, Light thought, never woulda brought LeVander over to see Franklin. Franklin be turning LeVander into a pussy-ass *cat burglar*, like Franklin. Light felt like wiggling his ass when he said it. Faggoty little *cat burglar*.

Light turned the volume down. Wasn't no reason to let LeVander hear him watching the movies. Franklin probably turning LeVander into a faggot just like him. Not that Franklin ever acted like no faggot. But getting that scholarship.

The TV sputtered, gray snow, a picture too dim to see, then snow, then . . . Light sat up. Man, that woman got some titties. Not too big, but with that light brown skin and them nips. Just laying across that bed, now going back. Them legs spread. How women can move so slow, rolling them hips. Got to tell LeVander about this.

Light was at the door when he heard it. Just a creak, then a whoosh as the door opened. Like the guy came in with a rush of air. Light froze. Guy had to see LeVander, soon as he went in the living room. Light turned down the sound, cracked the bedroom door, and looked out. He just saw the guy's back, big guy, stocky. Had a jacket, nice jacket, tailored for a left carry.

LeVander froze as he heard the door open. Couldn't be Light. Wouldn't be going outside, not without telling him. LeVander thought about the lamp, thought about cutting it off, but that would give it away for sure. No, guy might think he left it on. Or could be the woman. Sounded like a guy though. Had that heavy feel to it.

LeVander turned slowly and stared at the archway where the hall to the front led. Only a little hall, maybe four feet, but where he was kneeling, he was obscured. The closet door opened, then closed. Maybe the guy hadn't noticed. So what? So what if he hadn't? Would soon enough.

LeVander crept behind an armchair and waited. He saw the gun first. It inched into the room, leading the hand by six inches. LeVander crept to the wall next to the hallway. He was behind the gun now. The man didn't see him, not yet.

The gun turned into the living room and stared into the far corner a moment before scanning the bookshelves along the far wall. LeVander crept closer. A lamp stood between him and the hand, the arm extended into the room.

LeVander straightened, flattened against the wall, and slithered toward the hand. The barrel stared into the corner of the bookshelf where LeVander had been crouching, as if it smelled the scent of its now moved prey. That prey, flattened against the wall, waited for the shoulder, then the head. LeVander needed the head. He felt for something along the wall. A shelf. Knickknacks, a head, African. Franklin would disapprove, destroying art. LeVander grabbed it. No time for that now. No way to get out without being noticed now.

The barrel continued its perusal. The head followed the hand, the face swung to LeVander, the barrel now stared at his nose. The African head was safe. The face smiled.

LeVander stood motionless, like the prey he was, using his last defense.

"Put it down," the face said.

LeVander did not move. Would the face shoot? Maybe, but if he put down the head, it didn't matter. LeVander wasn't going to give it up now. The thumb moved, pulling the hammer slowly away. Metal clicked against metal as a round slid into the chamber. LeVander slowly replaced the head.

The barrel inched away.

"How did you get past alarm?" the voice asked with a Spanish lilt.

LeVander shrugged. "Know about alarms," he said, as the shadows shifted behind the man. The man didn't seem to notice.

"Alarm not so good, heh?" The voice was relaxed, almost happy.

LeVander glanced over the man's shoulder. Light was moving along the wall, inching closer to the man, holding something in his hand. LeVander turned back to the man and shrugged. "Good as any. Nothing foolproof."

"Or burglar proof, heh?" The man laughed a rich laugh, a laugh of true enjoyment. "You are lucky, you know that."

LeVander looked down, sweeping his eyes across the hallway behind Light. It was a cane, that's what Light had, a cane.

"How come?"

"If the carpet was red, then I kill you already. But carpet is white. Anacleta doesn't like stains. She like nice things like the head you had before. She like that." The man pulled the gun back, running his fingers along the barrel. "So I take you somewhere, kill you there. Where you like to die, by the seacoast, by forest? Heh. Whatever you want." The man laughed again.

LeVander saw the flash as the metal cane leaped above the man's head, then the crash as Light tripped and headed toward the floor. The man turned. LeVander grabbed the head. Light hit the floor; the man aimed. LeVander brought the head down. A rush of air left the man as he crumpled to the floor.

"Who put fucking carpets in the hall? Ain't no place for a carpet." Light pulled himself up. "Fucking white people . . . and wanna-be white people."

LeVander stepped over the crumpled man. "We got to get out a here."

Light brushed his pants. "Find anything?"

LeVander shook his head as he pulled Light toward the door.

Light held back. "Wait a minute. You got to see something." He led LeVander into the bedroom. The video was still playing.

There was a man with Anacleta, his tongue alternately probing her various orifices.

"Where that guy come from?" Light asked.

"Who is it?"

Light shrugged. "Ain't no porn star, that for damn sure."

"Take that tape," LeVander said, turning back to the living room.

"All of em?"

LeVander spun back. Light opened the door, revealing about thirty tapes. LeVander nodded.

David kissed Anacleta lightly as she stepped into the cab. "Friday," he said.

She smiled and nodded. The cab roared down Columbus Avenue.

He felt a falling in his chest as the cab disappeared. It had been a while since he'd had that feeling. Since Janie left, he'd felt as if he wanted them to leave as soon as he met them, as if he were running away.

He didn't feel that with Anacleta. It was the playful Anacleta with whom he had spent this evening. That other one, the taciturn Anacleta, had not appeared. It couldn't be love, he told himself. Shouldn't be. But the attraction was there. The visions of a life together were there. Unlike Janie, this woman wouldn't insist on David's going into a commercial practice for the regular hours and safety.

But if he were asked to choose, what then? If he were asked, as he was with Janie, to choose between her and his curiosity, his passion, what then? It was ironic that, as he asked the question, he was indulging both, the burglary stroking his curiosity while Anacleta was stroking him. Dishonesty made a bad start for a relationship; isn't that what they said? How about treachery? Sleep with me while I rob you.

The strangest thing, he supposed, was that he had forgotten about the burglary as they made love, remembering only when the phone rang. It had gone well, the phone call said. With a minor complication. David had covered the call with questions that seemed like the discussion he would have with the wife of a man who'd just been arrested. She had asked if it was work, and he'd said yes. She smiled that smile that hit him in the center of the chest and made him happy and sad at the same time. Then she said she'd go.

David picked up yesterday's *Times*. He tried to read but couldn't. He wished Walsh would come over now and tell him what was so goddamned important. But Walsh said tomorrow. David picked up the remote. There was always cable.

Walsh pushed the tape into the VCR and clicked it on. The image flashed up on the monitor. Good image; clear, sharp lines. Walsh liked the SVGA. Worth every penny he had paid for it.

He was glad he hadn't shown Cohen right away. Cohen had that dreamy sound on the phone, as if that woman had gotten to him, gotten to him deeply. It was hard to counter that feeling, especially hard with a series of films of his beloved indecently involved with others. Walsh smiled. Indecently . . . a remnant of his Victorian youth, he supposed. He certainly didn't think of it as indecency. He hardly thought of anything at all as indecent now.

The image from the monitor danced across his eyes. She was indecently talented at indecency, as was clearly evident. It wasn't her indecency that concerned him, nor her skill at it, as he watched the bodies turn and grope. There, three quarters, another second. No. Damn.

Walsh leaned back to enjoy the show. There had to be another scene. They would have needed it as much as he. Wouldn't be much blackmail value in a white ass dancing in the dark.

A moment later the crescendo came, and so did the white ass. A few words, then the man turned. Walsh tapped the mouse. The image froze. Perfect. Walsh moved the cursor over the man's head, tapped the button, and dragged the square until it covered the man's face. Examining the detail within the square, he shifted the mouse, trying to exclude all detail showing where the photo had been taken, or what he was doing, or that he was with someone else, or that he was naked. Just a head shot.

He tapped the button again. The rest of the image disappeared, the photo of the man's face growing to fill the monitor. Another few keystrokes and the photo was black and white. Just a news photo now. Maybe this important man at the beach somewhere. Let them speculate as to what he had. They wouldn't be able to print anything until he told them. He'd tell them it was sensitive. Not until he has the whole story, he'd say. They would agree; they'd have no choice.

The story wasn't a congressman in some woman's pants; that occurred every day. No legs, as they say, especially with the subject congressman dead. That's what he'd tell them anyway.

He tapped the mouse button, ejected the tape from the VCR, replaced it, and started the whole routine with another tape.

An hour later he had six 8½-by-11 black-and-white photos. He glanced at his watch. Five A.M. Good. Still night shift at the paper.

Walsh pushed the photos in his case and stood, slowly straightening his back. It was a good night's work. Walking to the bathroom to throw some water on his face, he pulled off his glasses, bent low over the sink, and rubbed the cold water across his neck. He wiped his face dry, groped for his glasses, slipped them on, wiped the hair from his eyes, and looked at the reflection. He looked better. It wouldn't be long now. He felt it in his whole body. Not long.

He picked up the phone. A groggy voice answered on the third ring. At least Cohen may have slept off some of that love sickness. Walsh gave him the address and waited while he wrote it down. Six, he told Cohen, then made it a quarter of.

It was 5:30 when Walsh stepped out of the shower. The buzzer rang, the doorman announcing a visitor. Cohen was early too. A moment later, still groggy, he stood, light rainwater dripping off the brim of his San Francisco 49ers hat, in the hallway at Walsh's door. Walsh waved him to follow.

The room was large, the entire east wall a window overlooking the East River. David wondered why East Siders cherished this view. It was ugly, if one were honest, even from this height. Factories lining the Queens shore, a dirty barge or two the main events of an average day. But this was an address in demand. Reporters for trashy tabloids apparently did well.

Walsh strode across the large living room to a desk with a computer stand tucked in the corner. Slipping into the chair before the screen as if David would naturally follow, Walsh pushed the tape into the VCR. David dropped into a chair across the desk with a good view of the monitor.

"This is important?" David asked.

"This is the point," Walsh said, snapping on the computer and turning to David while it warmed up. "This wasn't just Twining. The plan was larger than that."

The Windows program manager appeared and, Walsh snapped the mouse twice. A new screen appeared, a dial tone, beeps of a phone dialing, and a request for disk one.

Walsh pulled a 3.5-inch floppy from his case and snapped it into the drive. "What we didn't know, we know now."

"And that is?" David felt the cobwebs clearing, but he still wasn't following.

"The time bomb," Walsh said as the screen cleared and a photo of a brown-haired man in his mid-forties appeared. Walsh pressed another button, and the computer whirred.

"The diary told us nothing of Anacleta's plan," Walsh said, turning back to David, "only where she was and when.

That was significant only when combined with the whereabouts of others."

The computer stopped whirring. Two photos flashed up on the screen, side by side. To the left the photo just entered, to the right another photo. It looked like the same man. A legend at the bottom of the screen read, "First of three". A short blurb appeared under the photo to the right. David leaned forward.

> Eric Morrel, Yale Law School, 1968, Rogers and Wells, NYC, 1968–1979. Elected to Congress from the fourth district of Oklahoma, 1984. Currently serving seventh term.

A moment later Walsh had gone through six photos, all congressmen. Walsh silently slipped the last floppy disk back in his case and turned his attention to the computer.

David sat back. The cobwebs had cleared, replaced by a weak-kneed feeling. Six congressmen, six photos. The common denominator, Anacleta. David wanted to be angry, but at whom? Anacleta never claimed she was pure. She never claimed she was anything. David never gave her a chance to claim.

He could hardly be angry at her for deceit, not after he had set up the burglary of her apartment—and the destruction of his own illusions. Walsh bent over the keyboard, pecking away, his gray nose almost touching the keyboard. He'd had the decency to allow David his time. Or maybe it wasn't decency, just his unbridled curiosity driving him to the next computer investigation.

The computer spewed out more information, some of which Walsh jotted down in his spiral notebook, some of which he recorded on a floppy. David turned away, not wanting to know the rest of the bad news. On the river a red tug with yellow tires strapped to its side struggled with a barge. The tug seemed used to it, as if it knew what to do and when. David envied that red-and-yellow tug.

"Sorry to do this, lad, but I wanted you to see this," Walsh said and, without looking at David, poked a button on the VCR. The engine whirred; the monitor flashed a white ass bouncing between a pair of light brown thighs.

"I cued it so you wouldn't have to see it all." Walsh sounded apologetic, but a thin smile creased his lips.

The white ass tensed then, seconds later, relaxed. It wasn't so much the pain, David thought, as emptiness. As if that part of himself that filled his chest had left, not willing to face this with him. The white ass slid back over the white knees, the upper body attached slumping over next to Anacleta. She looked peaceful, David thought, happy. He wondered if she looked like that with him. His eyes didn't want to drift over to the man, the white-assed man.

"I cut out a part earlier on," Walsh said.

David wondered why he hadn't cut out this. What was so important that his imagination had to be robbed of the opportunity to protect him, to create the scene as Walsh described it. He wouldn't have put in the part about her looking happy. His imagination would have painted the scene with her face awash with the look of an assembly-line worker, doing the job without being present. Putting in the time. Not the way she looked when she was with him.

Walsh tried to hide it as he pulled the tape from the VCR, but he couldn't, not really. There was that look of compassion on his face, those sappy eyes. But deeper, there was a smile. David turned away. Hard as it was to look at that sap, it was harder still to see that smile. Better the tug, David thought. The red-and-yellow tug, right out front, just red and yellow.

The mouse clicked as Walsh tapped it. David turned back, hoping the picture was gone. It was not. Jenson's pocked face had filled the screen. Why did that make it worse?

"In the part I cut," Walsh said, "Jenson took a sample."

"A sample?" David's voice cracked.

"Of her vaginal discharge. To be compared to the discharge found on Twining's penis at the time of his death." Walsh tapped the mouse again, and the picture disappeared from the screen. "He gave it to Mario—you remember Mario, at the morgue?"

David nodded.

"Well, he wanted Mario to compare it. Do the PCR. Mario's the night tech there. So Mario calls me yesterday, tells me he has this test. Jenson doesn't want it, would I be interested."

Walsh flipped off the computer and turned to face David full on. "I couldn't understand that. Why would Jenson not want the test results? I mean, I didn't know what the results *were* even, just that they were on this case and they were results of a test he had wanted Mario to do on the QT."

David found himself drawn in by the story despite himself.

"The results were a comparison of the known sample from Twining's penis and the sample that Jenson brought to Mario."

"Well?"

"It didn't make sense until I saw this tape this morning after Light and LeVander got back."

"Did it match?"

Walsh nodded. "She's the girl."

It didn't really mean anything, David told himself. She had been there that night. She had been his girlfriend. They had made love. That didn't mean anything. It just meant that she and he had made love the night he died. Somebody else could have come in to kill him. It didn't have to be Anacleta. She didn't even have to know about it.

David told himself that, but it didn't help much. These tapes had to be blackmail. Why else would Jenson have given up the investigation? She must have called him back, shown him the tapes. And the tapes, Anacleta had to have been part of that. Part of cutting Light's dick.

The question was what to do now. He could just walk away, ignore Anacleta, ignore Walsh, ignore Light. David thought of Light's dick. No assurance Anacleta and her friends would ignore him. He could get the diary and return it. But how? Go find Evelyn and beat it out of her? Not likely. Wherever she was hiding, it was not likely to be a neighborhood he could slip into and out of easily.

Go to the police? Jenson wasn't likely to be supportive, not after this. And if David went to someone else? The only thing he had were films of congressmen sleeping with Anacleta. It might motivate an investigation, but the thought of giving up Anacleta still troubled him. There was this strange warmth that pervaded him when he thought of her. His heart caught by a professional blackmailer. Maybe that was her strength. Men still loved her, right to the end.

He wondered if he should meet her as planned. If he didn't, she would surely know he had been involved in the burglary. And if she knew, her handlers knew as well. And if her handlers knew, he was dead. Looking back at Walsh, still pecking at the keyboard, David knew he had no choice. He had to meet her.

Walsh looked up as the door closed behind David. Too absorbed. Too absorbed by the damn computer. Hadn't even noticed Cohen leave. He considered running after Cohen but decided against it. What could he say? Cohen, you shouldn't be in love with this woman? That never worked. Cohen would have to work it out himself, like everyone else.

There was the danger, but Cohen knew about that. Besides, it was doubtful that the cartel knew that Cohen had set up the burglary. Walsh had to chuckle at himself. Never thought the day would come when he would worry about a lawyer's safety, especially when Walsh himself was in more danger. *If the cartel suspected anyone, it would be me,* Walsh thought, *not Cohen.*

Walsh tapped the keyboard. The screen sprang to life again. Comparative voting records. Walsh punched in the names of the six congressmen. The computer whirred. The records spewed out. Walsh tapped the mouse. The screen cleared. Twelve bills popped on the screen, twelve bills they all supported. Walsh tapped "print."

The solution and the proof. The question now was what to do with it. Print the story? With the videos? Maybe call one of those TV magazines? They'd pay, and pay big for this story. Sex, power, politics. Walsh thought about it. It'd

HOSTILE WITNESS

be nice. Fame, maybe a job on TV. He wasn't very photogenic, but that didn't seem to matter as much anymore, at least not for men.

He pushed the thought away. The cartel wasn't likely to leave him alone after that. And he wasn't likely to survive the attention that would surely come to him. No, he needed a front to break this story. The police. The FBI. Let them do the investigation. Cohen would be pissed. His girlfriend would go down. Walsh shrugged. He'd be saving the fool.

Go to the police? It was a choice. Of course, if he went to the police, the fame would pass him by, the attention . . . the money.

The money. The real money wasn't in TV or in the story. The real money was in corruption. A simple phone call. *I have the goods.* That's all he'd have to say. Walsh reached for the phone. That was something they understood. It was funny, you can trust a greedy man. You always know what he will do. Just a simple phone call.

Julio slung the heavy garbage bag over his shoulder. The knot he'd tied in the neck of the bag cutting into his shoulder felt good. It felt like the punishment he deserved, especially with the sound of the boat cutting slowly through the water toward the Verrazano ringing in his ears.

Julio stood in the back of the boat, waiting. It would be soon, he thought from the way the man at the wheel signaled him to stand up. The sound of the engine had changed, becoming a putting sound as the boat slowed. The man at the wheel signaled. Anywhere here, the signal meant. Julio nodded to the man.

Julio walked to the left of the boat—port, he thought they called it. The water looked murky and deep. He bent low and tried to peer beneath the surface, the rocks in the bag bouncing against his back. The water gave up none of its secrets to his eyes. The man at the wheel turned impatiently. Julio swung the bag off his shoulder. The night absorbed the splash as it slipped to the depths. Julio took a breath. Half of his failure sunk. Half of half of his failures sunk.

He turned to the man at the wheel and nodded. The boat moved slowly.

Julio sat, his back resting against the back of the boat, staring blankly as the skyline of lower Manhattan rolled through his field of vision. It wasn't his fault, he told himself. Not his fault at all. Santeria had said the same thing. It probably didn't matter, Santeria had said. Probably nothing would have been different. But Julio remembered the look in Santeria's eyes: not anger, but disappointment. It was that look that had cut Julio. That hurt him still.

The boat would be back in port in a few minutes, Julio thought. A few minutes more and he could begin the second stage of his redemption. It wasn't a redemption, Santeria had said; there was no need for a redemption. Julio felt the need. There seemed to be a black ball in the center of his chest, pulling his chest in, rounding his shoulders, pulling his head down on his neck.

As the boat pulled into port, Julio felt the black ball in his chest. It hadn't been like he had a medical history, he told himself as he stepped onto the dock and into the Blazer. It wasn't like that at all. In fact, had Santeria told him what he knew, it might have been different. He told himself that as he turned the key, as he backed the Blazer from the space and as he worked it onto the highway. It didn't help. Maybe for *norteamericanos,* those who had been brought up in the culture of blame, but not for him. Perhaps it was the training. Julio did not know. But his responsibility was for the life. Santeria had more important responsibilities.

Rockaway, Santeria had said, near the road, where someone would see it tomorrow, but not until tomorrow. A simple sounding order, Julio thought, watching the grasslands near Rockaway rush by him, until one realized the city had been good about lighting this road. Julio thought about going back, saying it was impossible. That would be wrong, he thought. Just as life was his responsibility, so was death. Especially when he caused it.

He swung right off the highway, onto a smaller highway. Seagulls circled overhead. The ocean was near. Julio turned

HOSTILE WITNESS

left, toward the center of the gulls' vortex. The road was narrow, two lanes, no shoulder, just a sheer drop to the mucky grasslands a few feet below. A body dropped there wouldn't be found for weeks. Even the stench wouldn't give it up.

But Santeria wanted the body found. Julio kept driving. A gull spiraled down to the side of the road on the left. Julio followed the flight to a collection of broken appliances, discarded furniture, and other debris heaped upon a section of dry grassland. Julio slowed. No one would notice if he pulled the Blazer in. Just another minor law violation, one that was apparently being ignored.

Julio slowed the Blazer and swung left. No one was here to ignore the violation, and he'd seen no one since he turned from the main road. He swung the Blazer around and backed onto the hard ground near the garbage. Pulling on his gray gloves, he stepped out of the Blazer, walked to the back, pulled open the rear gate, and grabbed the rug.

A few minutes later the rug lay rolled to the left of the body, gloves on top of it, and the body stood tenuously on ankles pinned in a plastic milk carton, ass resting against a washing machine. Julio examined the body, naked from the waist up. It stood, waiting to be noticed, as it would surely be in tomorrow's early light.

Julio was disappointed that the many cuts, shining red when made, had been absorbed by the gray-blue of death. But what most disappointed Julio, as he pushed the card into a pocket of the corpse's trousers, was the number of cuts, 240. Not even a quarter of the goal.

Julio stepped up into the Blazer. He had no way of knowing about the man, of course. Santeria knew, but he hadn't told Julio. Julio felt a little resentment when he thought about that now. He had been blaming himself, but if he had known about the one lung, he could have kept the man alive and maybe found out more. At least Santeria would have been sure that the man didn't know. That was as important, Santeria had said, as important as knowing the information.

Julio's spirits were lifting as he drove away from the

body. Santeria had said he would have another chance. It was important that he learn. That's what his teachers had said: learn from your mistakes. And be prepared for your next chance. Julio turned the Blazer onto the highway. He would have another chance. That was what the card was for, for his next chance.

David dropped the phone back in the cradle.
"Who was that?" Joel asked.
"Evans." David answered to the Statue of Liberty over Joel's shoulder.
"What did he say?"
"Wasn't her." That much at least was positive.
"Doesn't make any difference, you know." Joel stood to his full height. "Doesn't make any difference."
David didn't answer. It wasn't the kind of conversation in which one side would convince the other. Joel couldn't understand David's decision. David couldn't either, not really. If he listened to Joel's reasoning, he couldn't argue.
"So she wasn't there when they killed that guy in South America, so what?"
"So maybe it's a coincidence."
"Coincidence," Joel said sarcastically. "So it might be a coincidence, I'll give you that. Maybe fifty percent it's a coincidence. But that leaves fifty percent it's not, and if that fifty percent comes up, you, David Cohen, might be dead."
"If that fifty percent comes up, I might be dead anyway."
"So you walk right in, right where they can find you?"
"So I should go to the South Pole?" David let the irritation creep into his voice.
"No, you should go to the police."
"Oh, walk up to Jenson and say I saw this videotape, and you look really good."
"FBI then."
David said nothing. Joel was right, of course. He could go to the FBI. But something told him not to. Maybe the FBI was compromised too. But that wasn't it. No, it was Anacleta. He couldn't walk away from her, just couldn't.

Some part of him just stood up and said, "No."

"I'm going."

"God, David."

"Don't follow."

"Don't worry. I'll just stay here and compose an ad for a new partner."

"Sarge, how could this body have stood there all day and nobody called it in?"

Rielly shrugged, stuck the half-smoked cigar in his mouth, and handed Jenson a card. "Friend a yours, I think."

Jenson took the card. "David Cohen, Attorney at Law."

"All we found," Rielly said, pushing his great bulk over a decaying Maytag to get a better look.

"No ID?"

"That's what I said." Rielly stood next to the propped-up corpse, turned to face Jenson, and smiled, cigar sticking out of his face. "Recognize him?" Rielly asked through clenched teeth.

Jenson allowed his eyes to play over the headless corpse, standing like a scarecrow over its field of decaying junk. It was half naked and covered with countless cuts, each an eighth of an inch or so wide, between an inch and two long, and just deep enough to get below the skin. The rectangles had been flayed, the pieces of skin discarded. The flotsam of torture.

Jenson shook his head.

Rielly climbed back, allowing the crime scene photographers access. "That thing you had with Cohen, could it be anything connected with this?"

Jenson shrugged. "Guy's dead, but we couldn't get a forensic determination."

"Yeah, well, get in touch with him, will ya? I mean, could be nothing, just a wise guy had Cohen for his lawyer. But the card was still there, know what I mean? Everything else gone. Even the fucking guy's feet, for God's sake. I mean, what can you tell from a fucking guy's feet?" Rielly watched silently as the mortuary techs wrapped the body.

"Like they wanted Cohen to know. Like it was a message or something."

Jenson dropped the phone in the cradle. He should have tried earlier, he supposed, but most lawyers worked until at least seven. Jenson glanced at his watch. 7:30. Hell with it. He left the message. Small enough favor, call the guy a little late. Probably this stiff had nothing to do with the Twining thing anyway. Wasn't the way that killer worked. If there even was a killer. Give Cohen the weekend. He'd get the message Monday. That's soon enough for him to start worrying.

Jenson pulled on his jacket. It was Erin's birthday. Ten years old. He'd told Shiela he'd be home by eight. If he left now, he'd just make it. Yeah, Cohen'd be all right.

She pushed the other earring in, checked her makeup, and walked to the sofa, making sure the *Daily News* with her picture was sitting faceup on the coffee table. Conversation piece, she laughed to herself. Conversation piece.

The bell rang. She got up and opened the door. David kissed her quickly on the cheek and walked to the sofa. She followed. He hadn't said anything about the fact that she wasn't smiling. Not that she was surprised. The men in her life rarely noticed.

He slipped onto the sofa and picked up the paper. "I saw this," he said.

"It's not stopping," she said.

David gave her that look, the one that said, "Give me a hint as to how you want me to act, what you want me to say." He was going to be good about it, give her what she needed. Maybe. If he really did have the diary, then he was feeding it to the paper, even while she was dating him. She didn't believe it, didn't believe that he had the diary. Didn't believe he had anything to do with the burglary. He wouldn't do this. But they said.

"It's getting old," she said, sliding in next to him, playing with his fingers.

"I guess it's still news," he said weakly.

"Murder investigation is over," she said. "Jenson told me today." She nestled under his arm. He dutifully wrapped his arm around her. "I can't go out," she said to his chest. She could feel the spirit lift in his chest.

"We could stay in," he said.

She turned her face to his chest and kissed his shirt lightly. She nuzzled here and there for a moment, until she found his nipple and then slowly rubbed her lips across it. "That's not what I mean," she said.

He stroked her hair, like he really liked her, like it mattered to him what she felt. She liked it. She started unbuttoning his shirt. "I mean anytime. I'm always afraid of reporters and photographers." She unbuttoned the last button of his shirt and pushed herself up to his mouth, kissing it softly. She ran her hands under his shirt and around his back.

"I feel like a prisoner in my own house," she said as she slid his shirt down over his shoulders. "The other night was so good, just to be out. I thought it was over. Then this." She gestured to the paper. "I wish I had that diary back."

"Where did you lose it?" David asked, wiggling free of his shirt and wrapping his now naked arms around her.

She kissed him again. He didn't know, that was certain now, she thought as she allowed him to unbutton her blouse. She'd done her best. Nothing more now but just enjoy. They could believe her or not.

He bent down, unfastened her bra, and began to kiss her breasts. He was gentle. She tingled and he went back to the spot and kissed it again.

She dropped her blouse, lightly took his hand, and led him to the bedroom. In a moment they were both undressed and laying on the bed. In a moment more she excused herself and went into the bathroom. She glanced at her watch. Nine P.M. There was nothing more she could do. If he didn't know, he didn't know. She stood in front of the mirror. Her skin was fine and smooth, her makeup perfect. It was like it had been with Twining now. It had lost its newness, lost its sparkle. She opened the medicine cabinet and pulled out the diaphragm. She absently pulled the small elastic bulb from the medicine cabinet and reached for the small vial of brown liquid. No anticipation, even in the preparation. She was bored, pulling the elastic over the lip, inverting the vial, and allowing the liquid to run into the reservoir. Bored, after all the training, she was bored. Finished, she snapped the elastic off the vial, sealed it, and slipped it inside the ring. Bored and disappointed. A moment later she was back in the bedroom.

David sat on the side of the bed and watched her walk into the bathroom. He wondered if he knew how to handle this. Telling himself that she was just like any other woman hadn't worked. She wasn't like other women. In a few minutes he was going to make love to her. Pushing his hands behind his head, he leaned back, stared up at the ceiling, and thought about his good fortune.

He thought of her body, that smooth skin covering those hips. He thought about how in a moment he'd be covering that skin with his. The question returned. What was she doing with him, a back-street criminal lawyer squeezing a living out of the lumpen of society? What was she doing with him? He tried to push the thought away, but it came back.

And where was the video camera? The wall in front of the bed was covered with bookshelves, more knickknacks than books. But the camera had to be there, somewhere in that bookshelf. No holes, no mirrors. They could hide cameras in tie pins; it could be anywhere.

Don't think about it. *You're not supposed to know. Act as if she just wants you for you.* She doesn't know, better to keep it that way. It wasn't blackmail, it was just that she had decided. That's what he had to believe . . . had to act as if he believed. Dismiss the rest. Just enjoy the night, the week, the month, or whatever she gave him. Forget the camera, the blackmail. Forget the questions about what she was doing with you; just enjoy.

But the question wouldn't be dismissed so easily. If not to kill you, then why? She was young, younger than David. She'd been with Twining for a while, that other congressman, the others. But they were business. This was just for fun. She was slumming.

David almost laughed out loud. That was it. She was slumming. He was her experience with the down side of life. She probably had had her own, growing up. But now, just once, she wanted a romantic experience just as other people had, before she settled on some rich and powerful man and rode him off into her Jackie-O vision of the future.

The bathroom door opened. That was it, he thought, as he watched her enter the room, naked save the short silk robe that dangled from her shoulders, alternately covering one hip, then the other. It fit perfectly. But it also fit that there might be a video. She might want to blackmail him too.

But how? He wasn't a politician. He wasn't married. If a video of their lovemaking came out, the only risk was that his poor lovemaking would be exposed for all to see. Other than that, it would be a plus. He had slept with Anacleta. More benefit to his reputation than detriment.

He watched her slide her right hip onto the bed, carelessly allowing the silk robe to slip down over her left shoulder, draping itself across the bed, as she gently nibbled his ear. It was perfect, he thought; just accept it as long as it's there. But his body seemed to disagree. It seemed to spring to her as if built for her touch. He squeezed her tighter. Fuck it, his body was always out of control. It was his mind that knew what was good for him, his mind would make the decisions. But his body was taking over, ruling his mind.

Anacleta laid back and stared at the ceiling. She'd have to tell *la doña* about the weakness in the training. After all, she hadn't been prepared for these *norteamericanos*. She supposed she was just supposed to enjoy it, but every area of sexual response had been trained. She was uncomfortable not knowing how to act, not knowing what they expected.

A shiver went through her. She didn't know if it was from what Cohen was doing or from the thought of discussing it with *la doña*. She had not discussed much with *la doña*. It had mostly been on-the-job training. Maybe it wasn't the training. She had certainly spent enough time with men's heads in her crotch to get used to it by now. Maybe it was impatience. This wasn't supposed to be pleasant, not this time.

On-duty sex was never really pleasant. After all, she was always thinking of the task ahead. It wasn't until after it was over. She shivered again. Her body wasn't thinking of the future, it was thinking of now. She touched David's head, gently moving it up. He mustn't think she was in a hurry, just that she wanted him up here, with her . . . and wanted him inside her.

He moved to her touch, kissing her stomach, her breasts, then her face. She stroked his neck. Important to make it look like something she did, not special. She reached down and touched him, stroking. She wondered if he'd insist on a condom again. She rubbed him against her. No, he was too anxious to care. He bent to kiss her, and she closed her eyes.

She felt him slide to her right. She opened her eyes. He was fishing through the pocket of his pants, laying by the side of the bed. Asshole. Worrying about some disease that might kill him in ten years. She stroked her ring across his back as he rolled the condom on. She waited for that feeling of detachment. She didn't expect to feel that rush of pleasure and joy she had felt with Twining; that would be too much. No, but she usually felt detached at this point.

She felt him enter and wrapped her legs around him. A shiver of tension shot through her. What was wrong? She'd slept with dead men before; it never felt like this. She pulled him in, rocking her hips back and forth. His back started to stiffen. Just hold it, a minute more. She stroked his back, rubbed her finger across his spine. Now, she should do it now. But her finger wouldn't obey. She took a deep breath. Push. She felt spasms ripple through her body. She pressed her finger to the spine. She had to push. But she didn't, her body out of her control. This man knew nothing, she knew that. He'd done nothing. She couldn't, she couldn't.

She watched as he pushed himself into her, touched her hand on his back, smiled, and pushed her hand tight against his back.

She tried to pull back, but she was paralyzed. She felt the skin give way. She tried to pull her hand back, but it was too late. He froze. His eyes glared at her: disbelief, shock.

She snapped to control. She had to have control. She took his hand and pulled it away from his spine. It resisted slightly. Slipping her hand out of his, she smiled at him. Had to play the role, it was done. It was the right thing. It had to be. It didn't feel right, but that didn't matter, it was the right thing. She slipped her hand over to the other side and plunged the pin in. She watched as his eyes darted helplessly back and forth. Wrapping her legs around him, she pulled him tighter. His eyes got wider. Closing her eyes, she allowed a wave of pleasure to wash over her. She'd always liked sleeping with dead men.

Julio glanced at his watch. Eight o'clock. Snapping his sleeve back down, he rested his elbow on the car window. He hated waiting, always had. It was important that everything be set, and that meant he was here at least a half hour early. But that didn't mean he didn't hate it. He could watch the traffic on Seventy-second Street for only so long. Santeria sat quietly behind the wheel, watching the traffic too, watching for any cops that happened along. Julio wondered why Santeria wore that old tweed thing. It made him look almost like a homeless man. But Julio never asked.

Julio never asked much of anything, just did his job and waited. He'd hated to leave, to come to the U.S., but it had been necessary. That's what they'd told him, anyway, since he was young. Told him it was necessary and that he wouldn't really understand, but it was for his own good. He looked out the window and watched an older woman walk by with a little dog, no bigger than a good-sized rat back home, but not as well behaved. It screamed as if the world were on fire.

Maybe it was, Julio thought, as he glanced at his watch again. That's what they told him, had told him since the beginning, how the world was on fire and he couldn't understand but needed to help put it out. That's what he was, Santeria said, a fireman. Saving the world from a fire, just as it said in the Bible, even though Santeria didn't believe in the Bible. It was a metaphor, Santeria said, for what was happening now. A metaphor for the fire Julio was putting out.

He was sure Santeria was right; that's what they all said. But when he watched that woman walk by, that woman with the dog, he was pretty sure she didn't know about the fire. Julio closed his eyes and put his head back against the headrest. It didn't seem as if there was a fire. It seemed as if this was the way life was to these people, just like this. Today just like yesterday, just as it was at home, but different.

"That's it, gather yourself."

The voice drifted over to Julio, enveloping him. He knew it was Santeria, but it seemed like more somehow, as if it were the embodiment of the spirits. The old men said that it wasn't, that it was just that Santeria had learned some tricks, but not the real knowledge. Julio didn't know. Santeria's voice seemed to fill him, cover him. It restored him when his faith was flagging.

"It will be like before, you will wait for me. I will come, and it will be all right."

It was as they had rehearsed. This time he went five minutes before. He would start alone. Santeria said it was a great test. Julio's next step. Julio hadn't been sure he wanted to take that step, wasn't sure he didn't just want to go home. But Santeria had talked to him, spoken in that voice, carried him to another place, just as the old men had when he was very young. Thoughts of home carried the sadness with them. But Santeria's voice came again.

"You must work fast. It will be five minutes. You will

work smoothly and rapidly, your hands carried by the spirits."

Julio saw as Santeria spoke, saw himself working as they had practiced. Saw Santeria walking in and speaking. The practice had been hard, but Julio had continued. He almost quit once, but Santeria had understood, had understood immediately and had spoken. He had told Julio that his life back home could start sooner if he learned this well, and that when they had finished, he could take Anacleta back, take her back as his bride, the conquering hero.

Santeria had said more, had painted beautiful pictures with his words, created fine images in Julio's mind, images Julio could not erase. Images that Santeria called back again and again, until they drew Julio toward them. If he wanted to go home and be rid of this, he must complete the work.

Julio pulled his head up, snapped his sleeve back, and glanced at his watch again. 8:15. It was time. He looked over to Santeria.

"Begin now. I will be there in five minutes." Santeria spoke quietly, in that transporting voice. Julio saw the image of himself and Anacleta returning. The image burning bright and clear into his consciousness. It held him and drew him out of the door. This would be the last. Santeria had almost said it.

Julio straightened his tie as he walked past the doorman who was talking to the super. He took Julio for a tenant. Good. He slipped into the elevator and pushed twenty-seven. The elevator hummed up to the floor. Julio checked his index fingers. A bandage covered each with a miniature syringe attached, with a tiny pin extending from the gauze. Julio thought about checking them again but didn't. He had checked three times since leaving the apartment; he wanted to be sure he had enough.

The elevator door opened. He walked to 27F. He knocked. The door would be open, but he waited anyway. He didn't want to arrive early. Not that he was protecting Anacleta's feelings; they all knew her job and how she did it. He was protecting his own. He had nothing against this lawyer, not personally, but he wanted to do the job right. To do it as it was drawn up, so he could take Anacleta back sooner. Take her back home and forget this. If he saw Anacleta performing her duty . . . Well, he wanted to do his duty calmly. He looked at the picture Santeria had painted him. He knocked again.

David wanted to grab her, hold on, and ride this out, but he couldn't. Couldn't even move his head. He was locked in like a paraplegic. It was a thought that had always terrified him, trapped in a room, helpless. He pushed against the paralysis again. Nothing. A flicker of motion in his arm, then nothing. There was nothing he could do, so he gave up, just felt the feelings that still came through.

And he enjoyed. The feelings still rushed and were more exciting. As if all the normal thoughts, plans for the future, even the immediate future, were gone, out of his control, out of his mind. The feelings rushed through him, and he had nothing to do other than enjoy them.

He heard the knock but didn't react. Couldn't react, but he didn't even think about it. After all, it was in that world that he no longer controlled, of which he was no longer a part. He felt Anacleta's heels dig into his back, pulling him closer.

The knock came again, more insistent. David watched as Anacleta's eyes shot over to the door. She sighed, like a housewife getting a call after vacuuming the whole house and all she wanted to do was watch "Days of Our Lives." David suddenly felt sorry for her. This must be important to her, having a whole man paralyzed, a full-sized dildo. It must be a disappointment.

She kissed him on his open mouth and rolled him slowly to the side. He felt the tingle as she kissed his earlobe and whispered something about how it wouldn't hurt, she'd been careful. He couldn't quite imagine how something could hurt in this state, or how she could think he was worried about that, but he thought how it was a sweet sentiment anyway.

She slipped off of him, pulled on her silk robe, and walked to the door. He stared at the wall as the sound of the bolt unlatching crashed into his ears. It was a curious sound, from another world. He was aware that he wasn't thinking of the danger, that he couldn't really imagine danger. Then he heard the male voice. Just a grunt, but male. The first thing he thought of was some homosexual event. He wasn't interested in that, and the anger started to work up. Then he heard her speak. She had frustration in her voice.

"You're early." The voice came through the walls, but was Dopplered as if they were coming toward him. David liked the idea that she thought he was early; he liked the idea of her finishing whatever it was she had in mind.

"Orders." The male voice came back. He spoke as if he was disappointed, disappointed that Anacleta was not happy to see him, not that he was early.

David stared at the wall in front of him but could tell when they entered the room. He hated meeting new people ass first, but that was the way it was. His mind started to come back, the waves of feelings gone now, replaced by that old feeling of fear at the paralysis. He was definitely here, definitely paralyzed, and definitely angry. But strangely the helplessness made him feel almost like an observer to his own fate.

He heard Anacleta swing open the closet door. A second later it closed with a slam. "Next time, I want more time," she said. David didn't know how to interpret that. Next time sounded pretty good, but would the next time be with him or someone else?

David felt a strong hand grab his left wrist. He felt himself being dragged to the bedpost. A cold collar of steel snapped over his hand, then over the bedpost. The strong hand released him, and he felt the weight leave the bed.

A new weight hit the bed, a lighter, gentler weight. He heard Anacleta's voice in his ear. "Good-bye, David. I wish it didn't have to end like this." It didn't sound like sorrow in the voice, more like resignation. David wanted to answer, sing "Ticket to Ride" or something, but of course he couldn't. In his current position he didn't like thinking of things ending.

In a second Anacleta was gone and the heavier weight back. David felt a prick in his neck, near the first, and a new burning through his veins. It was a second before his right arm felt a modicum of life. David pulled hard on the paralyzed arm, but it barely moved, and in a second the strong arm and the cold steel were on it and it was attached to the other bedpost. A second later his legs were pinioned. His head flopped to the right, and he saw Anacleta buttoning the top button of her blouse and brushing her hair back. Only one part of David's body was rigid.

Santeria pulled the car around the corner onto Seventy-third Street, near the rear entrance. The cab driver he'd paid to wait was still there. Santeria signaled him away and pulled into the vacant space.

He flipped the car into park and put his hands behind his head. There was no rush now. He'd told Julio five minutes, but he knew it would take longer, possibly considerably longer. So he would wait. Thirty, forty-five . . .

He pushed the CD into the player. The Goldberg Variation. He'd always loved the complexity.

Twenty minutes had passed before Santeria looked up. The small, white door cut into the white brick cracked open. Anacleta walked out with her arm around a man. Santeria smiled. The two hunched into the cab waiting by the door. They sat in the middle of the backseat, huddled together. A second later the cab pulled away. Santeria glanced at the car waiting across the street. The driver nodded back and waited. He would wait just a few seconds, Santeria noted with satisfaction, then pull away, a discreet distance from the cab.

Santeria snapped off the CD and stepped out of the car. Bach would have to wait. He walked to the white door, pulled it open, and signaled to the man sweeping the street, who put down his broom and followed Santeria. Complexity

HOSTILE WITNESS

resolving itself into a greater order. That's what Santeria liked, that's what the world needed more of.

Santeria climbed the steps. Order is the beauty of the Universe, he thought, the order of interactive chaos. He had created a little more of that today, a little more of what makes the world right.

Anacleta leaned against his shoulder. She wasn't sure, but then she never was. She generally didn't think. She could never resolve anything that way; it just came to more questions. Santeria had told her to leave that to him. She was the feeler, he'd said.

The feeler knew by feeling, not thinking. She supposed it was true, up until Santeria told her to do something that didn't feel right, then she didn't know. She wasn't sure that feeling was as good as thinking, but she had what she had.

She pushed herself against his shoulder. She wanted a reaction, a warm hug, thanks, love. Maybe it was too soon. Maybe that's the way he reacted. It took all kinds. She rubbed his leg. Take his mind off it. Maybe he was just fixated, stuck thinking about it, like a turntable with the arm off so the record keeps playing. Rubbing his leg would make him think of something else.

The cab swung right down Second Avenue. Anacleta looked out the right window, across his body. He was rubbing at the blood, as if he wanted to get it out. Absently stroking the stain, as if he wasn't in his body, as if a small part of him, like Lady Macbeth, was wishing the spot out, but the rest, the greater part, had chosen to leave, chosen to be absent, thinking other thoughts.

She left him to his thoughts. The ride would be short, and he'd have to act when it ended, but now she could leave him to his thoughts. She was curious about what men thought of murders, or how they felt. She had never seen a man so soon after. Usually she was alone, and the man, the only witness, was dead.

The cab pulled next to a blue van with Chinese writing on the side. The light turned green, but cars double-parked on both sides slowed the traffic to a crawl. She stroked his leg again. She felt his arm float around her, squeezing her gently. She put her arm around his waist and squeezed back.

"What's going on?"

She ignored the voice and squeezed again. Act like it's just a date, like this is what happens on prom night, and you knew it all the time, she thought.

He pulled her to him, tight. Not lustful tight or security tight . . . angry tight. "What's going on?" The voice cracked through more firmly now.

"Shhh," she said, as she reached up and kissed him. He didn't respond. She gestured with her head to the driver and kissed David again.

Nothing, like he wasn't grateful. She could have let that bastard Julio cut him up. He should be thankful she stopped that.

He rubbed the bloodstain across his shirt. He should be grateful, she thought again, as she pulled his jacket closed over the stain. Maybe it was the shock. After all, the blood was wet. Lawyers usually got there after the blood had dried. It had to be different for him.

It was different for her, the wet blood. She smiled to herself as she thought back. Kept her mouth closed and looked out the window as the car swung right on Seventy-second Street toward the East River. Thought back to how she had stopped to choose. Julio had that whole case full of knives and scalpels. She stopped and picked a long, thin one.

As Julio was climbing up, she hesitated. He gave her a quick smile, a lover's smile, then climbed up on the bed. She knew what Santeria had said, of course. He was always promising her to someone. She played along usually, knowing it wouldn't happen, not without her permission. After all, what man who knew her would go with her if she didn't wholeheartedly approve?

But Julio was too stupid. He thought she loved him because Santeria said so. She felt the handle of that thin stiletto in her hand, the coolness next to her skin. She understood how people felt about fine tools. You could tell the difference between that stiletto and a cheap one.

Julio was taping David's dick so it stayed still. Julio had straddled David, sitting on his chest, so that he could hold him still, then pushed David's chest flat and pinned him.

The stiletto had slipped in smoothly, just under the rib cage. After it was in, Julio turned around. She smiled, thinking back to it, that goofy look on his face, as if he couldn't understand. How could she do this to her future lover?

David braced himself against the wall of the elevator, Anacleta under his arm. It hadn't been hard to get by the doorman: a wink from Anacleta, a belch from him. The doorman held the door with a smile. David could feel his legs again. Shaking the right, he could feel it move. Not long, Anacleta had told him.

The door opened. Anacleta stuck her leg out, waited for him to exit, then followed. A few minutes later she dumped him on his couch. He was able to right himself and even follow her movements as she locked the door and turned out the hall light.

"What's going on?" he heard himself say.

She silently returned to the couch, picked up his flaccid left arm, and draped it over her shoulder. "We're alone," she said.

"What's going on?" he repeated.

She stiffened against his side. "It was a sexual enhancement. Most men like it."

"What about 'Shoulders'?"

"Julio," she said, crossing her arms.

"Julio," David repeated.

She threw his arm off her and walked toward the door.

"Anacleta, don't get cute here. Your brother walked in after you paralyzed me, strapped me to the bed, and opened a set of woodworking tools. I want to know what's going on."

"What do you want me to say? That I'm a killer?"

The word ripped through David like a sword. It wasn't

news, but he had resisted believing it. Now the admission.

"Twining?" David asked.

"The first part," she said. "Julio finished him."

"Why?"

"Because it's what I do, David." There was force in her voice, quiet force. "You're a lawyer, I'm a killer."

She dropped like an angry brick in the chair opposite David. "I'm a killer." More resigned this time.

"Why?" David repeated. The question made no sense. There was no answer, but it was the one that sprang from his mouth. "Why didn't you stop?"

"You think I haven't tried? You think I haven't read every book on sexual response?" Anger leaped from her eyes. "Do you know how fetishes start?"

David shook his head.

"No. Some say it's association a child makes with what he's doing or watching at the time he has his early sexual responses." She pulled a book off the shelf and looked as if she wanted to tear it apart.

"When did you start to study law? At twenty? Twenty-one?" She waited until David nodded before continuing. "I started when I was three. Three years old. A baby."

"You killed at three?"

"No, but I started training." She turned away from him, seemingly hiding tears begging to come out.

"Your parents?"

"I never knew them. I was probably an orphan. I don't know." She sighed, leaned forward, and stared at her hands, clasped before her as if she were trying to solve their puzzle. "A woman brought me up. *La doña.* That's the only name I ever had for her. She was my teacher, my mother, everything. I had no other relationship until I was fifteen. I had lovers, but that was part of the training." The tears flowed freely now.

"How many . . . ?" David could not finish the question.

"Not many. It wasn't a large part of the job, really." She got up and walked to the window behind David. He heard her separate two slats of the blinds.

His arms and legs had more feeling now, the feeling that had left his body. He turned to watch her.

"It was my greatest thrill," she said sadly.

"Killing?"

She nodded. "*La doña* took me to executions sometimes. Tortures really. She would hug me as the man had the most pain. I rarely got hugs. After a while I looked forward to those times. As I got older, she made me stand in front of the man, so he could see me as he suffered." She spoke slowly. "Finally, when I began to mature sexually, she would have me tease the dying man with my body. Stimulate myself as he suffered. *Always look at his face*, she would say . . . And I did."

David stood and walked unsteadily to her side.

"It was the only time I was satisfied . . . with a dead man." She slipped her arm around him and squeezed him tightly, pushing her wet cheek against his chest.

David felt the feeling wash through him. Overwhelming sympathy. Overwhelming relief. He was alive. He was alive because of Anacleta, a killing machine trained from the age of three. Why? Why was he alive?

"You were different," she said, seeming to feel his question through his body.

"I'm better alive than dead?"

"You were pretty good dead," she said, smiling. Then she frowned. "I don't know why."

"You killed Julio so he wouldn't kill me." David felt the tears soak through the bloodstains on his shirt. The tears were warm.

"They weren't just going to kill you." Her words were muffled by his chest. "They wanted the diary."

He pulled her closer. He didn't know why, but it made him feel better, to be closer to something alive. He tried not to think about what they would do for that diary.

"It would have taken a long time unless you told them where it was."

"If I didn't know?"

"It would have taken a long time."
David shivered. A long time.

"They'll be here soon," David said, allowing the slats of the venetian blinds to close.

"Surprised they're not already." Anacleta sat on the couch, her arms crossed, staring at the white wall before her.

It had been forty-five minutes since they had spoken. Forty-five minutes. He was sure they knew where he lived, even though Anacleta swore she never told them. Swore they never asked, which is why David was sure they knew.

Anacleta had been quiet in the last forty-five minutes, since she had told him about his planned fate. She told him no details, just that it would be slow. But David had made the mistake of getting his messages. Jenson had drawn it out. Much more graphic about the fate they had planned for him than Anacleta had been. Maybe that was her kindness and she expected thanks.

Maybe she deserved it. After all, she had saved his life. Put it in danger first, then walked out of the apartment, leaving him helpless and alone with a crazed killer. She had come back, but by her own admission only when she realized that they didn't just plan to kill him but torture him. He wasn't sure how he felt about his pain being more valuable to her than his life.

But she had made a good point about her own life. If they were willing to torture, then kill Walsh, David, and presumably Light to find this diary, then what would they be willing to do to her? Trained since the age of three, she said. What knowledge about this organization she must have. And David hadn't even asked her about it.

He would, he thought. It just didn't seem appropriate now. Too early. Too early for what? To ask her why she was willing to kill him?

"What are you going to do?" The voice was small, a voice David had never heard from Anacleta before. Like a little girl helplessly seeking shelter.

What was he going to do, indeed. He could walk away from her. Should really. Light wasn't involved, so that duty was completed. *But then they'd come after me,* a voice inside him said. He could agree to give Anacleta up in exchange for his life. Agree to give the diary away.

Slapping the blinds, David spun to the kitchen. "Tea?" he asked. Not waiting for an answer, he grabbed the pot, filled it, and dropped it on the stove.

"I could go," she said, walking up behind him, carefully not touching, as if she knew that was unfair influence.

"Where?" he asked, still facing the stove.

He felt her shrug. He didn't know how, maybe the reflection from the stove, but he knew she had shrugged, and he knew she had no real answer. She was offering herself up for him. Offering, if he chose, to go back as trade.

David reached into the cabinet for cups. It was different, he thought, actively turning her in as opposed to letting her go. If he could just let her go and be safe he would, but he couldn't. They would come after him. Even as that voice inside his head spoke in reasonable, professorial tones, he knew it was wrong. He could not let the woman go this time. It was fortunate, he supposed, that he had not been presented with the choice of letting her go. The decision would have been the same, exactly the same, but that professorial voice wouldn't have liked it.

He pulled out a plastic box filled with various herbal and regular teas and slid it to Anacleta. "I don't know." he said. "What should we do?"

He was amazed at how gently and smoothly she slipped her left arm inside his right, allowing her fingers to inch down to intertwine with his while simultaneously selecting a peppermint tea bag.

The buzzer rang. David motioned her to be quiet. Skipping to the blinds, he pulled them open and peered out. A blue Chevy stood illegally parked in front of the building.

Anacleta had followed him, a tense, inquisitive look on her face.

David nodded. "Get your stuff. Don't make a sound."

He waited a second while she disappeared into the bedroom. He had to answer; the doormen had seen him come in. Besides, if they thought he wasn't here, they'd post somebody just to wait. He'd never get out unless he went to the police, and that meant turning Anacleta in. No, he thought, pushing the speaker, this is the only way.

He grunted.

"Mr. Cohen, two men here to see you."

"Send them up."

Anacleta stood next to him. No time to explain now, he thought, grabbing her arm and pushing her out the door. She said nothing, accepting, it seemed, the role he had assigned her. Maybe that was the problem with him and Janie; she insisted on having a mind.

Glancing at the arrows above the three elevator doors, he punched the up and down buttons. Two were moving up, the right one now on the fourth floor, the left on the second. *Shit, one's out for repair.* He figured they were in the car on two. Eight floors to go. The gold arrow jerked up to five, then six, then stopped. *Christ, if the other one was going to pass it*... David looked desperately up and down the hall. Only an exit door on the far end, but the door opened only one way. Once in, the only way out was through the lobby.

He glanced back to the arrows. The right car had started to move but was running even with the left one now.

Anacleta looked from the arrows to David. "They'll catch us."

David looked helpless. He knew he looked helpless, his career as a Latin macho man over less than a minute after it had begun.

"Damn, David," she said, slamming her hand into the door of the elevator, "why did you say we were here?"

"Look, it was a mistake, okay? We can take the stairs."

"And they'll be there, waiting." The woman who had been willing to sacrifice herself for him a minute ago was now angry.

The romantic part of David thought it was a good sign. However, a more practical side thought she was right. David looked around for a weapon. The fire hose, with an ax. David started toward it. He stopped when Anacleta grabbed his arm, pointing at the arrows.

The left one had stopped at nine, the right continuing on. With a little luck, they'd be on the right when it arrived at twelve and away from these killers.

"Let me get the ax anyway," David said, moving toward it.

Anacleta refused to let go of his arm. "That'll sound the alarm, right?"

David stopped. It would. And before they got to the ground floor, their man would know about it. There was nothing to do but wait. The right elevator clicked to twelve, the left to eleven. David put his arm around Anacleta and guided her to the right one. The doors opened. The left one jumped off eleven.

"Come on." David pushed Anacleta in the elevator and pressed one. The light didn't light and the doors didn't close. "Shit." He pushed again. He was about to escalate to fuck, when Anacleta pushed fourteen, gesturing to the lit green arrow next to the control panel. The door on the left crashed open as the doors on his shut.

"Close," Anacleta said.

"And not over." The elevator opened at fourteen, and an elderly lady with a small dog got in. David waited impatiently, then reached around her to slam the button for one.

The woman shot David a cross look while the terrier emitted a low growl. Taking Anacleta's arm, David moved to the corner of the elevator. The indicator showed the elevator falling, thirteen, twelve. David wondered why he thought of them as killers. He had no evidence except that someone had come. The door popped open on the ground floor, and David pushed past the woman, pulling Anacleta with him. Ignoring the woman's scowl, he jogged to the front door.

"Mr. Cohen, what about those guys I sent up?"

"Tell them I'm still up there," David said without stopping. The lobby was empty, as was the Chevy parked out front. Both of them had gone up. And only two. That was good. It gave David and Anacleta a few minutes to get away. Without pausing, David turned left and headed toward Court Street. A moment later they were in the subway.

"Wait here a minute," David said, pulling a quarter from his pocket. Punching the number, he wondered what he'd do if Joel wasn't in. He was. Ten seconds later, meeting place established, David grabbed Anacleta's hand, dropped two tokens in the slots, and they ran through.

The station was crowded for late in the day. *Train must be late.* David pushed his way through the crowds, Anacleta following. Joel would be there with his bike in two minutes. David didn't want to be much later. A couple of minutes later they pushed through the revolving exit at the Court and Montague exit.

"Wait here," David ordered at the bottom of the stairs. Tucking himself behind an overweight matron with two huge packages, he matched her waddle up the stairs. Halfway up, peering through the green steel fence surrounding the stairs, he scanned the area. No killer types, but what were killer types? But more importantly, no Joel. Anacleta stood quietly, unmoved by David's terror. Maybe there was something to this training, he thought as he scanned again.

He heard the Harley before spinning to see Joel. Spinning around again, he saw the blue Chevy.

Running down the stairs, he grabbed Anacleta's hand, dumped two more tokens in the turnstile, and ran back through the station. Joel saw him. Maybe they saw him. Pushing his way past a bag lady waiting to exit, he pulled Anacleta through. Evans. They could get to Evans.

They popped up inside the Municipal Building entrance. A homeless man was spreading his blanket, preparing to display his used paperbacks. No Chevy. David dodged through the crowd, still holding Anacleta's hand. She kept up. Must have learned to dodge crowds somewhere.

At the corner David hid behind a water delivery man and scanned where he had seen Joel and the blue Chevy. The

Chevy was there, facing down Montague. Good, just slip through the crowd and in a minute they'd be at Evans's. Just hope he's home.

"Hold still."

David gripped the pillow with both hands.

"Such a baby." The Haitian lilt came through Evans's speech for one of the few times since David had known him. It was intentional. Just to add the additional mocking tone of a Caribbean nanny.

David felt the slice, then the cold steel instrument as it scraped away some of the accumulating fluid.

"A stitch and we'll be through." Evans dropped the collection of vials in his bag, poked a curved needle through David's back, covered the mess with a bandage, and slapped David's upper back. "Shirt on."

David got up and walked to the kitchen. "What are the chances?" David asked, gesturing with a Dr Pepper bottle.

Evans nodded. "Can't say exactly. It gives us another reading. If it's the same stuff, and I imagine it is, we can get a breakdown pattern." Evans marked the vial containing blood and another containing scrapings from the wound on David's skin. "Anacleta was there, you know."

David nodded. He had heard the story of Jenson's "investigation." "If it is the same stuff, then what?"

"If we can determine what it is, find or make some of it, and test it on animals, then we can estimate the time between administration and death . . . maybe."

"Maybe?"

"Not very exact stuff, this. As inexact as time of death is in a normal case, it is even more inexact with a calculation like this. Too many variables."

"So I may have gone through this torture for nothing?"

"Torture is never fruitless, my dear boy. If nothing else, it builds character." Evans drained the soda and held out the bottle, as if asking if David wanted another.

David shook his head. He felt light, as if the weight of

the case had been lifted. The reality was, it was heavier than ever.

"So, what is it I have to protect this dear lady from?"

David looked out the window. He didn't really want Evans to know he was looking for his killers. Evans would try to stop him, and with three hundred pounds on his side, might very well succeed. David didn't want to be stopped. He couldn't see another way, even if he were willing to leave Anacleta to the wolves, which he was not. He ignored that sensible part of him that said she was in on it, a killer who didn't seem very upset at having cut a man's ventricle while he was using it. She wasn't the kind of woman one should think of spending time with.

"No answer, huh? Well, let me see if I can figure it out. She cut this guy, probably killing him. An important man in the organization she worked for. Her job was to sleep with Twining." Evans paused and waited for David's nod.

"There were advantages to the organization to bringing pressures to bear on congresspeople. In the current atmosphere a younger woman is a negative to a congressman. If it gets out, loses votes." Evans waited for David's nod. "But then why the heavy stuff?"

"Perhaps there were times when that threat wasn't enough. Remember, Twining was separated from his wife, and he was from an urban district. His voters might not have cared so much. There was only so far they could push him with threats of exposing his affair."

"And since his affair was already exposed, by you . . ."

"There was no threat. So Anacleta would bring out her 'sexual enhancements.' Put the fear of God into him."

"Either because he didn't respond to the threat or because he slapped Anacleta around a little for having the audacity to think she could intimidate a United States congressman without a license to carry a PAC."

"Right." David stood as if the conversation were over.

"And I have to wait here with this delightful young lady because who's waiting to see her?"

David turned back to Evans, sprawled on two thirds of

the sofa. "Just a couple of assassins." David pulled on his jacket. "But you can wait up here until it's over."

"Oh, that's reassuring."

"Don't let anyone in."

Evans nodded. "You know there are other ways."

"Like what?"

"Police, fire department. All those people handle life and death. Part of the job, you know?"

Ignoring him, David asked where the computer was. Evans directed him to the bedroom at the end of the hall. An hour later David emerged with a fistful of papers and two floppy disks. Tossing one of the disks to Evans, he slipped the other and the papers into his briefcase.

"Hold on to that, okay?"

Evans nodded, the look on his face indicating he wanted to ask but thought better of it.

"Take care of Anacleta too."

"No one will know she's here. Or I, for that matter. I try to avoid assassins at all costs."

"Good. One more thing," David said, pulling his pen from his pocket and jotting a note on a pad. "Call this number in about an hour. Give them this message." David pulled the sheet off the pad and handed it to Evans.

"Will do," Evans said, folding the note, stuffing it into his pocket, and checking his watch. "One hour."

"Right," David said, heading to the door. He stopped suddenly. "And thanks."

"Con mucho gusto," Evans said without much feeling.

It was time, had been for about two weeks, ever since that bitch stole his book. The book rightfully his ever since he stole it from the Spanish bitch. Couldn't let that bitch Evelyn get away with nothing like that. And it was right that he'd smack Evelyn 'round some. It was her that started all this shit to begin with. Making him go get involved with them lawyers again. It was getting old, that's what.

Light saw the building. There, right in front, big red brick.

Have to go up the stairs, past all them junkies and such. Have to go right up. Light ignored the graffiti on the stairwell wall. Didn't want to go up in no elevator. Not when you got business to do. Couldn't be waiting for no elevator after the business. Wanted to know what was what.

There was this stairway here and the other one over the other side. This one here look clear. Closer to Evelyn's sister's apartment anyway. Better this way. Then run down the stairs after, down 'round the corner, over toward Pacific. Time he made it out a the projects, nobody be stopping him. Don't nobody care about no crack-headed Evelyn Jefferson.

Light pushed the fire door open from the third-floor stairway. Junkies light today. Only saw one the whole way up. Whole way up to the apartment, 3B. He knocked on the door. Didn't like to knock when he doing business, but he knocked this time. Look better.

The door open just a crack, two eyes peering out around the edge. Then the head turn so only one eye peeked through. Only one eye, but it have Light straight up. The eye blinked a question. Didn't say nothing, but Light answered the blink just the same.

"Evelyn Jefferson," he said.

The eye blinked again, and the door closed. Can't teach they children to act respectable to respectable people. Light straightened his coat. Maybe he didn't look that respectable, but time he was ten he could tell respectable from those that weren't just by looking, not having to depend on clothes. Kids now weren't the same. Too much TV, Light suspected.

The door opened and Evelyn stood there, scowl on her face, hand on her bony hip. The scowl said, "What you doing here?" just as clear as if she spoke. Light felt like he in some Twilight Zone where there was this house where nobody talked.

He ignored the question and pushed past her into the house. Evelyn's sister sat on the torn couch in the corner, fat as Evelyn was skinny. The daughter who belong to the eyes stood in the kitchen, peering now through the crack

HOSTILE WITNESS

between the swinging door and the frame. Girl just like to peer through cracks.

"Come for it." Light said it steady, like he wasn't there for no argument, no question. Was there 'cause he was gonna get it 'cause it was his. Had to act like that was enough. Confident.

Evelyn just snort. That kind a snort that's not a refusal exactly, but cuts at you deeper than a refusal. Says you're not even worth answering... neither you or your question.

Light thought about hitting her right then, but he wanted the book first. Then he'd hit her. Make like he doing for the lawyer, but he ain't, not really. He'd hit her for himself.

Light took a step toward her. "Ain't got all day." He said it menacing. That's what they'd say in court. Menacing.

Evelyn took a step back, hesitated like she was thinking or something, then smiled. Light didn't like it when she smiled. It usually meant that she gonna do some kind of humiliating. Light told himself he didn't care about that now. Only people listening was her fat sister and that girl with the eyes that peered through cracks. Nobody care what they think. Besides, in a minute, when he have the book, he gonna get to hit her. Get to hit her good, though he thought he'd have to hold back, skinny as that crack made her.

Evelyn turn, bent down, and pull open a drawer in the table next to the sofa. Light jumped across the room, grabbed the drawer, and held it steady. She probably have a gun in there. Might anyway, that's where they leave guns in them TV shows, in drawers like that.

Evelyn look up and laugh. "What you scared of? The book? Can't even read, you old fool."

Light rip it from her hand. Thought she hurt a little, just from how he did it with a twist at the end when she tried to hold. He wondered if them crack-weakened bones snapped just from that. He didn't hear nothing, but it would a been okay.

But she just grimaced a second then pretended that it wasn't nothing. "Doesn't matter. I sold copies of all those pages anyway. Paper got it all. All the money can be made been made." She laughed again.

Light didn't know if he was madder 'cause she thought he stole it 'cause he wanted to make money, or 'cause he'd never be able to explain to her that it wasn't money. She always had that power, make him mad about something he don't care about, because she act like he did. It didn't matter that he didn't care about it; the anger bubbled up through him anyway.

He could feel the knuckles of his left hand hurting from gripping the book so hard. He knew they was turning white. Knew it even as his right hand crashed into her face. It felt good landing there. Sounded good too, with the way her face cracked. Made the knuckles of his left hand relax a little.

Light looked over to the fat sister. She sat quiet. Even smiled a little, like she knew Evelyn had it coming. Light glanced over to the eyes peeking through the door. Could only see one eye, but it looked to be smiling too. Seeing as how he was giving so much pleasure to two of the occupants of the apartment, he smacked Evelyn again. She whimpered a little this time and fell down. Fell down like a thirties actress, maybe Betty Grable or somebody, landing all neat on the couch.

Light turned in disgust and walked out the apartment. Didn't even yell or nothing. Just fall, trying to look the lady. Light slammed the door and headed for the near stairs. A few minutes more and he'd be down the stairs, out the projects, and over toward Nostrand Avenue. Thinking he stole that book for the money, or stealing it now for the money.

Wasn't that. Never was. Just got to help your lawyer when he get in trouble. That's what. Light been doing that for couple a years now.

Smiling unconvincingly, the man in the gray suit turned the other key in the other lock. Clicking reassuringly into place, the wall again seemed an unbroken line of gold, glimmering under the fluorescent light.

"Your wife will sign the card when she comes in, Mr. Cohen?"

David nodded, returned the unconvincing smile, and followed the gray suit up the stairs to the main floor of the bank. Two banks in an hour, not a bad day, he thought as he pushed through the revolving door onto Jay Street. He stood for a second, squinting against the bright sunshine, deciding which way to walk. He didn't notice the blue Chevy until it stopped at the curb. Two men in running suits, one a heavy-set Hispanic. Could be, he thought as he turned and headed up Jay toward the Brooklyn Bridge. Glancing back, he saw the Hispanic man skip in front of the car and start jogging toward him.

Spinning front, David took off, dodging shoppers, heading toward the bridge. He hadn't thought of what he'd do if he got there; there was no time. Ducking right at the corner, he glanced back. No Hispanic in a running suit. Maybe he was caught in pedestrian traffic. Maybe he wasn't looking for David at all. In any event, he was nowhere in sight.

David slowed his pace, glancing over his shoulder. There, back again. The man started to jog. The street was crowded, too crowded for full flight, but the man was gaining, darting between shoppers. David darted into the street, dodging around a cab and running toward an office building on the left. Might be a guard there, for whatever that was worth. Spinning around the corner, he glanced back; the Hispanic man had stopped, helping a woman pick up her packages. David dashed down the block and left onto a quiet street behind a large office building. Another few feet and he'd be at Flatbush Avenue and relative safety.

He was ten feet from it when he heard the running footsteps behind him.

"Counselor," the voice called.

He glanced quickly, spinning back to the front so he could keep running. The face hadn't made an impression in the quick glimpse; it did now as he spun left, around the office building. He glanced again. Jenson side-skipped around a lone shopper who spat a creole obscenity as he passed.

"Counselor," Jenson panted. "I want to talk to you."

"Jenson," David said, pulling himself to a stop, "I know your problem. I've seen the tape. But we can work around that. They're chasing me right now. Come on," David called as he started to pull Jenson toward Flatbush.

Jenson stood steady, yanking David back. Another face appeared over Jenson's shoulder.

"Buenos dias, Señor Cohen."

David stared, speechless.

"You did not expect to see me, *verdad?"* The man in the running suit jogged up behind. Julio straightened his tie. "I look good, no?"

"No," David said, twisting to get away, but Julio's hand squeezed hard, pulling David around in front of him. Smiling cruelly, Julio held up an index finger covered with a bandage, then moved it slowly to David's neck. It was a question.

David nodded. He had no choice now. This definitely changed things. What was it they said in AA? Work the plan. David had never been in AA. Maybe that's why his plan wasn't working.

Evelyn pulled the ice from her cheek. "Shit, first be whupped on by white men, then black, now white again. Can't keep this here shit straight." She left the door open as she walked back and plopped down on the sofa. "Look, look all you want. Won't find nothing here."

Julio gently moved the ice from Evelyn's cheek with his pudgy hand. "Where is it?" His voice was gentle, but there was a firmness to it.

David leaned against the door frame, Jenson and another man behind him. Evelyn took a long time looking at the Hispanic, longer than David would have. David had often been told he spoke too quickly. But Evelyn, despite the twitching in her arms, took a long time.

"The man come back and took it," she said finally, moving the ice pack against her face.

"What man?"

"Light."

David tried to keep his cool as Julio turned to him. There was a stiffness to the Hispanic man's movements, and a bulge under his shirt told of his wounds. But other than that, he seemed unfazed by the incident, other than perhaps being imbued with increased resolve. The man's eyes bored uncomfortably into David.

David didn't want to nod, not until the man asked him a question. But the man didn't; he just looked. Waiting as long as he could, not as long as Evelyn, but long enough to make the man's lips purse just slightly, David nodded.

The man spun back to Evelyn. "Where is he?"

"Don't ask me where that nigger at. Look here," she said, gesturing to her face, "it look like he tell me his comings and goings? Just like you, he smack me then take what he want."

The man straightened and asked David, "You know where he is?"

David shrugged. "Know where he lives." He tried to keep his face blank as the man tried to read it.

Julio gestured. David followed Jenson and climbed in the back with him. The Hispanic man climbed in the driver's seat. Jenson turned to the window, avoiding David's eyes. This was a surprise. He'd expected Jenson; that's why he had had Evans call. But he hadn't expected Jenson was already so thick with the bad guys. Sleeping around wasn't so bad, even if it was a witness on a case. David had expected negotiating room when Jenson showed up. Expected he might find a way to make Jenson an ally. Jenson still sat, staring out the window. All he'd gotten was the back of Jenson's head.

Light stuffed the book in his belt and pulled his jacket over it. Don't like this shit, to be stealing for his lawyer. Had become too much a thing with this Cohen. Always asking this nigger or that to go steal something for him. First that shit with Franklin and LeVander last year. Then me and LeVander. Now with me alone. Ought to teach that boy his shit then let him do his own stealing.

So he say, "Light, go out and steal the damn book that you already stole once." Shouldn't never have to steal nothing twice. Ain't right, that shit happening. *But, I did. 'Cause the lawyer want it. Always 'cause the lawyer want it.*

Cocksuckers, Light thought, always saying trust me, this the way it work. Like it do. *I'll take care a you.* Every time a lawyer say that shit, you gonna wind up in jail behind some bullshit, Light thought, every time.

Light jumped out of the train and headed toward Nostrand. Then the lawyer say you gonna be safe in jail, just till we get this thing straightened out. Be safe in jail. Nobody safe in jail. Don't see no lawyer saying, "I'll be safe in jail. Why you don't straighten everything out while I sit in jail safe?" No, don't hear that shit. 'Cause they control freaks, that's what. All them lawyers just want to push everybody, make 'em do what they want. "You go here, you go there."

By the time Light walked a block, he'd worked himself into a frenzy. *Bastard,* he kept saying. He saw the red and white lights reflecting off the buildings before he reached the corner of Nostrand and Pacific.

No, he told himself, *ain't gonna trust no lawyer this time. Not this time.* He reached over to the pay phone hanging on the brick wall near the corner, stuck a quarter in the slot, and dialed. *Everybody be on the corner,* he thought, *but it be too late time I get there. Let me just make this here call, and take care a shit.* The phone clicked up. A moment later Light dropped the phone in the cradle. *Now just wait here a few minutes, just a few. Then we see.*

Julio sat in the passenger's seat. Another man—young, taller than Julio, but with the same stocky build—drove. With David and Jenson in the back, David could have jumped out. But Julio, with that half smile that said "pay back is a bitch" covering his face, didn't seem concerned. As if he knew David would not leave, that he had no place to go. Or maybe that he thought the gun he held in his right hand would discourage David. It wouldn't have. Not if David really wanted to go. It was crowded. They wouldn't shoot him here. But escaping now would just mean another chase. Maybe Julio knew, knew that David didn't want to continue the chase. He wanted to end it, one way or the other.

Julio sat with his arm over the seat, peering back at both Jenson and David, as the car lurched forward. Maybe that was it. Maybe Julio didn't trust Jenson anymore than he trusted David, which was not at all.

All of which was interesting, David thought, but didn't help with the immediate problem. Jenson was a detective. That would complicate the problem. All he had to do was walk up to Light, search him, and confiscate the diary. Who would complain? Not Light. No way to make a complaint about stealing stolen property. Not Evelyn. She'd know to stay out of the middle of something like this. And not David, he'd be dead. That was the immediate problem.

Squeaky dropped the phone back in the cradle. Evelyn Jefferson. Unscrewing his cue, he turned to George. "Got to go."

"What you going for?" George asked sadly.

"Shit, what I got to explain to you for?"

"Just walk out, middle of a game." George looked at the table, simple stop on the eight and a straight in on the nine. He hated to miss the opportunity to make Squeaky roar.

Squeaky snorted. "Just so happen that some people got some work to do."

"Only work you do is right here when some damn fool with his money walk in."

"Shit, George, I don't come in here to get insulted. It happens a sister just got her ass whupped and needs us to help."

"What sister?"

"Evelyn Jefferson."

"Evelyn Jefferson get her ass whupped every other Tuesday. Ain't nobody gonna do nothing."

Squeaky slammed his cue into the rack behind the table. "Well, I am. Can't just let Light get away with that shit."

"Light," George said, hurrying out from behind the counter. "He the one?"

"He the one. Now you coming?"

"Shit, I guess, but it don't seem like no big deal to be beaten on some old cracked-out whore."

"You know what this is?" Squeaky called over his shoulder as he skipped down the stairs. "It black-on-black crime, that's what."

"If I didn't know better, I'd say you been reading books." George paused his waddle at the bottom of the steps, huffing to catch his breath. "Since I know you can't read, I figure you must a been watch that Muslim evangelist shit on Public Access."

"I ain't got time to listen to you both sucking wind and trying to talk. Now shut up so we can get 'cross the street. There he is now."

Sucking another big mouthful of air, George stepped off the curb and followed Squeaky. With all a Squeaky's bullshit, he did respect the man. Wasn't too many down here would go after a man for beating on a woman didn't mean nothing to him. Which got George to thinking that maybe Evelyn did mean something to Squeaky. Heard of weirder things than a man falling for a cracked-out whore. Wouldn't be able to say nothing about it, not without taking one huge ration a shit, but then it could happen. The woman get hers and he get pushed to doing something. Whatever though, no woman was worth getting your ass shot over, especially some crack-eaten bitch wasn't too much when she was young and even. George hurried along behind. Had to protect Squeaky from that anyway. Had to protect him. But Squeaky was far ahead, and George was lagging far behind.

* * *

"So, you've committed, huh, Detective?"

Julio waved the gun for David to be quiet.

"See, at first I could understand. You didn't want anyone to know about how you fucked Anacleta."

Julio, having reached back with his gun hand, prepared to smack David, stopped.

David caught Julio's eye. "You didn't know, Julio. Quite torrid. *Señor* Jenson is quite the lover. He used instruments on the lovely Anacleta."

"Shut up, Cohen." It was Jenson this time.

"You see, Julio, he is upset now. It would be quite embarrassing for him to be caught with a woman of that kind, you know, *una gran puta.*"

Julio's eyes narrowed.

"Not me, you understand. You and I have great respect for Anacleta. I am here, that proves that, right? I mean, if I didn't have respect, I could have gone to the police. They would have arrested the bunch of you. Including Anacleta. But I didn't, right?"

"Shut up," Julio said, turning away from David and toward Jenson.

"But, see, Jenson didn't care about that. You remember from the video, that part where he uses the instruments?"

Julio's grip on the gun started pulsing, his knuckles whitening.

"Oh, they didn't let you see the film. Well, at the beginning, where he goes down on Anacleta? Well, you or I, or any man who had any feeling at all for the woman, would be in ecstacy at that point, right?"

Julio was glaring at David, but the gun pointed at Jenson.

"Right," David answered his own question. "But, see, he brought out this little vial. You won't believe what he did with it. You want me to tell you?"

Julio continued to glare at David, anger burning in his eyes.

"Well, maybe you don't want to know," David said, turning to look out the window. "We'll be there soon, just a block or so."

"Tell," Julio screamed.

"Okay, okay." David waited until the car turned onto Pacific before continuing. "He wanted the sample to build a case against Anacleta. He wanted to put her in jail. Isn't that awful? Take advantage of a woman, treat her like a *puta*, which is what he thought she was, right? Then put her in jail. Terrible, terrible."

"Oh, shit." Jenson pulled the handle, slammed his shoulder into the door, and flew out, just before the shot.

David dove after him. A moment later they were through the parked cars and into the crowd on the other side.

George paused to catch his breath behind Squeaky, but close enough to see and hear.

"There he is. You know what this motherfucker did? He beat Evelyn Jefferson within an inch a her life. Right up there in her sister's house where she hiding from this man." Squeaky was yelling top a his lungs. Everybody, even all those people knew Squeaky full a shit from jump, turning 'round to look.

Light jump away, ducking to the inside a the sidewalk, like that gonna get him 'way from Squeaky and his big mouth.

"Don't be running now, Light," Squeaky said, skipping right over behind Light, keeping his distance, about five feet but keeping close too. "Don't be running from your crimes."

"I ain't running from nothing," Light said, breaking into a trot. "Don't never run from nothing."

"Why should he, tell me, Charlie, why should he? Don't got to run if you only pick fights with skinny old women. Ain't that right, Light?"

Light dodging now like he really did do something. Up till now, George didn't really believe that Light did nothing. After all, Evelyn complaining about this and that ever since he knew her, and that be over twenty years. But the way Light cutting and running, it look like he guilty. Have the look of a guilty man.

"Don't run from your just accuser, Mr. Scott. Stand and take your medicine."

Light spun 'round now. Didn't have a lot a choice, getting close to the corner like he was. The usual group hanging there, watching what's going on. But that don't be nothing usually. That make this here a big deal.

"Take medicine from who, you?" Light faced right up at Squeaky. Just like they was never friends.

George moved up close, now that they stopped. Before he didn't think he'd catch 'em at all and would have to hear about it secondhand. But now he was here so he could hear it himself.

Squeaky stopped before he got into real good punch-throwing range. Like Squeaky said, he like to talk and like to play pool, but didn't need no fight. Funny that he'd pick this fight. Didn't have to or nothing.

"Well, what you gonna do?"

Squeaky didn't say nothing then, just stopped, glaring at Light like he didn't know what for a minute. Seemed like a minute. The lawyers would probably say it was like five seconds or something.

"Shouldn't be doing this to no sister." Squeaky spoke quietly this time. Not like it was for the crowd. But the crowd gathering around, moved a little closer.

"Evelyn got her problems, but she don't deserve to be done like that, Light." Squeaky talking real quiet now. And the crowd moving in closer still, till George had to push and waddle his way to the front around some kids.

Seemed fair to George, seeing as how he was there in the beginning so he'd have to know the whole story so he could tell it right. George felt like he was the historian of the neighborhood anyway, with the pool hall up on the second floor with them big windows overlooking the whole thing. Seem like he should hear. Like having a press pass. Anyway, those boys seemed to think so, they let him right through.

"Don't change the question, though. What you gonna do?"

Squeaky stood silently, like he didn't have no answer for that question.

Rolling up next to Jenson behind a Ford parked across Pacific, David peered out at the Chevy. The neighborhood had already absorbed and discounted the gunshot. A man walking behind David gave him a quizzical look.

"Nobody even notices a gunshot."

"A twenty-two down here means you need self-esteem classes," Jenson replied. "You blew my investigation."

"Your investigation?"

Jenson nodded. "I was gonna get the whole story, undercover."

"Where's your backup?"

Jenson said nothing.

"That's bullshit, Jenson, but I'm still gonna get you out of this."

"You meant what you said? About getting me out of this?"

"Shit, Jenson, the only thing you're guilty of is fucking somebody you shouldn't have. Another five minutes and you would have been in on a murder."

"They said they weren't going to kill you," Jenson said, his head popping up above the trunk.

David followed suit. The blue Chevy had moved down the street, past the crowd on the corner, and was turning right. "What else would they tell you?"

Jenson shrugged, stood and slipped his nine millimeter into his shoulder holster.

David gestured for Jenson to follow. "Besides, what else are they going to do with me? Let me walk around, knowing the story?"

"You know the story?"

"Forget it, Jenson. I don't know a thing. Just enough to get you out from under." They walked toward the corner, where a crowd encircled some kind of combat. David broke into a trot.

"But can you get me out?" Jenson asked, trotting alongside.

"Got it set up. Just stick with me."

"And I'll walk on this thing?"

"You may have to quit the force, but you got a future as a porno star. Got your radio?"

Jenson nodded.

"Good. Call in a disturbance. Officer needs assistance."

"What assistance?"

"If you want out from under, just do it."

Jenson reluctantly pulled his radio from his jacket pocket and whispered in a call.

David picked up his pace. This might work out. Just possibly.

Light stood face-to-face with Squeaky. Well, sort of face-to-face. Squeaky wasn't getting within about five feet. Just like George always thought, Squeaky a cowardly little bastard. Wasn't gonna fight no how. Light dropped his hands and turned toward the corner. Gonna walk right though this crowd, looked like.

Light took a step, but the crowd didn't move. Charlie stood right in his path. Right there, not moving. Charlie ain't no friend of Evelyn's, been hanging with Light on the corner for all these years, and he ain't moving.

"What you do to Evelyn?"

"Shit, you know that old bitch, Charlie. What do you care?"

"Ain't right to be beatin' her."

Light moved to the next man in the crowd, but he didn't move either.

"Ain't nobody gonna move, Light. You gonna take yours right here." Squeaky talking louder now. Yelling almost. This here shit getting out a hand, George thought. He heard the siren, but it sounded far off.

The crowd started to move in, pushing Light toward Squeaky. Light spun away, facing Squeaky. "This ain't right, Squeaky. Ain't right, all you guys against me."

"Ain't right what you did to Evelyn," Squeaky replied.

"Well, then it ought to be you an' me, you the one all upset 'bout it. Ain't fair like this."

"It ain't fair you beatin' on a woman like that neither."

George heard the siren cut off before he saw the spinning lights. A moment later the crowd moved away as the cops moved in. Gonna be all right.

"Let me get this straight. You want me to indict your client?"

"Right."

Stella "Chapter-and-Verse" Prescott, held the manila folder in her large black hands for a second before flipping it open and turning a page or two. "This is tracked D, 'dismiss if you have to.' You had to figure that."

"Yep. Look, you talked to Jenson. Twining was killed. That's what Jenson thinks, and this can prove it. Just one indictment."

"You know what the ECAB assistant said? Said that the complainant is a crack addict."

"Recovering."

"Recovering." Stella slammed the file closed. "I saw her this morning. She got some money."

"Not recovering?"

"Not recovering." Stella pushed her chair back from the desk and put her hands in her lap. David could feel the Southern preacher's daughter coming out. It had been rumor around the office that she did the best Barbara Jordan imitation in the country, but only when she wasn't trying.

"We can't, David. We have policies. There's no weapon here. Even if she said there was, we're not supposed to indict unless the weapon is recovered. And the complainant says there wasn't a weapon."

"Stella, we just need a week. We have to keep Light in a week."

"David, what can I tell the DA?" Stella spread her hands helplessly. "It's against policy."

"Stella, they're willing to kill for this diary. I can tell you that on the best authority. They're willing to kill."

"So why don't you testify? We'll put you in protective custody."

"Against who? I didn't see anybody except the girl, and she's in the wind," David lied. "I can't prove anything yet."

Stella folded her arms, her face setting in a glare. David had to turn away. There was power in that Southern preacher's daughter's stare. He looked out the window. How much did he tell her? How much did he reveal? It wasn't that he knew that much, not really. If he told her, he was confessing, confessing to a woman who put quarters in the meter when on official business. She could arrest him. He'd be a party to the robbery, an accomplice. And the case against a lawyer wouldn't be dismissed so easily. Even if the complainant was a crack addict, Stella could push it. She would push it. And she would stand before the jury and quote chapter and verse why she had to. Why the entire Western world would collapse if she didn't.

But what else could he do? He couldn't let Light walk out. If Light walked out, the diary would go back to somebody, and that person either gives it up or gets killed, probably both. These guys couldn't take a chance, not with whatever was in that diary. Whatever it was was dangerous enough that they would kill for it. Torture for it.

Shit, if she didn't indict Light, then David was just as vulnerable. He'd seen it. He'd had it, as far as they knew. He'd set up the scenario where Light got arrested. No, David had no choice. He had to tell her. Had to trust her.

"Stella, I set up the robbery. It was my idea."

Stella turned back. She spoke slowly. "David, I must advise you that you have the right to an attorney."

"I know my goddamn rights, Stella. It was the only way to keep anyone from getting killed. They would have killed Light, Evelyn, me . . . anyone connected with that diary."

"Why?"

"I don't know. But they sliced Light's dick and would have sliced mine."

"But they didn't."

David shook his head. He didn't want to implicate Anacleta. "As long as you have the diary, as long as you're prosecuting Light, then there is a way to the bottom," David said.

"How?"

"The diary. They want it. You have it, but I can get it. I can tell them that. In fact, it's true. You don't really want to prosecute this thing. I give the word, you dismiss."

"I might dismiss anyway."

David waved her off. "As long as I'm the only one they can get to with access to the diary, they have to do business with me."

"And what will you do?"

David spread his hands. "I don't know." He looked out the window. He'd figure something out. At least he hoped he would.

"Where?" Joel asked.

"Washington."

"Shit, David, first you tell me that these cocksuckers are shooting curare-soaked thumbtacks, and now you want to go to Washington to talk to one of them?"

"Needles, I think, not thumbtacks. And it was curare with something else. I forget what. Otherwise I would have died."

"David, I don't give a shit about the curare. I give a shit about you and pushing this thing."

David said nothing, instead looking out over the East River. The attempt to make light of the danger hadn't worked as he knew it wouldn't. It wasn't that he hadn't asked himself before why he was doing it. He had. Many times. But there was no good answer. He told himself for a time that it was because he loved Anacleta, but he knew that wasn't true. She was more sexually exciting than any woman he had ever known. Although no other woman had paralyzed him during sex, so perhaps the comparison wasn't fair. It wasn't love, but he couldn't let her go. Just release her.

"David, these people mean business. They already tried to kill you."

"And Anacleta saved me."

"And now you're going to save her. Very gallant." Joel rose, stretching to his full height, and, towering over David, continued. "David, the woman made her choice."

"Did she?"

"Of course she did. Just like you and I. She made her choice. She has to pay the consequences, not you."

"You made your choice, Joel?"

Joel remained silent for a moment, moving slowly away from David, giving him room, David supposed. "I don't want to discuss philosophy, David. And I don't want to lose a partner either. But that woman isn't worth either of us risking our lives."

"I'm in too deep. I'm going." David turned toward the door.

"What good is it going to do?"

"Look, if I'm dead, their problems are solved."

"From what I can tell, you don't even know who they are."

"Exactly, which is why I'm going to see Vance."

"Well, wait a minute. You don't think I'm going to let you ride the train," Joel said, hurrying after.

It was three hours later as David sat in the same park, waiting for Vance.

"Have that story sold yet?"

David looked up with a start. Vance clearly remembered him and apparently still bought the reporter story. David waited silently until Vance seated himself next to him on the bench.

"No, haven't even got it written. But I do think I have an angle on it."

Vance tugged on the sleeves of his tweed jacket, crossed

his thin legs in the European style, and waited for David to continue.

"Let's say there's a woman who has an affair with a congressman. More than an affair, becomes his lover. Develops his trust. At some point she tries to influence his vote." As David spoke, he felt the tension. He wasn't sure how he felt Vance's tension, probably the tiny movements he caught out of the corner of his eye, Vance tugging again at his sleeve, straightening his glasses. Not the movements so much as the way they were made. But Vance remained silent, waiting, it seemed, for David to continue.

"That's probably not so unusual. After all, congressmen's wives all have influence with them. That wouldn't be considered so shocking."

"No, I suppose not. Although some of the wives have had some strange ideas. You could include something about Huffington's wife, although, thankfully, he wasn't elected." Vance seemed more relaxed.

"That's one angle, but I was thinking of another. Let's suppose this woman didn't just happen to meet the congressman, but was set up to meet him."

"Nothing unusual there. Happens all the time," Vance said brightly. "Goes both ways. These girls want to meet power, and power wants to meet them. Yes, I think you've got a good story there."

"Yes, but usually the public perception is that the girls like to be close to power, the aphrodisiac. This girl would be a little different. See, she had some training for this sort of thing."

Vance tugged at his sleeve again, then adjusted his glasses.

Yes, David thought, signs of tension. "Trained both to influence and to please."

"A Mata Hari."

Interesting how the voice cracks even more obviously when the speaker is trying hardest not to. "Yes, but with a stinger."

HOSTILE WITNESS

Vance wiped his forehead and stood. "It's been nice talking to you, but I do have a meeting."

David jumped up. "I'll walk with you. You see, I meant a stinger quite literally. She can enforce her will by either threatening to expose their affair . . . or threatening his life."

Vance hurried. "I'm sure that never happens," he said.

"I'm sure it does. And I'm sure you're lying."

Vance stopped short, the tension now etched on his face. "You have proof?"

"I can prove Twining was murdered and that he was prepared to go to the police."

"But not about what?"

"Not yet. You care to bet on how long it'll take me to figure it out?"

Vance turned, moving at a more leisurely pace. "No," he answered slowly, his voice more relaxed, "but I would be willing to bet you're not a reporter."

"Lawyer."

Vance nodded.

"Who introduced him?"

"You expect me to tell you about this woman with the stinger just like that?"

"I could go to the Feds."

"Why haven't you?"

For a second David imagined Joel's reaction. Probably sitting in the BMW, nodding furiously. Pushing the image away, David answered. "Let's say I would prefer that this be handled without official intervention."

"Ah." Vance smiled. "You too have been stung."

"Whatever," David said uncomfortably. "The question was, how were they introduced?"

Vance smiled. "Me." He said it quietly, as if hoping it was loud enough for David's ears but not for the electronic ears behind.

It made no sense. If Vance was the killer, the man behind the stingers, so to speak, then why was he talking to David? A possibility hit David like a load of buckshot. Vance was planning to kill him. David tried hard to hide the shock. He hadn't thought it was Vance, but if it was, Vance had fooled David with that act, believing he was a reporter. But here Vance was calmly telling David he was the man. That meant, in the final analysis, Vance had cut his own man's throat. David's collar felt tight. "You," he croaked. It wasn't so funny about tension's revealing itself in the cracks of voices now.

Vance strolled a few more steps, seeming to enjoy David's discomfort. "All my idea, actually," he said finally.

As the shock wore off, David began to feel more uncomfortable about the way Vance was telling him the story. The first admission could have been a slip, but as he spoke more and more calmly, exposing himself to prosecution, David felt more and more vulnerable.

"I was idealistic in those days; so was my first employer. I had one client, a congressman from upstate."

David grunted, his concern suddenly diverted from the direction the conversation was taking to the direction they were walking. Aside from the obvious problem of assassins waiting on the other side of the Washington Monument, there was the question of whether the silver disk in his pocket, David's last keepsake from the dear, departed Crawford Walsh, had the power to broadcast through stone monuments.

David moved toward the benches on the right. Vance kept walking, a sarcastic smile creeping across his lips. "She was an environmentalist," he continued, raising his voice slightly to adjust for the increased distance David was putting between them. "A real earth mother in every way, except looks. She was gorgeous."

David plopped himself down on a bench. He wouldn't go farther. If Vance wanted to tell this story, he would do it here. David tried not to think about the fact that it was he who needed the story, not Vance. "Gorgeous," he said.

Vance stopped, hesitated, then joined David on the bench. "Gorgeous," he replied, "and totally dedicated to the cause. She was one of those people who lived in a morally unambiguous universe. If she believed it was right to save the environment, then that was it. All was fair. No nice ethical distinctions for her."

David felt envious for a moment, then pulled himself back to his situation. Vance didn't seem bent on murder, at least since he tacitly had agreed to meet David on the bench, but why was he telling him this? What good could it do him?

"It was harmless enough at first. She and that young congressman were actually in love, I think. He was at least. She certainly liked him well enough."

"What happened?"

"Well, she enlisted a couple of more girls, they met a couple of congressmen, and they pushed them into supporting environmental issues. Then a man came to me, very much like you did this morning, and told me a story, very much like you did."

"A reporter."

Vance stood. "Shall we walk?" he asked.

David was torn again. No mistake this time, Vance purposely wanted the other side of the monument. The park wasn't crowded; there were people, only a few. David stood. It could make the difference of only a few days. If he didn't get the story, there was no next step, other than to wait for the executioners to catch him and Anacleta. . . . and probably Light. He fell in next to Vance.

"Yes, a reporter," Vance said as they passed behind the monument. "He had the story, much as you do, although he seemed to have worked harder to get it. There was no murder then, no event of any kind that would draw him to the story . . . or to me."

Behind the monument now, David glanced around. No one suspicious looking, but then there wouldn't be. If they hadn't been willing to shoot him in Brooklyn, with the crowds there, then what did he have to worry about here? Taking a deep breath, he relaxed, or tried to. It was then that he noticed Vance had stopped talking.

"Are you all right, Counselor?"

"Yes," David said. "His story came out?"

Vance hesitated a moment before turning away from David and continuing the walk. "No, it was strange. He was an ambitious young man," Vance continued, gesturing to a bench near the monument.

David followed him to the bench. "Ambitious . . . and he didn't sell the story?"

"He offered me a deal. Have my girls, that's what he called them, my girls, have my girls do something for him on this piece of legislation. Well, it was nothing really, didn't make much difference either way, except that 'my boys,' the congressmen, had crucial votes on the issue."

"You and 'your girls' did?"

Vance nodded. "That was the mistake. You see, the man didn't care about the bill. No, what he cared about was compromising me." Suddenly Vance had a tired, beaten look. An old man, no longer with that enthusiastic blush of youth.

No longer afraid. David fingered the disk in his pocket.

"It won't broadcast through the monument," Vance said. "Walsh gave you a cheap one."

"You knew?"

Vance nodded. "You see, that was Walsh's plan all along. After compromising me, he introduced his own girls into the operation. Didn't need me at all, except to shut up."

"Walsh?"

Vance nodded sadly.

"But . . . ?"

"I don't know. For years I dealt only with Walsh. Then this other man last year." Vance smiled at David, as if reading his mind. "These people are killers, David. This monument is to protect you . . . not me. If they thought you knew . . ."

"They do," said David.

Vance nodded sadly. "My only advice is to give them what they want. Then at least you will live . . . maybe." Vance stood and continued on his path around the monument and back toward his office.

David sat silently. He felt for the old man but didn't intend to make his choice. The old man could have fought, could have told Walsh to shove it, but he didn't. Vance may not realize it, David thought, but he has paid for the rest of his life. David didn't intend to. If Vance wouldn't tell him who the new leader was, and Walsh couldn't, he'd get it out of Anacleta.

David pushed himself off the bench. He had more of what the bastards needed than they did of him. In fact, they couldn't kill him, not with all the stuff he had. They'd never get it all, not unless he gave it to them. But they had to know all that he had. It was no protection if they didn't know. David hurried back to the car, where Joel was waiting.

"Make copies and hide 'em around," David said, leaning in the driver's window of the BMW. "Somewhere where you'll be able to find them if I'm not around."

"Nice euphemism, David. I know a good hiding place in the U.S. attorney's office."

"No." David was vehement.

"Okay," Joel said. "I lost you for the second part."

"I know, I remember it."

"Where are you going?"

"I'm going to take the train. Safer."

"For who?" Joel asked as he drove off.

For who indeed, David thought. At first he'd thought for Joel, but now he wasn't so sure. Anyone watching would have figured out that Joel had some kind of tape, or might have. And if Vance was being less than honest about his current position, they'd definitely know.

David shook the thought off and hurried toward Union Station. Nothing he could do about that now. Three hours from now he'd be back in New York, back with Anacleta.

David dropped the phone in the cradle. Gone. It had been harrowing to get her out of there. Every face had looked like a South American assassin. But they had done it. Safe in Evans's apartment. Safe for the duration. No one could connect Evans to this. No one would look there. She had been safe until David could work the rest of this out.

Had been.

"What could I do?" Evans had asked. "You want me, a three-hundred-pound black man, to hold a white woman in my apartment against her will?"

David had been silent. Evans had been right. Holding her there when she wanted to leave would have been like kidnapping or unlawful imprisonment. David was losing the lawyers' nice distinctions. The anger tore at his insides, but there was no focus.

David imagined what it was like, closed up in that hole. For a woman used to a different life . . . What was she used to? She knew the risks out there. But she had left. Why?

David shook his head. She did. That's all he had to know now. She left and was out there. What was it Evans had said? She had talked about his taking the risks. She didn't want that. The new Anacleta, trying to save him. Sacrificing herself? But it wouldn't do any good. That was the problem with self-sacrifice, it didn't do any good.

The question was, what to do now?

He could lay low and hope they didn't find him. How long could he lay low? A month? A year? Eventually Light comes to trial and the diary gets released. David shuddered. No judge would give Light high bail for long, not if his attorney made even a modest request for a reduction. This wasn't the kind of case that screamed out for pretrial detention. Light gets released. They kill him. *Abated by death.* The case would be over and the diary released. No, David couldn't allow that, not after he had put Light in by setting up the robbery. Not after he had set up Light.

Going to the police meant giving up Anacleta. He felt the rejection in his chest radiating through his body. His chest wouldn't stand for that, no matter what his mind told him was logical.

Only one choice left. Into the lion's mouth. David picked up the phone and punched out a number. Vance's secretary said he was in New York. *Followed me,* David thought. *Why?* That question had no answer, but it didn't matter. He dialed the number the secretary gave him. A moment later

Vance picked up the phone. David said they had to talk. Vance grunted an affirmative-sounding grunt and told David a half hour. David grabbed a copy of the case synopsis, a copy of the diary, and the congressmen's names as he remembered them and was out the door.

A half hour after surviving subway mayhem, he was at the door of Vance's New York office. Vance ushered him in personally, took a seat opposite him across the coffee table in the corner, and offered coffee. David declined.

"It sounded urgent," Vance said while attempting to sip his coffee calmly.

David popped open the brass locks on his briefcase, pulled out the synopsis, and slid it across the table to Vance. "I've got a number of these and copies in a safe place."

Vance leaned back, snapped on the reading lamp behind his head, and began with page one. After a moment he reached forward, plucked the quill pen from its holder, and made a mark. He leaned back in the worn chair and continued.

David couldn't help feeling the irony of the ex-college professor, years later, somehow involved in this murderous business but still feeling bound to correct a "paper" handed to him.

Vance nodded silently as he flipped a page. "Excellent analysis, Mr. Cohen." He flashed a smile of approval before returning to the page. Five minutes later he flipped the front page back on top and slid the package back to David. "I've made only a couple of corrections. I'm impressed, Mr. Cohen."

David nodded humbly.

"The question, however, is what you intend to do now. I take it that you have chosen not to follow my advice?"

David shook his head.

"And the police?"

David shook his head.

"Yes, you are another of Anacleta's victims."

David bridled but held himself silent.

"But the question is the diary. The police have it, I understand."

"But I can get it."

"And, in return for various promises, deliver it to me?"

"Not you. Someone with the power to negotiate. That isn't you."

"Quite right. It isn't."

"From professor to flunky. How does it feel?"

Vance examined his fingernails, pushing a cuticle back on his right index finger. "We're all flunkies of one kind or another, as you will no doubt discover."

"I'm not a flunky." The man's tone, calm and superior, grated on David. But it was also strange, not the tone of voice he used in Washington. Was the office tapped? David nervously slid the papers back in his briefcase and snapped the locks shut.

Vance slipped his pen back in the holder with that look that chided David, as if his precautions were much too late. "No, you're not a flunky . . . not yet, anyway," Vance said, leaning back and staring at the ceiling. "You know, when I started in this business, twenty-some years ago, I had that same attitude. These flunkies, these congressmen. They had the smile, the suit that hung well on them, the straight WASP hair. They had nothing else, I thought. Look at me now." Vance looked deep into David's eyes. "Do you wonder how it happened?"

"I thought you told me."

"No, I told you the mechanisms, not the movement of the soul. Do you wonder how it was that Twining and the others fell?"

"With your help."

"Yes, with my help." Vance twirled the quill pen between his fingers. "Did you ever wonder how I fell?" For the first time David heard the emotion in Vance's voice.

"The way it always happens, greed."

That superior manner again. "Not greed . . . passion. Greed is a form of passion, I suppose, but it wasn't mine."

"The rain forest?"

"Among other environmental concerns. The world was literally going to hell in a handbasket, and these politicians were concerned only with getting reelected. I'd tell them that in fifty years there wouldn't be enough oxygen in the air to support life, and they'd ask me if that knowledge was reflected in the polls. I was young, or at least younger, arrogant, superior. Like you."

"So?"

"When Walsh came to me, it wasn't the threat he presented. Prison would have been short, in a country club. No, what he presented was a choice: give up my passion . . . or become corrupt." Vance studied his fingers again, long, narrow, bony fingers, but they held such fascination for him. He spoke to them now. "It was the same for Twining and the others. They all had a passion. For Twining I think it was just to have people call him 'congressman.' For others it was this cause or that. But it was the passion, that drug that comes from inside and makes you think you have something to live for. And it's that passion and that addiction to passion that allows them to play you, son." Vance looked up now, his eyes only slightly damp.

David opened his mouth as if to speak, but Vance waved him to be quiet, glancing toward the lamp on the desk. A bug perhaps?

"You have a chance, young man," Vance said. "You can walk away. They will allow that. But you must give up your passion."

David was silent for a long time. "And Anacleta?" he finally asked.

". . . is your passion," Vance answered.

David felt Vance's sadness tear through him. Vance had said the right thing, advised David as his handlers had ordered. On the tape his handlers would listen to, it would seem that Vance had carried out orders. But David read the pain on his face. Vance had not given up his passion without cost.

"When can I get to meet your handlers?"

"You're aware of the danger?"

David nodded.

"Tomorrow?"

"Where?"

"I'll call," Vance said, standing up. "I'll call early."

David pumped the pedal. The Toyota hesitated, rumbled, quieted, then rumbled again. He could still hear the beep in the background ... and Joel's voice, as if the beep had killed it. David allowed the engine to rumble. The voice had sounded desperate, David thought as he pulled the seat belt across his chest, snapped it in place, and picked up the map. Desperate to find him.

It would be three hours, that's what Vance had said. As David looked at the map, he saw the last half of the trip would be on two-lane secondary roads. He'd listened to the whole message, but couldn't bring himself to pick up the phone. He flipped the Toyota into gear and pulled out onto Livingston Street. The engine rumbled its complaints, but five minutes later, when it was on the Brooklyn Bridge, it gave up and ran smoothly, through the Lincoln Tunnel and onto Route 80.

The call had come early, just as Vance had promised. An address in Pennsylvania, just over the Jersey border, the voice had said. A farmhouse behind a six-foot-high stone fence. It had had an ominous sound, but it was the only way, Vance had said.

They had Anacleta. David had insisted on seeing her. He wouldn't make any arrangements without seeing her. He wanted to make sure she was alive. This was the only way, they said. They said without the diary, they couldn't guarantee her safety. Guarantee her safety. A strange euphemism that David had accepted without thought. He thought about it now. The only threat to her safety was from them. They were conceding that they couldn't guarantee their own actions.

If they couldn't guarantee their own actions with Anacleta, then what could they guarantee with him? Nothing, David concluded. But then, David had his passion.

* * *

David turned onto county road 54617 in Wayne County, Pennsylvania. It was indeed remote. A few houses dotted the landscape as he turned, but within a few miles the road was lined on both sides with pastureland. Another turn and a mile farther the stone wall appeared on the right.

David slowed, turned into the circular drive, pulled around a Mercedes, and parked on the far side. At least he wouldn't be blocked in.

The front door was open. David walked in. Vance sat in the small living room. Anacleta sat next to him, looking only vaguely concerned. She jumped up, ran to him and planted a kiss on his mouth. As she squeezed him, he got more concerned. It didn't seem as if he was rescuing a damsel in distress. It felt vaguely like a set up.

A man stood up as she released David from her hug. He was tall, maybe six feet, with the long, narrow fingers of his right hand extended to David. The man said, "Santeria."

David introduced himself and took the man's hand. The man gripped too tightly, using the handshake to guide David toward the couch with Anacleta. Vance and another man got up, the other man larger, wearing a suit jacket on the hot day. It probably hid a shoulder holster, David thought. Julio was not here. David wondered about the significance of that.

Anacleta sat on his right and held his arm tightly. Perhaps she really was scared. Maybe the laughter as he came in had been the act, not the tight grip now. But there was no way to tell, nothing to do but go ahead with the plan.

Santeria sat in the chair next to the couch, smiling broadly. "It is nice to see love bloom, Mr. Cohen. However, before we can allow you two to leave to enjoy the rest of your lives, there is some business, no?"

David looked around the house. It was old, not in good repair. The paper on the wall was cracked, furniture oddly arranged, as if placed recently, perhaps for this meeting. "Perhaps we should discuss the matter outside, Mr. Santeria."

Santeria shrugged. "A careful man," he said. "I like to

do business with careful men." He gestured to the front door, and David led the way. A large maple graced the center of the circular drive, its branches arching over a patch of grass. David walked to the right, past the maple, and looked across the road, up the hill of pasture. Holsteins grazed peacefully. Several men worked with some machinery on top of the hill across the road. David turned right, around the side of the house. He walked several steps and stopped, turning to face Santeria.

"Business," he said.

"Business," repeated Santeria. "In particular, one diary and several tapes."

"And several tapes?" David continued watching for a change in Santeria's expression. There was only a slight smile.

"You have copies?"

David shook his head.

"We have recovered them all then. A misunderstanding with a former employee." Santeria smiled sweetly. "An arrangement has been worked out."

"Walsh."

"Correct." Santeria took several steps toward the side yard. David followed. "The burglary was your idea then, as Vance suspected."

David nodded. No point in getting anyone else involved.

"There were other possibilities that would have been more distressing, I suppose. I am more comfortable now that I know you are a common burglar."

David smiled. "Not common, I hope."

"Whatever. You have the item for us, in exchange for Anacleta's freedom and your own?"

David said nothing.

Santeria smiled. "No? Come, let me show you something." David followed Santeria to the back of the house. Santeria pointed to two holes, six feet by six feet by three feet, freshly dug in the sod. "Prepared for you and Anacleta."

David gulped. "To be prepared like Walsh?"

"If you hadn't told us what we wanted. But had Julio had a little more knowledge, we may not have needed you."

"A little more knowledge?"

"We hadn't told him everything."

David felt a rolling in his stomach. "Hadn't told him what?" David asked, turning to the green hillside behind the house, rolling up into the maple-covered mountain.

"Walsh had had a lung removed, didn't have the stamina he once had. That was why we had to let him go."

"This is how you let someone go?"

"No, not at all. We provided what you call a 'golden parachute.' More than he would get unless he were a CEO of a *Fortune* 500 company. He was quite well-off." Santeria continued in a sad voice. "Do you remember what Vance told you yesterday about us taking over his operation?"

David grunted, a sound he meant to be "yes."

Santeria took it that way and continued. "The man who set it up was Walsh. He was the mastermind. But when we let him go, he wasn't satisfied. Wanted revenge, I suppose, although I don't know what for. He was well paid."

Santeria led David toward two chairs set in the late-afternoon sun.

"Why?" David asked, following.

"He believed that he was the founder and should have been afforded more respect. I assumed you would be more reasonable. Perhaps I overestimated you."

"You can assure my safety?"

"Of course."

"After you get the diary?"

Santeria laughed. "You are a cautious man."

"Cautious enough not to have brought the diary."

Santeria looked concerned for the first time. "Where is it?"

"The original is in the police evidence room. Copies along with a full statement of what I believe happened here are in safe-deposit boxes in my name and another in Anacleta's."

"To be opened in the event of your death?"

"Yes, and a representative of New York State must be present whenever the safe-deposit box of a dead person is opened. Unless you're intending to break into the bank, you can't get them."

Santeria signaled to an older woman inside a window. She nodded and disappeared.

"You've been watching too much television, Mr. Cohen. It won't work. What prevents us from killing you and Anacleta now? Without the testimony of either of you, the police would have a diary and a statement. A diary that tells you nothing, am I correct?"

David said nothing but had to agree. They never had found the time bomb. It was only the videos that tied the scheme together, and with he and Anacleta gone it would come down to the willingness of two congressmen to corroborate the story, something Santeria was apparently confident they wouldn't do.

David turned again to the green hillside stretching away in the distance. The sun warmed his arms. The breeze rustling through the maple leaves cooled them. The scents of a thousand plants assaulted his nostrils. Life had never seemed so precious, political corruption never so meaningless. David wanted out.

He sipped a banana daiquiri. It certainly was a civilized way to receive death threats. It almost felt as if it were someone else being threatened, except for the memory of Walsh's interrupted gray skin.

"My guess throughout has been drugs," David said.

"Cocaine, to be more precise."

"I should have known. Cali?"

"Actually, we are an independent contractor. Cali was one of our clients. We deal more with Mexico now."

"And the congressmen in your stable, they know?"

"No. Not at all. They don't even know they are in anyone's stable. We are lobbyists using the gentle arts of persuasion."

"Until they attempt to escape."

"Escape? There is no need to escape. We allow retirement."

"What good is the influence then? I mean, all this work."

"You will see for yourself in just a moment." Santeria paused while the tall man brought two new daiquiris and placed them on the glass-topped table between Santeria and David. "I was most distressed to lose Julio."

"Julio?"

"Yes, he is back in the jungles, I suspect. Happier."

"For failing to kill me?"

"No, for the gunshots. We don't like to do that."

"Then Anacleta..."

"It was part of the plan."

"She was in on it?"

Santeria smiled without answering. David could feel the anger creeping up. It wasn't Anacleta's betrayal, or non-betrayal. It was that this man knew, and knew how much it hurt. David thought about Coyce Loyn. It was better that way. Pay for it. Get it. Go home. He loosened his grip on the glass. He didn't want it to show. Not now.

"I am glad to see you can control your pain. *Norteamericanos* are better at that than we. We tend to be more passionate. Do you think it is in our genes or in our upbringing?"

"She did know then?"

"Would you prefer I tell you that she did not? Well then, she did not. But we did. We have seen this many times, this weakening. You see, Anacleta was not recruited from the ranks of prostitutes, as you may have surmised. Nor was she a self-made true believer, as were the girls run by *Señor* Vance. She was trained, trained from an early age. From the age of three in fact. Trained in the skills and in the beliefs."

"Beliefs?"

Santeria smiled. "It was the late Mr. Walsh's great contribution. Serendipitous, that is the word?"

David nodded.

"He had just finished a story on cults. He ran across Mr. Vance's operation and had an idea."

"And came to you?"

"Not me. To Cali. He needed financing. They provided it. People began to be trained."

"Trained to do what?"

"What Anacleta is doing. To love men so that they cannot get enough. So that they become addicted to her. Love is far more addictive than cocaine, don't you agree?"

David didn't care to expose his ignorance of both so said nothing. "But the training doesn't hold."

"Which is why Walsh added the religious aspect, saving the world from the pagan gringos. The ignorant gringos. The religion increases loyalty."

"But even that . . ."

"Fails? Yes. Sometimes, alas, it does. Just as with men, there is a time when the little head speaks and the big head listens, no? Well, with women there is a time when the mother speaks and the trained killer must listen. If you watch the trained women, you can tell. It is like the woman who is about to deliver a baby, she starts to clean the house. When she met you, she started to clean the house. We could see, even if you couldn't." Santeria laughed. "And you don't know whether to believe me now, true?" Santeria laughed again.

David turned to watch a chipmunk run across the stone wall stretching to the right. It paused on a tall, moss-covered stone, rocked up on its haunches, stared at David for a long second, trying to decide if he was friend or foe, then, having made its decision, disappeared into a crevice. David wished his decision was as easy to make. Even more, he wished he had a crevice to disappear into.

Santeria hadn't made his offer yet. There had to be an offer; otherwise, why keep David alive? The offer had to include Anacleta. Why had he raised the doubt? He could have left David believing that Anacleta had saved his life. It would have increased her value and the risks David was willing to take for her. But he undercut her, then resurrected her even stronger with the story that it was in the plan but that she wasn't in on it. That she had acted out of love. A trained woman, trained to not feel, and yet she felt so much for David that she had risked it all to save him.

That was the part that stuck in David's craw. After his training, he had very little trust for love. But the thought drew him; like a teenage fantasy, it drew him. His reason told him not to believe it, but part of him insisted on believing.

"But I promised to tell you how the scheme worked, did I not?" Santeria asked, breaking in on David's thoughts. "You now have a problem. Either Anacleta is a killer, still loyal to our organization and ready at any moment to cut your throat, or she is a woman who has given up that life, given it up because of her love for you. A love that you return, *verdad?*"

David said nothing. He didn't want to listen, but he couldn't stop himself.

"If you walk away from her and you have guessed wrong, she will surely die. At our hands, you think. Whatever. You will find out. We will tell you. And you will live the rest of your life in grief at having not only lost a woman who truly loved you, and whom you loved, but having killed her in the bargain."

Santeria's laugh cut through David's brain like a razor. David was fast learning to hate the man.

"However, if you take her away from all this, thinking that she is the true love of your life, and you are wrong, then you sleep with a woman who can kill you in undetectable ways. Any day may be your last. You are trapped, *señor.*" Santeria looked over the stream babbling quietly to the left.

He was waiting for David's predicament to sink deeper, to twist his mind even more than it already had. David tried to resist but couldn't. There was little chance of his sleeping well tonight.

"We have a problem, don't we, *joven?*"

David didn't like the use of the word "we."

"Normally we let the problem sink in a little more, a day, a week, whatever. But here we don't have so much time, so allow me to explain further. You see, I am in the same kind of conundrum as are you. I don't know what you are intending. You may be intending to go home and report on all of this to the authorities, make yourself a hero at my expense. On the other hand if, believing that, I kill you and I am wrong, my superiors, who don't like to kill, would be upset. If I believe that you really will keep these documents in the vault somewhere and, if I leave you alone, you will leave us alone, and I am wrong . . . well, you see the problem.

"It is much the same problem that comes up with the legislators, in your country and in mine. But we have found a solution."

"What's that?" David felt his voice crack. He was sure the crack was audible, destroying any hope of maintaining an image. It didn't matter.

"You must understand first that it is not the women who create the problem for these politicians. In my country, for instance, a politician might be in trouble if he did not have a mistress. He would not be considered man enough to be a leader. Here it is different. A man must be squeaky clean. That is the phrase, no, squeaky clean?"

"Squeaky clean, supporting the illegal drug industry?"

"Supporting?" Santeria looked up with genuine surprise. "No, no, *señor*, not supporting. Opposing. With every fiber of his being. It is our first issue. We insist that they support the war on drugs."

"Support the war on drugs?"

"*Señor* Cohen, do you believe drugs would be a multi-billion-dollar industry if these drugs were legal? Would we be able to take ten cents worth of coca and sell it for a thousand dollars? Of course not. Your government is our partner, a partner who pays all the costs while we reap all the profits. A good partnership, no?"

"Squeaky clean. He appears to be a conservative on drugs, opposing them."

"More than that, he is conservative on that issue, but that creates his problem with the woman. The congressman is worried that he will not get reelected if the story of his peccadilloes gets out. So we solve both his problems. His problem with the girl is nothing, only to get him to listen, to talk to us in private. Once he does, then we offer him something he needs more than the publicity."

The man appeared with another daiquiri. David waved him off, but Santeria accepted the drink, even though the one he had was only half empty.

"While we speak, a draft of $100,000 is being wired to the account of Cohen and Jacobs."

"A bribe."

"No, a retainer."

"Retainers from criminal organizations are illegal."

"But not from the flower industry of Columbia. One of our biggest exports, you know."

"And the biggest customer is the U.S.?"

"Correct."

David felt the trap closing. "Anacleta?"

"She goes with you. If she loves you, you live happily ever after. If not, you have my word that she will never harm you. Unless, that is, you harm us."

"If I refuse?"

"Both you and Anacleta die."

"Messy. There would be questions."

"You would die in an accident. Regrettable, but not a hint of suspicion could be raised. We have much experience in that kind of death."

"And Anacleta?"

"A much simpler problem. She doesn't exist, you know."

David felt the noose tightening. "Doesn't exist?"

Santeria nodded. "Her entry was illegal, of course. No bank accounts, the apartment is not in her name. She has no friends, except professional acquaintances. Most of them don't want to see her anymore."

"She has people at home."

Santeria shook his head. "We recruit from the bush, as the Australians say. The hills. No birth records there. We've had her from birth. No family." Santeria seemed peaceful beneath the smiling face. "Have you ever noticed her fingers? The skin on the tips is periodically burned off. She doesn't even have fingerprints."

David shivered through the warm sun. "You would kill her even if she is loyal to you?"

Santeria sipped his daiquiri and flicked at a small insect clinging to the arm of his Adirondack chair before answering. "The difference between us," he said softly, "is that you care about Anacleta . . . I don't." Santeria smiled. "The point is to make you suffer. Anacleta is expendable for that purpose."

A cold shiver ran up David's back. "And if I take your deal, then send Anacleta packing and turn you in?"

Santeria laughed. "Do you plan to give up women, Mr. Cohen? No? Well, then how will you tell if the next woman is not one of ours?" Santeria drained his daiquiri, pushed it aside, and picked up the fresh one. "Will you date only unattractive women, thinking to fool us that way? We have all kinds. No matter how big a case your FBI brings, you will not get us all. There will be a couple of indictments maybe. The authorities may be able to keep you safe. But someday you will want a woman. A beautiful woman will appear . . . and you will die." Santeria laughed. "It is funny, thinking of you hesitating as you reach for her, as you kiss her. Not knowing if she is there for love, or murder." Santeria waved a fly away from his drink. "You are better off with Anacleta. The devil known."

David felt the trap close.

"By the way, the deal is that you will have a retainer of $100,000 on your anniversary every year, as long as our business continues."

A trap, but a velvet trap.

David felt a vaguely satisfied feeling pulsing out from his stomach. He had the story now, the whole story. He would be safe. Anacleta would be safe, and the retainer would pay the bills. The other feeling was present too, the feeling that these criminals would get away with it. But there was noth-

HOSTILE WITNESS

ing David could do about that. If he accepted the retainer, he was bound to silence. And with him bound to silence, there was no reason they would kill him. His testimony wouldn't be admissible, not after today.

No, that other feeling said, you could argue that the retainer was foisted upon you by coercion. Perhaps. But David didn't care. He would allow his silence to be bought, and threatened. It wasn't a perfect deal, but a deal David could live with. He remembered a professor in law school, talking about negotiations, saying a settlement you can live with is better than a trial, almost any trial. David stood.

"I guess I should get Anacleta and get out of here," David said, shaking Santeria's hand.

"The diary."

"It will be released to you as soon as the case against Light is dismissed."

"It has been a pleasure, *señor*," Santeria said, guiding David into the house.

Anacleta sat in the living room next to Vance, looking a little uncomfortable. David smiled and she jumped up. "Do you need to get anything?" he asked.

She shook her head, and a moment later they were in the Toyota, heading down the hill on the curvy road toward the highway. David felt good, strangely good. It wasn't like having the murderer confess, but it was close. And he had Anacleta. For better or for worse, he had Anacleta.

The tall man came to Santeria with a metal box in his hand. It was silver in color and had a small red switch on the top. Santeria took it, walked to the front door, and watched as the Toyota pulled from the driveway and into the road. It headed down the hill on the narrow, curved stretch of blacktop toward the main road. Santeria fingered the switch. It was tempting, just for the pure joy of it. But he handed the box back to the tall man. "We will not need this," he said and returned to his daiquiri.

* * *

Anacleta slipped her arm inside David's, running it down until she reached his hand and intertwined her fingers with his. He felt this radiance from her, this glow, that pushed through him.

"You were right," he said.

She kissed his bare forearm as it released the gearshift. "They never kill first," she said.

"What about Twining?"

"Almost never," she said, massaging his palm.

EPILOGUE

David rubbed her palms between his thumbs and forefingers. She turned them, allowing his eyes to play over them along with his fingers. His eyes moved up from her hands, across the white cotton covering her waist and her breasts, covering all the way to her neck. The dress was a bit too formal, he thought, a bit too formal and a bit too informal.

His eyes hesitated where the white cotton met the dark tan of her skin. Her skin was still unconscionably smooth, radiant. Something about her beauty, he thought as his eyes played up to her face, something unconscionable. Unconscionable. That was a lawyer word, a word he never would have known without law school, a word his life would have been complete without. But it described Anacleta well. At least her appearance.

In the last year he had gotten to know the woman better, as she had gotten to know herself. She was a woman now, scarred by her past as are we all, but her own woman. Her own and his this past year.

His eyes rested on the hat. Much too formal for the way this was to be. He fingered his tie, straightening it to the dark suit. Both were too formal for David's taste also. But then, every woman had her fantasies. Every person, he supposed. Certainly he had his. It was she who approached with her fantasies first. She broached the subject gently. A suggestion, but not even. A statement that she was thinking about a suggestion. It was enough. They had talked.

David had waited for her to make the suggestion, although he had thought of it long before she. Or had he? Maybe she had thought of it and waited for him until she could wait no longer. He didn't know. He did know he was glad when they had discussed it. He also knew that in the past year, with all the problems, he had been happy. Happy to come home and have her there. Happy to sit with her after dinner, happy to fall asleep with her next to him.

He leaned toward her and kissed her softly on the lips. She accepted it but leaned back, indicating herself. Her appearance, she wanted to look good. Why was it, David wondered, that for women appearance was always so central? Because it was for men, David supposed the answer would be. But he wanted to really kiss her. He wanted more than just a peck.

She turned shyly toward the wooden door set in the white Sheetrock walls. They were alone. The hallway, not more than forty feet long, had two doors: the one she would go through in a moment; the other, at the other end, was his.

She slipped her hands out of his and joined them in front of her. She glanced up, the shy smile back. A smile that had been so trained into her was hers now, no longer a tool to be used but a part of her personality. It brought a glow to her entire being, and a glow to David's. He returned the smile.

She glanced shyly at the door.

"Do you want me to go in with you?" David asked.

She shook her head vigorously. "You're not even supposed to see me today," she said.

He nodded, bent over, and kissed her lightly before she turned and disappeared through the door.

David hesitated a second before turning to the other door down the hall. A heaviness took him as he trudged toward it. It was the right decision they were making, he told himself. The right decision. Why did it feel so wrong?

"Here I am, Lightfoot, over here," Evelyn called across the street.

Light turned his back, hunched his shoulders, and walked

off. Squeaky over by the corner, not saying nothing but looking kind of sad about it all.

"Want to beat on me?"

Evelyn always wait for the crowd before she start yelling that kind a stuff. Ostracized, that what Light been, ostracized since this shit over. And Cohen now telling him he can't say nothing because if he does, then them people come kill him and that Spanish bitch.

Fucking lawyer, Light thought as he climbed his stoop and sat on the top step. Wasn't no fun no more to sit this stoop. No boys coming over, no Squeaky or Charlie come over for a beer. When he go over front a the bodega, the bunch get quiet, nervous. Ain't right, and he can't explain it to nobody.

Squeaky, he know, but he don't say nothing, 'cause Light tell him not to. That a miracle in itself, Squeaky not saying nothing about something he know. But Squeaky treat Light all right. He the only one. But he be all right.

Light pulled the napkin out the bag and wrapped it around his fingernail. Six more months, that's what that Mr. Cohen say. Six more months. Light dug his napkin-draped nail into the groove around the top of that can. 'Cause she speak Spanish, that what they say. Put her anywhere, that's what. Here, South America, Spain. Any fucking where and she be safe. Where they gonna put Light? They don't talk about none a that shit.

No, six months from now when that trial over, they put her some witness protection shit, send her somewhere to South America or Europe or California. She be gone, and he don't have to see her no more, not ever. Mr. Cohen, he say he can't see her no more after that either. She just be gone. Disappear off the face a the earth, far as anybody know. Then Light can tell what he know. That's what Cohen say. Six more months.

Didn't know why Mr. Cohen feel so bad 'bout that Spanish bitch disappearin'. Mr. Cohen, he better off with a bottle-headed bitch. Give her ten dollar go get some crack, she be happy. Keep right up to when she get weird like Evelyn, then toss the bitch out. If those boys still around, that's what Light tell 'em. Just what he should a told Mr. Cohen.

Light popped the top of his beer, pushed it up to his mouth, and threw his head back.

"Over here, Mr. Lightfoot."

Trouble with Evelyn, he just can't toss her fuckin' ass out his life. She just sit 'cross there, wait 'till he get his head up to where he couldn't help but see her, couldn't even pretend to ignore her. Then she yell out. Light took another swig from the Old English.

"Yoo-hoo, Mr. Lightfoot."

Light dropped his head down low. Only time he lifted it these days 'round the neighborhood was when he sucking one down. Even when he did, Evelyn there cackling. 'Nough almost to make a man take the pledge.

Light shook his head. Wished that lawyer would ask him to break in some place next time. That he could do. That was easy. This here being quiet, that hard.